Hell's Belle

Jane Holleman

POCKET BOOKS
New York   London   Toronto   Sydney

An *Original* Publication of POCKET BOOKS

 POCKET BOOKS, a division of Simon & Schuster Inc.
1230 Avenue of the Americas, New York, NY 10020

Copyright © 1998 by Jane Holleman

ISBN: 1-4165-1087-8

First Pocket Books paperback printing May 2004

10 9 8 7 6 5 4 3 2 1

POCKET and colophon are registered trademarks of
Simon & Schuster Inc.

Cover photo by Barnaby Hall/Photonica

Printed in the U.S.A.

All my love to my sweet children—Sarah, John, and Blythe. I am so lucky to be your mom. You each inspire me to keep at this writing thing by making me mindful that we need the MONEY. Thanks, kids. You're my best friends.

And for Jack Raskopf, Ph.D., professor of journalism at my alma mater, Texas Christian University, and still my good buddy today. Thanks, Jack, for the day twenty years ago at TCU when you told me that my writing showed talent. You put lightning in my heart that moment, and it never went away. With this, my second novel, I think I'm over that B you gave me in a class, even though I pleaded fiercely for you to change it to an A. Just think, if you had changed the grade because I begged, I might have gone out there thinking that good things come to those who whine long enough. Instead you taught me to work harder at it, whatever it is we want, no sniveling or cheating allowed. And I know, like you said to me, that I have always been an A in your heart. Likewise, I'm sure.

ACKNOWLEDGMENTS

Thank you to Detective Curt Brannan of the Fort Worth Police Department homicide division (who is possibly the most honorable and handsome tough guy on the planet).

Also much thanks to Joseph Warren, Jr., Senior Forensics Biologist for the Tarrant County Medical Examiner's Office; to State Criminal District Judge Bob Gill of Fort Worth; and to Roger Eppstein, M.D., of the Medical Clinic of North Texas.

My gratitude to you all for your players' spirit and the valuable time that you gave for free to a hack novelist.

Hell's Belle

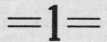

=1=

She made the same call each day. He always answered after the third ring and gave the same response.

And so it went on this January day with a sky so gritty with sleet that you could chew the air outside her basement-level window.

She: "Emory, hey baby doll, it's me. I thought I'd call again and ask, will you marry me?"

He: "No, sweetheart. But thanks for calling. I love you."

She: "Okay, babe. I love you, too. See you tonight."

She stood studying the spectacle of her desk and her cubicle, both so cluttered with boxes and papers that they appeared to have been ransacked. And she licked her lips at the thought of dousing it with lighter fluid and flicking a burning match into all the piles.

A man spoke behind her, half hidden by the waist-high cubicle wall. He looked like a soap opera leading man, too groomed and chiseled lean. She wondered what he was selling and how he got into the detectives' secured area of the police department.

"Rachel Collazo?" He put out a hand and she saw the manicure, sneered at it. His chumminess was practiced. "I'm your new partner, Chase Diablo. They call me Chaz."

Hands to her slender hips. She sneered deeper. "You're shittin' me."

He looked lost for a moment, took away his hand. "No. That's my name."

She rolled brown eyes that he found both beautiful and

1

fiercely intimidating and said with her profound Texas drawl, "Chase Diablo. More Chippendale boy than cop, I'd say."

He sounded sheepish. "With a name that translates to mean Catch the Devil you wouldn't think I'd grow up to be a kindergarten teacher, would you? And yes, I'm your partner. I've been here with the Dallas P.D. four years, and I've been through the ranks, most recently in vice and narcotics. They shifted me down here, with you. I heard your last partner dumped you because you said if she came late to her shift one more time you'd shove an umbrella up her ass and open it."

A smile from her. She said, "Yeah, lucky for her it wasn't raining that day." He noted that it was a pretty smile from a centerfold's full lips, which went along with the shapely legs that folded under the skirt of her expensive business suit when she sat down at her desk.

She asked him blandly as she put glasses on her cute nose and fluffed her shoulder-length black hair, "You got assigned to me, huh? Who'd you piss off upstairs?"

She was slamming things, drawers and files. He was watching her. He had only seen her in the teeming hallways over the years, never worked with her. But he'd heard about Homicide Detective Rachel Collazo. The bitch babe. If you stood back and looked at her—the five-foot-eight runway model figure, the aristocratic cheekbones, the swanky skirts and jackets, the soft black hair and sizzling black eyes—if you only looked, you saw erotica. Then she opened her mouth to speak and a chain saw cut through your gut. He knew all that. He knew the stories, that she had more guts than a slaughterhouse and the temperament of a samurai warrior, never giving up the fight until she had drawn blood.

He wondered as he watched. She stabbed at computer keys on her terminal with unpainted, utilitarian fingernails. There was no perfume in the air, no lipstick, no girly shit.

She snapped at him, "You married?"

"Happily divorced."

Nonplussed, she kept typing. "Kids?"

"None that I know of."

"Diablo. That's Mexican?"

"Half Cuban. The other half is Apache. I take it you're not married, since I just heard you propose to somebody on the phone. You took it rather in stride, I'd say—his rejection."

She punched a button and a printer clanked and spewed paper from its slot. "I ask him every day. He says no every day."

Chaz could only mutter dumbly, "Oh . . ." and shrug.

She turned to him, faced him in parade rest position. "I'm going to tell you what they say about you, Diablo, so we can get past it. They say that five years ago, before you came to Dallas P.D., you were an L.A. cop who shot your partner. He recovered and you were exonerated. They say you hustle women, beat up handcuffed perps. I hear you're a hell of an ace investigator and that you're a snob, that when the victim is some poor schlep you consider beneath you, like a bum or a whore, you don't work too hard at it."

She stared, stony. He swallowed.

He answered, "It was a drug bust in a dark, slum apartment. My partner caught my cross fire."

She didn't smile. "I didn't figure you aimed for him."

He said, "They say you have a foul mouth, a big heart, a bad temper. I hear that you give higher-ups shit because you don't want or plan to go anywhere in the ranks. You like being a detective. I want more. I concentrate on the high-profile cases when I can—the victims who matter and draw press coverage. Oh. And they say you have a great ass."

"Do I?" She barked it.

He hadn't expected to blush. He said, "Absolutely. Do I?"

She smiled gently. She liked this cocky fella, past the ignorant little earring and the idiotic pony tail and the stupid pinky ring. He was a hot shot, too slicked back and buttoned down for her personal taste what with the pin-stripe suit and the imported leather shoes. But he smelled good and didn't deny being a ranks climber and looked at her softly even when he talked tough. He put out his hand again. She shook it.

She said, "I can't tell about your ass in that snazzy overcoat, partner, but when the shooting starts you just keep your ass in front of mine at all times. Dying in cross fire is not my idea of a day's work."

A short, fat uniformed cop trudged in the door and over to Rachel's cubicle. He hoisted up his belly from his sagging belt and huffed at her, "Collazo, your sentencing in the Montoya case is coming in over at the courthouse. They just called." The fat cop stared stringently at Diablo.

Rachel linked herself into her black trench coat. "George Dorcus, this here is my fancy new partner, Chase Diablo, but he says everybody calls him Chaz."

Dorcus looked disgusted. "Your name's Chase Diablo, and you admit it?"

Rachel chided, "Be nice, Georgie. I finally got me a bilingual partner for the streets. No more counting on one killer to interpret for another."

Chaz's face squinched. He admitted, "I don't speak Spanish."

Rachel yelped, "What? You're a Cuban, and you don't know Spanish? Fuck that."

They stomped. Chaz padded behind. "Listen," he offered, "they wanted us to be total Americans, my parents did."

"Great." Rachel bitched. "I got me a culturally challenged partner. I've asked twenty times for a bilingual partner. So they give me a Cuban cop cake from fucking white town."

Chaz trailed. He called out, "Hey, Collazo, you forgot your purse."

She yelled harshly, "I don't carry a purse."

Such a gender-bender deserved pursuing. "Where do you keep your lipstick?"

She had a gracefully long stride. "I don't wear lipstick."

"Your hair brush? Your driver's license. All that girl stuff? Mirrors and powder puffs and designer ink pens?"

She called back to him as they left the granite halls and fell into the crunchy sleet outside, "I don't brush my hair,

4

cop cake. I don't have time on the job to primp. My driver's license is in my car; where else would I need it?"

"To write a check in the mall?" He was truly curious.

"Cash only." They entered another building, the courthouse, swarming with ne'er-do-wells and sleazy lawyers.

Chaz leaned at her in the elevator. "Your gun?"

She opened her jacket. Shoulder holster.

Chaz dropped back. He shook his head at her. "You're not normal, Collazo. No purse. No perfume."

Dorcus said proudly, his third chin flopping, "Detective Good Legs here takes boxing lessons." He said it like a snot-nosed little brother describing a champion sibling.

"She does?" Chaz tried. Must equalize, he figured. "Well, I have a black belt."

"Hey," Dorcus chimed to Rachel, "I know a little karate myself. You ever seen the martial arts move they teach you to use when somebody points a gun at you?" Then he lifted both hands straight in the air over his head and took one step back.

They were making fun of Chaz. He pouted. Rachel laughed. And laughed. And her beauty took Chaz's breath for a moment.

=2=

Rachel and Dorcus watched with prurient, stoic interest as they stood in the hallway outside the courtroom door. The cascade of women drawn to flirting with Chaz was oddly, amusingly captivating.

Two blonds stopped to ask him the time. Forget about the huge wall clock they had to duck to miss seeing.

Dorcus groused, "How many women you figure he fucks in a week?"

Rachel chuckled. "Not near as many as throw him down and fuck him."

A redhead in a tight minidress fingered Chaz's suit jacket and feigned interest in his tailor.

"What is it?" Rachel asked flatly. "You reckon it's his big shoulders or the hair or those pearlies of his?"

Dorcus switched the toothpick to the other side of his mouth and said dryly, "Could be the flat belly or the savage Tarzan suntan. Maybe his movie star eyes. Looky there. That brunette just tucked her business card into his pocket. Jeez. Last time that many women noticed me was during my wife's bridge game when I was checking to see if the fireplace flue was open, and I caught my shirt sleeves on fire."

Rachel felt itchy, antsy. She eyed the courtroom door. "I thought the jury was back."

Dorcus dug into his molars with the pick. "It takes them about an hour to all go pee."

Chaz approached, humming, looking like a man on his

way to a sorority party with a full beer cooler and a pack of condoms. Dorcus curled a lip at him.

Rachel asked Dorcus seriously, "Georgie, did we do all we could for this little dead girl's family?"

"I reckon we're getting ready to find out, Good Legs." He gave her a pat on the shoulder. "They found the killer guilty. That's a start."

She said wearily, "But our job was to bring in evidence that he needs ninety-nine years in prison."

Dorcus tried to sound consoling. "You did a great thing, getting all those other little neighborhood girls to admit the guy had been inviting them in for lemonade and then diddling them."

Heat flushed through Rachel. The memory of delicately but expertly drawing gruesome information out of a bunch of little girls made her nauseous. "I'm not proud of putting those precious children through hell and then letting the whole town see it played on video tape in a public court-room." She shored up, felt a thud of pride. "But it proved that even though this asshole has no priors, he's still a continuing danger."

Chaz jolted when Rachel began to outrightly cry. He fidgeted embarrassment. "Are you crying?" he stammered. "Is she crying? Why is she crying?"

Dorcus handed over a limp handkerchief to the blubber-ing Rachel who had turned her face. "She always cries," he offered dryly.

Chaz drew a blank. "Why? She knew the murdered kid or something?"

Dorcus said irritably, "No. She's just emotional is all."

Chaz huffed, "Women," rolled his eyes and coiled a stick of chewing gum casually into his mouth.

In the courtroom the jury filed in. From the front row of spectator seats, the murdered girl's washed-out, broken-hearted mother turned to see Rachel come into the room. Since little Teresa Montoya, a bright-eyed, ten-year-old fifth grader, had been abducted walking to school on a sunny morning near her home, the mother had come to rely on

Rachel's professional acumen at catching killers. She had also come to love Rachel's overt compassion.

Rachel and Dorcus had worked to bring in enough evidence that the Montoya's odd bachelor neighbor was the one who grabbed the girl, took her into a field, raped her and then strangled her with the strap of her new backpack.

As the girl's mother looked back at them, haunted and bereft, Rachel gave her a terse thumbs-up. Chaz frowned.

He whispered to her, "What are you? An impartial officer of the law or the family's third-base coach?"

"Fuck off," Rachel hissed. "And back out of my face."

Moments later, after the punishment was read aloud, the earth sputtered on its axis and humanity lost a split second of movement and awareness. In that moment only Teresa Montoya's devastated mother made a sound. Through the granite halls and the ancient, antebellum stained-glass arches of the courthouse, a piercing howl raced like a fireball, choking everything outside the courtroom doors and suffocating everyone's last hope for justice.

The Montoyas' odd bachelor neighbor got a measly, lousy twenty years of prison time. He could be out in half that time.

Rachel Collazo, there in the middle of news flashbulbs and stunned spectators, plunged into the quivering arms of the little dead girl's mother. They stood together and sobbed uncontrollably.

"I'm sorry, Mrs. Montoya," she sobbed as she held tight to the hysterical woman. "I'm so, so sorry. Please . . . oh god, honey, I'm just so sorry. . . ."

Chaz chewed his gum, expressionless, noticed that the flavor was gone from it, noticed that blustery old Dorcus was wiping his weepy eyes and wondered with steely resolve how a sap like Rachel Collazo ever got tough enough to win all those police commendations he had seen framed on her office wall.

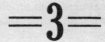

=3=

He was yapping behind her like a panting dog as they walked, but Rachel didn't care what Chaz was ranting about. She found the office door she was looking for in the courthouse and blasted through it.

The arrogant, uppity prosecuting attorney looked up and gulped. The notorious Rachel Collazo was in his doorway looking like a mother bear getting ready to defend her cub.

Her red wool suit was impeccable, but her face was scarred with black smears of mascara from crying. She looked as bruised as she felt. Her dark hair was wild, like she had just come from a roller coaster ride. He felt himself step back, which he knew a good offensive player never does in a battle, but his retreat from her was reflexive.

Rachel commanded in a low, steady voice, "Come around to this side of the desk, you sidewinder son of a bitch. I'm going to whip your ass."

Chaz paled, slapped his hands forlornly over his eyes and moaned. He wanted to vaporize.

The prosecutor flitted a goofy, nervous laugh. He loosened his tie to make himself appear relaxed. "Rachel, you're an extremely beautiful thirty-six-year-old woman. Act like one."

She stepped forward, fists clinched. "And what would an extremely beautiful woman do right now, Tillery? Come over there and run her fingers through your hair and tell you it's okay that you're a gutless cocksucker who just put a kid killer back on the streets in probably ten years or less? Is that what a nice girl would do here? Because see, I have nine brothers who didn't mention to me that I was a girl, 'cause if they'd told me that along the way, I might have asked for special treatment. I'm an old dog now, and you can't teach me there's any difference between you and me."

He thought of swiveling in his chair, turning his back to her and peering out the blinds at the looming dusk, but he didn't because he was afraid she would lob something heavy at the back of his head. "You should be more feminine," he said lamely.

She bristled. "You mean weak. Like you were in this trial."

He stood and yelled, "The punishment is not my fault! I can fire you, Collazo, and maybe I'll do just that!"

"Fire me? Good. Then I can go home for the day."

Chaz leaned on the wall, seeing his career cracking and falling to the floor one piece at a time by association with this psychotic amazon who was his new partner.

The lawyer's armpits were sweating. "Oh, I'm a piece of shit because twelve impartial people went light on a guy with no priors? That's my doing?"

She stomped toward him. "Yeah. And you're also a piece of shit because you didn't ask for the death penalty."

"He had no known priors, Collazo! The jury wouldn't have put him to death, goddammit!" He came uncoiled and kicked his chair.

Chaz touched Rachel's arm lightly. She slung away from him.

Her face contorted into disgust, and she screamed, "You weeny! It was your call." She reached across the desk and poked a fingernail into his tie. "Let's call a spade a spade here, Tillery. The twelve people who gave that light sentence today had the option of a life term for him, and they knew it. And those twelve impartial people were picked by the goddamned defense team while you stood and played pocket pool. All the pro-prosecution hard-ass jurors went through your hands and THAT is when it was lost, because you suck at jury picking."

She jabbed. He wanted to hit her. Chaz tried to speak, but the prosecutor cut him off.

"Oh so you're a lawyer now," he seethed at Rachel, dabbing his wet upper lip with his sleeve. "I thought you were just a token girl cop."

She dragged her tongue across her pretty teeth and let the moment simmer. "Come around this desk."

Chaz spoke sanely. "Rachel, I'll take you somewhere to cool off. You're talking to a chief felony prosecutor . . ."

She ignored him, scalded the drained lawyer. "He broke her nose while he fucked her in the mouth, Tillery. She was ten-years old. She weighed sixty pounds. She was their only child."

He pressed cold fingers to his hot forehead. "This jury would not have given him death."

"If you'd picked it right they would have."

The lawyer sought solace in eye contact with Chaz. Bonding. Gender alliance.

"She's everybody's conscience," he snarled. "All the goddamned victims' families are so in love with her. They swoon about how diligent and caring she is. Yeah. She's a saint. Except she treats everyone she works with like minions and dirt balls because we don't meet her *standards*." He spat the word.

Rachel snapped at him. "I don't do this job for you. I do it for them, the victims. You want people to be nice to you, Tillery, go work at fucking Chuck E. Cheese."

He looked only at Chaz. "I blow up the crime scene pictures and point at the carnage for the juries. I put weeping mothers and fathers on the witness stand and make theatrical fodder of their agony so some scumbag will go to prison. And what does she do? She stomps around here and knocks everybody's dick in the dirt because we don't care as much as she does. What the hell do you do, Collazo, that's so great?"

Her eyes were dead. He had not moved her. "I bring in

the suspects so guys like you can put them away. And when you can't I take it personally."

They faced off an interminable moment. She said without remorse, "You fucked up, Tillery."

Chaz offered, "Rachel, you can't think he doesn't care."

Her smile was sinister, not friendly. "I think he wants to get out of this trench of crime but he doesn't want to get his fingernails dirty doing it. I think, Tillery, that when you point at those crime scene blowups and start emoting, I think you're faking it."

He shot her a level glance of hatred. Turning, with Chaz blindly following after her, she left Tillery's office, softly closing the door behind them. Chaz continued after her into the ladies room, where she washed her face.

"I can't be your partner," he lamented.

She blew water, dried her face. "Fine."

"You're crazy, you know." He handed her a comb from his pocket. "I mean, there's this total lack of propriety about you. You cry out loud. You scream at people. If I go into this with you, the same trouble you get into will follow me. That assistant D.A., Tillery, he associates me with your insanity right now. I want to go into the FBI someday, Collazo. I want to be an agent. I can't be known for spending all my time talking my partner off ledges. I have to be known for being cool, calculating. You're a joke. I'll be known as the joke's sidekick."

"Diablo, I said fine. Put in the papers. Change partners."

He sighed greatly, put doe eyes onto her. "Is it like this with you every day?"

"Yep. Pretty much." Her eyes were swollen, but she felt better, somehow requited. "When you're asking the right questions and saying the truth real loud, the liars and the inept start squawking. That's my theory."

"You still got that black stuff, right here." He touched her cheek with his thumb and wiped.

"You're not responsible for my behavior, Diablo. I am. And I was right; what I said to Tillery is all true. Now you go do what you have to do. I'm going to drive to the Montoyas' house and give that little girl's mother a ride to the cemetery like I do every Monday afternoon."

He stood alone in the antiseptic stench of the toilets and the stained bathroom sinks. He wondered how to get out of this debacle gracefully.

=4=

The only order among all the chaos in the house was the preemptive grief; it was as sturdy and tangible as a coffin parked in the center of the wrecked living room. But no one was dead. Yet.

Everything was a mess except the horrible pain of grief, which was intact. The dishes her young son had eaten from—last night's canned spaghetti and this morning's instant oatmeal—were strewn on lamp tables and armchairs. The laundry (she couldn't tell the clean from the dirty) was piled crudely on the breakfast table, towels and T-shirts dripping over the edge. Toys were everywhere, soft toys that squeaked, sharp toys that lit up, muscled power figures with broken arms, plastic sports stuff like bats and T-balls. Everywhere she looked there was nowhere to move among the clutter.

But Mrs. Julie Ann Nystrom, former queen of housekeeping goddesses, didn't care. She was kneading a stray Nerf ball in her hands like it was a wad of her grief, and she was battling the Devil.

She spoke, devoid of emotion. She was alone in the chaotic rubble. "It isn't fair, Lord. It isn't fair. The world is full of whores and women who don't love their kids and women who never go to church. And I never miss church and my son is my life. So you do this to me?"

The first silvery tear streaked down a cheek so fair of skin it was like a palette of milk. Her eyes were an oddly

14

seductive emerald-green, her hair naturally more blond than corn silk. She dabbed the tear with the Nerf ball.

"I'm thirty years old, Lord. I'm a Christian. I tithe. I go early on Sunday so I can help out in the church nursery. I'm not like those whores who smoke and drink." The very remark wound her up, caught her breaths and made them come faster. "You can't be punishing me with this breast cancer. I've never done anything to be punished for like those whores who wear leather clothes and show their bodies in tight-fitting dresses. I never do that. And for my goodness as a Christian . . . you give me breast cancer. All I do for you, and you're going to let me die, take me from my child, leave my mother and son all alone on this earth without me. Oh, Lord, it is just so unfair."

She dialed the phone and heard the clicking and humming of the busy newsroom in the moments before she heard her husband's jovial voice. "Nystrom," he snapped, sounding centered and important, which annoyed her to a manic level.

"You need to come home, Daniel."

He tensed. "Jules, honey, I can't leave here early again today. I'm writing a story about a city councilman being sued for sexual harassment, and I finally got one of the women to come talk to me on the record. If I cancel, she might spook and I'd lose the source."

She was hysterically desperate for him to obey her. "You care more about that than about me?"

He wanted to choke her. "I don't know what to say. The question is so stupid."

"Don't call me stupid!"

He made flutters and clucks of sounds to calm her down, which she did, long enough for him to tell her, "Honey, my health plan here will pay for your cancer treatments, but if I lose my job then I lose the insurance. You see? Now more than ever I have to do good work."

She started to sob. He rolled his eyes.

The words fell like bricks into a pool of thick oil. "Danny. I have cancer."

He took a long, contemplative breath to steady his response. "I know, Julie Ann. But that's all we know, and the surgery next week will tell us how badly you have cancer, which may not be bad at all. You see?" He lowered his tone as if his words could stroke her. "As soon as I'm finished here, maybe just a few more hours, I'll come home."

She hissed at him cruelly, "You'd come home right now if I said I'd have sex with you. My breasts are rotting with disease, but you don't care, you want to touch them and put your mouth on them." It all ran together, the self-pity and his obstinate defiance. "You're so sick I hate you you're such a sinner."

"I give you everything you want, Julie Ann."

She was pacing. "And for that I'm supposed to give you sex."

"It's called marriage, honey."

"You get home right after work, Daniel. And don't you dare smell like beer. I'll have a grocery list for you."

"Can't you go now, yourself?"

She was perspiring with rage. "In case you forgot, I have cancer. And besides, you don't do anything all day but sit and write. A monkey could do it. I want you here before dark. When you get back with the groceries, you can give Pete his bath and read him a story."

She hung up on him. He held the phone and said snidely into it, "Yeah, and then you can give me a blow job and a goodnight kiss. Fat chance. Bitch."

The reporter sitting an arm's-length away at another terminal smiled slyly. "It's not nice to call a dying woman names, Nystrom. What was her excuse to not lay you before she had cancer?"

Daniel answered sourly, "The Lord. And the fact that I'm an ugly, worthless male pig." He put his headphones on and prepared to transcribe notes from the tape, and then he winked at her.

"Not from where I'm sitting," she mumbled as she typed.

It was an ostensibly harmless flirt, friend to friend, the

kind she had poked at him so many times over the four years they had worked together at the newspaper. He never shamed her for her coy come-ons, nor did he acknowledge them. Lots of women tried to hustle Daniel Nystrom; all of them failed. He was the quintessential good guy. Loved his kid. Kept himself clean-shaven and flat bellied. Laughed at others' dirty jokes but never told one himself. He was tall, wore wire-rim specs and rumpled khaki pants. He played golf on Saturdays and went to morning and evening church services with his quaint little family on Sundays. His allure was put into words by the women who craved him. They shared their lusty opinions as they dressed in the gym locker room at lunchtime: "Danny Nystrom is so adorable, I just want to take him home and eat him all up . . . yeah, and for a hunk like him I'd even swallow!"

In a newsroom, where reporters sit at computers as close together as tables in an intimate bistro, nothing was private. It is a purposeful design, meant to insinuate the freedom and accessibility of the press's thoughts and actions. It also meant that Daniel's admirers heard most of the grim, volatile conversations he had with his ailing, wicked wife. She had been terrible before she discovered her breast lump a few weeks earlier; afterward, she had become downright horrible.

They all knew that she called him at least ten times a day at his desk. But they were calls of rage, not love, a kind of desperation borne of a hateful craving to control him. Daniel tolerated the verbal assaults, not like a priest or a shunned little boy, but like a prison inmate who has long ago accepted himself as powerless against the guard's position in the system. In his case, the weapon she used to keep him submissive, like early parole, was their five-year-old son Pete.

In her abject misery at home, Julie Ann lay on the floor, glad to be alone and vengefully bitter that her husband had abandoned her—again—like before when she couldn't find him, and she knew that SHE DIDN'T MATTER TO HIM AFTER ALL. The brashness of it, him going away overnight out of town and FORGETTING HER, forgetting that she OWNED him, was so bold that even the thought of it these many years later drove her to hyperventilate.

That very morning she had reminded him. "I'll never forgive you and neither will God. You broke our vow."

He had stood there that morning looking like a fit and fair-haired young college professor and he said without halting, "You would know this, of course, that God hates me for being away one night and not calling you. I couldn't call home, Julie. It was impossible, all night. What vow did I break? Thinking you'd be okay and that when I explained, you'd understand?"

He thought her tongue slithered like a dragon, and her jade eyes sparked. "You left me alone. It's a sin. Sins are black marks on your soul, Danny. Nothing takes them away."

Lying on the floor, she heard Pete stir. If she pretended to be asleep, then the boy wouldn't bother her. He would get a cookie and a juice box and sit dutifully, quietly on the couch until she opened her eyes. She shut them tightly and tried to look very peaceful.

Danny. She thought of her husband and wanted to smack his face. Gone from her overnight, five years ago, out of town on a secret investigative story. She, pregnant. He made up excuses for not calling her all night. Nonsense, the excuses, and she had somehow known it. He was supposed to call her hourly, and he knew it. And he had gotten far enough away from her so she couldn't control it. It drove her crazy for hours.

She had a vision of him picturing her that night, knowing she was frantic—and enjoying the image of power it made him feel over her.

Forgive him? She asked herself as she felt Pete watching her. Forgive Danny? Never. His power had made her into a fool that one time—never again.

=5=

"Diablo!"

Rachel screamed it like a drill sergeant at mail call. Before he could answer she had marched to his desk and put her scowl squarely into his face.

"You're in my parking place on the lot, you Ken-doll-piece-of-Gucci-shit. I'm calling a tow truck. I fight the freeway gunslingers and the fat carpoolers to get here, and then I find your Romeo-mobile set smack in the spot with my name on it. What's wrong? Was there a bum passed out in your space and you didn't want to risk nicking your grill when you smushed him? We don't get many perks around here, Diablo. Hell, our secretary doesn't speak a lick of English and the coffee tastes like chewing-tobacco spit, but we do at least get our own parking spots. Move your car or I'll throw this orange juice on your fancy-ass Armenian suit."

By now, after a week of it, Chaz was numb to the tirades. He declared, "It's Armani. Not Armenian."

She carried on. Everyone in the maze of cubicles paid no attention. The clusters of other detectives knew her scratchy voice and irascible nature by heart and didn't notice unless the shrapnel flew their way.

She flopped into her chair and began peeling away layers of scarves, gloves, a coat. "Why didn't you park in Harrigan's or Morrow's spots? Because they're guys? Because you think they'll whip you and I won't? Does anybody in the world get up in the morning anymore and go through the day doing what's right? Am I the only person alive who doesn't operate under the every-man-for-himself theory? Morons. Fucking morons. A-One Towing? Yeah, this is Detective Collazo at the downtown P.D. . . ."

Chaz stood so she could see him over the cubicle. He smiled like a guy watching his worst enemy drown slowly. "Oh, Detective Collazo? There was already someone parked in my space." He jerked his thumb toward a nearby wall where a dowdy woman sat alone in a row of chairs.

She was smiling at Rachel, though it was more a look of dental pain. She stood timorously.

"You're Miss Collazo? I'm the one who called . . . about my sister's death."

She studied a wadded-up tissue that she played with between her hands. Her clothes and hair were frumpy, she wore no make-up, her coarse hair twisted into a clumsy knot. It was a look Rachel recognized—the wan, blanched face of prolonged grief after a loved one's death. "Maybe, umm, I should move my car?"

Suddenly and sincerely Rachel's tone became as beholden as the host of a children's television show. "No, ma'am. Your car's just fine." She moved instantly to the woman's side and took hold of her as if to help her move away from the burial sight while the dirt was shoveled.

"You go there into the conference room and I'll get you some decent coffee from upstairs."

The woman sputtered. "Well, it took longer than I thought to get here because it started to snow, and I'm just such a coward when it comes to driving over twenty miles an hour in the snow. . . ."

She blathered as they walked. Chaz was laughing silently as Rachel looked back at him with a ferocious glare. When they sat in the conference room together, Chaz hung back a proper distance for dispassionate analysis. Rachel took to the woman with the warmth and comfort of Santa Claus in his big red chair at a shopping mall. The woman kept her perpetual smile that cinched her eyes. It played as an apology.

She said tentatively, "I think my sister was murdered."

Rachel remained relaxed. Chaz went on point, militantly ready to absorb details.

Rachel invited confidence and calm with her tone. "Yes, you said that on the phone. Tell me what's going on."

The tissue was shredded into the shape of something with petals. "Well," she averted Rachel's gaze respectfully, "she had cancer, uh, breast cancer, you see, and then after she died her, uh, her husband just sort of . . . disappeared." She threw her palms up in a shrug. "Ran off. He phoned me before he left. He didn't mention that he was leaving, but he said that I could use my key and retrieve whatever of my sister's clothing I wanted to give to charity. I found these on the kitchen counter. It would have been about a week after he went away."

She produced pamphlet-size jackets bearing the name of a travel agency, pockets that had held two airline tickets. The tickets were gone.

Chaz reached, studied them. "So you're thinking he has a travel companion. Where is he?"

"Sailing I guess. He would have flown to his yacht in South Padre Island."

Chaz sat behind the woman, half his butt on an ancient radiator along the wall. With his long hair flowing down, he looked like an Apache warrior doing a men's suit ad. He raised his brows at Rachel incredulously. The message said that he thought the woman was a kook.

Rachel searched for words, an intonation of regard with an anchor of logic. "Mizz . . . Pickett, it is, okay. Did you call this travel agency and ask who the other ticket was issued to for a flight to South Padre on that date?"

The smile didn't fade, but the eyes teared up. "Umm, the woman there said Wesley bought only one ticket. I asked why there were two jackets and she said maybe someone came in at a separate time and bought their own ticket. Or maybe this second one is old, from another trip; they traveled a lot before Ashley got sick. But they were there, the ticket holders, right together by the door where he left them."

Chaz interjected, "They got a kid he might have taken?"

"No. No children. They only had each other. Oh, I knew you wouldn't believe me. No one else does either."

Rachel took the teary woman's hand. "I believe that you believe it. Now honey, tell me, your sister was how old?"

A fresh breath of relief that someone was listening to her was followed by, "She was young, I mean, fifteen years younger than me. She was thirty-five." A goopy tear slid and hung on her top lip until the mauled tissue erased it. "She found a lump this past October and then had surgery. It was bad, in her lymph nodes, so they did a radical mastectomy and started her on chemo for twelve weeks. She died the first of this month, about eight weeks into her chemotherapy. She got pneumonia."

She looked past Rachel, out the window slimy with freezing rain, as if the streams on the window formed into images that she could describe. Her voice went to a whisper. "She died very fast, a matter of days, her body was just so worn out from the surgery and the chemo. Before all that she was this beautiful, vibrant person, a pianist with the symphony. And she loved tennis and cooking. She was all the family I had. My husband is sometimes . . ." she turned her face as if gossip was too unsavory but necessary, ". . . he is sometimes rather cold, but Ashley, we were close. She brought me great joy."

Chaz's eyes were blank. He did not believe her or give a shit about any of it.

Rachel asked kindly, "And how would he have murdered her?"

The woman's jaw tightened. "Poison. I don't know."

Chaz's deep voice was arrogant. "Was she on some kind of life support or assisted-breathing that he could have disconnected?"

"No." The tone was bleak, catatonic. "She was weak, but she was improving as the chemo progressed. It looked as if she were in remission. They gave her some time to live, but they couldn't say if she'd meet the five-year mark for survival. But she was clearly headed for a span of remission. And then she got the pneumonia. Suddenly she was dead."

Rachel inquired, "When she got pneumonia, why didn't she go into the hospital?"

"She got a fever on a Wednesday night. By Thursday afternoon it had not worsened so her doctor decided not to hospitalize her, since she wasn't getting sicker. That Friday morning Wesley found her dead in bed."

Rachel said methodically, "So if she died at home then the medical examiner had to come and pronounce her dead. What did she say?"

The woman slumped. This was always where it broke down. "The medical examiner said she died of shock from the pneumonia. She said that during the night on Thursday Ashley's fever spiked and it collapsed her major organs. She said she was dead, that's all."

"If she died unattended at home then she had to have an autopsy. Did that take place?"

"Yes." The woman grew smaller and more frail.

"And?"

"Septic shock," she uttered forlornly. The tissue was fluffy flakes in her lap. "No poison. No foreign toxins. Nothing. But he did it. He did something."

Chaz said, "Why? Did she have money? Does he get the inheritance? Did he have another woman?"

"The money was all his. She had life insurance but the money went to me and Wes knew that. He didn't need it. Maybe he just got tired of paying thousands of dollars for every chemo treatment at home. I don't know."

He persisted rudely. "I thought he was rich. What's a few thousand dollars to a rich guy? Because of one extra ticket jacket on the kitchen counter you think he killed his wife who was already dying of cancer?"

The tears flooded. "She was not dying!"

"Did he have pneumonia himself, and he breathed it onto her?"

She shouted, "I don't know! But where the hell is he, and who used this other ticket? I called every goddamned day, and she told me Ashley was doing fine! There were no visitors because of the risk of infection, but I called every day! Then one goddamned day she tells me Ashley has a slight fever and they've called the doctor. The next day she tells me that Ashley is the same, no worse, so the antibiotics the doctor told her to start the day before must be working. Then the next morning my sister is dead, and Wes is buying two first-class airline tickets to sail away on his goddamned yacht! Does anyone but me see the suspicion in all of this?"

Rachel sat forward more tightly. "Mizz Pickett, you said 'she.' Who is 'she'?"

With the frustration of having to cover details, the woman sighed, "A visiting nurse. The one who did the home chemo."

Chaz asked pragmatically, "Did he run off with the nurse? Have you checked to see if she's gone, too? Did you ever see the nurse and him together in a way that made you uncomfortable?

The woman flinched and turned at Chaz as if he had just belched crudely. "Mr. Diablo, please, it was not just one nurse. There were two. It rotated." Her eyes jeweled to a hard sheen. "It was him. Her husband. Wes Merriam. He used a fancy poison that disappears. The needle marks wouldn't have mattered, she had a chest catheter where the chemo went every time. He put it in there. It lowered her immunity and she got pneumonia."

The tissue was snow in her lap. She was visibly angry and weary. "Can you help me, Miss Collazo?"

Rachel asked softly, "Who was with your sister the night before she died?"

"Wes. I called about nine. He said her fever hadn't worsened from the day before. She was sleeping with a sedative, he said, and the visiting nurse had checked on her and left. A woman named Kelly McLaughlin. Oh, and he was drunk. I could tell. He found Ashley dead just before dawn."

Rachel cradled her own head tiredly. "I'll try his place on South Padre. I'll call him. If he's on the boat the Coast Guard can get him a message to call me. I'll ask who's with him. I'll get back to you."

The woman said weakly, "I'll never hear from you."

"The hell you won't. A woman is only as good as her word, Mizz Pickett, and my word is solid gold. We'll take a look at the autopsy stuff and her medical records. If you think her death is hinky, then as long as it's reasonable I'll trust your judgment until I hit too many walls. Okay, honey? You going to be okay?"

She dropped the snowflakes of tissue into her prissy purse and sniffled. "He murdered her. Please prove it."

Ten minutes later Rachel and Chaz clipped down the brightly lit hallway, bumping shoulders with harried secretaries and bums and cops, some with sleet melting on their coats. They had an interview with a Hispanic family whose small house had been shot up to cinder in a drive-by shooting that killed their four-month-old baby.

Chaz scoffed, "She's a signal 13. Demented. You know that. We've got four major homicides working right now. We can't waste time on the unfounded ramblings of a hysterical old whacko."

"You're not a cop," Rachel huffed, hearing the echoes of her high heels on the shiny floor. "You're like some little yappy mutt wearing a dog sweater. Everyone else knows he's just a mutt, but he thinks he's a person. Besides, when does your new partner assignment come through?"

"Not soon enough for me." He offered half of his umbrella. She walked ahead of him, undaunted by the pellets that would melt and drench her hair. "Hey, I heard you ask that guy again on the telephone this morning to marry you. What's the deal with you? Have you no pride?"

She started the car. The window was a sheet of ice. "I'm going to ask him until one day he says yes. It takes a lot of pride, Ricky Ricardo, to fight for what you want even though it makes you look like a nitwit."

Chaz smiled at her. She smiled, too, reluctantly.

"Solid gold," he mocked, chuckling rudely. "More like chipped ice if you ask me."

She winked at him. He winked back.

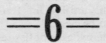

=6=

Kelly McLaughlin did for a pair of red lace thong panties what a bottle of champagne does for an ice bucket.

Kelly lay quietly in the luscious folds of her black satin bed comforter, noting with mild humor to herself that she was the only thing in the room that had any roundness. All the severely contemporary furniture in her apartment was angled, sharp and vividly colored. She could see it all misconstrued in the mirrors on the ceiling, the mirrors that now reflected the full length of her. She was moaning, stretching herself out from under the ominous ripples of black satin. The volcano-red panties and her porcelain-white skin were warm curves against the darkness beneath her. Pillows of flesh on a lacquered black abyss.

She smiled, stretched more, paid attention to how the gasps of oxygen ignited the red in her large nipples. Daylight creased itself through the red-and-black blinds, but she could see that there would be no sunlight that day. Winter clouds were so thick that the covering was now a gray, unwrinkled blanket over the world.

She took the bedside phone in hand and dialed, toying at the curly red cord like she would a man's genitals, up and down, tickling along the way, twisting the tiniest portion of it into her cinnamon-colored lips. He answered on the second ring. Burly. The way she remembered him. Crisp but cordial. Tall. Meticulously groomed but endearingly shy.

"Mr. Merriam?"

He recognized her voice and felt something shivery go

across his collar, something as capricious as a black widow spider darting along his collar line and down into his shirt.

"Miss McLaughlin. What can I do for you?"

"I was wondering . . ." she fondled her breasts lightly, ". . . how you're doing?"

The coffee in his mug had the slightest ripple of tension through it when he lifted it in his hand. "I'm fine. And you?"

Her blond hair splayed out on the black sheets and pillows like scattered yellow gold. The red panties were a V-shaped blood spatter on the milky-white paleness of her skin.

"I'm fine. I'm just making a routine follow-up call to see if our home-nurse service can help you in any way in the transition after your wife's death."

He exhaled. His hands were cold. "How did you know where to call me?"

What was not routine, though she didn't mention it as she watched herself in the ceiling mirrors, was to dip your fingers in your red panties and grin like a witch while comforting the mourner. "Our billing department has this number. It's your beach penthouse in South Padre, isn't it?"

What she said made sense; he should not feel as anxious as he did. "Yes."

She opened her legs. A million men would've paid a million each to merely observe. "It's hard, isn't it, Mr. Merriam?"

"What?"

She broadened her smile from witch to devil. "Getting on with your life after losing a loved one."

"Oh. Yes. I think Ashley and I were lucky to have had time to say all that we needed to say." He sat. The ocean outside the panoramic windows that circled him was as flat and silver as the blade of a knife. "You were a great comfort to her at the end."

She could see him, dashing as James Bond and demure as James Stewart.

She took her hand from her panties, trailed a moist finger along the ear-piece where she could hear his breaths.

"I cared about your wife, Mr. Merriam. If I did anything at the end to ease her pain or her fears, it was my . . . privilege."

"Yes, Miss McLaughlin. Thank you. If there is a performance evaluation for your nursing service, please send me one. I have only gratitude for what all of you did to help while my Ashley suffered so much." His eyes teared suddenly; he was shocked at his own vulnerability. "Oh, gosh. I guess hearing your voice brought hers back to me. We were together so many hours at the end, you and I, with her. Thank you for checking on me."

She coiled her body into a lily-white snail with a virulent red core of lace. She had gone in one night to say that the chemo was finished and the sedatives were working and that she was going home. And she found him, the indomitable Wes Merriam, steel baron and ex-college football stonewall, weeping in his bed like a six-foot-four-inch young boy.

He had felt her hand on his shoulder and clutched it, the languid assurance of the hand that so relieved and hopefully cured his suffering wife. When Kelly's fingers danced lightly through his hair he had not objected. When her warm, moist lips dusted his forehead he had not objected. When she stood to leave he had not objected, but the thought of reaching for her was crushing.

There had been nothing between them except the daily rigors of caring for the wasted relic of the only woman he had ever loved. Ashley. Many nights he watched Kelly rub oil along the fragile skin of his wife's aching back. They talked like girlhood chums while Kelly lavished lipstick onto Ashley's cracking, bloodless lips. Kelly lowered Ashley's emaciated body into the warm bubbles of a bath. Kelly crouched on the bathroom floor and wept encouragement while Ashley vomited after the chemo. Kelly administered the medications that made Ashley able to sleep and eat and move and breathe through the horrors of the therapy.

It piled up on him. Ashley's pain, the anger, the memories of their happiness, the godless abandonment.

And through it all, Kelly was a beacon of gentle strength. Nothing she had said made him feel guilty, not like he had cheated. The assumption had been a natural one. I have seen you loving my wife and, therefore, it is so that you also love me. She made him tea each time she came, after Ashley was irretrievably sedated. He came from the shower and a mug of hot tea steamed on his bedside nightstand. He bungled to her car one night late, just before she got in, and he enraptured her with an embrace. He didn't care when the gratitude of that moment leapt into passion. He didn't resist when she pushed him to the ground, opened his robe, took him into her mouth and relieved all the poisoned pain of months without love.

They never spoke of it. Kelly came back many times to care for Ashley. She was not there the dawn that Ashley went into shock from low blood pressure brought on by a raging bacterial infection. Kelly was not there when Ashley died.

The black sheets buried Kelly McLaughlin after the phone buzzed with finality in her ear. She did not laugh or cry. She did not pray. She lay very still, hands on her enormous, lovely breasts, willing her heart to slow from its concupiscent racing.

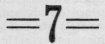

=7=

The phone ringing on her desk caught Rachel in a woozy daydream, thinking of when she had met Emory and all the unlikely dynamics that coming to know him had put into play.

Her big-haired, loud-mouthed and lovable high school chum Lyla Cavanaugh had recruited Rachel to volunteer with her at a fancy golf tournament in Dallas. They had been, almost twenty years ago now, seventeen-year-old horny virgins. Lyla had promised, parked on Rachel's bottom bunk in a bedroom she shared with two hounddog unruly brothers, that they could meet a couple of young golfers and then could quit their afterschool jobs at the movie theater and move into mansions next door to each other and never even have to go to college. All they had to do, Lyla effused, wearing orange juice cans for hair curlers and smoking a Kool, was run errands like picking up the golfers' laundry, taking them messages from the tournament command center and, oh yes, babysitting their kids while their wives went shopping or got drunk.

Wives? Well, some have wives, not all of them, and those are the ones we'll pay the most attention to, like, okay?

Rachel's close-knit family didn't belong to a country club. They didn't really belong to anything except each other and Our Lady of Guadelupe Church and, of course, her wonderful daddy was a member of the railroad workers union.

The inside of the country club was nothing like those rowdy, free-for-all union picnics they went to once a year.

First, there were no tables full of fried pies and melting iced tea, and second, rich country-club people drank their beer in glasses. The golfers' T-shirts did not show through their pressed, white button-down shirts, either.

She smiled now about how she must have looked, like a kid with no coins staring at a bunch of people eating sundaes. She wore a short denim skirt that day with black tights and black clogs, and she remembered that all she could see in the mirror were ridiculously long skinny legs and her full lips painted so red they were almost purple.

The country club foyer had been filled with lovely sprays of flowers and pretty people, all so groomed and relaxed that it seemed like they were afloat on a lavish cruise ship, leaving the gritty union world as far away as a polluted, savage city on the mainland. The golfers smelled good and tipped even better, she remembered thinking, and nobody was pushy.

Amid her errands—dropping off dry cleaning, finding the newest edition of *Sports Illustrated* at a drug store, watching two toddlers at the baby pool for an hour—Rachel asked herself: Why do all these golfers look like Roger Moore and talk like Roger Mudd?

They dispatched her, in an official tournament Cadillac that cost more than her parents' frame house, to the hotel suite of a hotshot who had four times won this tournament, the Byron Nelson. His name was Emory Jacobs, and Emory Jacobs wanted a ride to the noon mass at the downtown cathedral. Rachel was to drive him there and politely wait. Under the awning of the hotel valet, which was teeming with dressy folks all seeming to be in a hurry, she saw a very tall, stately, smiling man being crushed by a cluster of autograph seekers.

The young parking attendant sighed greatly when she rolled down the window. He answered, "Yes," and she expected him to genuflect or weep, "that's Emory Jacobs. Isn't it so cool, seeing a legend like Emory Jacobs in person?"

Emory got into the front seat; the others she had driven took the back seat, relegating her to a mere driver. She saw

Emory from the bottom up. Shiny loafers. Maroon argyle socks (her daddy wore white ribbed socks from Sears). Black linen slacks and a black sports shirt with a maroon monogram.

His shoulders were wide and square, his face clean-shaven, his hairline gently receding, his brown hair combed back straight like a gangster. All the seventeen-year-old boys she had ever craved in her life fell from her desires like clumps of dung from a bull's butt in the pasture. This gorgeous stud beside her, with the strong jaw and the serious brown eyes and the soft voice, was all she would ever want again in life. She was seventeen-years-old. He was forty-seven. He was, in her estrogen-laced arithmetic, full grown.

The phone on her desk rang again, jangling away the juicy remembrance of five years after that meeting when she finally convinced him to come to her college graduation and take her dancing afterward—grown-up ballroom dancing, too, not a bunch of nonsensical shimmies, but the hugging kind of dances where she could feel his inevitable erection and grin while they swayed.

She yanked up the phone, "Collazo."

The voice made her smile. "Nystrom," he faked pomp.

Her chair squeaked when she leaned back. Rain clouds parted and a slice of light hit the papers piled before her. "Danny boy. You're as cute as a bug, you know that?"

"Are bugs cute, Collazo?"

"I guess. Maybe if you're another bug. What's up, Danny boy? Whose constitutional right to privacy are you violating this time?"

Papers rustled. In the newsroom she could hear a flurry of laughter. "The drive-by. I hear that one skinhead in the car when the Herrera baby was shot is making a deal to testify against his skinhead buddy who did the shooting."

Rachel's grin widened. "Yeah? Now where'd you hear something like that so soon after the arraignment yesterday?" She grinned because she had told him herself.

"I never reveal a source," Daniel insisted, "at least not for free. So now today I hear that the accused shooter, the one the D.A.'s hanging the case on, has an alibi. Confirm? Deny?"

She frowned. She hadn't told him that part. "Nystrom, you son of a bitch. You're fishing. You print that and you'll fuck up the whole entire deal. Goddamn you."

He was undaunted. "So that's a confirmation. I just have to find out what the alibi is."

"I'm off the record, you bastard. It isn't an alibi, not exactly, but it's a possible glitch in the kid's actual opportunity to have done the shooting. You won't find it; it's sealed in the pending indictment." She shouted, "And if you print it without knowing it for sure, then you're a fuck-faced liar!"

Daniel flinched. "God, Rachel, where did you get your communication skills? Off the toilet seat? I heard you dated the Unabomber, but he dumped you because he thought you were a danger to society."

She snarled, "Yeah, but first I taught him everything he knows about journalism. Nystrom, tell me who leaked you that shit about the kid's so-called alibi. Some asshole around here needs to be fired."

He sounded annoyingly cavalier. "You know the one thing, Collazo, that keeps this government of ours from operating in a vacuum of elitist oppression of the people?"

She yawned. "Bribes?"

"No. A free press."

"Oh, fuck you. Say, how's your wife? Diablo told me about her cancer. I'm real sorry for her, Nystrom. Too bad it's not you instead of her. What a party the local lawmakers would throw."

She didn't notice that he didn't sound sad when he said, "She's having surgery next week. There are three lumps, so it doesn't look like a fluke. It looks bad. After the surgery they'll determine what to do next, chemo or radiation."

"Oh, man," Rachel lamented, reaching a hand to cover her own left breast. "That is so tragic, Danny. She's just, what, thirty years old? Man. Did she find the lumps herself?"

"No, her doctor did during a routine exam." His words

were oddly composed. "She's never been the healthy type anyhow. Something is always wrong." He perked up. "So I hear my handball buddy Diablo is your new partner. That's Clorox and Comet."

Rachel chortled. "Yeah. He's Cuban and Apache. I'm Irish and Italian. We're the formula they used at Los Alamos to make the first A-bomb. I already hate the vain prick. He's put in for a new partner. Did you know that he wears silk socks and suede loafers and constantly brushes his teeth throughout the day? And you're his friend? You, Danny, whose idea of style is wiping the spaghetti sauce off your tie after lunch?"

Daniel laughed loudly. "Hey, I like Chaz. We met on a story I did right after he came here from L.A. We went on a ski trip once, and I swear he puts his toiletries in alphabetical order. You'll be good for him. You, whose idea of tact is not using the choke hold on people at parties when you first meet them."

She studied the murky clouds that had opened to cold sunlight outside. It made the day colder, not warmer, as if the clouds were the lid of a steaming tea kettle, and when it was lifted all the warmth escaped.

"You want a beer, Nystrom? I'll buy if you bring money and trust me to pay you back tomorrow."

His reply was stodgy. "I can't. I have to go straight home and do a bunch of laundry." He added after a lapse, "My wife, you know, she used to be a sweet, cuddly thing. Now, marriage feels like I'm walking around with my shoelaces tied together."

She knew this good man. "Well, Danny, faced with what's coming at her, you two need to be real tolerant with each other. You're scared. She's terrified. I've known you lots of years. You're a good husband. I've seen those bar babes come at you, and you remain a stand-up guy."

He said like a man who had just been sentenced to death, "I'm committed to her, Collazo. And some days that commitment is all I have to go home to. No love. No joy. Just a commitment."

"Print your speculation on the Herrera case, Nystrom, you bastard, and I'll call your boss."

"And tell him what? That you have department leaks and I'm good at my job? I'll take that beer another day when I'm not on evening deadline. Thanks for talking to me today, especially for what you didn't say."

"What is it I didn't say, you tabloid scum?"

"You didn't say I was wrong about the kid's alibi; you just said I was off a notch on the terminology. In my business, that's a start to a great story."

Chaz was malingering by her chair when she hung up the phone. She looked up at him glumly. "You know," she griped, "your cubicle doesn't look like a cop's desk. It looks like a tea party."

"I'm sorry," he said snidely, "that I don't have furry cups of coffee and an opened box of Tampax on my work area. I came to tell you that you have a visitor. I think it's your dad."

She said menacingly, "He's my sweetheart. He's sixty-six-years old and fucks like a jackhammer. I come about four times a night. He proved his manhood to himself decades ago, which means I don't have to wake up every day and prove it for him again by being a good little girl."

"That's the man you propose to every day? I have to meet him. I have to know a man who could sleep with you and not mind the redness and swelling of his ego."

Emory stood when they rounded the corner. He was tall and lanky with an enviable amount of wavy hair that had grown white. His eyes sparkled with a peace that made other men's gazes frenetic. He had a dapper mustache, a crushing handshake, a honied southern accent that dripped class.

Rachel went girlish, breathing and wrapping herself into his arms. Chaz was astounded at her rush of femininity.

Rachel cooed, "Emory, baby, I put together some things today in a box for the Herrera family. Their baby was killed, and I want to take them a new little outfit to bury him in. Can we go by there on our way home?"

"We can do anything you need, darling, anything you want."

Chaz's eyebrow went up. He was witnessing opposites attract. This suave giant with the impeccable clothing and the voice like a neck rub was everything and everyone that Rachel never would find in her work. It was as if for love she had gone cruising a croquet club.

"Emory Jacobs," he said, holding out a greatly worn and tanned hand as if he were sidled up to a warm hearth in a Welsh castle's library. "You must be Chaz."

"I recognize you. . . ."

"He's famous," Rachel spewed nastily. "If you watched anything but yourself in the mirror you'd have seen him on TV."

Emory laughed like she was just so charming, then said easily to Chaz, "Can you imagine how wonderful it is to be her, to be Rachel? So freely unabashed. Consequences be damned. Conscience like a mother superior. No game playing. No horse shit. Every fight is fair. Every feeling is real. What a great pleasure for men like you and me to know a woman—a person—who gives to everyone what she craves for herself. Total acceptance. Unconditional honesty. What a remarkable woman I am in love with, wouldn't you say?"

Chaz muttered, even more astounded, "I was thinking right after I met her that I needed a tetanus shot."

Rachel laughed greatly, proudly. Emory tousled Chaz's hair like a king patronizing the jester, then he took Rachel's arm and they were off, linked and loping in stride, cuddling, cooing. Chaz stood blinking stupidly, knowing that after a decade as a cop in the worst neighborhoods he had finally, now, seen everything.

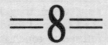

=8=

Daniel chuckled about the contents of his grocery bag as he walked from the garage into the house. Beer. Bananas. Bread. And barbituates. Julie Ann was having trouble sleeping, and the mild sedative helped her rest at night.

In the slices of early evening sun through the dining room blinds, he saw her crouched by the glowing fireplace in a thin cotton gown. She was a white hologram stained with delicate shades of amber and orange from the fire.

"Where's Pete?"

She didn't turn to face him. "Next door playing with little Will. You can walk over and get him before dinner."

He flipped on a lamp to wash away the grimness of early evening. The large sunken living room was tidy for the first time in two weeks. The two walls of windows that overlooked a jungle of greenery on the long patio gave enough light into the corners to see that she had vacuumed, too.

In the kitchen he could hear that the dishwasher hummed idly. Tonight he would not have to scrape dirty plates and utensils left all day for the food to crust and dry. He took a glass of beer, a glass of water and one pill down the long hallway to where Julie Ann sat folded inward onto herself. He sat by her.

Her skin was paper thin but creamy and lovely. He touched her face. "Here. Take one of these and go on to bed. I'll take care of Pete."

She didn't pull away from his touch. He pulled off the reading glasses propped on her head that held back her long, straight blond hair. Their eyes met for a moment, and he felt an odd sensation of his own weeping. Looking at her, he could recall with such sweetness Julie Ann the College Girl, the one who had sat in his lap at football games and always smelled of bubble gum when they kissed. He couldn't remember when she had stopped fondling his tongue with hers, when she first refused to touch his body or share her lean, sinewy body with him. It had come long before the lumps in her breast. Maybe, he told himself, they were going to pretend that the cancer shattered their intimacy with its oppressive dread, but the truth they both knew was that their marriage was already sick and dying.

She stared into the fire and her eyes became golden.

"I'm scared, Danny."

"I know. I'll do anything I can to make it all easier for you, sweetheart." His chest felt heavy with loneliness. "You just tell me what you need."

She spoke as if hypnotized, no blinking or inflection. "You can't help me. This is my punishment."

He wanted to retch the beer he had just sipped. "For what?"

Then she looked at him, serpentine and dark. "Sex is a tool of the devil. Sex makes us turn away from God. I should never have enjoyed it with you so much."

He whispered so he wouldn't shout. "No, honey, that's not right. You're wrong. I don't think that's the message your precious church meant to teach you. I think. . . ."

"Isn't it your church, too, Danny?" She asked accusingly.

"Sweetheart, somewhere along the way you misunderstood the scriptures. Even in that purist mecca of our church nobody is taught that a husband and wife shouldn't make love and like it."

She shivered. "We should make love only to make children."

"Oh god, Julie Ann." He came off the hearth to sit at her bony knees and put his head in her lap. Through the gown he could see and smell her cleanliness. "Let's get help, Jules, counseling maybe. Before this crisis, we were already in crisis. The more I loved you each year, the more you made me struggle every day to prove it. And day by day our church has made you so cruel."

"Danny, you knew when we married that I was a Christian." She stroked his cheek. "And you faked like you were, too. But I learned slowly that you're not. That you're indulgent and juvenile and so—" she leveled disgust, "—so undisciplined. No counseling, Danny. Our problems are private. Only God can solve them for us."

His erection was painful. "I want this marriage, and right now I want to make love to my wife. Please."

"No. If we stop, my punishment will go away."

The fire popped, and he imagined it was the sound of his heart breaking again. "I should leave you. I deserve to be loved."

She smiled tightly. "But you won't leave. If you did, everyone would hate you, especially Pete. Act in haste, you fool, and you'll regret at your leisure."

The erection was fire in his gut and groin. He whispered, "Maybe someday that will scare me less than the idea of how much I hate myself for living this way."

She laughed, a sudden wave of pleasure in her cruelty. "You're so weak, so lazy. You still think like that big, dumb, college-tennis-team fraternity boy, not like a father or a husband. Like a boy, not a man. I've grown, Danny, and you haven't. That's been the problem with this marriage for the past five years."

"Funny," he sighed as he sat up and finished the glass of beer and straightened his hair. "I was thinking that the problem in this marriage is that you don't love or respect me. You love and respect the preacher and the Bible and the Lord, but not anyone else. Everyone else, you judge and hate. Maybe you're not being punished for making love; maybe you're being punished for pandering hatred."

"Go get Pete," she seethed at him. "But brush your teeth first so the neighbors won't smell the beer."

When he had gone out she opened the other five beers and poured them one by one down the drain. Danny would be angry when he came back. The thought of it made her feel immensely powerful and avenged.

Daniel made Pete's favorite, scrambled eggs and pancakes, for dinner. They did a simple puzzle on the living room floor, and then Daniel rocked his son and kept rocking long after the boy was deep asleep. The touch of Pete was like a whiff of heaven to him, a surge of strength that even a wordmaster like him could not put into words. Pete was his best friend. Blond curls on his head like a thousand springs had broken through the fabric of his skull. Blue eyes. Tiny hands that amazed the preschool teacher with their ability to color within the lines. Daniel smiled. What a big deal had been made of that back when school first started in September. Pete, he of the million questions. How come that woodpecker in our tree doesn't get a big headache? That's what he had asked that evening as they bundled up and took a walk around the block.

He gently pressed the covers over Pete as he laid him in bed, feeling so fulfilled and lucky.

Then in the upstairs study where he worked at home, he put a triple-X movie into the VCR and masturbated, like he had for many nights over the past five years. He always finished with the same feelings—loneliness, confusion and shame. But at least the physical pain of desire would go away, and then he could sleep.

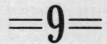

=9=

Kelly went up and down, straddling him, swiveling her pelvis, and with each thrust she tightened her inner muscles on his erection like a slick fist.

He moaned, "Don't stop," and pulled her so one delicious breast fell into his mouth. She kissed his forehead, bit an earlobe, slipped her tasty tongue along his shoulder.

He lurched and convulsed inside her and then relaxed. His vision still murky from sweat and exhaustion, he studied her perfection. Thin. Muscular. Skin the color of a perfect pearl, milk-white and glistening with health. She had the eyes Satan would use to seduce an angel from God's folds. Blue sapphires with golden sparkles—pornographic jewels. Her hair was magnificent layers of blond velvet.

He tried to touch her hair. It was swept into a swirl atop her head. She stopped his hand, kissed his palm, then guided his fingers and began to ravenously rub herself to orgasm against his wet knuckles.

He got to watch. How her nipples grew hot and erect. How her pulse played wildly in the soft spot of her beautiful, long throat. How her bright, white teeth bit deeply into her delightful lips, lips that he knew could suck a man's sanity from his soul.

She heaved one last time and said quietly, "I should go. Your wife might come home."

He toyed with her breasts calmly. "I told you, she's out of town. Kelly, it's been a month now that I've had you. You know, I almost didn't go to that oncology conference

41

downtown. I thought it would be boring. How wrong I was. If it wasn't for that conference, I wouldn't have met you. God, what I would have missed. You fuck like a thorough-bred race horse runs, lady."

She smiled demurely. "Raymond, are you sure you haven't told anyone you're sleeping with me?"

He tried again to touch her hair. She stopped him again, sucked on his fingers. He answered, "Honey, surgeons don't engage in locker-room gossip. It would cost me millions of dollars in a divorce if I was dumb enough to brag about what you do to me in this bed."

She leaned forward and kissed him hard. He felt the slender angles along her back with both his hands. She groped his testicles while they lashed tongues. Her beautiful breasts pumped his chest like bouncing decadent balls as they banged themselves to orgasm again.

He was dripping sweat. He sat up on the bed's edge and felt weak with satisfaction. "To celebrate our one-month anniversary today, here's a present."

From the bedside stand he pulled a small box. She dressed in her white nursing hose—he noted the added nastiness of the white garter belt and crotchless white lace panties beneath—and knowing it was all for him made him feel dizzy. She sat by him when she was dressed.

"Open it," he commanded, and she gasped lightly at the sheen of the diamond bulb on a gold chain for her neck.

"Raymond. No, no, don't put it on me." She wouldn't touch it, and he chuckled at how these nurses and secretaries thought baubles and beads were so impressive.

She told him, "I have a present for you, too. Get dressed and come into your study."

He showered quickly and dressed. Wool slacks. Blue monogram dress shirt. Tie. Socks. Tasseled loafers. The crisp look of the chief surgeon. Understated and painfully tasteful.

In the study, she pointed to his throne of an armchair. "Sit here and close your eyes. Don't peek, okay?"

He felt slightly uneasy. "Kelly, I can't keep sentimental objects from you around my house, you know. I can't make mistakes. Whatever you give me has to be something nobody will recognize as a clue to our relationship."

"I promise," she sang out. "Now close your eyes tight."

She stood to his right side. Put his semiautomatic .380 pistol an imperceptible breath away from his temple and pulled the trigger.

She had been careful what she touched, but went through anyway and wiped doorknobs and the bedposts. With a white cotton cloth—universal in its fiber components—she lifted his right hand to his temple, put the gun in his limp fingers and let it all drop. She ripped sheets from the bed, bundled them, dropped them into the washer and added bleach to the hot water, wiped the washer door and the bleach bottle and set things back into place. They would find no evidence of her. The white cotton fabric she wore had no forensic distinction at all. The pistol left no residue on skin.

In the doorway of his study, she looked over the mess. Pieces of brain tissue clung in globs to his computer screen and covered the wall behind him. He was slumped sideways, hand dangling, gun on the floor. Blood was pooling in his mouth and spilling onto his chin.

"As I promised, darling Raymond, no clue as to what we were doing."

Her car was in the private alley behind his sprawling estate, a private cove used by caterers and housekeepers and the man who cared for the now dormant elaborate gardens. She messed up her footprints purposefully as she walked lightly in the snow. She backed her car out to the street cleared of snow by salting crews. After putting on surgical gloves, she backed Raymond's car over her tire tracks, parked it by the curb, got into her car and drove away. The neighborhood was desolately empty and quiet. The diamond necklace, box and all, sailed easily into the dumpster behind a big grocery store along with the incriminating white surgical towel and gloves.

=10=

Rachel swiveled in her chair in time to turn and see Chaz coming at her, waving and smiling. She frowned.

"What, Diablo? You running for office? Why so chummy?"

"Two things," he remarked glibly as he sat. She smelled musk and shampoo and couldn't help but admire his jazzy baggy slacks and cool sports coat. He gazed longingly at her. "First, I really need a personal favor from you. Second, I'm having a better day than this call we just got." He flipped a notepad. "Dr. Raymond Esterhaus, Associate Chief of Surgery at Dallas Memorial, signal 51 with a brain burner. I feel good just knowing I'm not as bad off as he must have been."

Rachel kept reading distractedly. "What kind of favor?"

He sighed. "I need you to go on a date with me."

She guffawed at the ceiling. "Oh, Diablo, you cutup."

"I'm serious, Collazo. My mother is flying in from Miami. I'm taking her to dinner tomorrow, and I have to bring some kind of date so she'll think I have a normal love life. We don't want her knowing that her son is a common whore."

"You got a ga-zillion big-titted nymphs on the trot line, Diablo. Take one of them."

"That's the point," he said, moving close to get her full attention. "Any of the girls I date is likely to show up wearing so much skin-tight latex that I have to tell my mama this girl works in underwater construction. No, I

44

have to take someone respectable, like you. Mama will collapse from doing rosaries if she finds out that all the women in my life are come-queens and contortionists."

Rachel sat back, eyeing him comically. "What's her name?"

"Mama? Camille. You'll do it? You'll eat with us and pretend you're my girlfriend?"

"Diablo, what do I look like to you? Lucille Ball? I hate the thought of playing a prank on a sweet, little old lady. Just tell her that you don't have a girl right now."

"She'll worry that I'm gay. Or worse yet, starving and doing my own laundry. All you have to do is tell her how happy we are together, that we enjoy the same things."

"Oh, like body piercing and group sex?"

He frowned. "Collazo, do this for me."

"And you do what for me?" She was immensely enjoying his bout with humility.

"Name it."

She took a moment, then announced, "Stay my partner until we prove to poor Mizz Pickett that her sister Ashley wasn't murdered. Help me look into it. You're good. You can help me put that sweet woman's mind at ease. Agree, and I'll eat with your mama. I'll even hold your hand at the table."

He winced. Rachel intensified, saying, "Then tomorrow night you help me serve at the soup kitchen. Every Wednesday I dish out grub at the Gospel Mission. You need to see these people, understand their plight better. Might take some of the sass out of your ass."

Chaz rolled his eyes. "Forget it."

"Fine," she snapped, "so Camille will know that all the girls you date dance in cages."

He simmered. She laughed. He said flatly, "Why do you care about Mrs. Pickett anyway?"

"She's nice. She's hurting. She's a human being."

He hung his head and growled. "Okay. Meet Mama and me at the Mansion in Turtle Creek tomorrow at eight. Call me Chaz—" he pointed at her, "and nothing else. Not cop

cake and not asshole and definitely not Diablo. Just Chaz.
Or baby doll."

She rattled a handful of papers at him. "Fine, baby doll.
Now let's get back to work. The Anna Huffman murder.
Stabbed eighteen times by her former boyfriend Ronny
McEntire."

"So. It's closed. He's confessed. Why, Collazo, are you
holding out on pushing for his immediate indictment?"

She put on her glasses, and Chaz grinned at how cute she
was. She said methodically, pointing at a chart of wounds to
the girl's body, "Looky here, sugarcane kid. Seventeen of
the wounds are extremely similar in width and depth. Big
butcher knife, Doc Truett says, two inches wide and nine
inches long."

Chaz replied drably, "I know. I found it and bagged it at
the scene last week. It has McEntire's prints all over it, and
cuts on his hand match the blade and trajectory. He slashed
her."

Rachel blew out a breath of contemplation. "Sweet and
simple, I reckon. Except see, baby doll—" she flickered a
dastardly grin, "I'm practicing for Mama, see here—there's
this weird wound in her neck. Three inches deep and a half-
inch wide. Doc Truett says this wound was first and fatal in
her carotid. The other seventeen pops were gravy."

He took the gruesome artwork, a drawing of a female
body with X's representing stab wounds riddled across her
breasts, belly and throat. Chaz postulated, "I can't see how
that minor detail matters in light of his confession which,
by the way, fits the crime scene and the autopsy findings."

Rachel's blood raced. "This fatal wound was done by
someone else with a different plunging strength and an
entirely different weapon. Trust me."

He laughed. "You have eighteen stab wounds to contend
with, plus the boy's description of how he did it, plus his
bloody clothes—Anna Huffman's blood, by the way—
which were found under his car seat when he was arrested.
His sperm is in her. And you think he didn't do it? Woman,
did anyone ever teach you to cry uncle?"

Rachel stood. "He says he did it because she prick-teased

him, they got naked and then she started backing off, saying no, so he raped her and then stabbed her. Naw. I don't buy it."

Chaz considered his fingernails and began to buff them against his pant leg. "His confession passed polygraph."

Rachel fixed a gaze out the grimy window and into the dim sky laden with polluted frozen rain. She could see how it happened, but she had no face to put on the boy's accomplice. "He passed polygraph 'cause he popped her like he said. They didn't ask him if someone else in the room shagged her first with something else. I think this someone else caught them just finishing a slow, nasty go at it, grabbed up something in passion, swacked Anna in the throat, and then I think Ronny shooed this person away, got the butcher knife and finished the deal. And if it wasn't Ronny's new girl Nancy, then I'll wear lipstick and perfume for a whole week."

Chaz asked curtly, "Why would Ronny take the rap for her? I interrogated that boy for six hours. He knows he's going to prison for a long time. Nobody loves someone that much."

Rachel said hollowly, "Ronny does. Now we'll just see how much Nancy loves him. She's a hotbox of insecurities and hormones. Anna was a looker, a wet dream. Nancy's plain, not too smart. His former affair with Anna must've driven her nuts, and then Anna taunting him like that, and to stoke the fire Ronny was probably telling Nancy all about how Anna was still after him. I've got the human dynamics, Diablo. I just got to prove it."

He may have sounded defensive against her cunning insights. "I interviewed Nancy at length, Collazo. She didn't do it."

The printer behind them sputtered to life. Rachel tore off the pages she wanted and said to Chaz, "Yes, she did. And I'm going to nab her. I'm going to do it like a big hunting dog, just the way Daddy showed me. Now look, here's the stuff on Wesley Merriam. He has never been charged with or convicted of a crime, neither local, state nor federal. No criminal history."

Chaz fished in her desk drawer for a piece of Clove gum and remarked dumbly, "God, this stuff is a childhood throwback. I feel like pulling your hair and launching spitwads."

Rachel read on. "Wes hasn't called the police to his residence in the past five years, no burglaries or alarm codes or domestic disturbances. Not so much as a traffic violation."

Chaz laughed again, and the smell of the gum came in a sickly sweet wave. "Ah, profile of a wife killer."

Rachel scoffed, "Hey, Tarzan, prisons are full of sane people who did one crazy thing and got caught. Some of us go to the edge of rage and stop there. Some go over the edge, and before they do they're perfectly normal joes. Check out this nursing service, a Janet Bachman and a Kelly McLaughlin. Find out the routine stuff about Dr. Wahlstein, Ashley's oncologist."

Wise ass as possible, Chaz replied, "Like maybe he's a.k.a. Dr. Kevorkian? Let's go, Columbo. We've got a dead doctor and then I've got to get a manicure."

"You're spooky, Diablo, you know that? I'm going to tell your mama that the main thing we have in common, you and me, is how much we both love butt fucking."

He screamed laughter at her. It echoed nicely in the solemn hallways of the homicide division.

=11=

The boy was good with his hands, Daniel noted to himself with fatherly pride. The work area in the garage was their nightly mecca. Tonight Pete was learning to use sandpaper, working on deftness. He was doing well with his small hands. Daniel kissed his son's hair.

"Where are you going to put this little stool you made, Petey? Got a special place for it?"

The boy chirped nicely, "I didn't really build it, Daddy. You did the hard stuff. I want to put it under my toilet in my bathroom. When you're short like me it's nice to put your feet somewhere when you sit a long time going poo-poo."

Daniel rocked back in laughter. Pete smiled endearingly.

"I love you, Pete."

"I love you more, Dad."

The room darkened as if a vulture had swooped. Julie Ann was standing in the doorway.

She said sweetly, "Pete, sweetheart, your bath water is ready. Oh, your new stool is just beautiful, honey. I'll use it in the cupboard for things I can't reach."

Pete met his dad's eyes with dread and said nothing as he walked quietly into the house and shut the door.

"He wants the foot stool in his bathroom, Julie Ann."

"I doubt very much that you know what he wants, Daniel. For most of his life you've been busy writing, winning big awards. . . ." she mocked him, "even a Pulitzer for your crummy newspaper. That certainly made us as rich as the next starving poet. I thought you were playing handball with your friend tonight. Or did he already beat you and you came home early?"

Daniel took it well. He only replied, "Chaz canceled. His mother came to town."

"I hate him," Julie allowed icily.

"I believe he knows that, thank you. Most of my friends do know that you hate them, especially after you tell them so."

He felt the urge to slug her or fall to his knees and weep. "What did you come out here for, Julie? Had it been a whole hour since you bitched at me? Need a bitch fix, hon?"

She shoved a piece of paper at him. "These are the things that I need for Pete's birthday party tomorrow. Be home from work by two o'clock and bring these things."

"What time should I tell my family to be here for the party?"

She stiffened as if ice water had showered her. "You shouldn't tell your family to be here. They're not invited. I told you I didn't want your brother and his sleazy wife in my home anymore."

The sledgehammer teetered on top of his tool box. He contemplated it, said to her calmly, "It's my son's birthday. And this is not your house. It's our house."

Her pale swan neck strained. Her cheeks flushed red. Her teeth gritted. Instant rage. "He brings wine. There will be people here from our church. Your family is not the right sort."

A chuckle erupted from him unwittingly. "The right sort of what? Judgmental, Bible-banging, anal-retentive people-haters you're used to from our congregation? You can't tell my family not to come here anymore, Julie Ann. I won't let you be so sanctimonious when it comes to people who Pete loves. Your opinion for once doesn't matter."

A veil of hatred crept across her paleness. "Daniel, it's not fair for you to ask me right now to endure any more agony than I have to."

He whined comically, "My family at my son's birthday party is agony? It might, like, cause your cancer to spread?"

Shit. He kicked the sledgehammer to the floor when he

heard her first grueling sob. She covered her face. He backed away, couldn't imagine reaching for her.

"Please," she cried, "if it's my last birthday party for my son, the last I ever give for him or share with him, let it be my way, Danny . . . please . . . just my mother and my church friends and me and you. . . ."

"You hate everyone who loves me, Julie Ann. Do you know that? You're jealous of anybody who cares for me because when someone loves me then you're afraid you won't be able to control me."

She cried loudly, "Stop! I feel sick!"

He took a long breath, watched her quivering and sobbing behind her hands. She was emaciated from worrying, wasting away with anger and despair. He went to her and put his arms around her. She did not return his embrace but didn't resist either.

"Okay," he whispered. "Okay, sweetheart, I won't invite my family." And his insides shriveled at the sight and sound of his own debauched fear of defying her.

She sniffled, "I want you to move all my things to the downstairs guest bedroom tonight. My clothes, everything in the drawers. I need to be downstairs after my surgery next week."

"You're moving out of our bedroom?"

"I have cancer, Daniel. The stairs are too much for me." There was a cold conviction in her glare. "I can't force myself anymore to do the things I've always done to make you happy. All my energy has to go toward getting well."

His voice hobbled. "Sex, you mean. You can't force yourself any longer to have sex with me."

"Celibacy will be good for you for a while," she intoned with amazing rigidity. "Christ was celibate."

"I'm not Christ. I'm your husband. Has it occurred to you that I might go somewhere else for sex?"

She searched his face, then smiled coldly. "No. Because at the base of it, Daniel, you know that if you did, it would kill me. And anyway, you're not that kind of man. Not that brave, not that shallow, and certainly not that desirable to other women. Once they watch you hold a sandwich in your teeth while you type or hear you scream at a stupid baseball game, any other woman would send you home to me."

She went inside stiffly. The fact that she was physically alluring in her flimsy nightgown, the fact that he could remember feeling her tongue in his mouth long ago and her juices on his erections was no comfort now.

For comfort he touched the foot stool, sanded to a smooth plane by the little hands of his son. With his hand on its spongy, shiny wood, Daniel could connect with the reason he stayed in the marriage. He sat on a taller bar stool, lay his head on the work table cluttered with tools and wood shavings, keeping one hand on Pete's foot stool, imagining that it anchored him to the only happiness in his whole reality.

=12=

The dead doctor had grown cold and turned a flat shade of gray mortar. The medical examiner, Dr. Erin Truett, a brilliant Aggie lesbian with the disposition of Ellie Mae Clampitt and the intellect of a Mensa master, said with that hot-tar Texas accent of hers, "Hey there, Rachel. Y'all come on in. I've got his head and hands bagged."

George Dorcus turned sublimely to Rachel and Chaz as they skulked in. "Hey, Mod Squad," he snarled with puffs of white from his cigarette, "This here is Dr. Raymond Esterhaus. Was, anyway."

Rachel asked, "Erin, can we step in here? Y'all gotten all the trace evidence?"

Erin oozed, snapping shut her big black bag, "Yeah, honey, we got it." She lit a cigarette beside Rachel in the hallway. "You get Emory to marry you yet, sugar?"

"No chance. If I did you'd have seen me running naked down the streets, hooting for joy. Did you and Jill tie the knot?"

Erin rolled her lively blue eyes. "Naw. She's still worried about telling her family about us. Like they haven't wondered why we've lived together for two years, and every time they drop in I'm wearing a tool belt and a Texas A&M jersey and working on the wiring or plumbing."

Rachel laughed loudly. Erin went on, "The good doctor here died after ten this morning and, obviously as we can see, before now—noon. He did a surgery at seven, left the hospital at nine and told his secretary he'd be back. He won't be back."

Chaz asked quietly, "Who's that sobbing in the kitchen?"

Dorcus said complacently, "Wife. She says they was Ozzie and Harriet, no money problems, he wasn't depressed or nothing. So she says."

Rachel looked in at the doctor's ghoulish death mask, his face sucked deep in a clear plastic bag that was splattered with his blood. "He used that .380 I guess, so that means no powder residue on his hand. Are his prints on the gun?"

Dorcus said, "There's prints, all matching his it looks like. We can't find no chinks in this chain at all."

Erin gathered paraphernalia into her bag and said sedately, "I'm all done here, kids. Preliminary ruling to the press is suicide. Rachel, when it warms up let's play tennis again."

Rachel laughed over the sound of the dead doctor being zipped into a black canvas body bag, his pale hand with blood trickles falling out and open, waving to them, until the paramedic shoved it back into the bag.

"Why?" she teased Erin, "You need a good laugh, watching me try to return your aces?"

Erin patted her shoulder. "Call me around four tomorrow. I'll have a final ruling on this guy. Right now, nothing hinky."

Chaz returned from the kitchen, closing his note pad succinctly. "The wife says he wasn't depressed. But listen to this." Rachel and Dorcus came close and leaned in. "She gets home, the house is immaculate as usual, except the bed sheets in the guest room are stripped and dumped in the washing machine . . . doused in bleach." His eyebrow arced.

Rachels' brain ticked. "No shit? Dorcus, bag those wet sheets and vacuum the guest room. Take it all to Erin. What else, Diablo?"

"This," he produced it. "The uniforms found it in his car. A receipt for a necklace. Wifey in there didn't get a necklace and hasn't found one anywhere in the house. I called the jeweler. Esterhaus bought it yesterday. So where is it?"

Dorcus sighed greatly, "You two beat all. He fucked some babe at lunchtime, gave her a necklace, and she blew his head off? Come on, Frick and Frack, give it a rest."

"So explain the sheets," Chaz challenged.

They whispered at high pitch. An M.E.'s investigator carefully scraped cerebral fragments off the wall. Dorcus answered irascibly.

"That's your job. Besides, bleach killed all the traces. You know that. Do I really got to bag those wet sheets, Good Legs?"

"Well, Dorcus honey, it's an inconsistency. I can't let it go. . . ." He tromped from the room unhappily. Rachel sighed, too. "Come on, Diablo. Let's go through his car. First I want to say to his widow how sorry I am and all."

Chaz groaned, rolled his eyes. Rachel stuck her tongue out at him.

Two hours later she dragged herself miserably from the biting cold into the cozy warmth of Emory's kitchen.

She smelled the savory saltiness of frying bacon. He was making egg sandwiches, chilling champagne and playing sexy music. She fell into it like a hot kid lets go of the tire swing into the cool creek.

He saw her in the doorway, a disheveled and beautiful gypsy. She folded her arms around him without a hello. "So," she whined, "why not?"

He smiled, his tanned face pleased and not at all confused by the question. "Sweetheart, I'm sixty-six years old. Any day now I could become incontinent or senile. Tomorrow I could have palsy and drool on myself. I won't give you a life of patting my head while I mumble the names of the saints." He kissed her forehead.

She munched a piece of bacon and put herself between his long, muscular arms. She could smell how organized he was. Shampooed. Cologned. Pressed slacks and extravagant wool sweater and shined shoes.

"You're not geriatric, Emory. You have a great chest and a

wonderful ass. Four days a week you walk eighteen holes of golf." She faced him in supplication. "Do you think that if we're not married when you slip into your blubbering decline, then I won't sit by your bed all day anyhow?"

He put his arms around her sweetly. "Did you know that you don't do anything conventional, Rachel? All of your personal habits are so . . . topsy. You sleep in odd places—the floor, the backyard hammock, the bathtub. You eat tuna sandwiches for breakfast. You watch TV with the sound off. You never have a bit of cash on you, not a dime. All your friends are vagabonds, bums and lesbians. You order things from home-shopping networks and never open the boxes when they arrive. And you're a boxer." He laughed kindly. "The love of my life is a boxer! Ah! Men laugh until they see you in that ring, how serious you are, the brilliance of your heart as you swing. God, you are a joy. Amid all this you love me, your antithesis. The big dashing hunks of men you throw off to talk and walk and make love with me. You confound all reason, Rachel. I love you like no man out there can imagine."

She deadpanned. "So marry me."

They kissed a long time, until he grew hard and she grew wet and they stripped each other and made love on the warm kitchen floor. They sat naked there, eating off china plates and sipping champagne from Waterford flutes. She felt the joy that puppies must feel when they're let in from the cold and given people-food in a warm kitchen.

She said with her mouthful, "While I shower will you go through your house and find me everything that's six inches or less long, pointed and could be used as a weapon?"

As always he said, "Of course, sweetheart. You're going out?" A tinge of worry came through.

The champagne went well with the sweet kiss she gave him. She put her hands through his silver mane and said softly, "Don't worry."

"When you say those words, I know I should worry. Do you have to go? It's so cold, honey. You'll be so alone."

"I have a gun."

"So do the bad guys out there."

She loved his face, touched it. "You know what they call me, Emory, besides of course bitch and cunt. When it comes to solving murders, I'm the Go-to Girl." She smiled.

He smiled, too, uneasily, and touched her hair—not in a fatherly way, but with the passion of equal lust and respect.

=13=

The crummy one-story house was far back off the main road and lost in darkness. Rachel followed the driveway and then parked in back, in a valley of thick trees that would hide her car. Untended tree limbs dipped and scraped her car windows like long, bloody fingers.

The crime scene tape was gone. The investigation was considered solved. Ronny McEntire was in jail for the murder of Anna Huffman.

Rachel killed her lights and sat quietly. Thinking. Ronny said he and Anna broke up their relationship six months before the murder. It had been a bad break-up. They attended the same university, Southern Methodist, and he continued having jealous rages toward her. She played coquettish games with his mind, flaunting other boyfriends and making late-night calls to Ronny, crying that she missed him, and then spurning him coldly in the light of the next day. The night of her death she had invited him over, he said, to talk. Their talk moved to kissing and fondling. They took off their clothes on her living room couch.

Then Anna went cold. Started backing off, making fun of him, telling him that her boyfriend's dick was bigger. In his confession, made to Chaz with a raging flame in his eyes, Ronny said succinctly, "She said that she had made a bet with her sorority sisters that she could get me into bed anytime she wanted to . . . she laughed at me on the couch like some kind of wicked witch . . . so I went berserk or something, and I grabbed up a butcher knife and I started stabbing her. . . ."

Rachel stiffened. The moon went behind a cloud. She evaporated into thick darkness. The limbs scraped. She opened her car door and felt her boots crunch on the light dust of snow. Her flashlight led the way to the plain, brown back door of an old house that had fallen into sad disrepair. She used the key and went into an abyss of bloody walls, blood-stained carpet and dusty overturned furniture. A struggle in stop-action. Death spattered the walls and ceilings.

She called out, "Hello. Police." Only the cobwebs rustled unkindly. Her flashlight followed the massive blood trail, now eroded to brown streaks, from the middle of the worn-out carpet, down the hallway, like a pond of mud that spiraled out to muddy rivers. A bloody handprint gawked from the corner of the wall and then bled brown spikes down the hallway where Anna had clutched as he hauled her by her long red hair toward the bedroom. Rachel followed the death trail.

The place was god-awful. The windows rattled with every frigid breeze like ghosts swarming her. She found the small bathroom where Ronny said he had stuffed Anna in the tub, where she had been found by her brother with a nine-inch knife plunged into her chest and her eyes gaping in a horrid scream. There, Rachel turned out her flashlight.

She whispered, and the roaches and rats scattered so she could hear their bustling feet overhead and beside her.

"Talk to me, Anna, baby. Tell me. I'm here. I know what they did to you. Now you tell me how they did it, girl, and I'll set your little spirit free to go on from this spooky place. Come on, baby, lead me. I'm wide open to hear you and help you. It's here somewhere, the thing she used to take away your life, the thing she grabbed up in a rage when she came in the door and found you and Ronny. . . . She yanked it up and stuck it in your carotid, and it was something you had right there beside you on a table or a counter, something common. I know she did it, honey. I just got to know where she hid it. Show me."

She aimed her flashlight at Emory's handkerchief that she had rolled open. It contained the things he had collected for her while she showered. She fingered them one by one.

"A steak knife. No. Your neck wound is not jagged. A screw driver. No, baby, your wound is smooth and pointed. A meat skewer? Too twisted; your laceration is flush. A pocketknife? Was that it? Ronny had two in his bedroom, no blood traces on either one. Naw. You didn't have a pocketknife handy, Anna. Girls don't. Scissors? No, plunged like that into your throat, the other blade would've cut Nancy's hand. She had no cuts."

She picked up another article Emory had included. It glinted in her flashlight. "A letter opener. Slender and sharp. Okay. Maybe, baby. Talk to me."

She shut the light off again. The floor creaked from a harsh gust outside. A willow tree wept at the window, scraping to call her into another dark room, strangling off the wispy, vague moonlight as it dipped at her.

The request Rachel had made of Nancy that afternoon was clear and simple. "I need some help from you, Nancy. There's this weird wound in Anna's neck and I can't figure it out. The M.E. isn't concerned about it since Ronny has confessed so accurately, but me, you know, I hate these loose ends. They look bad on my records. I need someone who knew Anna to help me figure out what this strange wound could be. And you knew her, from college classes, from parties at her house. Tomorrow morning early I'm going back to the house to look through it again, and after that I'd like you to come look at the stuff I find. We need your help, Nancy, us cops, and since you're on our side you can't tell anybody, okay?" And now she could only wait.

Rachel padded through the darkness. The cops had looked everywhere, but she looked again. Under and inside the toilet tank. Under the kitchen table where something could be taped. Inside obscure cabinets. She flashed her light into a panel that opened to the wet black dirt beneath the house, hung her head down and scanned the spider webs, gasping at the beads of red and gold varmint eyes that glared at her hatefully.

She fiddled through the things left strewn on Anna's cluttered dressing table in the filthy bedroom. Anything important had been bagged as evidence. Loose photos. A box of letters. Only makeup, cigarette butts and Coke cans were left, a graveyard of muck ruck. There was a manicure set. Buffer. Emery board. Cuticle sticks. Cotton swabs.

Rachel bent. "I'll be dipped in shit," she breathed lowly. "Here's a slot for the metal fingernail file. So where's the file? She hid it . . . after she stabbed you with it, by golly."

She looked for it everywhere, maniacally, almost panicked to find it. She took pictures off walls, slung drawers to the floor, dumped a clothes hamper and rifled each musty piece of dirty laundry the cops had left behind. She removed light switch plates and poured caked dirt out of dead potted plants. She was sweating and swearing when the flashlight caught the slightest glint of an object along the wall.

The crotchety old air conditioner stuck in the window had not been used in a long time, if it worked at all. She held the flashlight in her armpit and ran her fingers delicately along the cracked and eroded foam lining that held the unit in the window. And there it was, just the tip of it.

She slid it free, saw the caked blood that made black marks in the metal fingernail file's crisscrossed blade. She dropped it quietly into a small evidence bag. Then she sat in the darkness to wait for what she knew would come.

The headlights crossed the room like lighthouse beacons on black, murky waters at Rachel's feet. The door opened, and in the blips of moonlight a shadow passed Rachel where she crouched. She wanted to jump and high-five someone.

Nancy stood at the old window unit and began digging. Rachel raised herself, hit the flashlight and asked the question.

"You looking for this?"

Nancy reeled at her, frozen in the glaring beam, shielding her eyes. She spewed, "Shit."

"That's exactly what I'd say in your situation, Nancy."

"What the fuck are you doing here?" She washed milk-white in Rachel's beam, a pale apparition of fear.

"Waiting for you. No, now, don't do that. Don't run. I'll have to shoot you. You'd be a suspect fleeing arrest."

The girl said coldly, "You tricked me. You told me a lie to get me to come here."

Rachel pulled out her handcuffs and started toward the girl who had collapsed in tears. She recited the Miranda amid the girl's crushing sobs.

She stood over Nancy, the cuffs shining like falling stars, "Nancy, do you know how many times in my life I've gotten so angry I could just kill somebody? Hell, we all do. I sure understand how it happens. Now just think of me as your priest or your best friend. Tell me how it went down. I'll take no notes. Later we'll get it in writing downtown. For now, you just explain to me what a nasty prick-tease she was and how you didn't have any choice but to do what you did."

They sat on the floor in the dark. Nancy sobbed. Rachel put away the cuffs and her gun. The house no longer felt haunted.

=14=

Deep in the black corner of her closet, Kelly sat naked, arms coiled around her lovely long legs, weeping.

He was going to tell her mama tomorrow, he had said, tell her mama that he woke up and found Kelly, his stepdaughter, fondling his penis with her hands and her mouth. He had jumped and run and vomited and now he was standing over her, weeping from revulsion, and threatening her.

Mama came in too late tonight from teaching a night class at the junior college, he had said, and she would be far too tired to face such a personal catastrophe. *But tomorrow,* he said so calmly that she knew he was resolved, *but tomorrow I'm going to tell her what you did to me.*

No normal teenage girl would carry so far with a crush on her stepfather, and maybe Kelly was sick and needed a psychiatrist, he said.

She could imagine them talking outside her tomb of a closet like they did so many nights when she heard them through her bedroom door. In low, sexy voices to each other, voices that sounded the way their bedroom sheets smelled. Like lipstick and leather.

Tomorrow he was going to tell. But tonight there was the insulin that Mama took . . . the insulin Kelly always gave to Mama in her leg.

She stood at Mama's rainy funeral, a fourteen-year-old, cream-skinned blond goddess with Aphrodite's voluptuousness. From under the hood of her mama's fur coat, she watched him fall on the coffin and weep, dirt caking his knees, tears blinding him like all that cascading black rain. When his mournful eyes met Kelly's across the muddy sinkhole that was to be his adored wife's grave, he shrunk and backed away, frightened of this young temptress, cold to his bones and short of breath beneath her placid gaze.

When he killed himself that night, when young Kelly found him dangling from a basement rafter with his eyes bulging and his tongue engorged, she unzipped his pants and laughed as she took him hungrily into her mouth, like an animal feeding on a kill.

"Mama," she cooed, as if whispering down into the floral wafts from the roses on the coffin, "in the end, he was mine."

Back in her closet she felt the scorpion drop onto her bare shoulder and scamper along her arm, its pincers tickling her hairs, stinger swaying. She knew it wouldn't sting. She lay very still as it slithered down her large breast and stopped to perch triumphantly on her erect nipple. She enjoyed the forbidden sensation of knowing it was the scorpion who truly should be afraid.

She flicked the scorpion away, uncaring, then crawled deeper into the shadows, a retreat into isolated madness that the daytime could never afford her.

Her mama's kindly face swirled into view.

"Insulin overdose . . . your wife is dead . . . your step-daughter administered it right, but sometime in the night your wife inexplicably gave herself more, a lot more . . . we'll never know why."

They would never know that it was Kelly who in the night slid into her mother's leg the injection of a lethal dose certain to send her into deadly shock.

Kelly crushed herself to the closet wall and clawed as if trying to climb it. She screamed crazily, "He's mine not yours mine not yours mine . . . not yours."

The manic clawing had made her fingers bleed. She coiled herself into a catatonic clump on the floor, her bloody hands smearing her chest and face like gruesome graffiti.

=15=

Coiffed like a regular classy babe, shiny hair fluffed with a blow dryer and tamed with a curling iron, looking stellar in a wool boucle jacket and fitted skirt, Rachel threw open the doors to the men's locker room at the YMCA like a pissed-off gunslinger. She yelled loudly and heard her echo over the spewing showers and brimming terse conversations of all the half-naked or naked men.

"Cover 'em, boys! Police business! Diablo! Where the fuck are you?"

A groan of disdain went out. Some lunged to cover themselves and some didn't. One guy called out, "Collazo, you're a complete fucking asshole."

She walked through the rows of lockers and puddles of water, and she hollered at him, "Shut up, you corporate worm. I've seen weenies bigger than yours in cocktail sauce. Diablo!" She rounded a corner and found him toweling himself and stepping into bikini underwear. She stared meanly and then said, "The Ashley Merriam thing is unclassified. Jesus, Diablo, wouldn't you be embarrassed to be found dead somewhere in those panties?"

He slid into camel hair slacks and a blue-and-beige flannel shirt. "These are underwear. Men do not wear panties. Collazo, do you ever think to wait until I get to the office for these conversations? What's unclassified? Her cause of death?"

"Yeah. On the autopsy report. I talked to a clerk on my

car phone on the way in this morning. What the hell kind of shoes are those, boy?"

He slicked back his hair in a mirror inside the locker door and poured a mound of goo onto it before winding his pony tail into a rubber band.

Rachel frowned. "You look like a fucking matador."

He frowned back at her. "Good. Because you act like a snorting bull. These are Belgian suede loafers. And you know that an unclassified death certificate is not a routine police matter." He turned to her, groomed suddenly like the prize winner in a dog show. "You did nice work on Nancy. I was impressed."

"Is that a compliment, Diablo?"

He grimaced. "If it was, it's because I haven't had my coffee yet and I'm addled. We got credit in the newspapers this morning for popping Ronny as a major source of heroin and cocaine among the rich bush-league kids here. You should've been in the photos of Nancy's arrest. You cracked her for the murder, and in the papers it looks like I'm the hero."

Rachel griped. "Aw, the Bureau's impressed by that shit. I'd do anything to get rid of your ass out of my department." She smiled nicely at him. "Hey, can you imagine that dipshit Ronny? He sells a half-million bucks a year worth of dope to most of North Dallas for two years, hides his money at Nancy's house. Then Nancy shows up while he's screwing Anna and man, the gloves were off, Nancy whacks Anna. Ol' Ronny had almost $750,000 in Nancy's closet. Jesus. Good thing that boy was an accounting major."

Chaz laughed dryly. "He knew he'd go to prison longer for the drugs if Nancy told on him than he would for the murder. So to keep her quiet about the dope, he said he did a murder while he was 'berserk.' Nice touch. He even called a free legal advice hotline to find out if dope laws were tougher than temporary insanity sentences."

Rachel chuckled. "With legal advice you get what you pay for. So, did you check into that nursing service Ashley Merriam was using like I asked you to?"

"Yes," he told her flatly. "From their driver's license numbers on our files I got a criminal history. None. From the DL numbers I also got their car tag numbers so I know where they bought their cars and I know they each make their own car payments each month. I got home addresses and checked to see who pays their utilities. Bachman has a husband and McLaughlin supports herself quite nicely—no payments to them from anybody else, specifically Wes Merriam. I got credit reports. They're both in good standing and pay their own credit cards. No sugar daddies. I got an employment history from their DEA numbers for handling controlled substances. We're talking squeaky clean here with these two broads. Then I waited in the nursing service parking lot and watched them arrive this morning. Bachman's pudgy, fifty and looks like a fractured fairy, kind of fat with big hair and too much cosmetics, real smiley and chipper." He stopped.

Rachel tuned it up. "And McLaughlin? Come on."

"If you'll pardon the pun, McLaughlin looks like the kind of woman a lot of men would kill for. You know what you say when you see a blond with tits and an ass like hers? You say, 'Don't bother to wrap her, I'll eat her here.' She's hot. Way above the good-looking crowd."

Two naked men padded past them, one fat, the other stringy, Laurel and Hardy fresh from the steam room. Laurel panicked and went into spasms trying to cover himself when he saw Rachel. She waved him away.

"So, Diablo, can you get more on these women, I mean, without violating anyone's right to privacy?"

"No, but I can get more without anyone knowing I'm violating their right to privacy. But this is dumb, you know. You've got no evidence Ashley was murdered. Erin doesn't think so. The forensics and crime scene don't suggest it. You got a ditsy sister-in-law with two airline ticket jackets. Either one of these nurses can sue the shit out of our department if they find out we're treating them like suspects and we don't even have a homicide ruling."

Rachel scoffed, as usual. "Fuck 'em. Asking is our job. What'd you get on her doctor, Wahlstein?"

"He's a hotshot in oncology. The only game in town. In twenty-five years he's never had an ethics complaint or been sued."

Rachel groused, "Ashley Merriam got a hospital bacteria two months after leaving the hospital. Her husband took off two days after her funeral and won't return my messages he's getting on his yacht from the Coast Guard. Anyway, I promised Mizz Pickett I'd see it through. It's not a mountain up there, but it's a grain of sand in my shoe. You know?"

"Did you make that up, Collazo?"

She smiled. "No. But here it is. A woman recovering from cancer, going into remission, who can't have any visitors because of the infection risk, suddenly she's got an infection. She sees nobody for two months except nurses, her husband and her doctor. Check their backgrounds just a little more for me. And tonight at dinner with Camille I won't say fuck or goddamn too many times."

A muscled, mafia-looking guy to Rachel's right dropped his towel as they walked past and let his dong hang for her inspection. He called out, "Hey, honey, wanna do the wild thing tonight?"

She answered dryly, "Yeah. But not with you."

As they passed through the workout club, the women in leotards, sweat suits and bikinis ogled Chaz. He muttered to Rachel, "Be nice to me. It's my birthday."

"Happy birthday," she offered. "Loan me twenty bucks and I'll buy your lunch."

=16=

Sometimes Julie Ann did everything right. She calculated it that way. Just when Daniel had enough of her bitchy rejection, when her meanness became common enough so he was openly immune to it, she went lovey-dovey for a spell. When he hated her the most, she feigned love to make him feel guilty for it.

She read the morning news and knew that he was having a good day in the news room. She knew colleagues were slapping his back and the community was applauding from its collective breakfast tables. Daniel was again the hero.

In one banner headline that morning, Daniel's abilities as an investigative reporter had leveled one corrupt government official. In the second front-page piece, he called into serious question why a police department didn't do its job.

After months of talking to a whispery, frightened young anonymous woman on the phone about the sexual advances of City Councilman Jack Lawson, Daniel finally got her name with promises never to use it without her permission. The barrier went down and the bond of trust between them gelled. Without once telling a lie, he tracked down the other sexual harassment victims of Lawson and convinced them to tell him the gory, lurid details.

"I can't tell you who gave me your name," he said to the source after she gasped at his name. "This is Daniel Nystrom. I'm a reporter with the Dallas News. I have some information that in your job at the city you have been sexually harassed on more than one occasion by Councilman Lawson. If you'd care to tell me about it I can hold out using your name in the stories for as long as possible. When I can't avoid divulging your name any longer, then I use everyone's names—all of the other women, too—so nobody is singled out for trouble. I'd like you to meet with me. I'd like to help you stop this abuse of Lawson's power—if it's true."

Some of them cried and screamed. Some hung up abruptly. But one by one, like deer to his block of salt, they tiptoed back to him. When they met him, individually and then all together as a mob for justice, they knew immediately why his phone demeanor was marked by such objective honesty. The plain, little-boy haircut. The wire rims. The broad shoulders and loosened tie. The depth with which he listened and never judged, and yet nothing they told him was whisked past him. He confirmed every detail, every date and event that they outlined as an episode of Lawson's abuse. From the woman whose rent Lawson had paid, Daniel wanted a canceled check with Lawson's signature on it. From the girl whose abortion Lawson had paid for, Daniel wanted the doctor's name so the facts could not be denied. From the woman who had felt so dirty for her longtime affair with the married Lawson that she ended up in lengthy therapy with a psychiatrist, Daniel wanted permission for the doctor to discuss with him how much emotional damage the woman had suffered because of Lawson. They were assorted secretaries and clerks who all worked for the city. And they were scared to death of Jack Lawson's retribution. Then they met Daniel and they knew that his ethics as a journalist was their way to destroy Lawson's powerful hold over their lives.

And that is just what the morning's newspaper had done, all prefaced by the byline of Daniel Nystrom. Lawson would resign by noon that day in a public press conference and hire a renowned lawyer to help him with the civil suits all the women were filing. Daniel knew the monetary judgments would eventually leave Lawson penniless.

The cops were furious about the other story. A young tough named Manny Herrera had been riding with gang members, one of whom sprayed the front of a rival gang member's family home with bullets and killed an infant inside. It was typical daily news grist, except that Daniel had discovered that the shooter was wearing an electronic tracking device that sent a signal when he went outside a certain perimeter and alerted the police that he had left his home. The police got the alarm. And for a reason nobody could justify under Daniel's questioning, the police ignored it. Sloppy cop work let the kid go far enough and long enough to murder a baby.

The police chief had called Daniel, ranting and squealing. "Nystrom, that's illegal information for you to have." And Daniel had grinned into the phone while the rabid old ex-marine colonel screamed at him. "You could have called me and asked for an explanation of why when that boy's leg alarm went off none of our officers responded. Goddamn it."

"Uh, chief, it says in the text of the story that you were out of town and did not return my repeated calls. I've got a copy of the Denver hotel's message roster, and I'm on it about six times while you were at that convention."

Bombs went off. "So you quoted our goddamned public information officer? That's as high as you went?"

"That's what you hired her for, to talk to reporters. I'm a reporter. So tell me the explanation now. Tell me how the D.A.'s office has this kid charged with a murder that he obviously committed during a time when he was to be monitored by your department. I'll put you on the record right now. Your public info officer said you were looking into the matter and would get back to me. So here I am, chief. Get back to me."

He laughed when the dial tone slapped his ear.

Carrying his gym bag, he loped his long legs and deck shoes across the parking lot of the newspaper building to the health club where he played handball and swam as many days a week as he could before going home. In the locker room afterward, after he showered and dressed, his friends from the D.A.'s office said a bunch of them were going for beers to celebrate Chaz Diablo's fortieth birthday and why didn't Daniel come along. Daniel declined begrudgingly. Chaz was a buddy, but Julie would make his evening pure living shit if he so much as veered from her duty roster of his marital chores.

He got home just before seven and thought immediately that he had walked into the wrong house. Instead of blaring cartoons and a cold oven, he felt low music and smelled garlic simmering in tomatoes.

Then he saw Julie Ann and dropped his gym bag to stand very still and stare at her.

"You look tired, Danny honey." She was wearing a negligee.

He was afraid to make noise and wake himself from what was sure to be a great wet dream. She came forward and looped her arms around him so that he had to bend and take hold of her, lift her off the floor.

She kissed him, opened his mouth with her tongue and chewed his bottom lip. She whispered, and the lulling love in her tone made his knees weak.

"We're alone, Danny. Pete is spending the night with your mom."

He lowered her and she began to unbutton his shirt. When her lips and then her teeth hit his bare chest a surge of hot vapors warmed him from the inside and made his testicles burn and ache.

They made love on the couch. She did things that he thought she had forgotten forever. Whether she had gone insane or returned to normal, he couldn't say, but the woman who hadn't touched his body in almost five months was writhing on top of him at that moment like maybe she did still love him after all.

He growled through the ecstasy, "I love you, Julie Ann. Do you know that?"

They talked afterward while they sat cross-legged at the coffee table by the fireplace and ate their dinner. Daniel almost choked when Julie Ann came from the kitchen and put a cold beer in front of him. Her legs were perfect. Her long hair draped nicely over her shoulders onto the straps of the negligee, white flames melting onto her small, creamy breasts.

"I want to say something to you, Danny." She sipped water from a crystal wine glass.

He looked sheepishly at her. "Okay."

She dabbed at her lips with a napkin and rested her hand on his. "I do try."

He started, "I know—"

But she continued quickly. "I try to be the things I believe I should be. A Christian woman first, a good mother, a wife." She lowered her eyes. "You know, they taught me all my life that Jesus would bring me—just poof, out of the sky—the perfect husband. They pointed to the Bible and said that if I was chaste and faithful ... well, I believed them, all that fundamentalist stuff, taking the Bible so literally."

He felt a cello note slide sourly. "And I'm not the perfect husband. Because a nice husband wouldn't ask you to be ... erotic or sensual. I know, Julie. I know that's what they taught you. My family grew up in the same church as yours, you remember. But honey, carnal love in marriage is not sin."

She tightened. "I could not live, I mean I would die, before I'd face my church community with a divorce in this family. But—"

"Divorce! What the hell—" The word meant death to him, death of his son's love for him, death of his whole tidy if complicated world.

"But Danny, all I can do is try. I can't keep pretending to be those things you said. Erotic. Sensual. They're as hard for me as it would be for you to be, I don't know, something horrible like homosexual or Roman Catholic. So one of us has to change."

Her eyes were as clear and blinding as hot sun blazing on a tin roof. "And since my behavior is from the Bible, then it's you who should change, Danny. My mother and my sisters and the women in church who are my fellow prayer warriors agree."

She was so blithe about it, and even though it was so tragic, he still had to smile drearily. "Prayer warriors? Appealing to God is now a . . . a weapon you use to make people think and act like you think? Julie, where are you? Where's the joyous, loving girl I married in college? The one who I married because we were so open and caring toward each other? Did you really just use the word divorce? Can you see no other way out of this, either I change or you wreck our family? Is it possible you're the one who's out of line here? Jesus Christ!"

She held up a frail hand. "Save your blasphemy. I love you, Danny. I love this marriage. But we've had our baby, and now if I'm facing cancer he's likely to be the only baby we'll get. So now the sex is just debauchery. You need to know that's how I feel. The prayer warriors have prayed and God has told me to stop fighting with you about sex. What we'll do is, when you have to have it, I'll service you, like just now. Meanwhile, I'd like you to ask the congregation to pray that you become more spiritual and less . . ." She stabbed him with her superiority. "Less unhallowed."

He felt his jaw set in anger. "I can't believe this is happening. They warned me, my frat brothers, they warned me that someday all that fervent Bible brainwashing would surface in you—"

She scoffed rudely. "Please. Those marauders, the losers. They're all divorced or having affairs, Daniel. And we're still a family."

He had moved to the sofa. She came to sit by him, to tempt him with her gentle if belittling logic. He said sadly, "I don't want just a family. I want a marriage, this marriage, like it used to be."

"Sweetheart," she cooed, "it was always to get a baby. Now, he's here, and I've tried it your way, the debauchery." She knelt and put her gaze on him lovingly. "I'll try, Danny. When you need it, I'll try. And will you try, too? Will you stop having beer in our house when our friends come over. Will you quit going to baseball games and football games on the Lord's day? Will you give up profanity, those cigars you smoke sometimes? Will you try to change, too?"

"Julie, when your church hillbillies come to my home, I shouldn't have to hide a lousy six-pack of beer from them. Why does what they think matter more to you than loving who I am? I like beer. I'm not an alcoholic. . . ."

She lashed at him verbally, her eyes ignited. "Daniel! I said I'll try! I said I love you! Can you at least try, too? If you want to crawl all over my body like Satan as a snake once in a while, and no matter how it repulses me I say okay, then can you just concede a few things for me? Come home from work straightaway. Don't drink beer in my presence. Don't curse or be late or go places where I can't find you immediately—"

He groaned and then yelled, "It's not normal!"

She yelled back. "No, what's normal is for people to give up. I don't want to give up. I want you to be the kind of man who's fit to raise my little boy if I die, and that is NOT a man who drinks and smokes and curses and goes to R-rated movies!" He started away but she caught his arm, screaming at him. "I want a God-fearing man, and I want it to be you! Help me, Daniel! Try with me! I'm trying, even while I'm so scared of dying!"

She started to cry, just sort of disintegrated into his arms. He stroked her pretty long hair, rubbed her back gently.

"Oh, Julie. My Jules. How can we possibly hate loving each other so much? Shhh, sweetheart. I know you try. I'll try, too. I know I do things that drive you batty, and I'll quit."

She sobbed with her face pressed into his chest. "You be there every minute in the morning while I'm in surgery. Please. Don't go far away from me. Promise."

He picked her up to carry her to bed. She looped her arms around him. He said, "Don't be scared about tomorrow, Julie. And most importantly, try not to be angry. You're not being punished. Maybe we're just being tested somehow."

He lay her down, sat until she was drifting away in slumber.

=17=

The patients sitting along the walls in the cheerfully uphol-
stered office of oncologist Dr. Edward Wahlstein looked up
at Rachel with a cumulative sympathy. By merely walking
into the reception area of his evening clinic, it was assumed
she had cancer.

Some of them were bald, sunken zombies, the bones of
their faces almost pointed. Others looked completely vibrant. The coat rack was crammed with winter coats, so
Rachel kept her overcoat across her arm. A portly, older
woman with zingy red cheeks from too much blush pushed
aside a pane of glass and looked at Rachel expectantly.

This was a dreaded moment. In a split-second the woman's perky smile would fade. "Evenin'," Rachel said as
friendly as a flight attendant. "My name is Rachel Collazo."
Then she flipped the gory badge and the woman's face went
from perky to mightily perturbed. "I'm a detective with the
Dallas P.D., ma'am. I just need a bit of information, you
see."

The woman said as if she'd just seen a fly floating in her
chicken broth, "Oh . . . my," and a hand fluttered to the
collar of her flowered polyester blouse.

"I was wondering," she eased into it, "if I could get a copy
of the medical records of Mrs. Ashley Merriam. I can read it
here, ma'am, or I can pay for an official copy to take with
me."

"Oh . . . my." The frail hand went to one of the gruesomely rosy cheeks. "Well. I better get Dr. Wahlstein."

Rachel stood, impervious to the plucking of whispers and stares twittering behind her. Dr. Wahlstein lumbered to the window in seconds. He was a ringer for a turn-of-the-century poet with his pouty bottom lip, bushy brows and frazzled head of tussled hair. He was frowning through the opening when he instructed, "Let's speak in my office."

Rachel followed, hoping never to walk down this plank of bad news as a patient.

She showed her badge again, quickly and painlessly, probably the way Wahlstein tried to do his job.

"Mrs. Merriam is deceased," he said with decorum.

"Uh, yes sir. I know that."

"Are you involved in a lawsuit of some sort, Ms. Collazo?"

"Oh, no sir." She noticed for the first time that he wasn't wearing the obligatory white lab coat. Instead he was decked deceivingly in a soft wool sweater vest over a pink dress shirt and subtle woolen slacks. His shoes were tasseled. This was his way of making his patients think they weren't meeting the grim reaper when they met him.

She continued, "I'm following up a simple request of one of her family members. If you'd be so kind, I would also like to see your copy of her autopsy report which should be part of your records."

He cleared his throat and sat like a chairman in his giant swivel chair. He spoke with the aplomb of a very benevolent king. "Of course I have no choice but to let you see the records, do I?"

Rachel chuckled. "Well sir, you do have a choice. It's your office and you can just throw me right out." She demured. "Then I'd go out in the lobby and call the grand jury foreman at home. He'd fax you a subpoena in about five minutes and then you'd have to hand-carry the medical records to him so he could release them to me. Usually not too many people make me do that. It has the appearance, you know, of you not cooperating with law enforcement."

He was the absolute master of giving bad news and just as suave at getting it. "The records are confidential, of course."

"Yes, sir. I respect that fully. But subpoenas are public

documents, like a big ol' blood drop right smack there on your malpractice records."

He glared at her. Bullshit was his art; he had just met his match. "I know your boss. The chief. Maybe I'll call him."

Rachel slapped her knees, jolly. "Okay, you do that. I'll wait in the lobby with all those evening patients. While I'm out there I'll call my office on that phone in the middle of all those people and report to my partner that I do after all need the grand jury foreman ready for my request for a subpoena. I just hope my voice doesn't carry too loud and alarm anybody, me being a homicide detective and all."

He hit a button on the intercom. In less than three minutes Rachel sat quietly in his stateroom of an office with a copy of Ashley Merriam's medical records and her autopsy report. He sat across from her, scribbling, looking up disgustedly at her over the rim of his half-glasses perched on his nose.

"Doctor, what is a radical mastectomy?"

He answered, deeply sublime, "It means there is invasion of the lymph nodes. Chemotherapy followed in Ashley's case."

"How do you take that chemotherapy?"

"She had a subclavian catheter. It's put in the patient's chest wall and left there so with each treatment the patient doesn't have to be stuck with a needle again."

"Hmm-mm. Says here at one point that she was doing well."

He acted as if she were interrupting his scribbling, but the truth was, and she knew it, that he was riveted on her every movement. "Yes. She was. I was very encouraged as her chemo progressed."

"Then," Rachel finally met his harsh gaze, "she got pneumonia."

"Yes, Ms. Collazo." If he were a dragon he would have just consumed her in a fiery breath and be done with her.

Rachel said, distracted from reading the mumbo jumbo medical jargon. "She died of pneumonia, but there's something else here. This says 'septicemia.' What's that?"

"A rampant infection. In Ashley it came from the pseudomonas bacteria."

He was clamming up. They were facing off. "A bacteria you get how? In the air? From another person? From contaminated food? How is this bacteria transferred?"

"The pseudomonas bacteria is particular and exclusive to the hospital after an invasive procedure. It leads to death by means of a virulent nosocomial pneumonia that is fatal in those who are already immunosuppressed by other disease or illness. It leads to septicemia. In Ashley's case, the antibiotics were ineffective because the chemo had left her with a minimal white cell count."

Rachel wanted coffee but didn't dare ask. "Whoa, doctor, maybe you could put that in street talk for me."

His nasty grin was condescending. "You only get nosocomial pseudomonas in a hospital. If you're already ill and can't fight it, it is known to kill in about four days unless the antibiotics by an unlikely course of anomalies beat it."

A dull thud went through Rachel's heart. "Okay, sir. But I thought Mrs. Merriam died at home."

"She did."

"Two months after leaving the hospital she died of a virus you only get in the hospital?" Now her pulse was pumping. Something was up and she knew it.

"Not a virus, Ms. Collazo, a bacteria. Transported in the hermetic encasing of a hospital environment."

She had to slow her speech so the tantalizing question came out slowly and distinctly. "So if she's at home getting chemo, how'd she get a hospital bacteria?"

"Pseudomonas is everywhere. In a person as ill as Ashley, even benign household pseudomonas could ravage as harshly as the virulent hospital bacteria."

"It could, you say, but it isn't very likely."

He swiftly removed the half-glasses and plunked them onto the desk. "I am advancing to you the theory of our chief pathologist. Ashley had virtually no white cells to fight any infection. Patients receiving 5-FU, which is the chemotherapy agent, have almost no immunity."

Rachel found the last page of the autopsy report, signed by her friend Dr. Truett, chief pathologist.

"Dr. Wahlstein, why is Mrs. Merriam's cause of death on here listed as unclassified?"

He stood. Bullshit adjourned. "Because it was an and/or pronouncement. Septicemia or pneumonia or even cancer. Treat those records with utmost discretion."

She stood, too. "I will, sir. I'll treat them with the same top secret discretion as, say, a sealed indictment. And can I ask you, doctor, why Mrs. Merriam was getting her chemo at home instead of at the hospital like most people do?"

He held the door for her, not politely but dismissively. "Because she was wealthy. You have to pay independently to have home chemo. Or your insurance may pay if you have a coexisting condition that precludes weekly visits to the clinic. The latter is a doctor's call to make. Good-bye."

With that he skulked away into the cushy silence of a treatment room where someone waited to see how their life would be dealt from the cards in his expert hands.

She was due in twenty minutes at The Mansion, a tony restaurant where she was expected to put in an Oscar-winning portrayal of Chaz's doting girlfriend. She punched the elevator button.

"Lord," she said upward, feeling exhausted, "if I lie to Diablo's sweet little mother, you'll get me back, I know you will. Just try to think of me as doing the right thing for all the wrong reasons, okay?"

=18=

A light sleet had begun to fall just after Daniel woke. In the depth of darkness outside the windows he could hear the frozen rain hitting the glass like bubbles popping.

He made coffee, shivering in his boxer shorts, fumbling for his glasses on the counter where he had left them before bed, as he stood there drinking milk and missing Pete. He had gone to his mother's house and read to his son, some ditty from a Richard Scarry book about a pig who made a mess of tending his friend's milkshake shop, and he had kissed and cuddled Pete for almost an hour.

His mother, an elegant, thin woman, almost six feet tall in her slippers, had found him sunk into her leather sofa, head in his hands. She had tousled his hair lightly and handed him a beer.

He had looked up at her, wondering how she had achieved at sixty-five-years-old such peace and prettiness. Her gray hair was cut severely short. Her smile at him was completely unconditional.

"Danny, everything will be okay."

"She treats me like shit, Mom. Tonight was the first time in five months we've had sex. The last time while I was making love to her she asked if I could move my elbow so she could see the television."

She had sighed. "Don't tell me. Please. I can't do anything about your pain, and it drives me crazy being so helpless to help you."

He reached across the sofa and patted her knee. "What

81

am I going to do, Mom? If I'm missing for an hour she goes ape shit crazy and starts screaming about how she can't live without me. Then when I'm with her she verbally abuses me, calls me lazy and stupid."

"Don't you ever tell her to shut up?"

He hadn't meant to glare at her. "No. Just like I never told you to shut up, either."

Stoic, even angry, she replied, "I've apologized all I'm going to for my mistakes. I admit I was too hard on you."

"I had time limits in the bathroom, Mom, so that I couldn't masturbate. You stood outside the door while I showered, making sure I didn't moan or groan." He grinned winsomely.

She did, too. "We great mothers do eventually realize that our children's problems are not necessarily our crises."

They squeezed hands.

She asked, "How is Julie Ann tonight?"

He let his eyes wander around the cozy room as if the right words were hidden somewhere. "Calculating. Manipulating. She's afraid that if she dies I might make Pete into a heathen or, worse yet, a free thinker. So she asks for a compromise in my behavior. I still get sex if I pretend to fear God—and her."

"It's her way, Danny. You remember last year, her miscarriage. She blamed herself, for some inane reason—carrying Pete to the car in the rain, I think it was. She's a blamer, Danny. Your brother drinking wine last Christmas at the table was my fault. The miscarriage was her fault. The cancer is your fault."

"Why, Mom?"

They sat quietly. The ice in her cocktail tinkled as she sipped bourbon and water.

"Because, Danny, she can't blame God."

He moved closer to her so he could whisper. "We were brought up in the same faith, the same church. I can't understand this change in her the last few years."

She touched his hair lightly. "We got out of the church, Dan. Julie's family stayed in, pounded that zealot ideology into her clean-slate-of-a-brain for decades." She lowered her voice respectfully. "Look, son, she has lived her life trying to please God—to the letter of the law—and He has done nothing but let her down."

He looked up woefully. "And I'm one of the letdowns. As a husband. So we do what, Mom? I don't even love her, the woman she's become. It's this bad-boy syndrome, and I'm supposed to mourn that she might have cancer?"

"Daniel, I'd like to tell you to leave her, to get your life back. I'd like it to be fifteen years ago when you were twenty, for you to come home to this bedroom full of tennis and golf trophies and bring some jovial sorority girl who adores you."

He watched her. She was not prone to heartfelt soliloquies. But she was prone to honesty. And this was a bout of it.

"But I can't tell you that, son. All I can tell you—all I will say to you—is that you're a grown man. And you have to solve your own marital problems. In forty years with your father, we worked out our own problems and we stayed together. I'll help with Julie. I'll keep Pete. I'll clean your house if she's too ill, or I'll cook, or I'll pay someone to do both for you until she's stronger. I'll do anything but enable you to put the burden of your adult choices in your life onto me."

He whined heavily, "God, Mom, I want all the good things back. My old marriage. Julie before her Ascension." He stared hard at her. "What if I leave her? Would she change, lighten up on me?"

"You can't leave her, especially if you find out it's cancer tomorrow. Now as your mother I'm telling you to go home and take care of your wife."

He stood lost in thought at the counter long enough so that the coffee was already brewed. Suddenly Julie Ann was behind him in their kitchen. Her soft, white gown lay ghostly against her even softer white skin. She echoed his name. "Daniel?"

He swirled, afraid that she would know he was dreaming . . . maybe he didn't have to know the shame of leaving her or the indemnity of living with her . . . that maybe she would make it easy and just die.

"Oh, Julie, I didn't see you there. Uh, you can't have any liquids or anything, honey. And I meant to tell you. . . ."

He was blathering nervously. ". . . my insurance company called yesterday. They've agreed to pay for your chemotherapy to be given at home. I mean, you don't have to make that awful trip to the hospital for treatment. A nurse will come here."

She was so small in the room that she seemed to be a tiny, vulnerable echo. "I thought you said it was real expensive to do that."

He poured coffee, tried to look casual, dying of fear that the relief on his face at the thought of her death would show through. "It is, and usually insurance won't cover it unless there's a medical reason, like another illness that makes the hospital environment risky. Dr. Wahlstein recommended we do it at home because of your asthma."

Her brows crinkled into a vague smile of confusion. "Danny, my asthma hasn't acted up since I was a teenager."

"It's good though, isn't it, Julie, that you don't have to take a trip into town for chemo?"

She faded into a frown. "You told him I had asthma."

"I told him that you had begged me not to make you go to a cold, strange hospital ward for the treatment if it comes to that. If there's no cancer then this is all moot. But you told me if it is cancer that what you fear most is being away from home. So I found a way to keep you here. Okay?"

She glared with narrowed, hateful eyes. "You told him about the asthma and you did it to make me sound weak and . . . different than other women. Thanks a lot, Daniel, for telling my doctor I'm a freak."

She was gone. He heard the shower water.

His forehead was sweating.

=19=

Rachel woke up slowly and lay quietly, thinking about things. She thought about loving Emory so much, about how often when she first introduced him as her sweetheart strangers thought she was joking. She would see their eyebrows go up and their jaw drop, and a tickle of pride would go through her.

She had loved the same unlikely lover for twenty years. Never wandered. Never wanted to. He wasn't a daddy figure. She had delved that subject enough times in her own head to know that it was the girls with bad daddies who grew up and tried to marry him over and over again until they got it right, which they never did. And it wasn't because Emory was safe either. She grinned cattily at that thought.

No, Emory was too handsome for her to lay back and let it ride. Everywhere he went, all those senior-tour tournaments and book-signing events and awards banquets, women from age twenty to ninety were captivated by his classic good looks and easy sophistication. She loved him, that was all. Adored him. Trusted him completely. Lusted for him. Every day with no dips or sways. He drew her bath water and the temperature was always perfect. He gave her wonderful foot rubs. He brought her coffee in the morning, compliments all through the day, and in the evening he knew exactly how to move himself to bring her to instant, overjoyed orgasms. He was centered, stable, wise and kind, never criticized. He worried about her, listened rapt to her and made her laugh with his bone-dry wit. There was no one else. She sat up and sighed. No one else. Ever. When he was gone she would pine forever.

She dialed his number, said "I love you," and was steeped in warmth when his mellow voice returned the sentiment richly before they hung up.

She sat in the predawn darkness of her small townhouse feeling the oppression of winter outside. The heat was gushing through a vent, wheezing as it tried to blow back all that bitter cold weighing down on the city. When she had grown tired the night before she took a blanket and a pillow to the hallway and fell asleep quickly, naked. For breakfast she craved a pimento cheese sandwich, which she was going to make for herself shortly after she brewed some campfire coffee—put a pan of water on and when it boils, dump coffee grounds into it, leave it awhile and then pour a tremendously delicious mug of hot java after all the grounds settled to the bottom of the pan.

She had spent the evening before with her lesbian neighbor Narda, who would look like a guy except for the tiny gold hoop earrings she wore and those hapless freckles scattered on her nose and cheeks like spilled red pepper.

Rachel smiled to herself calmly and raked back her hair that was all askew. She traipsed through unopened boxes of junk she had ordered off the TV—Why is it, she asked herself then, that you don't mute the sound when they're selling decorative spice racks or blown crystal from New Jersey—and she found her robe.

While she showered the answer kind of streamed onto her with the spew of hot water.

When people grew up they did whatever they did because of how they lived when they were kids. All idiosyncrasies, she decided, came from what happened to you day after day when you were growing up. She slept in her guest room or on the floor in the kitchen or curled up on her breakfast bar because growing up with nine brothers in a four-bedroom house had taught her that if you sleep in a bed you get peed on frequently.

She ate weird stuff for breakfast because her favorite prank had been to pick a brother's lunch bag each morning, wolf it down, and then scream and run when the offended realized all he had in his bag was crust and an apple core.

She watched the TV with the sound off because from the day she was big enough to be propped in front of the set she had not heard one whole sentence of one single show. Nine brothers didn't sit like choir boys and listen carefully to what Robert Wagner and Stephanie Powers were saying, so Rachel learned to figure it out by watching their faces. Without a word she could figure it all out.

She bought home shopping stuff and then gave it all away without opening it because everything she ever got in her life, until she finished college, went to the police academy and got a job, came from a Sears catalog. She remembered with great pleasure coming home from elementary school and finding those Sears boxes and bags on her bunk. She would rip through them while her mother's eyes glowed and teared up at the sight of Rachel flouncing in flowered cotton or dancing with a bright-red wool shawl.

So it wasn't the shit in the boxes she wanted anyway, it was the process of finding boxes stacked on her patio when she got home. Only now, with her delightful, doting mother long dead, it seemed sacrilege to open them.

And, she admitted it, her friends were mostly a gang of trashy true hearts. Narda was always in love with some girl who was breaking her heart, but Rachel listened with puerile interest to the goings on between women, how lesbians could get themselves into relationship jams just as screwy as men and women could.

Melvin she had dragged into adult life from high school. He had a college degree in English Literature but was too good, he said, to teach, and was just going to starve, he said, until one of those nitwit big-time publishers in New York recognized his talent and published one of his fifty or so coffee-stained, cigarette-burned, tragedy-laced manuscripts.

Pauline had some years back murdered her brute of a husband—shot him twice in the face with a nail gun, piercing his brain like a burning rocket—and Rachel helped prove that Pauline's sorry husband regularly beat the daylights out of Pauline, so it was all in self-defense, and Pauline was not indicted by the grand jury.

It wasn't as if Rachel hadn't sat around before with society women. She had. She was often invited to speak to women's clubs around town about things like family violence and ways to combat crime. Afterward they pooled around her, holding plates of cookies shaped like the damnedest things, and she always noticed how unrequited something was in their eyes and their words. They had gotten married thinking life would be some magic carpet ride that ended with them posed like people on a romance novel cover, all windswept and wet-lipped. Then they found out that what they had signed on for was actually emotional boot camp, twenty or thirty years of scaling one stout wall of complications after another, and all they had brought with them were saline implants and jeweled evening bags.

At least Narda, Melvin and Pauline never talked about curtains or labor pains or made everyone else pretend to care what they were saying.

Rachel checked herself one last time in the mirror. Hair was good, piled up and pinned loosely. Head up. Shoulders back. Chest out. The navy wool suit was soft, the white ruffled shirt was crisp. She could look proudly and honestly at herself in that mirror.

She ate pimento cheese on toast and drank campfire coffee while frames of the morning news went past on her silent TV. She knew exactly what was happening. Bosnian kids were getting blown up and everybody was talking about maybe possibly sort of doing something to stop it. Some bum had been executed on death row the night before and a few candle-clasping fat people were whining. Then Martha Stewart was standing there with a forest of broccoli, but Rachel couldn't tell if Martha was going to show how to cook it, grow it, decorate it or use it as organic wallpaper.

In about thirty seconds her sandwich was gulped and eaten. That's the way it was growing up with nine brothers.

You had to eat fast. And you had to learn early when to run and when to stay and slug it out for righteousness sake.

She was ready when Chaz honked from her driveway. The gray air was so cold that she couldn't get a breath for a moment, but then she adapted and set out for the gritty day at hand.

=20=

Kelly's orgasm raced from between her legs through her chest and brain like fire consuming fumes. It faded slowly. She felt him buck and then collapse beneath her as he climaxed.

They dripped sweat even though the pre-dawn air outside her car was viciously cold. In an hour the horizon would be pierced with a gold line, but for now the car seemed sunken on an opaque ocean bottom. Half-built houses under construction loomed around them in the deserted area like contemporary ruins.

She straddled him, her blouse opened and breasts dropped in his face like swollen chocolate kisses. Her tight skirt was pulled waist high, garter belt and nylons there for him to hold on to as they bucked and she arched backward into the steering wheel behind her. She came again. His quiet laughter at watching her pleasure was low and sexy. She felt the waves of heat and spasms gloriously.

They kissed. She clutched his face with her gloved, delicate hands. They rocked together, their breathing a primitive kind of jungle beat, until she was finished and he was depleted.

She whispered, "Don't go, Jeff."

"I have to go, honey. It's my job. You better get yourself back together. These construction people show up at sunrise."

He wanted her off him, just like that, and she knew it. He

didn't see the change in her eyes, but he would feel soon its wrath.

She tongued his tongue, his lips. "I want to be your wife."

It was more glib than he meant it to be. "I already have a wife. You know that. You've always known that. You went in with your eyes open."

"Fuck me again."

"No, baby, I can't. Physically. You are beautiful though." He caressed her breasts as if to bury himself in them. "Now come on, let me zip up and get out of here. I'll call you when I get back. First thing. We'll . . . have some fun."

She fell into the passenger seat. "I thought you would leave her."

He zipped, pulled down a mirror to work on his tie. "My wife? My kids? Kelly, I never said that. Her father is CEO of the company that pays me a half-million a year."

"But she won't fuck you."

"Which is why I've kept seeing you these last six months, honey. You are absolutely every man's dream fuck. A goddess, the best looking woman I've ever seen, without a staple in the center of her navel. Plus you're smart. And you're quiet." His eyes shone pearlized at her, menacing. "And you always will be quiet, right?"

He reached to her lap, fingered her, groaning, traced his other hand along her belly to the garter belt. "Now pull your dress down and button up, babe. I have to go to my car and roll out of here."

She said glumly, "I brought coffee. There's two cups in the paper bag behind my seat."

He fished, found them, held one out to her. He started to leave her car, but she reached for him.

"Wait. Jeff."

He closed the door, sounded perturbed. "Kelly, don't get weird. This is all it can be."

She sounded girlish. "You won't even let me meet your friends?"

He balked. "Jesus! My life is a fucking Pleasant Valley Sunday, babe. My minister is my wife's brother. My next door neighbors are my kids' pediatrician and kindergarten teacher. Please, Kelly."

"So nobody knows." Her heart fluttered with excitement. Soon the cocky bastard wouldn't be so cocky.

He blinked heavily once, sipped more coffee. His motor skills were deadening from the gram of Chloral Hydrate she put in the coffee. In a few minutes he would be fast asleep.

He slurred. "Je . . . sus, I feel drunk or something. No, nobody knows I see you or even know you. You better keep it tha . . . man, Kelly, am I having a stroke? Get me some air I'm feeling really. . . ."

He was out. She took his car keys and dragged him across the street by his coat collar. He was lean but muscular, heavier than she had thought at dead weight, but she used his coat like a stretcher and made it. She put him in the driver's seat, upright, ditched the coffee and set the cup in the console cup holder. She loosened his tie, leaned his head back, rolled up his left sleeve and laid his hand open on his lap.

In her purse she had his pocketknife, the one he always set beside her bed when he emptied his pockets for their sexy rendezvous. She clicked it open to extend and lock the blade.

Lengthwise, up and down instead of across, she slashed his left wrist deeply. His heartbeat was extremely slowed by the barbituate, but the gash was deep enough to sever the artery. Smoke rose from the hot blood as it drained down his crotch and soaked his upholstery and pooled in his hand. In his right hand she put the pocketknife. She shined her pen light onto his wool coat, knowing her hair was pinned up tightly and sprayed so none of it would flow onto his clothing. He heaved a long rattling breath as the first waves of heart failure kicked in. The seizure was brief. He was dead.

She stood straight, looking down on him. Her breaths were smoky. "Guess I'll go for a jog, then get some breakfast. Killing cocky, selfish men really stokes a goddess's appetite."

=21=

"Mornin' glory," Chaz chimed. He was a canvas of tasteful brown. Tailored single breasted brown suit, cream-colored shirt, brown silk tie showing flecks of gold and subtle red. His mahogany brown eyes also flecked gold when he smiled.

He tooled the steering wheel with one finger. "So, Rachel, this suit is Brooks Brothers. How about it, huh? I mean, is the monochromatic color scheme a good fashion look for me? All brown? Does it make me look too . . . approachable?"

She smiled away, out the window. A drab morning mist floated on the manicured little townhouse courtyards as they passed, heading for the warzone of tangled freeways. "What's this hot news you have for me?" she asked blandly.

He stayed with the vain asshole bit. "Is my tan too deep? I want just the right hue—Southhampton tennis club without any hint of George Hamilton."

The freeway loomed out of the cold fog like a Boeing 747 descending from a cloud. Already it was snarled with angrily idling commuters. Rachel stared at his shoes.

"I see you've got on your fairy slippers again."

"Do you want to hear what I found out, or do you want to verbally spar again today?"

"I always go in looking for the knock out, Diablo. You show me your stuff and then I'll show you mine."

In the traffic where they sat at a standstill they finally got to move up about five feet. Chaz said sincerely, "Thanks for being so nice to my mother last night. I know you hate to lie."

She scanned him disapprovingly. "I didn't lie. I said I am Roman Catholic, an Aries, a junk food addict, a closet cigarette smoker, and I told her that I box as an amateur."

"Yes. She loved that part when you showed her your stunning combination. I think she likes the idea of me with a woman who slabs petroleum jelly on her face."

Rachel grinned. "Girls do two-minute rounds, Diablo. Your mama got a little bit into the Chianti. I liked her. I'd like to see her again someday. She's got heart. And guts."

He launched unceremoniously. "Nurse Bachman's husband is a school principal. They're fine financially. She's been an RN for decades and a home health care nurse for about ten years. Her bank deposits are consistent, no big jumps like if Wes Merriam paid her to infect his wife with pseudomonas pneumonia. I checked her bank accounts and McLaughlin's. It's all steady and normal. McLaughlin, on the other hand, has a little fly in her ointment."

"Yeah? Walks like a duck and quacks like a duck, does it?"

Chaz was strangely serious. "She was in nursing school at UT ten years ago. Got married. She was about twenty-one then. He was a law student there. From the divorce decree I got the name of the law firm she used for the divorce. Then I found a dweeb lawyer at the courthouse who knew somebody in that firm. He inquired, and he found out that they divorced because of infidelity. Hers. She was banging a married med student. He took his internship in Dallas at Parkland. McLaughlin followed, got on the nursing staff there. This was eight years ago. Listen to me, Rachel."

She glanced, focused. He was troubled. She said, "Go on."

He steadied the words. "The young doctor, her lover, died suddenly during his internship. A staph infection. He was hospitalized with a bad flu, was released and died."

"Oh, shit, Diablo. Of a nosocomial infection?"

His gaze at her was crystal clear, rock hard suspicion. "He

died at home of a hospital infection. But he had been in the hospital so recently, nobody questioned it."

"And you're thinking. . . ."

He pulled over and stared right at her. "Some coincidence, huh? Two people she knows dying at home of hospital infections, and she's a nurse, in and out of hospitals all the time?"

"The cases were far apart, Diablo. It could all have happened the way it seems."

He lowered his sunglasses at her. "If you think that, then let's go home. Otherwise I've got something to show you."

"Drive," she commanded. "Show me what you've got."

She took out her notepad as they rode. She told him what she knew. "Ashley Merriam died on a Friday morning at six. Medical examiner ruled it death caused by septicemia, a bacterial infection that comes from having pneumonia, but this pneumonia came from a germ called pseudomonas, like I told you. A person gets pseudomonas in a hospital ninety-nine percent of the time."

Chaz asked, "And the other one percent?"

"Well, you can get it from household pseudomonas, but it's a pretty remote possibility according to the stuff I read about it last night. So she died on Friday. The Monday before her death, Kelly McLaughlin did chemo on her at home. She came on Wednesday for a routine check and found that Ashley had a temperature of 99.8 so she calls Wahlstein. He says it's not too alarming but he wants her started on antibiotics and checked the next day at home by the nursing service. The next day, Thursday, McLaughlin goes again and calls the doctor to say nothing has gotten worse. Her temp is still 99.8 and her pulse and respiration are normal. McLaughlin notes on the chart I saw that she gave Ashley a strong sedative and the antibiotics Thursday evening. Friday at dawn, Ashley dies from shock when the infection weakens her heart and its beats dropped too low. Merriam called the paramedics at 5:40 A.M. when he got up. She was dead when they got there."

Chaz rummaged through a pile of his own thoughts and

said, sounding distracted, "The key will be to find how Ashley got the pseudomonas bacteria and if Wes and Kelly were in on it together."

Rachel thought aloud. "Maybe Wahlstein is doing that Angel of Mercy thing and puts deadly bacteria into the chemo bag. Maybe the nurse puts poor Ashley away so she can have Wes all to herself."

She added pointedly, "The husband had to know his wife was dying that Thursday night. McLaughlin had to lie about Ashley's vital stats. Her fever was higher than 99.8 on Thursday. She was slipping into this septicemia thing. Erin told me that in the latter stages of septicemia—when it's way too late to help the patient—everything goes up, except the blood pressure. A nurse couldn't miss it. So she lied to Wahlstein."

"Which doesn't implicate the husband," Chaz added logically.

Rachel jumped. "Oh, yes it does. It's a horrible death, Diablo. You drown in mucus. Ashley would have been clawing at the walls for air, crawling on her hands and knees begging for help. Wes Merriam had to turn away. He had to be in on it. He had to wait until her body cooled to call the ambulance so the high fever wouldn't be detectable to Erin at autopsy. We're far away from the truth, Diablo, but at least we're hip to the lies now. This is a nasty murdering nurse. Can we prove it?"

"Has he called you back, the husband? Want to put out a warrant for his arrest?"

Rachel answered somberly. "No. He hasn't called. And no, I don't want to arrest him. Before I start asking questions of a murderer, I like to already know the answers."

=22=

They drove down a wide boulevard adorned with an island of bare trees in the center and flanked by restored turn-of-the-century homes, ornate with arches and beveled glass. The avenue ended at the front steps of an ivy covered sandstone cathedral. Chaz pointed at a two-story brownstone tutor house that had been revamped into two spacious apartments, one upstairs and one downstairs.

"She lives up there."

Rachel hunched down in the front seat. "And how do you know when she jogs? You've been following her?"

"I cruised her place and Bachman's a couple of mornings in a row before work. She jogs at 7 A.M. and then sits naked in a hot tub whirlpool on her balcony."

Rachel smirked. "It's hidden in the trees and rose vines, you mutton head. How'd you spot her?"

He grinned. "The rose thorns were murder. Let's move closer to that park over there. That's where she warms up."

A woman bundled like a Russian peasant passed them slowly, pushing a triple stroller full of bundled identical babies. Rachel gasped. "Look at those precious babies!"

Chaz said as cavalier as possible, "Yeah. Little rolling financial liabilities. You want kids, Collazo?"

"Hey, that's none of your business."

Hands up, he relented. "Okay. Sorry. God forbid that anyone you work with know a morsel about your personal life."

She frowned at him. "When people start knowing your personal business then it isn't personal anymore."

"Fine, Collazo. Excuse the hell out of me." He drove exceedingly slowly, scrutinizing the various people passing on roller blades, bicycles, behind hapless dogs on extending leashes. "Tell me what you found out from Rex Warner at the M.E.'s office."

Rachel's note pad was crammed full of her writings. "First I found out that people with multiple Ph.D.'s in microbiology and physics wear 1970's shirts with plaid 1960's pants."

She read from her notes. "Science does not mingle with fashion, I reckon. All right. Rex said she had to get the pseudomonas bacteria one of two ways: from an infected person's spit or mucus or from a tray of it in a hospital laboratory. I called the hospital lab. They don't keep extra trays of toxic bacteria around to play with. They use a small culture of the patient's . . . uh, sputum it's called, for diagnosis and they dispose of it immediately by strict toxic waste codes. Inside a special container that's incinerated. So she got it from a live person."

He pulled to the curb, set a road map conspicuously across the steering wheel to make them inconspicuous and then told Rachel methodically, "So I check to see if any of the patients on the nurse's roster at the time of Ashley's death had pseudomonas pneumonia."

She mocked him. "Whew. No wonder you're a sergeant."

"Blow me."

"Diablo, I wouldn't put my baseball mitt around that thing, much less my mouth. No telling where it's been. Now, she could have taken the infectious sputum and put it in a sterile dish and kept it for a couple of days. Rex said it lives fine in the refrigerator for that long. Then she took it to Ashley's and put it in her."

A little poodle shivered past, towing its fat owner wrapped in warm-ups and wearing headphones. "She put it into Ashley's blood through an injection?"

"Through the sub-whatever catheter that's there for the chemo. Or into Ashley's lungs somehow. I can't imagine

Ashley lying still while the nurse shoved a wad of someone else's mucus down her throat, but who knows."

"Could she have put it into the chemotherapy solution?"

Rachel scribbled notes to herself. "No. The solution would kill it. Rex said if it went into Ashley's lungs she'd be deathly sick within twenty-four hours. In the blood it would take longer. She was already feverish on Wednesday, so Kelly had to put it into her blood on Monday somehow."

"Hey," he calculated so fast she could hear his brain ticking, "maybe it was fake chemo stuff. You know, saline or sugar water."

"I'll check to see if she had chemo solution in her blood at autopsy on Saturday. Nice work, Watson."

He laughed. "You, of course, would be Sherlock."

"Except I play the fiddle instead of the violin."

Chaz said suddenly, "There she is. Kelly."

Rachel took his binoculars. The woman coming at them, huffing white breaths and bouncing in a run like a graceful gazelle, was thin but muscular and had the cheekbones of a French cover girl. She wore earmuffs and gloves and a sweatshirt. Her breasts were round and large and up high. The spandex jogging pants showed fabulous legs.

Rachel whispered. "Man, she's gorgeous. A real Southern belle. Too bad she's from about as far south as you can get. . . ."

"Yeah, she's flawless. Until you get to the part about her being a homicidal maniac."

The image in the binoculars drew closer in slow motion, a mixture of lean athlete and sculpted ballerina and Vegas showgirl physique. She had creamy skin and eyes that made Rachel think of silvery mountain waterfalls.

"What do you know about the young intern who died?"

Chaz answered, opened a folder beside him. "Dr. Marcus Chang. I called his widow. She was none too happy to answer my questions, but she answered them. Said she has a new husband and has worked hard to put that tragedy behind her. I asked specifically what happened in the days leading up to his death, after he left the hospital."

He took the binoculars and salivated as Kelly stopped

under the barren rows of Maples, chugging white smoke and acrobatically bending and stretching. "Nothing stood out except when she said that a friend of his from the hospital, a nurse, brought him some prescription cough medicine the first day after he was dismissed from the hospital. He died a week later after being readmitted for pneumonia. In his autopsy they found it was a nosocomial infection."

"And that nurse," Rachel said dreadfully, "was—"

"You got it, our very own, Hell's Belle."

"We got nothing, Diablo."

"Instincts."

"Oh. Yeah. Like that alone on an affidavit will get us a warrant to search her house."

"She's connected to two deaths of the same nature, Rachel."

"Eight years apart. And both of them ruled natural deaths."

She stared at Kelly's form fading down the street and felt a surge of anger. "Ashley Merriam was struggling to live through all that pain and fear. If her son of a bitch husband and this bitch nurse killed her, I want them."

He wheeled slowly into a stream of traffic on the main road off the sedate boulevard. "Her fingerprints won't be on the bacteria, you know," he reasoned. "Even if we found the syringe or the tubing glowing in the damned dark under her bed with a search warrant, it wouldn't mean anything. She took it from a patient she was treating. Her prints are supposed to be on all those implements."

Rachel sighed deeply. "Man, she's going to be tough to catch. Maybe when Wes Merriam comes in to see us, then I can crack him. Poor Mrs. Merriam. Poor woman with cancer. Stop and get me a chili-cheese burrito for breakfast, would you?"

Chaz grimaced. "You sure you're not pregnant?"

"Positive. I had my tubes tied years ago."

Surprised, he asked. "What if you're sorry?"

"I won't be. I eat chili-cheese burritos in the morning all the time."

"I mean about the tubal ligation."

He glanced. She was pouting. He changed the subject.

"How are things going in the ring, slugger?"

"There's this one big lummox who keeps knocking me on my ass. She backs up a lot and draws me in swinging so I get tired too fast. It's a great offense. I've nicknamed her Cujo. So now Doak, my trainer, has me set up to spar in the ring with a guy."

Chaz cracked up in loud laughter. "Oh. Shit! I pity the fool! I really do. He's going to start off thinking you're a girl and go easy on you. Somebody should warn him."

Rachel faced the sunbeams streaming at them, hidden behind her movie star dark glasses. "Okay, I'll tell you one personal thing. It's the least I can do since you might save my ass as back-up in a dark alley someday. All the babies I've seen since I became a cop, Diablo, are beaten to death or neglected to death or swaddled in body bags. It's not that I won't inflict a baby on myself. It's not that at all. It's just that this baby I'll never have, well, I already love her too much to dump her into this pile of human dung. You know?"

She looked at him, pretty as a blushing schoolgirl. He reached over with his arm bulging all those muscles and very gently pushed her hair back from her soft cheek.

He tried a little tenderness. "Look, she's going to find out we're asking around. We've requested nursing schedules, interviewed Wahlstein, contacted Wes Merriam, copied Mrs. Merriam's medical chart. Someone will tell Nurse Nasty that we're scrounging around in her life. Don't be a dead hero, okay? If she's who and what we think she is, she will try to hurt us. I want you to be very careful when the lights are out at home."

The tenderness snapped off quick as the lid slams shut on a sweet little music box.

"Hey, Diablo, don't parent me. I hate that sappy shit."

=23=

She woke up screaming in the recovery room. No warning, no slow awareness or subtle wearing off of the anesthesia. Julie Ann simply opened her eyes and began to scream.

"Daniel! It hurts! It hurts it hurts it hurts! Daniel!"

He was up from the bedside chair and onto her in a matter of seconds, but it was too late to keep the intravenous line in her hand from flying loose. The bandage that had held the IV grew red with blood. In only a few more seconds, nurses swarmed her and promptly put Daniel aside. Julie's cries were hoarse and loud, and a monitor went off because she had yanked the thin oxygen line out from one of her nostrils. Her nose squirted a stream of blood and then she began to sob.

As Julie settled into delirious moans, Daniel's heartbeat slowed to a normal rate. One nurse deftly reinserted the IV needle while another went for the dose of morphine.

"Daniel." She reached, and he saw with a pang of what felt like tears that her wrist had trickles of blood from skin she had torn yanking the IV out.

"Right here, Julie Ann."

"Daniel, is it gone? Is my breast gone? Is that what hurts so much?"

The nurse said crisply as she fiddled with the monitors, "Mrs. Nystrom, Dr. Wahlstein will be in to talk with you when you are fully awake. We'll take you to a room. You can rest better in a room; there's less commotion."

Julie sounded dreadfully distant. Daniel kissed her frail

hand. The nurse with the morphine put the injection smoothly into the joint of the IV line and went away, pulling the curtain around them so it made clanking sounds.

"Danny, I'm cold." He could barely hear her. She was drifting away again.

He pulled the blanket up that she had kicked away. A long moment went by. He thought she was sleeping. Around him he could hear noises as foreign to him as the beat of African war drums and chants. Someone moaned. Someone else in a different compartment mumbled something and then another person laughed slightly. The heart monitor beeped repeatedly, a backhoe backing up. A nurse was on the phone about Mr. so-and-so's Demeral dose needing to be upped. Daniel could hear crying, distant and muffled yet right under his feet, some stranger beyond him in pain. Nothing around him had any texture. Bald stainless steel. Bland white blankets. Washed-out pink curtains that cocooned him.

He put Julie's willowy hand to his face.

"Daniel," it came as if from her grave. "Is my breast gone?"

He whispered. "Yes."

"Do I have cancer?"

He ran his fingers through his hair, wanted to weep but couldn't. Under his glasses he rubbed his eyes. What to say to this woman girl, the only woman he had loved since he was twenty years old? The shy, beautiful blond who peeked out from behind him at life and counted on him to keep the bad world away. The woman who had given him a son. The woman who used to give him strength with her profound innocence.

"Danny, where is my mother?"

He didn't want her to hear his tears. "They're all waiting, honey. They can speak to you in a few minutes."

"How long was I in surgery?"

A sniffle. "Uh, three hours."

She finally opened her eyes and looked at him. The bad world he had felt so manly to protect her from had just rushed in at them.

She rasped, "Don't cry, Danny. It shows a lack of faith in God to cry. Do I have cancer?"

"Yes. Julie Ann, can I just lean over there and hug you?"

She closed her eyes and took away her hand. "No," she sighed. "Just stay right here and leave me alone."

So he hugged himself, a man huddled in the cold. He wanted to hold her. God had promised he could hold her if he married her. The promise was long ago broken in Daniel's heart.

Hours later when they moved Julie Ann to a room, it seemed as if life might be about to go on. Here there was a television, and how could you die while "Seinfeld" was on over your head? There were flowers already, mostly from people at their church who Daniel had asked not to visit until the next day. They settled Julie Ann into the bed. She settled under a dome of greenish fluorescent light and closed her eyes.

Daniel felt wildly dispensable. He had tried several times to help her and she had shoved away his hand. He pulled back the vertical blinds and saw the nighttime and said to her, "It's snowing."

She lay like a mummy and said only, "Please shut up."

Dr. Wahlstein trudged in. He folded his long frame into a chair and took on the visage of a dispassionate professor about to explain evolution versus the creation theory. He would not be responsible for how the student processed the information; it was only his job to offer likelihoods.

"Mrs. Nystrom, I have done a radical mastectomy, removing your right breast and the lymph nodes in your axilla, or armpit. This is due to an invasion of malignancies in your lymph system. There were three positive nodes, which I have removed, but the usual course for this type of finding is chemotherapy, which you and I have already discussed. Later we may need radiation."

They waited for Julie Ann to say something. Wahlstein was painfully abiding. Seinfeld got a big laugh overhead.

Julie Ann asked at last, "What should I tell my little boy?"

Wahlstein drew air and prepared for his usual spiel. "We

have counselors to help cancer patients prepare for that sort of thing."

Julie tensed. "I don't want any counselors."

Wahlstein was nonplussed. "You'll need some help dealing with the realities of cancer, Mrs. Nystrom."

She lay a thin arm across her eyes. "No. I can't talk to anyone about it. Just tell me if I'm going to die."

He stood. "There is a concern that the malignancy can invade the lungs, bones, liver or brain. The chemotherapy will be very aggressive and is often also very effective. The treatment modalities we have now can arrest the spread of the cancer. Our goal now is to keep it from metastasizing in other organs."

Her eyes widened. "I don't have to do it?"

Daniel snapped, "Yes, Julie Ann, you have to do the chemo. We have a son."

"The church can pray. . . ."

Daniel lurched. "Julie, stop that shit! Somebody before us has already prayed and that's when God invented chemotherapy!"

"Mrs. Nystrom," the voice of reason chimed lowly, "I believe in miracles too, and I believe that the cancer treatments we have at hand today are often very miraculous. I'll be around to see you in the morning. You can go home day after tomorrow. You're doing chemo at home, so we'll begin four weeks after your first post-operative checkup in my office. You'll come in town to my office once a week for a brief checkup, also."

"Dr. Wahlstein?" Her tinny voice came as he was almost out the door. He turned to her. "I don't want the counselor. I don't want to talk to anyone about my private concerns. Please. Other women aren't like me. Other women, they're all too needful. I have my church and I have God, and that's all I need."

She turned away toward the window. Wahlstein touched his wizened gaze to Daniel's sad glance. The omission of Daniel's name had hit its hurtful mark. The doctor left glumly.

Daniel stood at her back and lightly touched the revealed

top of her spine under the tie of the hospital gown. She tightened into an aspish coil.

"Would you like your own nightgown, Julie, or some more water?" She didn't answer, but lifted a weak hand and shut off the light beside the pillow.

"I'm going."

The tall parking lot lamps outside gave her face a blue sheen. "You're leaving me? Oh, you would. Leave me here alone."

He put his palm against her warm skin. "Julie, honey, it's late. I'm hungry and I'm exhausted. I want to go get Pete from mom's. I want to talk to him a while. He must be scared and confused by now. We agreed to tell him that you're ill, so I want to go and reassure him. There are people here to take care of you. You won't be alone, honey. I'll be back in the morning. Please don't make me sleep in this awful chair."

She was crying. "You always hurt me, Daniel."

Her whining incensed him. He despised himself for being prey to it. He minded her like a puppy and he knew why; he knew that his religion had taught him since he was a boy that love is the same as fear. "Julie, I'm so tired."

"Maybe they'll cut off your penis someday, Daniel, and after they do I'll go home and get a good night's rest. All you ever do is disappoint me."

He found himself next facing a wall of vending machines. Cheese crackers, an apple and a cup of coffee spit out into his hand from the slots.

He stepped onto the elevator with a goddess and was horrified that as his wife lay riddled with cancer he could even notice her.

The perfume came at him first, then her silver eyes the color of sea foam in moonlight. Her blond hair was full and layered like a beauty queen on a shampoo commercial. She wore black so her shiny eyes appeared to be diamonds dropped onto dark velvet. Daniel flinched at himself for noticing her breasts, how full they were above her slender waistline. He swallowed the thought of tasting her smooth nipples by quickly crunching a bite of his apple.

When she spoke, a chill twisted up his spine as if it had finally begun to rain in the desert and great sheets of relieving cool came over him.

"You're Mr. Nystrom. Daniel Nystrom."

He swallowed, but it wasn't easy. "Yes."

A lugubrious flute played in his head, making the cobra lilt up from its basket. She was poison; he knew it instantly, but the power of holding her attention would make a man master of his own eerie, erotic universe.

"I'm Kelly McLaughlin. The home nursing service I work for takes care of Dr. Wahlstein's patients. Your wife is on my roster next month. How is she doing?"

"She's . . . uh, angry."

Her eyebrow arched and he saw a tiny diamond drop earring in her lobe, against her shapely neck. She had small shoulders. Her mouth was a damp, pink, soft vaginal opening just made for him to suck while she groaned.

She said only, "You've crushed your crackers, Mr. Nystrom." The elevator pinged and the doors opened. The cobra loosed itself. The goddess stepped off the elevator.

Daniel rode the rest of the way up holding his breath in his chest and his lousy dinner in his clenched hands. The packet of crackers was dust in his fist.

=24=

Chaz crunched sunflower seeds and spit the hulls into a pointed paper cup he had pulled from the holder beside the water fountain. Rachel stared at him obliquely, each of his idiosyncrasies grating on her like nails on a chalkboard.

She griped, "Diablo, you eat like a weird bird."

He dusted his hands together. "Well, Collazo, we don't all have that boarding house reach and gulp you're so famous for. Want some water?"

"No, I want Erin to hurry up and see us. I'm having dinner with my boyfriend tonight. I'm hungry for food and his good lovin'."

He glared. "Did you have a recent head injury, Collazo?"

She laughed loudly, tossed her head back and enjoyed his annoyance. Then Erin Truett opened the morgue door and said, "Y'all come on in. Mr. Laurence is naked, but he's not shy."

A puff of white air hit Erin as she opened a cooler door and slid out a slab holding a sheet-draped corpse. She chattered the whole time about how her New Year's resolution had been to quit smoking, and she'd only had a pack and a half that day. When Erin Truett, esteemed forensic pathologist, noted scholar and former Texas Aggie women's rifle team world champ, said the word "well," it came out in two syllables. Way-ell. She was as Texas as Lone Star Beer. If not for the sprays of medical degrees, fellowship honors, gaudy maroon Texas A&M banners and blankets and trophies everywhere in the room, Erin might have looked more like Marshall Matt Dillon in a pleated skirt and low heels. She was big and she was brave.

She snatched the sheet back from Mr. Laurence's icy blue body and went to work behind her goggles, sawing into his skull with a loud whirring sound. "Hoowee!" she called out happily, "Hold on, Mr. Laurence! The rubber's about to meet the road, honey!" The whirring sound grated into his head.

Rachel shouted, "We need to talk about Ashley Merriam. In this file here, what's this reference to the Green Raider?"

"Ah, yes, the Green Raider. Pseudomonas. Under the microscope, Rae, honey, it's as bright green as a frog's ass. Oh, and I checked for you. Mrs. Merriam did have sufficient chemo fluid in her liver to have had a bonafide treatment on the Monday prior to her death. Guess that kind of leaves us thinking that your Nurse Nasty put it into her lungs somehow. That's really safer anyway, if you're the murderer. In the bloodstream there really is a chance that the chemo agent would negate all your hard work and wipe out the bacteria before it killed your victim."

The electric saw hit bone and made a dull heavy buzz. Rachel asked, "How would she get Ashley to inhale it?"

Erin's eyes flickered excitement through the plastic lenses. "Pick up that file there that I set out for you. Look at page eighteen under secondary existing medical conditions."

Rachel got it and was stunned. "Holy shit. Ashley Merriam was asthmatic."

"Uh-huh. She sure was. So what she did was she intubated Ashley with the pseudomonas bacteria. There now, let's weigh your brain, Mr. Laurence. Don't worry. This won't hurt a bit."

She plopped the brain into the hanging scale. Erin raised her goggles, wrote in the chart on the clipboard. "My guess is that she suctioned someone with pseudomonas pneumonia and then used that contaminated tubing to ventilate Mrs. Merriam. The germs would spread in Ashley's lungs like wild fire."

Chaz said, "She has an in-home patient, Lester Graff,

who had it. I just got his name from a pal today. The guy is a road map of bad diseases. Heart problems. Diabetes. Bleeding ulcers. Wahlstein is treating him now for colon cancer."

Rachel asked Erin, "If a guy is that sick, why would he be sent home from the hospital with all those illnesses?"

Now she weighed Mr. Laurence's bloody brown liver. "Because he's a chronic. So you send him home with a tracheostomy, a hole in his throat for the tubes, because even if you keep him hospitalized you can't do anything more for him than the home health nurse. It takes its own course. He'll live or die from it all no matter where he is. Is he dead yet?"

"No," Chaz reported.

Rachel had a thought. "Hey, Erin, if Kelly put Mr. Graff's mucus into Ashley would his DNA be in Ashley's body?"

Erin snapped the goggles back into place after cleaning some hunks of human gunk off them. "No, sugar, not without a massive bone transplant. And even in that case the host's DNA would take over and erase the donor's DNA real fast, a matter of hours. I know you think Kelly did it, Rae, but I tell you your theory has no more proof than plain apple cider."

"Let's pretend you're under oath," Rachel tried. "Could a person die in forty-eight hours from septicemia without a medical professional being able to detect this condition eighteen hours prior to death?"

She silenced the saw, and suddenly Ellie Mae gave way to Erin Truett, the articulate expert.

"When the infection from the pneumonia goes from the lungs to other organs, you are septic. On Wednesday of the week in question Mrs. Merriam's temperature was 99.8, her respiration twenty, her pulse seventy-five and her blood pressure elevated to 160 over 95. It is possible that her septic shock took place between the hours of 7 P.M. Thursday when she was given a sedative and 5 A.M. Friday when she died. Yes. It's possible."

"Is it likely, Erin?"

The cowgirl smile; she liked the game. "No. Not likely."

Chaz threw in, "Is it possible she got a hospital infection so many weeks after being out of the hospital?"

Erin lit a cigarette, leaned on the metal sink and played with the smoke as she exhaled. "Well, now listen. Y'all know that this pseudomonas stuff is on everything. You can get it sipping a soda can. But a healthy person has immunities that would kill it."

"So it looks the same under the 'scope?" Rachel asked, agitated.

"It does. The regular bugaboos look like the hospital strain. The difference is how they respond to antibiotics. Those little asshole hospital pseudomonas germs have already survived all that rigorous sterilizing that goes on in a hospital. Think of them like little mutant green warriors who just keep whipping every sterilizing agent and antibiotic soldier that comes at them. I mean, hospital pseudomonas rules. So if you're already immunosuppressed, like she was, your little body hardly has a chance fighting off the regular stuff from a soda can, even with an inundation of antibiotics. You get the big daddy nosocomial kind and it can ravage your system, overstress your big organs, in a matter of days. It should take about four days, but if you're a little slip of a thing like Ashley Merriam—Lord, five-foot-four and a hundred pounds—the nosocomial strain would just eat you alive."

"From the soda can? In twenty-four hours?"

She shrugged, plopped her cigarette into the sink. "Given her delicate physical profile and her severe immunosuppression, I mean the chemo wiped out virtually all of her white cells, under oath I'd have to say she could have gotten it from a benign source at home and declined overnight. Yes."

For the first time Rachel looked at Mr. Laurence. He had a gaping hole in his chest, burned black around the edges. "What happened to him?"

"Hunting accident, so his son-in-law says. Of course he was shot from about two feet away with his shirt off at an angle you might get standing over his bed at midnight. Unless his son-in-law is a sleepwalker, I'm ruling it a homicide."

A faucet dripped. The wind rattled. Chaz jumped horrified behind Rachel when the dead Mr. Laurence groaned.

Erin was fishing in the refrigerator for a diet soda. She stood up, laughing. "Honey, that's just body gases escaping from his chest cavity. You're safe."

Rachel asked dryly, "Wouldn't Ashley's decline have been bad enough for her husband to know he needed an ambulance?"

The soda can splotched. "Well, he's not trained. You can't prosecute him for not recognizing septic shock."

"What do you think about Dr. Chang?"

She snapped her goggles in place. "I read his autopsy report that you faxed me. To refute it you'd have to have the bottle of cough syrup she took him, find it tainted with pseudomonas mucus, find her fingerprints on it and then prove she put the bacteria in it. Rachel, if you're right about all this, then this nurse is committing the perfect crimes."

Rachel whined, "Well shit, how'm I going to stop her?"

The power saw whined too, aimed for Mr. Laurence's shredded chest bone. "Maybe you'll catch her the way we catch 99 percent of them. Maybe she'll get stupid and brag about it."

Mr. Laurence's arm lifted by itself off the table, as if he were pointing to the ceiling. Chaz yelped.

Erin laughed over the gruesome drone of the saw. "Honey, calm down! It's a muscle spasm. I haven't cut the pectoral yet."

"I want the fuck out of here," he said, terribly pale.

They turned to leave. Erin called out and they turned back in time to see her slice into Mr. Laurence's underarm so his pointing hand dropped like a rubber ball. "Rachel, can't you put this woman under surveillance as a suspect?"

She said dejectedly, "For what? I can't even prove anybody's been murdered. Thanks for trying, Erin."

=25=

Given the option, Mark Tillery would have rather looked up from his shabby desk and seen Jason—goalie mask, ax and all—standing in his door instead of Rachel Collazo.

He had to shake his head at how she looked. Winter-white, soft wool slacks and fitted hip length jacket, tasteful beige flats, lips that bloomed pink and the black hair and eyes of a matinee seductress.

Then she spoke, and Jason's ax met bone.

"You wanted to see me?"

He tossed a file. "No. Trust me. I have to see you."

She sat down casually. He talked fast to get rid of her.

"I want you and Chaz to take a look at these two suicides. Raymond Esterhaus and Jeffrey Iverson. Respectively a surgeon and a pharmaceutical salesman."

"Okay. Something hinky?"

No arguing. Yet. He steeled himself. "Neither guy was depressed or in debt or recently separated from his wife."

She said plainly, "We worked the prelims on Esterhaus. There was a receipt for a diamond necklace nobody ever found and some sheets in the dryer. We tested for trace on the sheets and came up with nothing. The hairs were his. What's up with Iverson?"

Mark relaxed. Maybe she wasn't going to reach over and smack him upside the head. He told her, "Dorcus has done thorough backgrounds on both of them. Esterhaus's car was parked on the curb while a three-car garage stood empty. Iverson drank a potent dose of a barbituate, chloral hydrate,

113

in his coffee, then slashed his wrist. Erin said the drug should have knocked him out cold in just over a minute, but somehow he managed to stay conscious and cut himself. Oh, and the back of his wool overcoat had street particles on it—mud, tar bits, gravel."

"Prints in the car?"

"All his. All his hair, all his fibers." He had stopped cowering.

She asked deftly, "So what's the connection?"

His coffee cup didn't wobble in his hand. He almost chuckled. "An oncology conference six weeks ago here. Esterhaus lectured to a bunch of general surgery doctors and nurses. Iverson came to peddle his wares, new cancer drugs. There's no proof they even met, but it's the only time they were both in the same place."

Rachel pondered aloud. "This Iverson, he had access to that kind of drug, chloral hydrate?"

"He had access to any kind of legal drug he wanted. He was licensed to carry samples of controlled substances. But there was no chloral hydrate anywhere in his car or his bags. The only remnants were in his coffee cup."

She stood. Her slender curves unnerved him. She asked bluntly, "That's it?"

Oh, how he wished. "Uh, no. Update me on what you and Chaz are doing with the kidnapping case. Lisa Canton. You've arrested her stepfather? Are you moving to indict?"

She sat again, politely, smelling his apprehension. "We're holding him for hot checks while we figure him out. The other kids in the family said he beat Lisa. The day she was taken from the field hockey game at the park, he left for a half hour in his van, alone. Says he went to get drinks for the kids on the team. Came back with drinks for the team. It was then that Lisa was discovered missing from the adjoining playground." She leaned, a conspirator. "I've got an angle going. I just need to keep him in jail long enough to follow through. A couple weeks max."

He hated her, but he trusted her. His discomfort returned in the form of a throb in his head. "There is one last thing."

She sat back. Fighter's stance. Mark knew he had to butch up now. The easy part was over.

He started strongly. "I got a call from a doctor. He says you're harassing two of his nurses and him about the death of a woman with breast cancer. He says she got a rare pneumonia infection and died at home, and that you're trying to make it look like murder."

Rachel sunk in boredom. "Wahlstein, right?"

He glowered at her. "Yeah. This guy has a Nobel for cancer treatment innovation, Rachel. I called Erin. She said there is some merit to your hypothesis, but that she couldn't back you under oath. You need to . . . uh, back off this one."

It fell in front of her like he'd coughed up a dead mouse.

"Look, Tillery, there is a history with this nurse McLaughlin. . . ."

He barked at her. "I understand that. But it's a mild aspersion, not a pattern or a serial. If you can't arrest her, then leave her alone. You know the rules of engagement."

She told him, "We have a hearing in the morning with Judge Kent to ask for a search warrant of her residence. We want syringes or medical tubing or whatever we can find. If Charlie doesn't grant the warrant, I'll leave it be. You've got my word."

He felt his balls loosen and drop. Finally, for the first time since she sat down. He said, "Fair enough."

And then she was smiling at him like a college cheerleader. "You still mad at me, Tillery?"

He said drolly, looking up from his writing, "Yeah."

"You carry a grudge, honey pie, it'll make you old before your time."

"Are you apologizing, Collazo?"

She sang out jokingly, "Shit, no! But I would like you to stop dropping down on all fours when we pass in the hallway."

He gave her his best hangdog pout. "It's not just every day that someone barges in here to tell me I should work at Chuck E. Cheese and calls me a cocksucker."

She slapped her knees and laughed. "See? That's how it is in life, Tillery. You suck one lousy dick and you're forever a cocksucker. Aw, come on. Lighten up. I'll tell you a joke."

He glared. She sparkled. "Here's the joke. What does it mean when a post office flies its flag at half staff?"

He smirked. She said, "It means they're hiring."

He tried, but couldn't keep a smile away. She walked out, and he watched her nice tight ass swivel. A vision came to him. He saw a caramel-coated lemon, said to himself, yeah, it looks so sweet on the outside, then you take a bite and your head explodes.

=26=

She was angry as she prepared for the task. Wahlstein had called that day and told her that the police were asking him questions about Ashley Merriam's death. Some hysterical relative thought Wes Merriam had murdered her.

The scalpel was in a sterile package. She dropped it into her hip pouch with the packet of powder she had mulched from her prescription. She moved in the pulsations of moonlight through her apartment, thinking, seething. She dressed in white. Cotton leggings. Cotton tunic. The surgical gloves were sealed, and after she used them she would incinerate them at the hospital's toxic waste drop, like she did all of her materials—covert and legitimate.

She stood at the window and looked onto a slope of white, crusty ground and trees that were sharply bereft of greenery. Their limbs stabbed at the dim film of moon glow. She swallowed scotch, tongued an ice cube and smiled. It was going to feel good killing him.

Bastard. Ungrateful bastard. Sanctimonious son of a bitch. She knew the alarm code for his house, and she had a copy of the key that she had made when she was working there. She knew his routine, where he laid his overcoat, which vodka brand he drank, which lights he turned on as he strode through the mansion. She knew how he lived and how he was going to die.

She set down the glass, looked at her watch. He would be home from dinner at his club by nine. He would have a drink and go to bed.

Cars were scarce on the icy freeways, but Kelly inched along. In the neighborhood, after she turned through the ornate arches that led to the ritzy sprawl where everybody had servants' quarters, the headlights were gold on the ice and made it look like her own personal yellow brick road. She tooled quietly along this avenue of wealth, hearing over and again Wes Merriam's testy phone call to her that morning.

He assailed her. "I got several messages on my yacht through the Coast Guard to call a homicide detective named Rachel Collazo. It concerns my wife's death and, goddamn it, Kelly, I tried to come home for a couple of weeks without anybody knowing about it, to play some golf and work downstairs in peace and quiet, now I've got some sort of paltry. . . ." he heightened it, the anger, "scandal on my hands involving my wife's sister and the nurses who took care of Ashley. The message specifically said this detective wanted to question me about the last days of Ashley's life, and of course only you and I saw her then . . . so just what the hell is going on? I could mention to them that I let you seduce me once, idiotic of me as that was, but before I talk to them I'd like you to apprise me of what the damned problem is, and I want you to know that I always thought you were . . . lascivious toward me, but I never mentioned it because Ashley was so goddamned in love with you. . . ."

He had ranted on. She had felt his murder come over her like burned red lenses across her vision.

The numbers on the gate panel had not been changed. She used a ball point pen to punch them. The gate swung open to a pristine layer of snow along the circular driveway. She parked around the back knowing Wes would park in front under the immense dark green awning. She smirked. Wes was not a backdoor man, so he had told her smugly one night. A slither of hate shot through her.

The swimming pool was an icy turquoise jewel. She walked past it, knowing later there would be footprints to deal with. Her breaths should have been nervous gusts, but they weren't. She was calmed by a sense of relief. The alarm panel beeped when she stepped inside into a wide hallway that led into the kitchen and the breakfast room. The ball point silenced it. She put the key back into her hip pouch and with a towel hanging from the oven door she wiped away wet smudges her shoes made in the shiny entryway. Her flashlight led her deep into his familiar lair. It was the same, his study, leather and plump pillows and yachting trophies, ocean scenes lit by frame lights that jutted up to make it incessant daytime on those shores.

She found the vodka bottle. With a cotton surgical cloth she unscrewed his brand and poured in the powder. She set the bottle back. She heard a noise behind her.

A thump. From the direction of the room across the grand foyer where Ashley had lain so many months and where she had died. Ashley, who at the end had looked like a bald Barbie doll left to melt in the desert. Kelly stepped into a shadow to hide from the strange noise.

The thump again, and then cool-skinned Kelly gasped as a lone note on the piano rang through the dark house. A single, lugubrious " . . . bong. . . ." that resonated and then died. The piano went silent again. Kelly's hands were cold, but they didn't shake. She didn't believe in ghosts, and even if she met one she felt sure she was meaner and more dangerous than some malevolent vapor.

She whispered, "Ashley, go away." She watched the pools of dark through the swatches of moonlight through the window, half expecting to confront a willowy apparition who swooped in sobbing and thrashing as it suffocated in mucus. Kelly slid to the floor and sat. She closed her eyes to compose herself, and when the apparition brushed her leg she opened her eyes. The cat had leaped at her from the piano. It was contemplating her with its cocked head.

She reached. "Oh, Josie, I forgot about you. I thought you were a grisly ghost." She nuzzled the cat. "You know, little pussy, there are hundreds of single men who piss their stupid pants wanting me. They simper when I glance. All the potbellied bubbas with their blue collars and drugstore cologne. All the white-bread tycoons with their midlife sports cars and their private clubs. All these brainless dicks and dickless brains for me to choose from, and what is the fun in that?"

She was panting. "The fun is not to defeat these lonely lap dogs who would lick shit off my fingers, no, the fun is to lure big daddy dogs from their bitches, to watch the wives and the puppies whimper as big daddy leaves them to sniff after me and mount me from behind. Taking men away from women, little pussy, is not my reward. My glory is in watching wives squirm when they see how ordinary and incapable and undesirable they are compared to . . . me."

She plopped down the cat. "Now you shoo, I have to hide. I have to find some unopened packages from the garden room and put them on the porch so big daddy Wesley will think my tire tracks are from a delivery service." She rose, the cat prissed to its favorite windowsill.

She set packages outside on the porch where he would park and enter the house. She reset the alarm and then skulked to the only room where he would not go for sure, the room that gave him such grief. Ashley's death room. She sat on the closet floor and waited patiently.

=27=

Wes Merriam tossed the package aside without a thought. He shut off the beeping alarm, lit the foyer light and tersely, absently flipped through the mail before he tossed it aside, too. He lighted the den, bending his long, athletic frame to pat Josie on her stump of a furry head, loosened his tie, threw his coat onto a chair as he passed through the breakfast room to the kitchen, where his ice bucket sat studiously beside the sink. He filled it halfway with ice, stuffed a hunk of lunch meat from the refrigerator into his mouth and headed to his study.

He poured Stoli over ice, the ice making a dull crack like someone had struck it with an ice pick. He sipped, thumbing his thick and tidy address book on the desk for Kelly's home phone number. He dialed, got no answer and leaned back frowning. There was paperwork before him, heady business stuff, but first the vodka. First the vodka. He sat with his eyes closed and gulped heavily. One, then another. The rush of relaxation was good. He began to see things, ocean waves and himself at the helm, a windy froth battering him. He jolted awake.

"Man, Josie, I'm sleepy."

The cat arced itself from its perch on his desk where it had jumped, he didn't know when. Josie yawned. Wes Merriam gasped deeply, the two of them yawning like tired toddlers.

He poured another vodka for bedside. Brushed his teeth. Crammed his slacks and shirt into the bag that he left outside for the dry cleaner to pick up and return. He hung his tie on the tie rack, set his shoes properly into the space left among the rows of shoes, threw his underwear into the hamper. By then half of the third vodka was gone. He guzzled the rest quickly, anything to numb the pain of not having his wife to make love to anymore.

She shined the penlight at him from the doorway. No reaction. His breathing was shallow. He was out cold. With the surgical gloves she ripped open the sterile package containing the scalpel. With tweezers from her cosmetic bag she handled the scalpel as she opened Wes Merriam's flaccid fingers and molded them around the scalpel. With her hand protected by both pairs of surgical gloves she pressed the scalpel into his hand. He twitched. She stiffened. Then he sunk again.

The deadly sharp scalpel that could saw through bone like cutting butter glinted at her. She guided his hand past his sternum, past his soft, naked belly, past his brown, wrinkled penis and his round, drooping balls. She stopped his hand there. Gently she pulled back the skin and muscle to expose his groin. The inside of his thigh where it met his testicles was clean. She could smell his morning's soap.

She opened his legs more. Set the scalpel point so it depressed the thin skin that covered the artery beneath it. She would cut the artery deeply with his hand. He would die in less than one minute.

She jabbed and yanked. The scalpel dove easily. Blood soaked her gloves, but she had stood aside so it wouldn't bathe her face or clothes. Two more oily, hot geysers erupted from his groin, but then the flow steadied and began only to run along his balls and soak like gooey syrup into the sheets.

She lay his hand on his penis. His fingers were tentacled over the scalpel. Wes Merriam had just committed suicide. The tweezers, gloves, scalpel wrapping, pen light, cotton cloth and the powder vial were in her pouch to be burned along with the gloves stashed in a paper bag. The vodka bottle was beside her. Her sleeve cuffs were bloody and some of it had spattered her chest. Pity to burn expensive cashmere, but no choice.

It was snowing when she set the alarm again and stepped outside. Heavy sheets of snow. Fuck the tire tracks. They'll be gone in an hour. As she drove away her headlights washed across a pair of golden eyes hissing at her through a window in that dark, silent tomb of Wes Merriam's house. She shivered and laughed and sounded girlish.

"Bye-bye, pussy. If not mine, then nobody's."

=28=

They stood obediently before Judge Charlie Kent. He could see them for the hearing at 7 A.M., he had said, no sooner or later that day, so Chaz and Rachel appeared dutifully if sleepily. Except for the three of them the cavernous wood-walled courtroom was empty. Judge Kent was enthroned on his bench several feet above them. The room's silence echoed every rattle of the papers they handed him.

He was an extremely soft spoken black man gracefully approaching his late fifties. He had a stern, operatic voice and tediously thoughtful manners. His Southern accent was as profound as his reputation as a respected intellectual.

He shuffled the pages of the affidavit. "Let me see here," he drawled. He squinted, finally relented with a labored sigh and relegated himself to put on his thick reading glasses.

"You lovely officers of our fine police department are seeking from me a probable cause search warrant and an extenuating arrest warrant on charges of homicide—two counts, premeditated—in the matter of a Miss Kelly McLaughlin. All rightee, then, what have we got?"

Rachel coughed. It bounced off the walls. Judge Kent leaned back sublimely and puffed an unlit cigar the size of a salami. Rachel began.

"You'll see there that we believe she purposefully took the lives of Dr. Marcus Chang eight years ago and Mrs. Ashley Merriam three months ago by the delivery of toxic bacteria which Miss McLaughlin intended to cause death to these individuals. We contend that in a search of her residence we would find physical evidence to implicate her in these deaths. The specific items are listed there."

He gnawed the cigar, looked at her kindly. He said, "All rightee, Rachel, as we are to commence here, let's first rid ourselves of this pesky formality: As you have a reason and a duty to suspect this person of two counts of first degree murder, Miss Collazo and Mr. Diablo, do you solemnly swear that the facts presented herein this affidavit and this court of law are the truth and will be shown to be factual evidence?"

In tandem, "Yes, your honor."

"Let's proceed then. You believe that your suspect murdered Dr. Chang by introducing into him a bacteria, streptococcus—am I saying that right?—so let's discuss your evidence."

Chaz said succinctly, "I interviewed Dr. Chang's widow. She remembers Miss McLaughlin offering to pick up her husband's prescription from the hospital and bring it to him at home. I also have testimony that the doctor and Miss McLaughlin were having a romantic affair and that he had rebuffed her campaign to end his marriage and marry her. That would apply to motive, sir. Her access to forms of this toxic bacteria would apply to opportunity, and her knowledge of medical procedure secondary to introducing the bacteria would present that she had the method."

The judge's brow furrowed. "I don't suppose widow Chang still has that illustriously valuable liquid prescription bottle?" He sighed deeply at Chaz's crestfallen expression. "No. Well. And his autopsy does rule his death as due to a nosocomial staph infection now, doesn't it, so we're up against that. Plus there is an implacable absence of suspicious forensics, is there not?"

Rachel said, "The consistency comes in with Mrs. Merriam's death, Charlie. Miss McLaughlin had the same motive, method and opportunity in Mrs. Merriam's death, or at least we suspect she did. Mrs. Merriam's husband will not return my repeated calls and is traveling on his yacht."

The judge raised his chin to look down at her through his bifocals. "But you will have testimony that she and Mr.

Merriam were also engaged in a serious dalliance which might have caused them to wish to remove Mrs. Merriam?"

"I have no testimony to that fact yet, sir. No. But Miss McLaughlin's phone records indicate that shortly after his departure she called Mr. Merriam at his beach house."

He said sweetly, "Rachel, I am not certain that such a call validates a motive for homicide."

"But Charlie, two people to whom she's connected have died the same suspicious death from a hospital grade bacteria, and they both died at home."

He parked the great cigar in his lips and studied the affidavit pages one by one, sifting them, and he said graciously to them, "You know, there was a time when this earth was more civilized and a man could actually light one of these cigars at his leisure and pleasure. One would suspect that if the lust of smoke which I could expel in this courtroom esoterically killed a few criminals and lawyers, I would receive commendation for such, but no, even my wife—pure of soul as a butterfly—shoos me into the dusky basement of my own domicile when I have an urge. Now, enough pontification from my dotage. This nurse cared for both of these people and they both subsequently died of the same type of infection, nosocomial, which Dr. Truett says in this affidavit is uncommon but not rare. Your concern is the length of time that Mrs. Merriam got the infection after leaving the hospital. I find that troublesome myself. Could you elaborate?"

Chaz said, "She had not been inside a hospital in two months. She was having home chemotherapy, oftentimes by Miss McLaughlin as her attendant."

He made imaginary puffs on the cigar and said somberly, "You assert that she infected Mrs. Merriam with the bacteria she took from another patient, Mr. Lester Graff. Is there a chance that Mrs. Merriam visited an ailing friend who had this type of pneumonia or perhaps a friend made an ill-fated visit to Mrs. Merriam?"

"The housekeeper said Ashley was strictly forbidden to have visitors. The rule was enforced at her home."

"You are requesting body fluid samples from the nurse."

Rachel answered. "Yes. On that Wednesday when she became ill, the nurse was ordered to deliver to a lab a sputum sample—mucus and saliva—to be tested for pneumonia. We think that to stall medical intervention that might save Ashley, the nurse sent someone else's sputum to the lab."

The judge flicked a heavy eyebrow and offered a slight chuckle. "Goodness, surely she wasn't dense enough to use her own spit. But that's what you suspect."

"We need one sliver of her DNA to compare it with the sputum the lab analyzed. Erin discovered in autopsy that the sputum culture does not match Mrs. Merriam's DNA."

He puffed more, looked away to the towering windows that showed snow swirling like blown cotton swabs. He spoke solemnly. "The sputum is not Mrs. Merriam's. And Dr. Truett equivocates here that this could be a simple laboratory . . . mix-up, for lack of eloquence."

"Without your orders we can't take sputum from Wesley Merriam or the nurse."

"No ma'am, you cannot. This same right that protects the innocent from police state bodily invasion does sometimes also protect the guilty, or so it seems. Now, lead me into this shady pool a bit deeper. Any evidence that you procured from her residence that connected her to these two deceased people would logically have physical connection to her— her fingerprints and such. In the doctor's home she was an invited guest under pretense of friendship and in the Merriam home she was a routine medical attendant. We will have trouble proving complicity based solely on the fact that links to these people are in her possession."

Chaz responded. "We've got method, motive, opportunity and an established weapon, the bacteria."

The judge countered calmly, "But you lack the pathology. Have you spoken with Lester . . . uh, Mr. Graff?"

"I have," Rachel said. "He's gravely ill but lucid. He said Kelly and the other home nurses routinely suctioned his lungs and disposed of the tubing in a special waste bag for infectious materials. I think she took a hunk of his mucus and put it into Mrs. Merriam's lungs by telling Ashley it was a preventative measure for her latent asthma."

He asked dryly, "And you will have a witness that prior to her death Mrs. Merriam received such a respiratory treatment with used or contaminated tubing taken from a bag marked as infectious materials?"

Rachel sunk. The judge said dryly, "No, again. Well."

He said with his resonant air of respect and wry humor, "What I need, as you well know and have made a valiant attempt to do here today, is for your investigation to positively foreclose on any other possibilities for these deaths, leaving only Miss McLaughlin as the sole standing likelihood. I do regret reporting to you that I don't believe such foreclosure has been accomplished despite your diligence and brilliance."

He banged the gavel and stood mountainous in his black robe, the star bass singer in a gospel choir towering over them.

He pointed the log of cigar and told them, "Hear me out. I think a sample of Miss McLaughlin's DNA could deftly enable your investigation to flourish or falter. It would allow you to prove or disprove that she purposefully impeded life-saving efforts to be brought forth to Mrs. Merriam and thusly caused her death. Please remember that once a person discards an article—say, a cigarette, a glass they have drunk from, a used hairbrush or a comb, remember then that the item is no longer that person's property."

He twinkled a kind of dignified mischief at Rachel and concluded, "You two, as sworn law officers, can retrieve this item. In so doing you become the chain of custody for said discarded property. You swear it's hers. I'm bound by law to believe you. Y'all have yourselves a good day now."

=29=

Chaz slammed into the wall and then unglamorously slid down it into a clump of sweaty flesh. Daniel stood over him, dripping beads of sweat, his white shirt and shorts soaking wet.

Chaz joked, "Had enough, Nystrom?"

Daniel panted, bent over, hands on his knees. He said between huffs, "Did I win?"

"You're the one still standing, pal. You won. Again."

"Oh. Okay." Daniel's breaths were slowing just barely. "Then I guess it's my turn to call the ambulance for us." He gave Chaz a hand up. "Could we give up handball and maybe take up chess as a sport?"

Chaz said gruffly, wobbling to his feet, "Sex at lunchtime would be more aerobic."

"Yeah. But you're not my type, Chaz."

Chaz laughed. Daniel gave him a back slap. They headed for the showers.

Their cheeseburgers were huge. They sat at a formica counter in a downtown diner, not facing each other and not talking much until they had wolfed down most of the fries and all of their banana pudding.

Stirring cream into his coffee, looking like the Sigma Chi poster boy in corduroys and a chambray shirt, Daniel finally spoke. "So tell me about partnering with Rachel." He leveled a wry smile.

Chaz grimaced. "Please. I'm eating."

Daniel laughed. "When you go to work every day, I bet

you bring along a chair and a whip. That girl is one piece of work."

"Nobody takes advantage of her. Let's put it that way," Chaz opined. "What's the deal with that boyfriend of hers?"

Daniel said considerately, "Emory Jacobs. The greatest golfer to ever walk the course. Their deal is that she considers herself his lover, not his warden, and he considers her a goddess. Emory's a great man."

The waitress brought a check. Daniel picked it up, saying, "Ante up, Elliot Ness. Ethically I can't let you buy my lunch and you can't let me buy yours. We're the perfect dutch couple."

Chaz plunked down money and said dryly, "Yes. If you buy my lunch I might be grateful enough to tell you that our police chief sleeps with dead women and live little boys."

Daniel smiled. "That isn't even a headline anymore. The world is desensitized to sexual scandal. Now, you tell me he doesn't pay social security for his Mexican housekeeper, we're talking federal investigation. Hey, how're you guys doing on that kidnapping-murder deal?"

"Lisa Canton. We still have her father in jail on some hot checks. And there's an angle going. My zealous partner has a brainstorm that hasn't panned out yet, but we'll see." Chaz softened then and added, "She is a damned war horse. She has called every person who was interviewed by the cops the day of the kidnapping and gotten from them the names of other people who were there but didn't talk to the uniforms. From an original list of ten people she's gotten names and contacted almost fifty others. In person, too. I say, Rachel, can't we call them on the phone? She says, no, I'll go see them each in person."

Daniel's instinct kicked in. "What's she looking for?"

"Can't say. Not yet. She starts about six in the morning and quits about midnight. The leads are ice cold and eroding, but war horse Collazo won't back down."

"Ah, Chaz, I think you're warming up to her, huh?"

He rolled his eyes. "I'm learning to live with it, is all. Say, how's your wife doing?"

Daniel's expression was notably flat. "She starts chemo

this week. Over what the insurance pays it'll cost me thousands of dollars. I get to shell out all the money, she gets to use cancer as a reason to stop having sex with me."

He didn't notice Chaz's splintered, stunned silence. Daniel asked, "Want a ride back to the P.D.?"

Chaz said remotely, "No. I'll walk."

"It's sleeting like crazy out there, man."

Chaz turned up his trench coat collar and said glumly, "I'll be fine. You take care of your wife, Danny. She's real cute. See you around."

=30=

George Dorcus spit tobacco juice into a Dunkin Donuts paper cup, hoisted his uniform pants up under his dangling belly and said to Rachel with snarling indifference as he pointed to the dead body on the bed, "Signal 51. His way. And not in a shy way, I might add."

Rachel lifted the silver tarp from the gray, drained body of Wes Merriam. "How?" she asked.

Chaz reeled at her. "Jesus. He cut his femural artery."

Dorcus growled, "Like I said, he wadn't kidding. It wouldn't occur to me to slice that near my own cahones. I always said I'm more homicidal than suicidal anyhow."

A flashbulb blinded Rachel as the police photographer took a photo of a highball glass on the bedside table. Erin Truett was crouched, taping brown paper bags over Wes's dead hands. Rachel asked, "Y'all vacuumed for trace already?"

Erin drawled like Texas salsa, "Yep." She dangled a baggie. "He used this scalpel, got the artery on the first swing at it, too."

"Any evidence he was helped along?"

Erin said supremely, "Honey, if there is, I'll find it. You're talking about Nurse Nasty, but remember, her hair and prints are supposed to be at this scene. She worked here. Now maybe there's her big fat thumbprint on the scalpel. That would help." She made notes on a clipboard, looked at Rachel over thick eyeglasses. "He died between nine and midnight last night. The neighbor came over about noon to collect his mail and feed his cat. She didn't know he was back from his trip. Nobody did, she said. He'd been home about three days but didn't call anyone."

Chaz asked, "The cat stayed here alone for three months?"

Erin chuckled. "It seems Pussy Galore here didn't like the neighbor's house and got real destructive."

"What's the neighbor's story?" Rachel inquired.

Dorcus explained, "She didn't do him. She's real old, walks with a cane. She just fed the cat and brought in packages and mail. Yesterday she let in the maid, but the maid didn't see Wes Merriam. Said he wasn't here so she thought he was still away on his trip."

"He wanted the house cleaned the day before he killed himself?" Rachel snapped.

Dorcus hitched his drawers again, spat, gnawed on the lump in his cheek. "Good Legs, don't complicate this. I got a hun'ert real killings to solve. This stiff did himself."

Erin gathered paraphernalia into her medical bag. She told them, "I'll do a complete tox on him. Y'all call me about six or so. Want anything special?"

Rachel answered. "Yeah. Check his saliva against the sample Nurse Nasty sent to the lab as Ashley's. Maybe Wes spit on the slide for her so nobody would know his wife had pneumonia. If it's his DNA, that'll prove collusion on the nurse's part."

"Y'all going for an affidavit to search her?"

Rachel frowned. "We did that this morning. Charlie shot us clean out of the saddle. We really need anything you can give us."

"You mean like you'd appreciate it if I'd help you prove that first she killed his wife with a bacteria and then she came back and killed him with a scalpel because he wasn't grateful for her murderous gesture?"

"That's what I'm thinking, too," Rachel said.

Chaz asked, "Where'd he get a scalpel?"

Dorcus lectured. "Scalpels ain't controlled weapons. He bought it at a medical supply store just like you or I could do. The basement's full of scale-size replicas of sailing ships he was building, along with a cabinet full of box knives, Exactos, shearing knives and wood carving tools. The scalpel ain't that illogical for him to own."

Rachel sighed, then asked. "He's nude, Georgie. Where are his clothes?"

"In that bag there, marked for the dry cleaners to pick up."

"When the neighbor came over today was the burglar alarm set? Did she have to turn it off when she entered?"

"Yeah, Collazo. She remembers it was on because she didn't have her glasses and had a hard time seeing the numbers to code it off. So he didn't want to get robbed while he was offing himself."

Chaz sniffed the bedside glass. "Smells like vodka. Where's the bottle?"

"There's about six or eight bottles of vodka in the bar downstairs. Cheap stuff. The good Commie imported stuff is still all sealed."

Rachel turned to Erin. "So this rich guy drinks the cheap stuff and saves the unopened Stoli for guests? I don't think so." She pulled off her protective gloves. "Are there antidepressants or other narcotics anywhere?"

Dorcus blew his nose into a tissue and said gruffly, "No."

Erin started out, then stopped and told Rachel pragmatically, "If she came for a drink and doused the vodka with a Mickey, she probably took it with her to destroy. Maybe you'll get lucky when you search her house and find a half-full bottle of Stoli laced with Seconal."

Rachel said dimly, "Maybe we'll get lucky and finally find a reason good enough to search her damned house. Bye, Erin. We'll come by tonight."

The room felt surreal to her. Blood splashes had made a gruesome pattern on the ceiling as it exploded hotly from his artery. Wes Merriam gaped at them, eyes and mouth open and silently screaming. His facial skin and torso had collapsed as his body drained.

Chaz asked, "Any suicide note?"

"No," Dorcus said, knowing he was whipped. He looked

gloomily at Rachel and said, "You want crime scene tape, don't you, Good Legs?"

"Any footprints or tire tracks, Georgie?"

"It snowed after midnight. Whatever was there is gone now."

"Well. Okay then, Georgie. Bring in the tape. Until Erin rules this a suicide—and she will, you know, because this fucking nurse is real, real good at this shit—until it's a suicide officially, it's a preliminary homicide. I'll take heat in the press, but fuck 'em."

Rachel and Chaz stood on the lengthy flat porch that was sliced by pillars as big as Redwoods. Their breaths were wintry white.

He said to her, "Dorcus said none of the neighbors saw a car."

Rachel smirked. "Did you ask if they saw anybody fly in here on a broom? I hate this bitch."

"Why are you so sure she did him? Maybe he was despondent over his wife's death?"

She glared harshly at the fuming low clouds and said, "I punched the redial button on his desk phone. Guess whose answering machine I got? Yep. Nurse Nasty. Sometime since he got home, he called her. So Dorcus is wrong about nobody knowing Wes Merriam was back in town. Kelly knew."

Chaz said sagely, "If he spoke to her or left a message. We have no proof that she actually knew."

"I'll tell you why he called her, Diablo. He wanted to know why a homicide investigator was calling about his wife's death. He wanted to talk to her before he contacted me. Drive me to a 7-11 for a hot dog. I haven't had breakfast. Oh. And could you loan me five bucks?"

=31=

They slammed their car doors. He drove slowly on the icy streets and asked her coyly, "You sparred a guy yet?"

She sounded testy. "I popped him once and he went down like a whore on a paying preacher."

"Did not."

"Did too."

"No way."

"Yes way. And he was no shrimp, either. He's a bouncer at a strip joint. I did that Moe thing. I said, oh look, your shoe's untied. Then I upper cut him like a flying barbell."

"Don't you ever fight with the head gear off?"

"Not yet," she said. "And I'll tell you a trade secret. That fucking cotton swab jammed up your nose with antiseptic on it hurts worse than the damned face slam. Guess what I did today while you were he-man-woman-hating on the handball court? I worked on those two suicides Tillery dropped on us."

He looked over at her. She was yawning, a delicate, pretty yawn with her full lips that strangely made his penis flicker. He said only, "And?"

"And Iverson, well, I called his wife. He used his right hand to slash his left wrist with his pocketknife. So I ask her, and so she tells me, Iverson was left-handed. Dum-dee-dum-dum. Then I go to the jewelry store and get a necklace just like the one Raymond Esterhaus bought that we've never found. The jeweler says he paid cash, no credit card records for like his cutesy wife to find, you see. Plus I got the registration list for everyone who attended the oncology conference."

He said it again, feeling like a parrot. "And?"

"Kelly McLaughlin was there the whole three days. She's like that chick on *Murder She Wrote*, J.B. Fletcher. Everywhere she goes, somebody ends up dying. Oh, don't look at me like that. Of course I have no proof they knew her. But when Miss Kelly and I have our ultimate and inevitable . . . chat . . . in an interrogation room, I'll have this bit of extra information to drop on her."

He scoffed. "It isn't much."

She poked him in the arm. "Neither is six lousy pounds, but that's all Cujo has over me. At some point those six lousy pounds takes its toll on me when we fight. It isn't much to start with, but in the end it really matters."

She yawned again. He looked away from her hair tousled so sexy and her eyes so velvety. "Daniel said a weird thing to me today at lunch. I actually wanted to punch him. I asked about his wife, so he says that keeping her alive is costing him money and that he'll never get any sex. It's like her cancer is all about how he's inconvenienced."

"Nystrom is an arrogant prick."

"He's not, Collazo. I hope he said it in a weak moment."

Rachel opened one droopy eye to look at him from where she leaned back in the passenger seat. "That church of theirs, it's a cult, Diablo. I've drunk enough beers with Nystrom to hear the horror stories about it. According to him their church teaches that you stay virgins and you trust God to send you the perfect mate. You buy without the test drive because if you test drive you go to hell. So Nystrom's perfect mate doesn't fuck, and he feels all betrayed by God, but he lives with a bitch because it's how the cult says he can prove he loves god. That's his story. His church does not let anybody escape the cult."

Chaz teased her. "My, that was a secular soliloquy. You actually think our Nurse Nasty is involved in the Esterhaus and Iverson suicides?"

"And Wes Merriam. Besides being an arrogant prick, how did Daniel say his wife's doing?"

"Chemo starting this week."

"Not at home, I hope."

"No. He's co-paying. They're not rich enough. What he said, you know, about the money and not having any sex, it's the kind of thing one hundred men in his situation would think, but Rachel, ninety-nine of them wouldn't dare say it out loud."

She was sleeping soundly. He turned the radio up loudly to drown out her irreverent snoring.

=32=

The final breath of winter was one last blast of sleet and snow.

Daniel stood in the doorway of what was now Julie Ann's convalescent room in their home. He could neither stand to watch nor turn away from the sight of Kelly McLaughlin's hands kneading lotion into Julie Ann's parched back. Julie was nude, lying on her belly, eyes comfortably closed while Kelly massaged in the moisture like adding water to cracked, colorless clay. They were the hands of a graceful ballerina, waving sensuality across Julie's desolate stage of a sickbed.

Kelly had taken off her heavy wool sweater and sat over Julie. Kelly wore a white body suit that showed every muscle and voluptuous curve. Her upper arms were slender but toned. Her waist was an hourglass that led to the small, juicy melon, so firm above her trim thighs. Her feet were bare and bronze. Her toenails were small, glistening pink petals. She had put on for Julie the lugubrious lull of a Gregorian chant, but Daniel was hearing only the coursing of bloody lust pumping in his heart and his brain.

Kelly did not look at him or make any sounds as Julie slipped farther into the sedation Kelly had masterfully given her. He found and admitted to himself that he did not crave to be in Kelly's position. He did not hunger for the feel of Julie's familiar but now estranged round, fleshy ass. He wanted Kelly. On top of him. Just like he could see her now. And he wanted to turn over to face her, pull her down to him, bury his hands in her healthy, shiny hair, bury his face in her luscious bombs of breasts.

Julie moaned. Kelly whispered like a hot gush. "Am I hurting you, Mrs. Nystrom? I'll be more gentle then."

He had to go. Grabbed his parka and fled to the wide decked patio that was only a jungle of winter-charred, blackened shrubbery. The wind was brutal. His hands shook.

His thoughts raced, manic marbles.

"My mother would hate me. God would hate me. I cannot, oh my god, cannot leave this wife of mine. I was so ready for her to die and now they're curing her. Oh god. She'll take my son if I leave. My house. Everything I ever worked for and loved. I'm doomed."

He jolted when the glass bay door opened and shut behind him. Then he relaxed.

The chipper voice was a relief. "Hey, little brother. Did you know that Farrah Fawcett is in there having lesbian sex with your wife? Got a video camera?"

"Hey, Mitch. Oh, thanks." He took the beer.

His brother sat across from him and took on a look of despair. "Nice work in the headlines this morning, bro. How'd you find out our famous Bible-banging senator invested a hundred-thou in porn last year? Shit, I wouldn't want you after my secrets." He peered closely. "Man, Danny you look like roadkill. What's going on?"

"It's . . . uh, stressful around here. She's three weeks into the chemo, sick all the time. It's hard for me at work. She calls all day, bitching."

"Why are you out here in a fucking blizzard?"

Daniel said disgustedly, "Oh. Julie Ann told me yesterday that if I was going to start smoking again I sure as hell wasn't going to do it in her house."

Mitch winced. "And did you point out that you pay for this house?"

"Oh yeah. And then she pointed out that she has cancer and I'm an ungrateful drunken sex maniac halfway already in hell." He felt nauseous. "Jesus, Mitch. I can't live like this. Remember her? Remember how hot she was in college? God, what a beautiful girl. What fun we had. She believed in me. She told me I was a great writer. I told her every day that she was a great school teacher. We made love. We were so . . . happy."

Mitch sighed white torrents from the cold air. "Leave her, Danny. She's a cold bitch. Nobody would blame you. What you had is gone. Don't stay for the memories." He leaned. They became quiet conspirators. "Look, Danny, I go to lots of architect conventions, parties, you know. I'll take you. You'll meet a girl to sport fuck. Tell her the deal. How long can Julie live?"

Daniel covered his eyes. "God. Jesus, Mitch. I can't pick up some girl at a bar. I got women swimming up my ass at the newspaper. You think I'd get mixed up with a woman you or I work with? It's all so far outside my value system."

Mitch bent closer to say, "Your value system was given to you when you were nine years old by a fat, Bible-thumping lunatic preacher in a toupee. What about you, Danny? What about what you really think and want?"

He lit another cigarette. "I want Kelly."

Mitch sat back, somewhat satisfied. "And she's up for it?"

The wind made Daniel's nose runny; he sniffled. "Yeah. I can tell by everything she doesn't say to me."

"Then what's the fucking problem? A sleeping pill for Julie Ann some night while Pete's at Mom's house."

Daniel looked up, feeling as gloomy as a man waiting to view the body. Mitch's expectant face was almost a mirror of his own, but two years older and just a touch balder. "The problem is that I love my wife."

"You love what she was." They were so close together that the gritty breezes ruffling their hair almost drowned out their gravelly low words. "What about what she is? This woman for the last five years has jacked you every way but off, brother. I've watched. I've watched you lose weight, lose interest in your job. I know what you do for sex, Danny. I gave you the goddamned movies to do it with. Have you looked in there lately at what has become of your sexy little kitten Julie Ann? You think that a woman who hated sex before she had cancer is going to like it better now that she has a real excuse to shut you off completely?"

Daniel was shaking all over. "Is it all about sex, Mitch?"

The leaves around them shuddered like crackling flames.

"She's dying of cancer, Danny. Before all this happened, you were dying of rejection. I've watched you try to please her. I've watched her slap your hand like you're a lame-brained kid. What's wrong if another woman wants you? So you didn't meet her at a bar and she doesn't work with you. Guess what? She loves your wife, too. She's in there now giving Julie the only good feeling Julie's had in months. So go for it, Charlie."

Daniel surprised himself by laughing. "Jesus, you're a fucking Eddie Haskell."

Mitch's face brightened. "I'm telling you. Men, we're always trying to figure out women, except we do it from their point of view. And of course to women sex is all about love, so when they don't love you anymore, poof, no sex. To you and me, see, sex is like food and air. It has nothing to do with religion or love, Danny. It's a whole different compartment of life."

"I guess that's what you tell yourself when you fuck stewardesses while your wife is at home making quilts and baking cookies for your twins."

"What I tell myself, thanks for asking, is that she's happier without sex and I've got to have it." He took Daniel's cigarette and tossed it. "You won't get some big blinding flash here. Men are not blasted out of our fine Christian belief systems all at once. We slide out of them slowly, when we find out those beliefs mean we have to do what the little woman says and stop being nasty. It'll come to you. Divorce is costly, and if I didn't have my girlfriends for sex I couldn't stay with my wife."

"I wish I could pray, Mitch."

He open another beer from his coat pocket and said to Daniel, "You can't. Neither can I. Look at it, Danny, until we each left home at eighteen, our crazy mother came into our room and made us pray out loud so she could check up on what we were asking God for. I wanted to pray for Barbi

Benton to come over and give me a blow job, but I had to pray for Grandma to have a bowel movement because my mother was monitoring my calls to God. Is that sick, to learn first thing in life that you have to lie even when you pray?"

"I never lie," Daniel said dryly.

"Sure you do." Mitch's eyes were strangely penetrating and illuminated in the dull shadow of clouds. "Every time you let Julie Ann berate and control you, you're lying to your son. You're telling him that this is the way it should be."

Just then she stepped out onto the patio, a California babe beckoning from a giant billboard, her perfect body perched above him and making him cringe.

"I'm leaving, Mr. Nystrom."

They went inside. She packed her equipment silently into a large bag on the couch and slipped her bulky sweater over her mouth-watering body suit. Julie's voice was like a buzzard squawking suddenly.

"Danny! Get Pete dressed and take him to evening prayer services right now."

Danny went to her doorway. "All right, Julie Ann, just a minute. Mitch is here."

Mitch stepped up to the door and saw Julie Ann compressed into a sheath of barren paleness. He spoke, "Hi, Julie, how are you feeling?"

She did not look his direction. Daniel said, "Julie, Mitch spoke to you."

She stared unblinking and straight at the pages of her opened book. "I know. I heard him. He needs to go home. You have to take my son to church. Tell him to take away the beer he brought. I don't want it in my house."

Daniel stood on the porch in the swaying arctic breezes with Kelly for a few minutes after they watched Mitch pull away.

"Do the husbands of all your breast cancer patients fall in love with you, Miss McLaughlin?"

"Yes, Mr. Nystrom, eventually. Because they're scared and lonely."

He looked right at her and heard the plucking of low notes of bad trouble.

She said without expression, "But I don't fuck anyone I don't want to fuck, no matter how lonely he is or how long it's been since he came in someone's mouth."

He had to grab the porch pole. "How long will she sleep tonight, Miss McLaughlin?"

Sapphires with flints of flame inside them met his gaze. "As long as I want her to, Mr. Nystrom. And the answer to your next question is yes. Yes. I want to fuck you . . . You are . . . what I want."

He gave her the house key and noticed that the key ring didn't jingle unsteadily in his calm hands.

=33=

Reverend Rose was pontificating from his fiery pulpit, blubbering in tears about the decline of morality in the world, precisely the lustful, gluttonous, greedy, slovenly state of the lives of the Christians in that congregation. Which, he said pridefully, could be rectified with a generous donation into the plate he was about to pass among them.

Daniel felt like sawdust inside. The epiphany had left him feeling wooden and shredded. The realizations were starkly tragic.

He had never acted toward Julie Ann the way he felt about her; he had only spent days cringing from the grief over having to fake love for her. He knew that his life would never be right with Julie in it or Pete out of it.

"I'm not talking to you, Lord. I wouldn't call this exactly a prayer. You don't even have to listen if you don't want to." Daniel cradled Pete's sleeping head. Reverend Rose was on mute in Daniel's mind, a violent mime up front.

"We want our lives to be right, men do, and we go around thinking that blind devotion to an unloving wife somehow proves that our thinking is clear. What a lie. What a perverse pressure your churches put on men, to teach us that to serve You we have to serve wives who won't touch us anymore, that we should pay their bills and take their verbal abuse and frigid indifference and live without love—just to prove that we love You."

He thought about a day when he had come home from the newspaper and found Kelly cross-legged on Julie Ann's bed, the two of them talking like giddy prom girls. Pete had been nestled in Kelly's lap while she petted his hair. Kelly had bent her head forward toward Julie, letting all that glorious mane of hair fall forward as she said loudly into Pete's tape recorder, "Julie Ann Nystrom does solemnly swear that tomorrow she will call and get herself a post-treatment breast cancer volunteer counselor. Now, it's on the tape, Julie, you promised me and you have to make the call."

Julie Ann had been a slate of illness pinned flatly to bleached sheets. Her bald head was covered by a scarf Kelly had taught her to tie. Next to her Kelly had been a muscle-toned Olympic ice skating queen in tight jeans and a sparkling sweater, robust and vibrant.

"Pete knows a joke," Kelly had announced, "tell your joke, Pete. Say it into your recorder."

Pete's radiant blue pools of curiosity and innocence ignited. "Mom, why is six afraid of seven? Because seven ate nine."

They had all laughed. Kelly had enfolded Pete in a loving embrace. Daniel had disappeared into the living room until she came in, Pete hoisted in her arms asleep. He had taken the slumbering boy from Kelly, kissing Pete and thanking her, for what he didn't know, for reminding him that he wasn't dead to the thought of love and laughter.

Her fingers had trickled from Pete's hair into Daniel's, and he had looked longingly at her as she said, "I left your wife my home phone number. I'm not supposed to, Mr. Nystrom, but we had a breakthrough today; she's going to open up to counseling. I also wrote the number for you. It's in your room by your . . . bed. Night."

Daniel had never used the number. His wife had cancer. He had a son. He was a Christian. His profession was as defender of the truth. If she loves my wife, a thought echoed oddly through Daniel, as if he knew other men had summoned this logic and would concur, then you must also love me. And now he had unflinchingly handed her a house key so she could come to him and unleash the fairy tale sin.

He closed his eyes against Reverend Rose's impassioned ranting and had to stifle an outrageous laugh. ". . . if I didn't have sex with my girlfriends I couldn't stay with my wife . . .." Mitch. That's how to deal with the cancer and keep the marriage, and in doing those things he would be a better father. No divorce.

She was awake when he carried Pete into her room, groggy but chatty. Pete perked up as he snuggled against Julie.

"Mom, we had doughnuts at church afterward. Dad let me tape record Reverend Rose. Hey, Mom, Reverend Rose had a booger in his nose when he came over to talk to us."

Daniel said solemnly, "Julie, take your sleeping pills."

She frowned. "I already have. You shouldn't have let him have a doughnut. Go away now. He can sleep with me."

"The boy should sleep in his own bed. It's a bad habit to get him used to—"

She flared. "Good fathers don't give their children junk food at this time of night, Daniel. Any idiot knows that. In case you forgot, I have cancer. I can sleep with my baby if I want to. Close the door."

He ate peanut butter—it was out and opened on the counter along with three days of what nobody had bothered to clean. The phone rang, and he took it in his bedroom. Mitch's familiar profanity jarred him.

"Hey, fucker, I need to borrow your car Wednesday. Mine's going for maintenance."

Daniel swigged milk. "Take your wife's."

"Shit. Can't. Carpool."

"All right, come by Wednesday early. I won't be here Tuesday night. I'm playing handball with Chaz. Hey, Mitch," Daniel asked, "Tell me your all-time biggest sex fantasy."

Mitch guffawed crudely. "Mine is the same as every man's all-time sex fantasy. Sex, right here, right now."

Daniel laughed, and the laughter felt good.

In the kitchen he got an apple and turned out lights behind him. He checked on Pete, kneeled a moment by the bed and held and kissed his son's face. He touched Julie Ann's dehydrated, flaky skin. She didn't feel his touch. She was deeply drugged.

=34=

The house was dark. To her left Kelly could see the expansive dining room windows. A fine icy mist was growing on the glass as if legions of willowy spiders were spinning webs against the panes.

The living room was shadowy from the last amber hue of a fire dying in the fireplace. Julie's convalescent room just to the right was dark.

She could hear Daniel's deep voice down the hallway to the master bedroom. The center of her ached for his hands and lips to be on her, all over her. She waited in the hallway, listening to his mellow friendliness as he talked on the telephone. She had arrived in jeans and a sweater, but beneath them sizzled flesh touched only by narrow strips of black bikini panties and a long sleeve knit crop top. The sound and smell of Daniel in the next room made her wet. She resisted the urge to rush at him like an animal.

She had watched him, so tall and polished. He often ran his hands through his neatly layered gold locks when he worked at his desk in the living room. His shoulders were broad, his belly flat and rippled with muscle. She'd seen it when he came shirtless down from the attic where he'd been cleaning all of one afternoon. He was adorable. The waiting had been almost physically painful for her.

She wanted him off the phone. She wanted her bikini panties off, his fire on her skin, burning her. He was in boxer shorts on the bed with the phone on his belly. His glasses were off and he was rubbing his eyes tiredly. Kelly peeked, gasped, felt a gush ooze from her. She wanted Daniel to lap it away.

"Yeah, good, you pick me up about six. You're what, Chaz? You're bringing wine? Cops drink wine while they play poker? What happened to malt liquor? Okay. You bring the wine." He paused. "My kid? Man, he did great. He's got a natural swing and if nobody touches it, he'll be fine. Can't you get your partner's lover boy to take my kid out on the course once and look him over while he swings? Shit. So what. Six-years old is the perfect time to start 'em. Okay. Tomorrow night. Six. Don't be late to get me, pal. My warden goes ape shit if I'm not home by nine. That doesn't give me much time to win away all the bribes you earned this week. Bye."

She heard the shower, heard him pee and flush. He began to sing, choppy and sloppy. Kelly grinned. She pulled off her sweater, kicked off suede boots, slid her jeans away. Daniel's song limped. She opened the shower door.

Small spatters rained on her. Her nipples pointed at him through the skimpy shirt and the arcs of steam.

He smiled the smile of a man freshly submerged in a warm surf, relaxed and rewarded by the abundance of nature. He stepped out, didn't towel himself but took her soaking wet on the soft carpet beneath them. Their fire dance of kisses stopped a moment, and he pulled the tight midriff knit top over her breasts so they could tumble at his face like two nymphs groping for him. He stretched the crop top over her arms, and she spoke for the first time.

"Stop, Daniel." He searched her eyes with a split second of alarm, until she whispered. "Stop at my wrists and tie them with the shirt sleeves. Pull the bikini panties down and tie my ankles together."

This is how he took her, in her compliant bondage.

His eyes burned afterward with drops of salty sweat. They lay together, sealed by oozes of body fluids. They could hear the sea sounds of crusty sleet hitting the window.

She had not asked to be untied, instead she curled her long, lean body beside him peacefully. A branch scraped the glass in a bluster of wind. Daniel shivered suddenly at the thought that it sounded like something evil trying to get inside and roar at them.

He asked between gratified panting, "How did you know?"

Her bound hands with red fingernails were on his glistening chest, two delicate albino tarantulas.

He stroked her. "You weren't there." He felt and sounded weak. "You can't know how a boy's mother dominates him into a pulp, and how the pulp becomes a formless man who can only imagine himself as dominated. You couldn't have known all that."

"Daniel. Sweet Daniel. I want you again. Take me again."

She was on top of him. "I'll never be faithful to anything or anyone again," he confided cryptically. "You know that. I'm a liar now. I chose her. I knew she would dominate me . . . I thought I would stop it, that I would prevail, that the memories of cowering in front of a tyrant as a boy would go away when I brought Julie to her knees. No. No. It doesn't work. Julie asks for mud pies and then punishes me because my hands are dirty after I make them for her."

Kelly whispered, "Do whatever you want to me, Daniel. I am your insatiable sex slave."

He laughed, rolled onto her, gripped her hair. He put himself into her and felt her spasms of pleasure. The power surge that ran through his gut and ravaged his brain didn't frighten him. Daniel knew what it meant.

He knew who the slave was. But he didn't care.

=35=

Mrs. Pickett opened the front door while drying her hands on a dish towel. She was the same as Rachel remembered, skittishly articulate and with a perpetual smile that seemed to hold back embarrassment.

"Miss Collazo." She slid the towel onto her shoulder and took Rachel's hands in both of hers. "Come in. I've made coffee. I've been so jittery waiting to hear what you have to tell me."

Rachel took off her coat and welcomed the warmth of the cozy kitchen with its lace curtains and embroidered place mats. They sat with two steaming mugs of coffee. Rachel plunked out her note pad. She spoke plainly because she knew no other way.

"Mizz Pickett, I'm going to shoot real straight with you. Since I got the letter you sent me about all the details of Ashley's last days alive, I've been on this thing like a duck on a damned june bug, I really have. And everywhere I go there's another wall in front of me. All I've got is theory and speculation. I think you deserve to hear my instincts even if I am full of shit. Okay? I do think your sister was murdered. I don't think we can prove it yet."

Mrs. Pickett needed a moment to recover from the graphic frankness. She sat, painfully obedient and humbled.

"You understand, Mizz Pickett," Rachel lamented, "that there is no statute of limitations on homicide and something can always break later to give me what we need to bring charges against a killer. This is not the end of the road.

I am not giving up. But for now my boss has warned me that he thinks I'm pissing up a rope on this case. Not that I give a rat's ass what he thinks, but I do agree with him that the pathology to support my theory is just not there, ma'am."

Mrs. Pickett nodded sweetly. Her face was crinkled as if she were facing direct sunlight. She said, "So Wes killed her."

"No."

She jerked. "No? Then . . ."

Rachel said grimly, "I have another suspect."

"Oh my god." Mrs. Pickett sunk her face into the damp towel. "Wes's sons? For their daddy's inheritance money?" A tear limped from eyes almost pleading with Rachel. "They came while Ashley was alone and poisoned her?"

"Miss Pickett, I can't name who I think it is. I'd get my ass sued off. But it wasn't Wes or his kids or the servants—"

A strain of fright jaded Mrs. Pickett's watery eyes. "No. You can't mean . . . the nurses? But, but . . ." she was panicky. "But they were so good to her! My god, Rachel! They eased her pain, gave her emotional support with talk of recovery and reconstructive surgery." She began to openly cry. "Oh Jesus, it was the pretty one, Kelly." A hand went to her mouth. "They were lovers. . . ."

In Rachel a nerve twanged. "I can't say anymore, ma'am, except that I talked to Wes's counselor. She said that after Ashley's death Wes was very angry, extremely choked by grief, that he kind of hated other women for a long time, that he wondered why they could live if his Ashley had to die. It's a clear sign that he wasn't having an affair with Kelly or anyone else. And when you told me that he was drunk the night before her death, the night you called, well, ma'am—I'm betting he wasn't drunk at all. He was drugged so he couldn't hear your sister crying out for help in the night, drugged by somebody who knew how. Somebody who wanted your sister gone and Wes to herself."

Mrs. Pickett wailed new pain. Rachel's eyes filled with tears that spilled. She wiped her nose on a tissue Mrs. Pickett gave her from her sweater pocket.

"I'm sorry, Mizz Pickett. It's not written on the chart that the nurse gave Wes any sedative, but I know what she did. She suggested that he get some rest and gave him some sort of potent shot that knocked him out. He never heard your sister dying."

The sobs overwhelmed Mrs. Pickett. Rachel moved beside her and said, "She sent a sputum culture to the lab that wasn't Ashley's so nobody would know there was actual pneumonia. I thought for a while it would be Wes's, but it wasn't. The M.E. cross checked for me after Wes died. So listen, he wasn't in on it." She held Mrs. Pickett and stroked her coarse hair. "He loved Ashley. That's the profile I've gotten. Ashley was truly loved."

"You're quitting on me."

"No ma'am. I'm going to back off, but I'm not going to go away. This suspect knows that I'm onto her. She's nervous now. If I just wait, she'll screw up. I'll be right there when she does, cuffs waiting."

"He was afraid of Kelly."

"Did he say that to you?"

"No. But the times I was there briefly, to take groceries or do errands for Wesley, he was fidgety when Kelly was in the room with us."

Rachel considered and then asked, "Like a man who felt guilty for something?"

Mrs. Pickett smoothed her hair, licked her lips. Settling down. "No, not like that. Like an animal sensing a predator." A clock ticked ominously. A brazen, crass crow fluttered in a rim of snow outside the window sill. "Your suspect . . . she gave Ashley pneumonia?"

"She got the bacteria from an infected patient. And I'm sure the contaminated tubing she used is long burned at a medical waste site."

The round, sad eyes pierced Rachel's heart. "Oh, Miss Collazo, how are you going to prove what she did?"

"I'm going to wait a while, and then I'm going to bring her in and ask her. One way or another, she'll tell me if I'm right or wrong about all this."

Mrs. Pickett looked far away. She shivered, but not from the cold outside. She said, "Let's have brandy in our coffee." It was barely 10:00 A.M.

Rachel said nicely, "All right. Let's do. And you tell me about all these little glass angels you've got everywhere in your house. I'd guess you collect angels, huh?"

A dollop clunked into each mug. Mrs. Pickett's voice was barren. "Yes. I thought angels loved and protected us. Maybe I was wrong."

=36=

The piano music in the restaurant reminded Rachel of the second time they had been in Rome. The first time they traveled there together had been just after she had convinced Emory to come to her college graduation, after she had chased him like a bloodhound every day since she met him. She took to calling him every day after falling crazy for him at the golf tournament. Volunteers had access to the golfers' press biographies, so she found out his hometown was in the exclusive and mansion-heavy Turtle Creek part of Dallas. She drove to the country club there, a seventeen-year-old cheerleader dressed as a chatelaine, and she drove a golf cart straight up to where he was standing, all languid and lanky in plaid, with a group of pot-bellied rich men sweating in bright Texas sun.

"I want you to be my boyfriend," she had announced unceremoniously while the rich men squinted.

Emory had been icy sweet. "I believe, my dear, that to do so would constitute a felony in this state."

"Your wife's dead. Your biography said so."

He had leaned on his long driver. Another of the men chuckled and suggested that the rest of them might want to head on back to the bar. Emory stood alone then, facing her like a man might face a veiled bride if she turned from the altar and proved to be a chimpanzee in lace. His shoulders being wider than his hips just killed her, and his pearly teeth and his eyes as serious as anything under glass at the Smithsonian.

"Rachel—"

"My daddy doesn't think you're too old for me. He said that nobody my own age could possibly stand my forthright bullshit anyhow. My mom, well, she has ten kids. She stopped a real long time ago trying to figure out what we're all doing at one time. I told her I love you and she just said 'Don't get pregnant.' And my brothers, they think you're cool because they win money betting on you on TV golf tournaments. So it's okay if you take me out. Even Father Jerry, our priest, he said he'd appreciate it if you'd show me about sex so I'd quit asking him."

Emory had sort of collapsed against his driver; it made a small pit in the grass among the spent tees. He had tried a couple of times to open his mouth and talk, but nothing came out.

"How do you know that you love me, Rachel?"

She had shrugged. "I watched you for three days at that tournament. You don't play air guitar or scratch your balls or brag about your car engine. I hate boys my age."

Then he had begun to laugh, and he had put his eyes on her like cheek tweaks, and he had gotten into the cart with her so she could drive him back to the club and he could buy her a burger while he sipped martinis.

On her twenty-second birthday he took her to Rome, she who had never been out of Dallas County except once when her criminal justice class drove to Huntsville and toured the prison. That time, the first trip, she mostly stood around with her mouth open while Emory pointed at roped-off paintings and tried to keep up with her skipping pace through all the ornate streets and squares.

They went again on her thirtieth birthday, long after she had become a Dallas cop and was already bucking for a spot on the homicide squad. On the first trip Emory made love to her like a delicate bird building a nest. Just a gentle twist here and the right peck there. The second time in Rome, and she smiled about it still, he had ravished her brown, pretty body like a wolf gurgling down its kill. He was fifty-two years old by then, but as fine and firm as any of the god-like statues they had sat beside that day while they kissed and laughed.

He spoke and jarred her from her thoughts. He looked at his salmon aspic shyly, aware of her moon glow gaze on him.

She grinned, too. "I love you, Emory. Did you know that? Since the moment I saw you twenty years ago I've loved you. Did you know that? I bet other people who have been together almost twenty years don't still say that. Do they?"

"Not to each other." He winked at her.

She leaned forward so that her ample cleavage in the fancy dress would unnerve him. "You know why I love you?"

He looked just where she hoped he would, right down at the pooches that would soon be pressed into his anxious mouth. "I've always known. You told me. It's because I never play air guitar. And do you know why I love you, Rachel?"

She laughed happily. "Because I never want to have a baby and I never borrow money."

"That, too," he said, "but mostly because you are so good to me. What? You look surprised. My god, Rachel, have you spent our lives together thinking that love is in the grandiose gestures? Oh, no, it's in the minutiae, the day to day. You never criticize me."

She was awed. "Emory! You never do anything to criticize!"

"Sure I do. I insist on living alone. I'm rude and abrupt with people on the telephone. I spend hours every week away from you on the golf course. I go to bed promptly at 9:30, no exceptions. I blow my nose too loud. And because I'm so tall I walk duck-footed."

"It's all as cute as it can be," Rachel offered sincerely. "Everything about you is just fine with me."

The waiter poured more wine and bowed himself away. Rachel sipped the divine purple pool in her glass and thought that life didn't get any better than knowing who you loved and why you loved him.

"And do you know, Rachel," he began the ritual of fooling with his pipe, "that most people dislike me immensely. And they dislike me instantly. Because I'm arrogant and introverted."

"You do have a presence," she conceded kindly.

"But you," he offered as he puffed, "people are fond of you, Rachel. On the face of it they get all perturbed about what you are, but they like and trust who you are. When someone around you is in pain, you weep."

"Lots of people hate me, Emory. They think I'm a pushy, big-mouthed bitch."

His eyes glowed with affection. "But they don't think you're a liar or a coward, which is what the world is sinking under. No, Rachel, there's a big difference in people not liking your delivery and not believing your message. On the point of the latter, you are greatly loved and respected."

They ordered brandy. He asked that she move her chair around next to him, which she did, so they both faced the great fireplace set in the middle of the dimly lit dining room. His pipe's aroma delighted her.

"Now tell me, Rachel," he said as he cradled his arm around her bare shoulders in the low-cut dress and began toying with a curl that dipped down from her French twist, "how it is you think you tilted the pinball machine of justice so badly today."

"Well, everybody's just madder than wet hens at me. Tillery. The news media."

"Diablo?"

She said with a pout, "No. He's on my side. He saw my questioning. Look Em, this is not something I think or feel, this is something I know."

"Secret technique," Emory said, puffing his pipe.

Rachel's red fingernail skirted along the lip of the shimmery brown bulb of brandy in front of her. "An interrogation tool of mine. You might leak it to the enemy."

"Yes, I am infamous for my verbosity."

Rachel laughed then. "Well, she's this pretty middle-aged Hispanic lady, a travel agent. I talked with her and asked her to tell me all about it, the rape, so she begins with

'We . . .' And right there I sat up straight. I mean, you've just been date-raped viciously and shot the alleged rapist to death in the back seat of his fancy car to save yourself, and you're still using an intimate term to describe the rapist? Naw. I don't think so. You'd be putting all the distance you can between you and this cruel dead asshole."

Emory watched her through his wisps of pipe smoke, amazed and adoring. She continued, talking like a cowgirl leaning over a corral fence and looking like a sequined magazine cover girl with delectably full lips.

"So I give her this piece of paper and I say, 'Write it all down for me, just the way it happened from beginning to end, in your own words.' So she does. Her beginning and her end of the whole ordeal, you know. Now first off I notice that she wrote '. . . we went in his car to a party, we stood around and had some beers and some tequila shots.' I mean, it's 'we, we, we' through her whole written text. Then it's 'we started kissing in his car, blah-blah, we got into the back seat, blah-blah.' So finally she says that he started taking down her panty hose, she asked him to stop, he says no, says he wants to fuck her, so she writes that she started kicking but he started choking her around the neck with his hands and she went unconscious for a few minutes. When she comes to, he's raping her. Only she writes, 'When I woke up after he choked me, we were fucking.' Get it, Emory?"

He puffed, titillated by her acumen. "Yes. You're saying that a raped or assaulted woman's recall usually reflects her hatred of the suspect by alienating him by reference."

She glanced at him dully. "Whatever. I'm saying that after the guy rapes you, if you ever talk about it, it's 'me' and 'him' then. The 'we' shit goes out the window. So then she bolts over the car seat, pulls a .22 that she has a permit to carry and shoots him four times in the chest, point blank I might add, and now she claims it was self-defense. All the women's groups are rallying in the streets."

"Then you drop it on them that she's lying."

Rachel said dejectedly, "Me. The bitch from hell. She wrote that she went back inside the party and started screaming for someone to call the cops, she's been raped.

And that's where her written account of what happened ended."

"And your suspicion is that there should have been more."

She swirled the brandy and shot the rest of it down in one burning gulp. "Women who are raped won't stop there, baby doll. Because being raped doesn't end there for a woman. I've asked 500 women to write it out for me, and I'll be damned if the ones that turn out to be telling the truth just never think the rape ended with the fucking. They write shit like, 'I went inside and I took a shower. I felt filthy and I was bleeding. I called the cops and I called my mama. I got sick and threw up. I hate the son of a bitch.' A woman who didn't mind it so much, the fucking, she won't know how horrible those last few details really feel. You see?"

"If I'm guilty," Emory growled lowly as he signed the check and finished his snifter, "I don't want you on the case."

She hugged him wildly. "Take me home, Emory, to your house. Take my pink satin panties off real slow with your teeth, then slide yourself in me until I wiggle and scream. It's the least I can do. You bought dinner."

They got some lurid stares, the young beauty in after-five and the handsome older gentleman in his designer dinner jacket. Neither Rachel nor Emory noticed those questioning aspersions anymore from strangers. They noticed only each other.

Two fat old bats at a nearby table conspired. The one in the couture gown that had been a size seven on the salon model but was a tarp on her smirked to the other who looked as though she had just come from the taxidermist.

"I heard he won her in a spitting contest." A scurrilous snicker.

The other fat bat wagged her brows. "Hmm. I wonder what first prize was."

They were deep into Wilma-and-Betty giggles when the old man with them, a weed with a tuft of white hair wearing an ascot, grumped at them.

"Shut up, you jealous cows. Emory Jacobs is a sports hero and a fine gentleman. Rachel Collazo is one hell of a homicide investigator. I heard they're together because he's damn lucky and she's damn smart." His eyes bored into his fat bat wife. "Now drop it. Eat your shrimp before it spoils and starts to smell like you."

=37=

On Tuesday afternoon, visiting nurse Janet Bachman gave Julie Ann her chemo dose and stood by vigilantly to handle the residual violent vomiting as best she and the medications could do. She left the Nystrom house at 8:00 P.M. with Julie Ann sedated into a slumber that would last until early morning.

Daniel was home from the gym that evening an hour before Janet Bachman left. He brought with him a dinner of chicken fingers, french fries and hunks of cherry pie from the restaurant where he and Chaz had beers and talked about the start of basketball season the next month.

As he set the food onto Spiderman paper plates and put their mugs of milk onto the table, Pete chattered away.

"So Dad, why do frogs make good baseball players? Because they can catch flies. Why do dragons sleep during the day? So they can stay up and catch the knight."

Later, he bathed Pete lovingly, let the boy play longer than Julie Ann would've liked, then rocked his son in their usual tender vigil.

"Dad," Pete had chirped just before he fell asleep, "if Mommy dies does that mean you die, too?"

Daniel's heart had felt stabbed. "No, Petey. Is that what Mommy said?"

His cheeks were soft as a pink baby bunny. Danny stroked them. "No, I just wondered. Mommy said God is going to make her well, and if He doesn't then she'll be in Heaven

162

and you'll take care of me. But why would God want Mommy up there and not you and me?"

He cradled the boy close to his chest. "Oh, Pete, we'll make it, you and me, no matter what happens. We'll be all right. I love you, Pete. I love you so much."

The morning came and found Daniel groggy **and** running late. Pete didn't want the kinds of cereal they had and didn't want to go to preschool and didn't like the snack that Daniel packed, and he screamed and stomped when the yellow preschool bus came to get him. By the time Mitch arrived at eight to borrow the car, Daniel was pissed and Julie Ann was trashing his every move.

Kelly floated in at 8:30, and though she made no specific eye contact with Daniel, he sensed that if they had been alone she would've begged him to devour her. Under her white lab coat she wore something tight and red, and Daniel wanted to rip it off her and fuck her standing up against the wall. She spoke to Mitch and him indifferently, like she always had, and went straight to Julie Ann's room.

Mitch had the look of a hound dog. "Good God almighty. In 1920 she'd have been a fifty dollar an hour whore and worth every cent."

Daniel used the stainless steel oven door to work on his tie. "She checks Julie the day after every chemo. Did Loreen drop you off?"

"Yeah." He was looking after Kelly's perfumed, gracious steps. "Are you and her—?"

"Jesus, Mitch. You think I'd tell you?"

"So you are."

"Just wait here. I'm taking Julie's car. We'll walk out together."

Kelly was checking Julie's blood pressure. Julie did not look when Daniel spoke.

"I need your car keys."

"Why?" Her face was impervious.

His agitation jumped like the mercury in that blood pressure dial that Kelly was pumping. "Because Mitch is borrowing mine."

"Did Pete finally eat?"

"A frozen waffle."

She cut her green eyes to him. Kelly didn't look. "Daniel, he hates waffles."

"He ate it. After a shit fit that we didn't have any Count Chocula, and thank God we didn't."

"Don't curse at me. I never buy that nonsense. He hears it from other kids. You're leaving?"

He sighed. Kelly put away the cuff and lowered the sheet to press a stethoscope against Julie's concave chest. "I'm trying to leave. Your keys?"

She rose like an apparition. Hobbled past him, holding the wall down the hallway to their long-ago shared bedroom. She hobbled back empty handed. He had gone into the kitchen and found Mitch pouring coffee at the bar and Kelly quietly waiting in Julie's room. She helped Julie lie down.

Julie groaned. "You should stay home with me today, Daniel. Kelly's leaving and I don't want to be alone. The chemo made me sicker than usual yesterday."

He felt his fists clench. "Your mother is coming before Kelly leaves. Julie, I have an interview for a story and a two o'clock deadline. Tell me where the keys are so I can go."

She closed the thin membranes of her eyelids. "I don't want Mitch driving your car. He's irresponsible. I hid the keys. You'll never ever find them."

Daniel took a long breath. For the first time Kelly looked his way with certain dread and pity in her eyes. Mitch said from behind him, "Danny, I can get a cab—"

Daniel gritted his teeth. "Give me the keys, Julie Ann. It's all planned, now give me the keys."

"Stay with me today, Danny. I don't want my mother. I want you." She screamed and everyone jumped where they stood. "All you ever do is leave me! You're not driving my car and your asinine brother can go to hell!"

Kelly brushed past him. She and Mitch stood back like strangers on an elevator trying to ignore it all.

"Julie. I pay for that car. I pay for everything."

"You'll have nothing if you leave me. It's my house, my

son, my savings account and MY CAR! YOU'RE NOT DRIVING MY CAR AND YOU'RE NOT GOING TO WORK TODAY BECAUSE I SAID I WANT YOU HERE WITH ME!"

She had sat straight up and was shaking her pitifully withered fists at him. His lungs and heart were on fire. He took a vicious step toward her, using all of his strength to not hit her smack in the face with the back of his hand. He took one of her wrists that he could've cracked like an icicle, and he jerked her hard. She didn't cry. She narrowed her eyes in hate and spat in his face.

Daniel let it hang there on his cheek. He snarled. "I'm not afraid of you anymore, you bitch. I was afraid if I didn't pretend to love you then I'd go to hell. I'd rather be a slave to some pleasure in this life and go to hell for it than live another moment being afraid of you."

It wounded and frightened her. He could see it in the way she shrunk suddenly and made a tiny animal noise. He thrust her hand away, into her own face.

"Give me the keys."

She lay back, a bald, scrawny, shrunken mummy. "No. No car keys. So you can't leave me. You can't ever leave me. No matter how you try. The keys are hidden."

He was in the living room, shaking all over and fighting tears of anguish when Mitch said sensibly, "Keep your car, Danny. Never mind. Kelly, can you run me over to my office? It's not far."

She nodded silently and put the slightest squeeze on Daniel's arm without looking at him. Julie's wails from the bedroom were obscenely dolorous, like a warbling siren.

Mitch said, his cheeks flushed with embarrassment, "Danny, man, this is no way to live. That broad is crazy."

The wailing siren echoed his name over and over, both galling and appalling. "Daniel, Daniel! I'm sorry, pleeeze! Daniel!" He went to her when Mitch and Kelly had gone; he sat on the bed, rocked her in his arms, kissed her hands. And he thought shamefully, turning his face from the weeping, wounded woman in his arms, of the night to come. He would find Kelly by the fireplace in her house, curled, cooing, comforting him. She would ease him down in slow motion and make tender or maybe, better yet, vicious love to him as she had so many nights in a row since they started.

He whispered as he rocked, "Shhh, Julie. It's okay. I'm here."

She pushed him away, her fist a rock in his chest. "I hate you, Danny," was all she could say, and then she fell into a sobbing lump under the blankets.

She would call him six times that day at work, hysterical, threatening, giving him orders, pleading with him to come home so she could emasculate him in person, so she could enjoy the familiar pleasure of seeing him squirm—and thinking somehow that his squirming meant love and obedience.

But as the dreary evening winds began to blow rain and make the world soggy and bleak, Daniel wouldn't be in the gym like he said when he phoned home. Instead, for that hour he would be in the roaming, clawing, imploring hands of Kelly, who never said no to him.

=38=

Just to throw off his annoyingly distinguished pal, Chaz arrived on time. Julie Ann answered the door.

He had expected a shriveled waif. He got an upright if gaunt pale beauty wearing a tasteful silk robe over nicely loose pajamas. He made a Hugh Hefner joke. She didn't get it. She had a burr haircut. He didn't make a Susan Powter joke. She wouldn't have gotten it anyway.

The house was a wreck, something straight out of a drug raid with dirty dishes piled and clean clothes strewn. But she smelled good, he noticed first off, because he had expected her to smell like a funeral arrangement, maybe carnations.

She said, unfettered, "Come in, Detective Diablo. My husband isn't home yet. Forgive my house. I have cancer."

She walked away, into the cluttered living room. He saw silk jiggle cooly. What flesh was left on the bones was shapely.

He sat. She filed a nail vigorously, ignoring him.

He asked, "How are you doing?"

She chopped at him. "I'm dying. Any more questions?"

Chaz cleared his throat for effect. "I'd like to say hey to Pete."

She was a fucking wrecking ball. "He's not here."

He smelled spoiled food. He felt a soured existence. She looked up suddenly, like something forgotten had just occurred to her. "Did Daniel tell you I have cancer?"

"Yes. I'm sorry."

"For what? Did you cause it?"

Maybe Daniel could take it, but Chaz knew he couldn't. He said, "Mrs. Nystrom, don't dress me down. I'll wait for Daniel and not bother you."

She had cat eyes, green as Ireland and just as foreign to him. She glared. He glared back. She was sexy to him, not like a vixen or a showgirl, but sexy like a sorority girl, all chin up indignantly and eyes opened with interest.

"What's in the bag, Detective?"

"Wine. Want some?"

She flittered those green beams sideways, a diabolical thought hit her. "I don't drink. But sure. Pour me some."

Among the grotesque kitchen litter he found a crummy dimestore cork screw. The pop was the only sound in this lost house that he recognized. She brought him beer mugs. He smiled at her unsophistication, poured, handed her one and drank deeply of his own.

They sat. She even coiled like a cat. Her skin was as milky as alabaster, almost translucent, as if sun had never shown on it. Her fingers were perfect relics of femininity, slender, long, pretty. He smiled again. She sipped, eyed him over the rim.

"Are you a Christian, Detective?"

"I don't know, Mrs. Nystrom. Ask me on my deathbed."

She smiled. Not flirting with him. Just remotely amused because his stupid arrogant soul wasn't her problem like Daniel's was.

The phone rang. Chaz heard it and instinctively hunched up his shoulders at the icy dispensation he got from his end. When she returned to sit in perfect posture across from him, her neck muscles were distended and her eyes were ignited.

"Daniel is sorry, he can't go with you tonight. He's on deadline. It will be a few hours and you are to go on without him. So. There. It is so awful to be as important as Daniel is. When you're important, your needs are all that matters. Nobody else counts."

He thumbed the coolness of the wine, knew what to say but didn't dare. She took the lead.

The wine had hit her. "Do you know why I stay married to him?"

He wanted to dance with her but said only, "Yes. Because God sent him to be your perfect mate. And to leave him flies in God's face."

She crinkled her delicate brow at him, even broached a distant smile, but stopped there. "We trusted God, Danny and I did. God will send the perfect mate, the church told us. Just stay pristine and virginal and let God handle the most important decision of your life. You know what God did, Detective Diablo? God gave me cancer. First he gave me a husband who doesn't love me and then He gave me cancer. Danny and I stay together not because we love each other, but because it's a way to pretend we still love God."

He gulped wine. This was fascinating, not frightening to him.

She said, "I don't want to die, Detective Diablo. I'm so scared. So, so very scared to die. Where do you think we go when we die?"

He pitied her suddenly. He said only, "Home."

She buried her face in a pillow. Chaz could only move to her and found himself wrapped around her, groping, touching her sunken face with his cinnamon hands. She reached at last for him, to him. When those ballerina arms encircled him, he had never before in his jaded life felt more sorry for another human being.

She cried out, "Oh . . . I am so scared. And alone."

He lifted her chin, didn't give a thought to it, and kissed her, tongue and all, like a timid teenager.

At the worst she could run screaming. She didn't. Her tongue was chilly from the cold wine.

She said softly, "I have only one breast. It's very ugly and sad."

He could not stop, took her into his arms, didn't apologize or feel fear. He said, "I know there is a clever, comforting response to that. But I don't know what that response would be, Julie. We don't know. Men don't know. But I am sure that for now I would like to make love to you before you're gone from Earth forever."

She said as she lay down beneath him, and it moved him in a place inside long since deadened, "Detective Diablo, I'm so angry. Let me do to you what God has done to me."

By now her tongue in his mouth was warm. He said, "What if you hate yourself for this?"

Her anger and bitterness were like her truth serum in his embrace. She said as she stretched herself out for his taking, "I've despised my prim and proper self for years. Please. Please don't let me die unloved. Oh, that's nice. Thank you."

=39=

There was no sound except the lavish rippling of the trees that dipped like black tentacles onto Kelly's upstairs balcony. Winter had traveled on and left in its wake a tidal wave of violent thunderstorms. With the sunrise still hours away, lightning whipped on the horizon like flashes of distant bombs exploding.

She wore a satin and lace, deep purple chemise with nothing beneath it but perfume and her silky skin. Her hair was loosely braided. Only her reading half glasses mildly detracted from her facade of diva-bitch-beauty-queen. She smoked a black imported cigarette and squinted in the curls of smoke and the dim light of her oven hood where she held a file of papers. Through the balcony doors she could hear the wind gasping as if someone in the next room lay dying.

She read one and then another of the newspaper clippings she had copied from back issues at the public library. She didn't notice that as she read her teeth gritted the cigarette more and more tightly until its end flattened.

Her reference words in the computer search for printouts had been simple. "Collazo, Rachel." There were snips of her enemy's name in countless stories over the past two years, both crime stories and events where Rachel had been a guest speaker or won community awards from women's groups and victims of violence organizations.

In some of the stories there was a file photo. She held it under the oval of yellow light with a profound sneer. The face was somber but soft, the eyes strangely erotic and fierce. Black hair lay like mink on narrow shoulders, and the lips were smoothly full and parted just enough to give the impression of wanting a dainty kiss. Cheekbones aristocratic. Nose slender. Business suit jacket very practical, no pearls or earrings or glossy lips. It screamed self confidence, the lovely face did. No adornment.

Kelly crumpled it suddenly and sank to the kitchen floor on her knees, pulling her hair violently with both hands and grunting as if she were slowly choking to death.

After a flurry of activity, it had all stopped. They got patient records and personnel files and did background checks and talked to clients and interviewed Wahlstein. They requested autopsy reports on the Merriams, sent a detective to see Delilah Chang about Marc's death, grilled Janet Bachman about Ashley's pneumonia.

And then it all stopped. Rachel the tiger had tracked her. Now she lay waiting in the brush. Kelly knew it. Kelly could feel it, Rachel's soft breathing down her neck, hot and silent and ever . . . so . . . patient.

They knew about Lester Graff. The goddamned hungry tiger had figured it out. Couldn't pounce yet, not yet. Lie still, smell the air. Don't blink. That was Rachel's pursuit technique. Kelly knew it.

She sat mummified, pulling so tightly on the dainty neck of the purple chemise that its thin straps snapped, it fell down, baring her enormous breasts, and she clutched them.

She stood, let the chemise fall off and then paced.

Across town, in the same ink of solitude and dense lightning, Rachel smelled the stench of years of tough-guy sweat that hung in the darkened boxing gym. She shivered in her shiny shorts and sweat shirt, jumped in place in her tightly laced high-tops, rocked her head from side-to-side and sucked spit from around the mouthpiece. Through the grid of the sparring helmet she could see Cujo's bowling balls of boxing gloves bunched chin high, itching to pummel Rachel's face. Cujo's tank top had a sweat spot between what would have been breasts if so much weight lifting hadn't honed them down to rocks of flat muscle. Her triceps were hunks of marble. Coins thrown at her thighs would click and bounce.

To the side Rachel could see Doak, her trainer with the personality of a swamp gator and the face of a highway pothole.

His crooked finger came at her as she sucked water and then spit it as she sat on a stool. "She's on target, angel face. She works well inside. Don't step in so much, use your counter left hook more, it's your best shot. You're scared so you're hitting too much. Don't do that; she wants you tired."

"Doak, I bit my lip. Am I bleeding? Is there blood on my shirt?"

"Yeah. Kid, don't look down at it. Don't look at the blood. Forget about it. Now go. She's 10-3-and-2, angel face, with nine knockouts in exhibition. Cover your belly unless you want to wear your ribs inside your lungs for decoration. Now go."

Cujo slammed her right off. Rachel fell, scrambled to her wobbly, skinny legs, tried backing up but Cujo came, grunting and swinging. A rush of drunkenness dazed Rachel. She sucked air through her nose and tasted blood from the impact of the vicious pop to the head gear.

Doak was growling. "Fuck your mother, Collazo. She told you don't you never hit nobody 'cause it ain't nice for girls to hit nobody. Fuck your mother, angel face. Hit the bitch." He screamed and it was a lawnmower grating gravel. "Never draw back to punch! Keep your chin down so's she can't clip it! Goddamn it, Collazo, get your weight on both fucking feet, look straight ahead. Fuck your mother!"

In her brazenly red tiled bathroom, Kelly slid white panties over her luscious curves, put her breasts into a white corset, tucked nylons into the slots of a garter belt. Daniel was coming for lunch. She smiled dimly at the double entendre. Coming. For lunch.

She painted her eyes like beautiful butterflies, embellished her cheeks and lips with shadows of purple and red, lay her blond hair down her tender shoulders in soft reams. Her white uniform couldn't hide the decadent package beneath, couldn't suppress the shape that made women shrink to mindless trash and made men weep when Kelly passed by. She emerged, war-painted, determined.

Rachel bit her tongue and jolted backward from the pain. Doak's battered jowls and ferocious eyes swam at her through the grid, past Cujo's dancing eagerness and thug smile.

"Fuck your tongue, Collazo!" He wailed. "Yeah, yeah, you're smart, but are you tough? Fuck the pain. Baby your lily-white ass later. Now, here, we fight. Smart ain't tough. Quick is tough. Brave is tough. Don't quit on me. Don't give up. Maybe it's smart to give up now, Collazo, but you can't never be tough laying there on your ass . . . think, don't follow her in, she wants you to, she wants you to do all the work coming at her. Back up and breathe, angel face, fuck pretty, fuck smart, wait on her, move sideways in a flash when you see it coming. Come on. Quit hugging her. You do that, you look like a goddamned girl."

In the ceiling mirrors Kelly could see herself laid out like a milky-white corpse. The dead eyes were mystical and childlike, a doll's eyes, opened and empty and oddly innocent. The brewing storm carried howls through the chimney. She dragged a fingernail along the front buttons of her dress like a bloodied switchblade, from her throat to her small waist.

She uttered among the flicks of lightning, "It's time, Rachel, you darling dark-haired hunter. Your deadly prey is coming for you."

Rachel landed one, a crushing one, and felt Cujo's feet lift a split second from the mat. Cujo didn't stumble, but wanted to, shook her head like a dazed dog. The bell sent them both panting and bleeding to their corners.

Doak swabbed her with a towel, squirted water in her mouth, rubbed her shoulders and never shut his mouth bitching.

"That was a good one. Where'd it come from?"

"I did what you said," Rachel huffed, "finally, I stopped drawing back to swing. Jabs are hard, not natural, you want the force of drawing back. Maybe I've whipped it."

"There ain't no force in drawing your arm back. Good for you. It took a long time. You got it now."

"My arms ache like fire, Doak. I got snot all over my face. Why is my mouthpiece bloody?"

"Aw, fuck it, your tongue will heal."

"Am I tough yet?"

He showed teeth blackened by cigars and cheap red wine. "As a buzzard, angel face. Beats all I ever seen. They laughed at us in the beginning, you and me, these punks that stand around here thinking they're all fucking Rocky. They laughed, remember? Look. They ain't laughing no more."

The shadows were speckled with pale white faces and grim black ones waiting to spar. There were no smiles.

Cujo came, touched gloves with Rachel and limped away. Rachel called out to her, "Hey, thanks."

Cujo's gorilla form didn't turn. She waved backward at Rachel and then fell mightily onto a long bench for a short rest.

"Doak, why can't I hit her for serious?"

"'Cause you're scared. Hit the showers. A squirt of club soda will clean that bloody sweatshirt, kid. See you next week."

Fingers of sunrise spread across the charcoal Dallas skyline, but only briefly, before a bleak glove of rain clouds covered the misty rays. Rachel's buzzing beeper greeted her when she stepped shivering from the moldy shower in the drafty locker room. She stared at the number in the panel. Her office. Another homicide somewhere in the gritty city.

* * *

Kelly greeted Lester Graff gently and kindly, as always. He was beef jerky, an old man withered almost to dust. But she kept him alive for a reason. She was going to need his pneumonia bacteria very soon. Then, she told Lester as she sedated him unconscious and inserted the suction tubing into his lungs, "Because I am so merciful, I will finally let you die, poor Mr. Graff."

=40=

The jukebox cried. Patsy Cline, as only she could, crooned "Crazy." Rachel came into the dive beer joint like pool hall was her middle name. Chaz regained consciousness, looked up from his beer bottle.

She said first off, "Do black belts in karate smoke?"

He exhaled heavily. "Do girl boxing champs wear spike heels and seamed hose?"

She sat, his side, next to him. "Emory and I were out dancing. You said it was urgent, so hurry. He's running my bath water."

Chaz looked like a burly, long-haired wrestling champion in biker clothes. The short sleeves of his T-shirt barely held back the knobs of muscles, and Rachel thought his pectorals were like cement shelves. His long hair was down and shiny black.

"Two things," he said, dry as the peeling wallpaper. "First off, the cigarette butt Dorcus got from McLaughlin shows that the sputum she sent in as Ashley's wasn't her own. It's not Kelly's spit."

"Gee. Imagine my surprise. I'd like to have seen old Georgie get it though. Kelly trying to eat a quiet dinner alone like that while Ralph Kramden put the moves on her in a black suit and white bobby socks."

Chaz smiled, but not very wide. "He followed her for two whole days. Once again, the nasty nurse thwarts the dogged detectives."

"Seems that way, doesn't it? They got a waitress in this place?"

"No. You get what you want from behind the bar and mark it on the chalkboard."

"Where's the bartender?"

Chaz said dryly, "Death row."

She came back with two boiler makers. A shot of whiskey for each of them, dropped into a mug of beer and shot down all at once. Chaz was impressed but not surprised.

"So the other thing, Diablo?"

He hung his head to a new low, looked at her with the eyes of a recently beaten basset hound. "I fucked my best friend's wife."

On cue, Patsy sang about falling to pieces.

"Shit, Diablo. Nystrom's wife? The one with cancer?" Her face was all splintered in total disgust.

"It just happened."

She wiggled in a spasm, "God I hate it when men say that! And why the fuck did you need to tell me? Am I your priest? Am I your mama? You want my approval, you numb-nutted amoral slut?"

He held out sweaty palms to implore. "Collazo, she was there, so angry with this God she's loved all her life. So angry with this husband who hasn't loved her in years."

He sucked deep on the beer and announced, "At the time, it seemed like . . . I don't know . . . like I was doing missionary work. Redeeming her faith. That kind of thing."

She posed, pondered, then said, "When?"

"Two weeks ago. That last weird snow. I went to get Nystrom and he called and canceled. She . . . was so desperately alone and afraid." He hung his head anew. "God, Collazo."

"I thought she was frigid."

He couldn't temper the memory and tried hard not to smile, saying only, "Uh, no."

"So for ten minutes you were . . . god? Is that how you've rationalized this?"

"Ten minutes? Try an hour and a half," he said, and then he did smile like the vain prick she knew he really was.

"You still doing her?"

"No. We spoke once by phone. She was very sweet and asked me to just let her live with a very nice memory. She said that before she died she wanted to do one exciting, forbidden thing, and she thanked me for being it. We won't talk again."

Rachel got more beers from the cooler, dusted chalk from her hands as she sat back down by Chaz. "How about Danny?"

"He'll never know. I don't have to worry about avoiding him because he never calls me anymore. I think he's involved with someone. About a month ago, before Julie and I . . . well, he started canceling handball."

"Nystrom? Cheating on his wife? It's like imagining Superman sleeping around on Lois Lane."

He struck an air of dignity. Rachel wanted to thump his stupid head. He said, "She told me that she has a 25 percent chance of living to the five-year mark. Any day now they could find tumors in her lungs or brain or bones. Any day; she goes to see her doctor once a week and gets chemotherapy, and they scan her each time for more cancer. Every seven days she lays there waiting to see if the monster within her is eating more of her alive. I just felt . . . feel so sorry for her."

Rachel smacked the table. "My daddy always told me, Diablo, if you have to lie about something then you can be sure it's the wrong thing to do." She drained her beer bottle and poked it into his chest. "By the way, I'm going to call Kelly and ask her to come in and see me next week. Real casual. It's nut-cuttin' time for her and me."

"And if she squawks for a lawyer?"

"She won't. She knows it'll make her look guilty. Kind of like you look right now."

She swished out, sequins flashing, hosiery seam as

straight down each long, pretty leg as the mast of a cold steel battleship on a calm sea.

Somebody in the joint was a Patsy addict. "Faded Love." In a different time, a better world, Chaz thought, he surely would've brought sweet Julie Ann here and led her to the dance floor to spin her delicately.

=41=

They were in a heap of bubbles, the sexiest place in the world, doing the most sexy thing a man can do to a woman.

Emory was washing her hair. With the silver pitchers of water that he lavished down her face, her shoulders, her back, he washed away the soot of human depravity that so often made her cry when she was out there alone working in it. They sat together in his large, round bathtub, bubbles enveloping them with the scent of roses. In the candlelight her red wine was enriched to the hue of a precious ruby. She sipped and leaned back against Emory's firm chest.

If they had looked past the door into his candlelit master bedroom suite they would have seen the shrouded figure floating outside, behind the long row of glass doors and sheer curtains. Shadows from the fireplace bathed the plush room. Outside an eerie fog snaked the grass. The shrouded figure crouched.

"There," he told her lowly, "all clean. Tell me, my Rachel, why you are fretting so tonight."

"I had a day of it. Two steps forward and one step back. Erin, bless her heart, can't find one bit of evidence that Wes Merriam didn't kill himself. The videotape I sniffed out does show somebody leading little Lisa Canton away from the field hockey park that day, but the image is so far away and fleeting. Still, it's a male and they can cross-check the description with the sex offenders tracking files. It's a major break, but you know how I worry. It just bums me out that we can't prove Merriam wasn't murdered."

She could sense his sensible smile. "I can see how suicide and natural death could be the bane of your profession." He lavished her back with a soft sponge of perfumed soap.

"You know, Em, that money you won at that seniors tournament would give us a great honeymoon. Greece. The British Virgin Islands."

He kissed her shoulders and the back of her slick, smooth hair. "I used it for that diamond you're wearing there, the one that's big enough for a team to suit up and play ball."

She pressed bubbles into her face and rinsed them away. "Is this an engagement ring?"

"Whatever it takes to keep you."

She chuckled. "Just put water and food on the porch. And keep these diamonds coming. God, you do give great diamonds."

He brought her wine glass around and fed her a sip. She kissed his hand and sunk deeper into the hot water. He asked her absently as he played with her hair and kissed the back of her neck, "What did Diablo want so late at night?"

He felt her tense in his arms. "Oh. In case I doubted it, he wanted to be sure I know he's a complete dumb ass."

Emory laughed gently. The ghoul crouched on the veranda could see but not hear them. She only imagined the scented soap, the warm wine and the tasty kisses. Fog swirled at her feet like a persistent cat. Her long, hooded coat made her appear as from another century, some sort of evil figurine. Her breath fogged the cold window, she was so close.

"You like that, Emory? Me rubbing you there?" Rachel was playing, sexy and lovable.

"Oh, yes," he was melting on the inside and growing hard on the outside, under the bubbles.

He asked, mostly to keep from collapsing in ecstasy, "What makes you think it wasn't suicide?"

"Yeah, so he's dead, our Wes. There's not a stray hair or fiber or fingerprint in the room except his, the maid's and the cat's. He comes home from a normal day at his office, and eats a hunk of lunch meat that's still lodged in his belly when he's dead. He makes a drink, maybe two, Erin said,

182

and takes a shit wad of Seconal, but first he grinds it. And of course there's no Seconal anywhere in the house, so where's the bottle? He neatly hangs up his tie, stuffs his dirty clothes in a bag for the dry cleaning service to pick up. He puts his shoes in the vacant slot where they belong in the closet. He brushes his teeth, puts his dirty underwear in the hamper, sets the burglar alarm, lays down and cuts his femural artery with a scalpel he just happens to have handy."

Rachel was leaning, loving the motion of Emory rubbing his soapy hands around her breasts. In another room, something fell lightly. She opened her eyes. "What was that?"

"Logs in the fireplace collapsing. You're completely safe with me. I would never let anything happen to you."

The ghoul cursed. She had inched backward and hit a row of dormant potted geraniums. For a moment she held her breath.

Rachel relaxed, feeling lazy and aroused. "Why that day? There was no disorder, no sinking into dementia or depression, no chaos of things undone in his life. He wasn't on antidepressants. He saw a psychologist after his wife's death last year, but she said they had concluded his treatment and he was doing quite well with his grief. There's no suicide note from a guy who had worked all his life to build an empire, and he didn't care at the end who the hell took over?"

"Had he taken a lover?" He rubbed his fingers on her nipples and felt the quickening of her breaths.

"No. No girlfriend. He puts his clothes away neatly? And the burglar alarm, he needs that for what? And he has a medical-grade scalpel handy?"

She swirled to face him. They were wet from the bath and arousal. "Most of all, if you told me to lie down and make a clean cut into my femoral artery, I couldn't do it. I don't know where the artery is exactly. I'm liable to be above or below it, especially if I'm drunk on martinis and fucked up on sleeping pills. But this guy, he nailed it on the first try. Like a pro."

The ghoul was thinking, studying. She could see on the

wall by the bed the panel for the security system. Of course a stately mansion like this would have elaborate alarms.

No, no, there would have to be another way, something more overt. The handsome silver-haired hunk bathing Rachel like a beloved princess would have to let the ghoul into the house with him. She flicked an eyebrow, an arc of arousal, fucking him would be nice. He had good shoulders and a center-stage handsome face. But no, she breathed out the thought, just kill him. No fun and games first. Or she could simply shoot through the glass, get a gun, shoot him, throw the gun in the sludgy river or bury it. He would be home alone when Rachel worked. He would be making coffee or standing in the window of his plush cherry wood and leather library downstairs and the window would shatter. Rachel would leave her work to grieve. The ghoul licked her lips that were simmering with impatience and the thirst to hurt the dark-haired hunter.

Car lights crossed her back, reflecting weakly through the thick fog. Kelly rolled herself into a black woolen ball until the beams eased past her as the sound of an expensive sports car muddled past into the distance.

"For a guy who planned to die, Em, he sure made a lot of preparations for the next day. I went to the basement and saw all these sailing ship replicas he builds down there. And you know what? On one of them the paint was still damp. The night before he had worked on one of his models down there, enjoying his hobby, doing his thing."

"Can I help you at all, Rachel?"

"Yeah. Tell me if he killed himself because he killed his wife and couldn't handle the guilt."

"No," he sagely said. "He didn't kill her. You said she got a virus and died while she was sick from chemotherapy. He couldn't have engineered that."

The sound of something falling sent Rachel into Emory's arms. "Fireplace logs? You're sure. Okay, so tell me, honey, why does a man kill his wife?"

The ghoul had stood, taken a step and slipped on the shimmery wet, high-gloss wooden veranda. She stopped, crouched like a fairy-tale witch, fingernails clicking nervously.

Emory shrugged against her embrace. He said frankly, "A man kills his wife because he doesn't love her anymore."

"There are other ways to end a deal."

"None less expensive. But your boy loved his wife, so that option is out."

The rush of Rachel's emotions caused a tall candle to flutter and make the shadow of a dancing ghost on the wall. "This nurse I told you about, Em, she's really smart at this murder thing. By day she's functional, by night she's . . . deranged. I have to be so careful or she'll slip through my hands. And all I can think of is that poor Ashley Merriam wanting so badly to live. It makes my blood boil."

He enfolded her in his warm, wet arms. "There are other reasons to be careful, sweetheart. I would guess she knows you're investigating her. Is she brilliantly insane, Rachel, or is she disintegrating into total dementia?"

The catlike fog twirled, showing murky, momentary patches of diffuse moonlight. Kelly took another careful step. Rachel whispered. The candles wiggled in her breath as if all at once they had become nervous little children. "She's evil and beautiful . . . and she's totally nuts."

A brittle crack outside in the weeping wind. A twig beneath Kelly's boots. Emory heightened his awareness. To Rachel he said ominously, "She wants other women's husbands. And you're in the way."

"I have to play the game, Em. I have to bring her to thinking that I'm on her side, that I'm her way out."

The figure floated down the dewy lawn, descending into the mouth of a beastly fog.

Emory asked quietly, "What do you plan to do next?"

"The only thing I can do. Look her in the eye, see what kind of animal looks back at me and then go in for the kill. The old fashioned way. One-on-one."

He saw candles reflected in her eyes like bonfires at a cannibal ritual. "I will worry about you, sweetheart, until the day I die."

"That's a long way off," she said kindly. "And when you go, you take me because, honey, I swear I couldn't live a moment without your love." She teased him then. "Did you know I can hold my breath underwater for longer than two minutes? I learned when my brothers used to try to drown me in the creek."

"I believe I have seen this talent of yours. But show me again, Rachel."

They kissed. Then she dived below the bubbles, a pretty mermaid looking for the human toy under there that brought her so much carnal joy every day.

The fireplace logs crackled and tumbled quietly. The candles died cold. Rachel and Emory took each other to his bed and made their own gnashing flames.

=42=

Kelly straddled Daniel, raising and lowering herself on him. In the ceiling mirrors he could see the length of her lithe body as she bent to suck his lips and gently bite his neck. He sat up, nudged her backward and explored all of her with his hands. She didn't blink, only stared through him, even as his sweat dripped into her eyes. When she reached orgasm, she arched, and Daniel felt himself exploding inside her.

She held him against her perfect body. He whispered, "I should go home now."

She begged, "Take me again, Daniel. I've been looking for you all my life."

He would be bruised and raw afterward, but no hellfire could have stopped him. They showered together afterward and did not leave room between themselves for even a sheen of hot water. He couldn't leave her lips or look away from her languid eyes, and when she slid down in the shower and went to her knees in the steamy spray to find him one more time, Daniel thought he would weep for joy and agony.

When he was dressed and sipping the crisp martini she made for him, she came behind him to kiss his shoulders and cause his skin to prickle. She pressed herself against him, glided her hand up and down his back, like ice on his parched soul.

She swirled around him. "Before you, Daniel, I wore ben wah balls. I put them up inside myself every day, and when I sat and rocked back and forth I could come over and over."

Her profanity aroused him so much, the forbidden words he was not allowed to say even to his wife being said to him by a depraved goddess who craved him.

She looped her pretty arms around him and kissed him, a long, chewy kiss, and she said, "I don't wear them anymore, my darling Daniel, since I have you to satisfy me. Come back tomorrow. Please. I'll be so wet, so willing."

"You know I will, Kelly. But I can't stay long, honey. I can't make Julie suspicious." He reached. She fell into his arms.

She said, "I want to dance naked for you—"

He felt a twinge of embarrassment. "The sex is plenty."

She moved her tongue around his wet lips. "I want to wait for you. I want to be your whore. I want you to fuck me constantly, more than you ever fucked your little . . . wife. Love her, Daniel, but love me more, totally, let my sex be your obsession."

He set down the martini, feeling suddenly weary, wishing the glow of unreality had lasted longer. He tried humor, holding her around her curves and trying a smile. "You know I can't live here. You have a cat. Cats make me sneeze."

She didn't smile, only arched a brow and said coldly, "The cat is old. I'll kill her. To have you, I'll kill her tonight."

He backed up a step. The fat striped cat on the couch hissed and waddled out onto the balcony. Daniel laughed at Kelly, whose stone expression he found more sexy than scary. "Kill your cat for me? Kelly. Don't talk crazy, honey. I'll never go away if you want me to stay."

She seemed unfazed. "I want you, Daniel. It's simple. To make you want me, I'll wait. I'll be quiet. I'll . . . abide."

She sipped her martini. The shimmering liquid touched her lips, and Daniel felt his belly leap with desire to have those nasty lips on his testicles again.

She said cooly, "I thought your marriage was over."

He said as warmly as possible, "Honey, marriages aren't over until they're finished. Until then, well, things can change. Things can get better."

"Do you love her?"

He felt a pang of panic. Oh shit. Don't complicate our sizzling sex with lousy love. "I love my son. I won't leave him."

"And me, Danny? If I said you can't have us both?"

"Are you saying that?" And that fast she went from simple trick to big trouble in his mind. He said, and meant it, "Because if you are saying that then we need to talk. You are everything I ever wanted in bed, and there will never be another one like you for me, Kelly. I know that. I can't forsake it yet, the fantasy. I can't go back to triple-X hand jobs on myself. But you see, baby, if it's working for me . . . and it's not working for you . . . then that means to make you happy, I have to be unhappy. Do you see, baby?"

The most gorgeous woman on earth said softly to him, "If I were your wife, you wouldn't be at her house fucking her."

He sighed, pictured himself crawling on his knees, though he wasn't. "Kelly, honey, you're a first for me. A sort of experiment."

She lifted her chin and eyes coldly. He pictured the cat with a knife in its belly, quivering and kicking while it died and she watched. He said quickly, "I didn't mean that."

She was naked in the chair, arms coiled around her luscious legs, blond hair mussed, eyes glittery and inviting.

"What did you mean, Daniel, darling?"

He felt his sweat. Anxiety made his mouth dead dry. He saw her expression soften as she felt his confusion. She rose and came to him. "Never mind, Daniel, my angel." She touched his hair. His soul simmered down. "I'm not demanding. I'm not vindictive. I'm just . . . madly, madly in love. Come tomorrow. I'll be everything, anything you want. I'll give you time. And peace. And most of all, I'll give you ravenous, filthy sex."

He sat in his car, stoned on martini, reeling from her lust, pierced by the notion of crossing the desert and returning to his old life. The empty life. Sexless. Loveless. His fingers were ice cold when he touched his face and said hollowly, "I have created monsters. And both of them own my frightened soul."

Julie Ann was awake when he came through the door looking like a walking anxiety attack. The TV blared. Without the scarf on her head, she looked like a stripped and broken mannequin. Ugly. Instantly derisive. The house smelled like the garbage rotting in the bin underneath the sink. He was tipsy from the martini.

"You're late," she bleated. "It's almost seven."

"Thanks, Big Ben. Where's Pete?"

"In his room. He's being punished."

"For what?"

"Sassing me."

"He's coming out of his room, Julie. He and I are going to play checkers and then I'm going to bathe him."

She leveled a monsterish gaze at him. "I told him to get in the bathtub. He turned and said to me, 'No.' I tried to call you at your desk, but you didn't answer. I thought you were working."

"I don't work at my desk, Julie Ann. I work on the streets, interviewing people."

She stared only at the dusty, repulsive image of a sitcom droning on the television. "Take out the trash, Danny. Leave Pete alone. He's in time-out."

The martini spoke. "You're not going to punish my boy for saying no! Everyone has the right to say no! You don't own all the fucking power in this family. Pete has some power, too, and so do I!"

She struggled to stand, "Lie down, Daniel. You're drunk. I can smell it."

"Oh, putting me in time-out, too, wifey dearest?"

She covered her face and began to cry loudly. She could barely stand. Daniel went to her, caught her.

She leaned on him. His heart ached dully.

"Danny, could you carry me to bed, please?"

"Jules, have you eaten? Let me get you—"

"No. Just to bed."

He lifted her, walked steadily. She said weakly but with the strength of strident conviction, "You're a failure, Danny, as a father and a husband. You've ruined my life."

He was too sickened by it all to argue. He said, "I know. I'm sorry."

She asked as he lay her down and covered her gently, "You won't go out again tonight, will you? You won't leave?"

"No, Jules. I'll stay where you can see me."

He waited until she drifted away. Down the hallway and inside the bedroom door he found his little boy, and all the charms of the world were unleashed at Daniel in one of Pete's ecstatic smiles and leaping hugs.

=43=

Rachel knew it wasn't a good sign to look up from her slumped, sweaty perch in the boxing gym and see Daniel Nystrom standing in front of her. He signaled trouble.

She mumbled through breathless heaves as she untied her boxing gloves and shoes. "Well, Nystrom, seeing you here means I won't need that laxative after all. What is it?"

He sat beside her, all jocular and groomed in his specs and loafers and khakis and a sport coat. "Collazo, what the hell are you doing?"

"I needed something to help me relax. An outlet."

He kneeled and yanked off her shoes for her. "Did you consider yoga?"

She stood, wobbly. "Come on, honey pie. You can interrogate me through the shower curtain. Watch out for that big bitch over there. Cujo. She'll hurt you bad."

Daniel stepped lightly around a spike-haired woman built like a boxcar who was pummeling a punching bag with ease. "Her lip's busted. You did that?"

The shower water ignited. Rachel called over it, "No, she busted it herself when she fell down laughing at my left hook. So, hotshot, talk to me."

Daniel bit the cap off his pen and held his notepad. "You're on the record, kid. I hear you've got a video tape of the Canton kid being led from that public park by a white male."

She ripped the curtain back and glared furiously at him, shampoo foam bobbling all over her head. The moment was too emotion packed for either of them to care that she was nude. "Nystrom . . . you. . . ." She fumed, slung the curtain closed and emerged rinsed and dripping. Wrapped in a towel she sat next to him, defeated and angry. "You can't print that. You fucking son of a bitch. Tell me who told you. Shit!"

She threw the shampoo bottle, turned and bunched Daniel's collar in her hands, despite the cavalier grin on his face. "I'm off the record now, Nystrom, you asshole, and I'm telling you if you print that, I won't get even with you now, but someday, some way, I'll fuck you up bad. Don't you mess with my investigation of that kid's murder."

Daniel smoothed his shirt. "That, I take it, is a confirmation of my information." She was behind a locker door, dressing and cursing.

He asked, "So how come if you've got an unidentified suspect you don't release her stepfather from jail? He's obviously not the kidnapper or the murderer."

"I hate your goddamned guts, Nystrom. You haven't seen any videotape. You just heard about it."

"Then deny it."

The locker door slammed. Rachel was in pantyhose and a white camisole. She was flushed with anger. "I'm going to find out who told you, and I'm going to turn the mother fucker every way but loose before I get a warrant for impeding a police investigation." She slipped into a short, A-line, black wool dress and turned for Daniel to button it up the back for her. He obliged while she huffed at him. "Her stepfather has outstanding warrants. Plus his other kids said he used to beat Lisa, which is why we popped him in the first place as a suspect. He's a puke. He was supposed to be watching Lisa at the park during the other daughter's field hockey game. What the fuck is it to you if I find a reason to hold a kid beater inside for a while?"

Daniel took off his sport coat. The room was steamy. "What's in it for you to suppress the video?"

She was madly slapping mascara onto her eyelashes and rubbing creamy blush onto her cheeks in the mirror. "Right, like you can't figure it out. Like if I explain why we don't release knowledge of the tape then I've confirmed there is one. Like you don't know that the perp would leave town immediately. Go to plan B, hotshot."

Daniel laughed easily. "Rachel, tell me about the tape, then make me a deal to hold it."

She put her pretty face smack into his, and he could see the guard dog glare. "The tape shows a white male leading Lisa out of the park. He's murky, in the distance, but it's definitely little Lisa. I visited everyone who was interviewed at the field hockey game that day and from each of them I got names of others who were there. One by one I tracked 'em, and four of 'em had videotaped the game. I viewed each tape and, bingo, I got lucky. I'm working with the FBI now to get paroled or probated child molesters nationwide who fit the description of the guy on our tape. I'm holding her stepfather because of some hot check warrants and because I generally disapprove of his parenting methods as they were described to me by Lisa's siblings, so I'm dicking him around. Just because he's a bully, and because I can dick him if I want to. Now, hotshot, wait until I say the word and I'll give you a statewide exclusive, blow-by-blow, of how I track down this low-life bastard."

"I'll take the exclusive," Daniel said, their noses almost touching as Rachel fumed, "plus you get Emory Jacobs to play golf with me."

"Nine holes, cocksucker."

"Eighteen. Saturday. My son gets to go and watch a real legend."

She stood, turned from him in disgust and started on her wet hair. "How's your wife?"

His face changed, as if it fell into the shade. "Uh, fine. I mean, she got checked yesterday and so far the cancer isn't metastasizing anywhere else. Most commonly it would be her lungs or her brain, but everything's clear. Wahlstein's guarded about it, though."

Rachel stiffened, stopped the blow dryer. "Wahlstein? Edward?"

Daniel was stowing his pen and pad into his pocket and putting on his coat. He was a head taller than Rachel and couldn't shake the collegiate look that made Rachel like him so much. He boomed in his big, deep voice. "He's the best, they say. We came in last week to see him. The trips to his office—I mean, getting dressed, riding in the car—are tiresome for her when we come into town. But the chemo's almost finished."

Rachel felt relieved. It sounded as if Julie wasn't having home nursing care. "Well, Nystrom, that's good. Does anyone else know about the Canton videotape?"

He piled into his tweed overcoat. "No. And there isn't a leak. I found it out on my own. You take care, Collazo, and by the way, it wasn't the shower that steamed up my glasses; it was looking at your terrific figure. I mean, who knew you were an actual girl? See ya." He turned from the doorway. Rachel could only grin at his good looks.

"Nystrom, sorry I called you all those names. It's just that, well, I meant every one of them."

He boomed a laugh and disappeared. Rachel stared after him, coddling the disturbing thought that Nystrom seemed way too happy—too gratified and plucky—for a man whose wife was suffering so much pain and fear. He had always been so politely distant and emotionally oppressed. Now, and she mused at the idea as she pictured it, he carried himself more jaunty, like a man fresh from a blow job and a chess victory on the same day.

=44=

Chaz was sitting across her desk, frowning more deeply with each growl of his stomach. He griped openly, "Collazo, it's almost eight o'clock. Can I be dismissed? We're going to be heroes in the headlines tomorrow for solving the Case of the Murdered Millionairess today; I'd like to celebrate by going home before ten o'clock for a change. And anyway. What happened to your hair? You came back from lunch looking like somebody hosed your head."

She said rudely, "Bite me, Julio. I took another boxing lesson today, and that head gear kind of whacked up my fluffy do." She tossed a wad of papers on the desk. "There's nothing in this fax from UT-Austin. Kelly's transcript is pure, routine nursing courses. No specialty in bacteria or virology. Shit."

Chaz rocked dangerously back in his chair, gleaming a smile like a cat who swallowed Tweety Bird. "You can't whip Cujo. Emory turned down your proposal again today. And you didn't catch Kelly the killer nurse. But you did bust a trashy trust fund bad boy today for murder. You're batting .250."

"I'll kick that damned chair over, Diablo. You know I will."

He took a breath. "What d'you weigh, about one-fifteen? With a wrecking ball you couldn't knock Cujo to the mat. I've watched you two spar. You know why you can't take her down, Collazo? Because she's a woman, and you like women. If Cujo were a guy, she'd be a greasy spot in the ring by now."

Rachel deadpanned, "What did you get today from Nurse Bachman? And make it fast. I spent four hours and breathed twenty cigarettes today cracking that rich kid who finally admitted he beat his rich girlfriend's rich mother to death and then stuffed her in a tar pit. Tomorrow I get to go watch while they drag this poor woman's melted body out of the pit. So if there's anything, tell me fast."

Chaz wiped his tired eyes with a silk handkerchief from his pocket. "Talking to Janet Bachman is like talking with Mother Superior. She's sweet, unassuming and honest. Kelly did Ashley's last chemo, and normally Bachman would've followed with the checkup later that week, on that Wednesday, but Ashley requested Kelly. Wahlstein instructed Kelly to do the re-check on Thursday when Kelly reported that everything was stable with Ashley's vital signs. And no, it is not unusual for a patient to request a visiting nurse, but it's only done if the nurse is available on the roster, which killer nurse was." He slapped his notepad down in front of Rachel and began loosening his tie. "Janet Bachman is not a suspect."

Rachel took a mirror from her desk and was, in fact, sort of horrified about how the head gear had wilted her usually spiffy hair. "What does Bachman think of McLaughlin?"

"Superlatives. Our killer knows the flies-to-honey theory."

"Tell me about Wahlstein."

He opened his briefcase on her desk. "Okay. Just once for me, yell 'Adrian!' Never mind. Okay. Uh, Wahlstein. He's had one patient in twenty-five years die of a hospital infection."

"How'd you get that?"

Chaz borrowed her glasses and leaned at the papers. "Crap, I do see better with these on. Aging is hell. I got it from an inside source at the company that carries his malpractice. They were very cooperative. The only thing insurance people fear worse than drunk drivers are cops, so it was an easy-greasy process to get Wahlstein's archives."

Rachel applauded. "Good lead."

"Yeah, don't hate me because I'm beautiful. Now, McLaughlin," he glanced up and said somberly, "there's no pat way to know every patient she's taken care of in the last fifteen years as an RN. Sorry, Rachel, we've only got the dead doctor-lover at Parkland and Ashley Merriam so far. She's got seventeen at-home patients right now, six of them likely headed for a hospice after their chemo treatments, the rest hanging on with various degrees of recovery expectations."

Her phone rang. She yanked it. "Collazo. Who? She has what? Well, yeah, let her come on back here." To Chaz. "Iverson's wife. She has a picture for us."

Chaz mumbled, "Who? She has what?" And then he smiled and said, "Already we've been together too long, you and me."

A woman appeared around the corner, not a pretty woman but a well-cared-for product of lots of money. Nose too big and eyes too close, but great tan. Facials had smoothed out the rough edges. The hair was a perfect pageboy, the clothes all traditional and classic, Lord & Taylor. She was in her early forties and not friendly.

"Detective Diablo," she said it, and Rachel saw a flash of libido in otherwise flat gray eyes, "when you interviewed me at my house after my husband's suicide, you asked me to contact you if I found anything unusual that might explain why he killed himself."

She hadn't bothered with Rachel yet, and Rachel was thinking, "Yeah, contact, not drop by after hours to visit."

The woman thrust a slick square at him. Chaz took it, muttered, glanced furtively at Rachel. To Mrs. Iverson he asked, "What is this?"

She preened. She didn't look very much like a widow in mourning to Rachel. Maybe it was good that he was gone after all. Maybe the babies had made her too fat for his taste and the bills had been too high for him to leave her. The woman said to Chaz, "It's a photograph of my husband and a woman. You can see that it's from one of those commercial cameras they use in night clubs, the kind you pay for when the guy comes around to your table. It's dated, so I checked the date, and that was the week Jeff spent at an oncology conference here. There were dinners and stuff every night, but I didn't go to them." The bitterness dripped. "Jeff went. Obviously not alone."

Chaz had gone a little pale around the gills, held the picture like it was on fire. "You know this woman, Mrs. Iverson?"

Primly, and with unmasked annoyance, "No. And he didn't want me to know her, either. It was in his desk at his office where I virtually never went. Today I found it in a box of things they delivered after we cleaned out his office safe and transferred all the files. The camera dated it. The time and place are unmistakable. And for me, so is the situation."

"Thank you, Mrs. Iverson," Rachel said crisply, "we'll look into it."

The fading young socialite stood a moment, gawky and blushing. It had been too long since she actually made a play for a man, much less for a GQ god like Chaz. She clucked a few more times and left.

Chaz said, handing over the picture, "It's Iverson. And Kelly McLaughlin."

Rachel went to the grimy window. Chaz joined her. She mused, "So this is her pattern. She falls in love with married men, and when they won't leave their wives, she kills them. Only with Merriam she reversed it, tried a new approach, killed the wife first so the husband wouldn't have to bother with leaving the wife. Then she went back and killed the husband." She put a hand on Chaz's concrete arm. "It's escalating. She's getting bolder and crazier."

He touched the window, felt its coldness shock his warm, sweaty palm. At the basement level, all he could see in the black shadows was a stairwell that led up to the deserted sidewalk. "Slugger, we can't prove any of it. And she's out there. Getting more psychotic. Getting away with it."

Rachel felt short of breath. An alarming sense of cold went through her. "We can't even take her off her job yet. We can't do anything but wait for her to screw up."

Chaz said, but didn't sound confident, "We'll nail her."

Rachel stood behind him. He reached a hand back casually and she put hers into it.

He said, "We've got a case load that looks like an encyclopedia of human horrors, not much time to chase the wind."

Rachel said hollowly, "You ever seen a hay devil? The wind on a hot day down at my granddaddy's farm, it would start twisting, and it would catch all the fine bits of strewn hay and spin it into a big furry funnel. We'd run through it, and that hay devil would chase us like it was alive and wanted to play. You get enough loose pieces caught together in the wind, you surely can actually see where it's going."

Her reflection in the glass was square shouldered, thin, overtly pretty and feminine. But he could picture her in that boxing ring, skinny legs and arms flying with precision, eyes blinking sweat, mouthpiece bulging.

He asked, jangling pocket change to ease the impact, "You ever think about planting evidence?"

She pulled her glasses from his head and turned to pack her briefcase, answering, "Hell yes, I think about it every day. And I decide against it every day. That's how I sleep at night." She faced him squarely.

"Thanks, Diablo. Just the fact that you'd do that for me on this case makes us friends and comrades. But no thanks. By nature, I guess, I fight clean and with the gloves on. See you tomorrow."

He was gone when the phone rang. Rachel was working alone, reading police reports on the kidnapping and murder of little Lisa Canton. She had just sifted through the crime scene pictures, looked closely with a magnifying glass at the horrible site where the girl's body had been found. From fiber evidence Rachel knew that after he took Lisa from the playground he had knocked her unconscious and rolled her into a pink wool blanket. Wherever he took her next he had raped her, sodomized her and kept her without food and water for at least seventy-two hours, according to Erin. Dirt under her nails and in her mouth showed she had probably been kept in a mud cellar or an underground tomb. Then there were the pictures, the girl dumped like a rag doll into a clump of brittle, frozen weeds by a railroad track. She was battered, bruised. He had beaten her savagely, shoved something so far up her vagina that it ruptured her liver, then he had broken her neck with his hands.

Rachel stood, walked in a tight circle, trying to draw air, trying to swat away images of a cold, scared little girl calling for her mama in the dark of a monster's prison.

High heels and all, she sat right down on the floor in a gangly heap, took off her glasses and sobbed.

She picked up the phone without bothering to blow her nose or wipe away the tears. "Collazo," she said as forlorn as she had ever felt. Not a sound came.

She was aware as she walked alone that the deserted basement hallways were cold and dark as a crypt. She took her gun from its underarm holster and kept it in her hand, in her coat pocket, as she crossed the parking lot to her lone car.

=45=

The smell was grotesque, putrid. Either Erin Truett was used to it and didn't notice anymore or she had a gas mask under her surgical mask. Rachel had to stand back from the strange, powerfully awful stench.

Erin had peeled away the corpse's skin like skinning a rabbit. The body looked like a scientific replica, red chest muscle with spokes of white rib bones splaying sideways. She took a scalpel and sliced from the throat area down the ribs and made an oval that she removed. Her assistant, smiling behind his mask, held out a regular plastic trash bag. Erin dumped in the slab of cut away chest wall.

Dorcus stood next to Erin, watching like she was working on his car and he was peering under the hood with her. Erin fished in the dead man's innards as if she were kneading ground beef for meatloaf, pulled up the purple bulge of a heart, stuck a huge syringe into it and pulled out blood.

"Two bottles," she said to her smiling assistant, "that's plenty for toxicology. Bladder's distended, so we've got enough to test the urine, too."

Dorcus pointed. "Nice looking heart. Bet mine don't look that good when you drum it up here. Bet it looks like the inside is lined with eggshell pieces and hunks of butter."

Erin did crinkle a smile. "Georgie," she placated, "if cops and health profession folks ever give up our stress aids— smoking and drinking too much—it'd kill us." To her assistant, with her gloved and bloody hands deep in pools and piles of human organs, "I've got the bullet." It blurred in her palm, silver in a blob of gooey red. "Looks like a .380. Mark it for the ballistics guys. Rachel, sugar, open my big file over there and I'll explain how we did all that stuff you wanted."

Chaz skulked back into the room, hand over his mouth. He'd made a hasty, pasty-faced exit moments earlier. He mumbled, "Sorry. We didn't get this stuff in vice. I'm okay now."

Erin got to the stomach and Dorcus muttered, amazed, "Hell, look there, he had oysters. They're still whole in his belly."

Chaz darted out again.

Rachel said, "Raymond Esterhaus. Forensics report."

The drawl made technical stuff sound like a cozy recipe for corn pone when Erin said, "Yeah. That's me. Chemical and microscopic analysis clear of drugs, legal or otherwise. In his throat I got a pubic hair. Does that interest you?"

It did. Rachel perked up. "Follicle?"

"Sugar, his nickname should've been Hoover. He sucked it right out by the root. It's blond. Not his color."

Dorcus chuckled crudely. The assistant held the trash bag steady while Erin dumped in a clump of soupy large intestines after she weighed them. The liver dumped into the hanging scale sounded like a wet towel hitting concrete.

"Can you compare the DNA on the pubic hair to the strands from Kelly's cigarette butt?" Her blood was pumping.

"I've already sent it to Lifecodes for cross-checking by the autoradiograph. If it matches—"

Rachel said ominously, "—then she knew three men who killed themselves. Esterhaus, Iverson and Merriam. Did you get anything at all off the Esterhaus sheets?"

"Uh-huh, some fibers. They've been cross-sectional shaped and checked for composition and dyes." She jabbed the bladder with a giant needle and drew out bright yellow urine into the syringe for smiley to label. "Sorry, sugar, they are completely indistinct white cotton. We put them under the Polilight and got nothing exceptional. This cookie is smart, she knows white cotton fibers are universal. Now that covers the biological, physical and trace evidence. The firearms examiners rap the gun out as his, and all the powder residue was on his temple, none on his hands and none to be expected with the .380 that he used, so no help there."

"Fingerprints?" Dorcus asked, but he was really paying attention to Erin slicing into the milky, jellyfish-like lungs.

Erin answered absently. "Zilch."

Rachel: "Even under the Polilight? With chemicals and powder?"

"Nada. Surgical gloves, two pairs probably. My guess is she sat him in the chair and said close your eyes and I'll give you a big surprise. Georgie, there's kidney stones, want to feel them?"

Like a kid, "Yeah . . . wow, just like little gumballs. . . ."

Erin asked, "Was the Esterhaus scene unaltered? I need to scoop out some of this bowel matter here. . . ."

Dorcus told her, "Wife found him, took a look and took off to the telephone. Soon as Good Legs here asked for a crime scene we got everything recorded, collected, labeled and stored and got the Crime Scene Investigator to do a drawing, we brought in the firearms guys. Real tight ship. Same with Iverson and Merriam. Aw, doc, you're going to cut his 'hones?"

She did. Dorcus cringed badly and stepped back. Rachel spoke solemnly, "Jeffrey Iverson."

Erin dolloped the skinned, pearly testicles into the scale, looked them over like antique crystal doorknobs she might want to buy and then unmercifully began to slice them. She said to Rachel, "No ballistics, but the toxicology from BioRad shows chloral hydrate, like I said, almost a gram of it. After ingestion, he had about one minute to cut himself."

Rachel grumped, "Yeah, and with the wrong hand."

Erin described the testicles into the constant tape recorder and then told Rachel, "No paint or polymer. Same fibers, on his clothes, mostly. White cotton. He had some funny lacquer pieces cracked on his hands. Hair mousse, industrial strength. Available at every grocery and drug store."

She dumped more human guts mixed with shredded muscle and stringy arteries into the trash bag, droning into her tape recorder about them and then telling Rachel, "We took everything we found on him, even the odd particles from the back of his coat. We had it measured, compared, classified, analyzed and hypothesized, sugar. Under the Polilight I even looked for fingerprints on his and Esterhaus's skin. He was freshly showered and either she never touched Iverson or she wore surgical gloves, probably under regular winter gloves. You've found absolutely no eyewitnesses?"

Dorcus was bending, squinting into the man's empty body cavity. Erin moved to the head for a brain section. Dorcus trailed her.

He said, "We canvassed each scene. Good, too. All the way. Photos of the nurse, everything. Nobody saw nothing at the doctor's house that morning. The Iverson scene was completely deserted until the construction boys showed up about 7:30 that morning and found him in his car."

"Tire tracks?"

"None at Esterhaus's. Too goopy to cast at Iverson's. The snow ruined every track at Merriam's. Jesus, his head bone saws pretty easy. I thought we were tougher than that in our noggins. Huh."

Erin said, "BioRad shows that Merriam had Seconal and three heavy ounces of vodka." Her eyes flashed like jewels behind the mask. "Imported. Are we good, or what?"

Rachel snapped, exasperated, "Goddamn it. All this shit, ballistics, DNA, forensics, criminology, toxicology, biological analysis, chemical classification, microscopic analysis, autoradiography, firearms and tool markings, fingerprint experts, and we can't catch this nurse? Is that what you're telling me?"

Erin's bottom lip may have pouted in sympathy, "Sugar, it doesn't happen this way often, but when it does, that's when forensics drops back and good ol' cop interrogation takes over. You got to get her to talk."

Dorcus said, his face bunched up near the exposed brain,

"I'll be damned. It looks just like that brain coral you see on them Jacques Cousteau shows. It does. What do you do with all that stuff in the trash bag, doc?"

Erin, brain in her hand like Lady Frankenstein meets Fanny Farmer, said easily, "Trash bag and all, we stuff it back into the body cavity and send you to the mortuary. The bag is buried with you. Oh, but first we sew you back up. With plain old kite string."

Dorcus scratched his head. Rachel stomped from the room.

=46=

The telephone rang. Emory answered.

"Miss Collazo, please."

A woman. Emory stared out the windows of his library onto his sloping lawn, down to the tall pink brick wall that lined his estate. The darkening sky seemed to magnetize the tree tops in one direction. They all leaned. Windy. Storm coming.

"She's not here. May I ask who's calling?"

Some drugstore name. Said Rachel had photos there. And Emory thought, "Bullshit." He knew every inch of Rachel's body and every minute of her time.

He was polite, but crisp. "Well, I would be happy to come and get the photos myself if you tell me what date she brought them in and what the photographs show."

No tension. No anger. He said, "Oh, I see, you're not allowed. Then put your supervisor on. Supervisors can do things—"

The line went dead in his ear. He walked to the expanse of windows and felt the energy that whipped the trees. The gusts were like race cars zooming past the manicured hedges. Past the protective brick wall he could see that the tree-lined street was empty. Rich people didn't go walking their babies or rollerblading. The children might have, but were not allowed. The money was old. By day the nannies organized outings to museums and private picnics at country clubs. In Emory's microcosm of wealth, only the stone statues spouting water played on perfect lawns. Even the gardeners and chauffeurs were discreet when they mingled, never in the driveways, always in the four- and five-car garages.

To his pool, lined with pink marble and rose quartz and beautiful green and purple shrubs, he took his pipe, a hefty crystal glass of bourbon and the *New York Times* crossword puzzle. He sat, sipped, puffed, filled in a row of blanks. In this oasis he was protected from the winds wrestling the front trees, but he could smell the pungent waves of the storm toppling toward the city. He had maybe forty-five minutes until sundown. He sat serenely in the blades of white light that poured through the tremulous clouds. They looked like beams to heaven that you could walk right up.

Kelly set the pay phone into its cradle, chewed her thumb. So he only looked like a perfect gentleman while being peeped at in the bathtub with his lover. In real life, he was astute and arrogant. Never mind. He's a famous celebrity, used to stupid prank phone calls, he'll think nothing of it. She got into her car, all in white like a novice nun on casual-dress day, white slacks and sweater, hair lacquered up into a stringent twist, spongy white shoes, plain white socks.

She drove. The harbingers of a nasty thunderstorm, brutal wind gusts, invisible but clutching, rocked her car. She drove toward Emory's mansion.

His flip phone rang. He popped it open, answered.

"Rachel, sweetheart, you got my beep."

He never beeped. She was flustered. "Honey, are you all right?"

"Do you have photos waiting at a local drug store, darling?"

He heard and felt the tightness. "Oh, hell no. She called."

He stood, looked around, didn't know what for. "I think so."

"I'm sending the uniforms—"

He wasn't used to chaos, couldn't tolerate disorder, had never felt fear. He commanded, "Darling, no. Please. She isn't a commando. She isn't going to scale my fortress walls and scale a tree and snipe me. She's . . . not a gun girl. Okay? It's you I'm worried about. I don't want you to go home tonight, Rachel, I want you to come here. Don't get out of your car until the garage door is down."

He could hear bar noises, she was having a drink with Diablo. She needed to relax with Diablo, with anybody, Emory thought to himself.

She said briskly, "Then I'm sending a uniform to her house, to check what she's doing. I'd love for her to take a hit at me. I've got nothing else on her. It would be too great if she came for me. She's been watching me. We know that now. She knows I stay with you sometimes."

He wanted an anchor of logic. He resented all this hoopla and drama. He said sweetly, "Please, get Diablo to follow you here. Finish your drink, sweetheart. Relax. You deserve it. When you get here I'll have steaks delivered from Chez Chic and a twenty-year-old vintage weeping for your lips. I'll give you an agonizing foot rub and read to you from Uris's newest epic. Take your time. Watch your back. I love you."

She couldn't argue with his sublime logic. She never argued with him. Period.

He traced the pink brick wall. The mansion next door was a football field away. Only its dormant chimney showed lifeless against a bruised purple sky. Beyond that, in the peaceful horizon, a wall of clouds malingered, mushrooms of turbulence and twisted rain. In a couple of hours they would detonate right over Emory's house. His palms were sweaty. His palms were never sweaty. Tense moments were his game. Decorum under pressure was his name. Under the crushing silence of a rapt gallery of fans, Emory Jacobs never even broke a sweat.

He was sweating now.

He turned, scanned. Sat. Sipped. Puffed. Waited.

=47=

Chaz had never actually been yanked out of a chair, especially by a hysterical girl while another girl, a redhead, was describing to him how she could swallow a banana whole and not break it.

When Rachel yanked him, it ruined his nice beer buzz.

He slapped the siren onto the roof of his unit and said through wind gusts that hammered his words, "Follow me! I'll go code!"

Tires squealed. Rachel was behind him, her nostrils flared and her teeth clenched, her fingers white on the steering wheel as Chaz rocked and rolled through busy downtown streets. They hit the highway and opened up to almost ninety miles an hour, but the fist of oncoming wind was like driving through a wall of bashing ocean waves.

In her car behind him, watching his car swish like a pinball, she cursed and cried.

"Oh god, oh no. Get there, Georgie. Go. Go. Go, Georgie, get to his house. She's coming. I can feel it. Please. Oh god."

Fat pellets of rain hit the windshield like hunks of clear clay. Chaz didn't relent, even accelerated when they hit the interstate that led to Emory's pricey enclave. She hit her windshield wipers and everything smeared in her view. Chaz turned too fast into the gilded archway of Emory's neighborhood and his car spun backward. Rachel sped past him, saw his lights level themselves and begin to race in behind her car.

The blips of blue and red choked Rachel first, in front of Emory's house. The huge ornate gate was closed, and Georgie was there at it, pounding on the buzzer, ducking against the bombs of raindrops. Rachel skidded in behind him and poked the remote gate opener clipped to her sun visor.

They caravanned toward the mansion.

The double front doors were locked. Lights shown from within, like on a Christmas card. The house looked sedate and settled. Her key got them in. She checked the library first. The lightning outside the wall of tall windows was followed by angry belches of thunder.

She called, "Emory! Oh, baby, answer me!" And she raced to his master suite where he sometimes showered before he dressed for dinner.

Chaz went through shuttered doors that led to a gourmet-style kitchen. Dorcus headed for the stone steps, lighted by solar lamps, past the granite lions and the cabana, toward the pool.

When Rachel hit the bottom step, Chaz was there. He fought her bodily, and he was strong. He grabbed, she flailed, but he was a mass of quickness, a vice.

He said only, "No, not out there. You're not going out there."

She kicked him hard and tried to jab, but he gripped more tightly.

She met his wild eyes and wanted to spit at them. "Tell me," she said, hoarse, hysterical.

"He's in the pool."

She swung again. He winced in pain, then whipped her around into a hold and they fell to the floor together. He had never fought a girl before, couldn't imagine one so strong.

She tried to punch. He blocked it.

Dorcus dove for Emory's floating body in the pool. A trail of black wavered in the blue lighted water, like inky smoke in an azure sky. Blood.

He could hear Rachel bellowing. It didn't sound real. He got a pulse on Emory, at the carotid. The flip phone was on the patio table. Dorcus called 911. His hip radio was soaked.

Rachel tried desperately to get out from beneath Chaz on the floor. She was hot and hoping for a fatal heart attack, crying so deep and loud that the image of falling backward into a horrible hole came to her mind. Chaz was a boulder on top of her.

He held both her wrists in one of his hands, his black eyes seemed to have fire in the center of them. He said through gritted teeth, "Keep your head, girl. Now more than ever."

She got very still and couldn't breathe anymore. She dug her fingernails deep into Chaz's wrist. There was blood trickling down his hand.

"If he's dead," she said, "kill me."

Chaz lay his head on her chest. Maybe weeping. He stayed that way until they heard the ambulance through the sweeping crashes of thunder and rain.

=48=

Through the sheets of the gulley washer, the cruiser that was parked down the street from Kelly's apartment saw the car pull into her side of the driveway. A lanky caucasian ducking under his sports coat leaped. Under the upstairs awning at Kelly's door he went for a key, but a blond with dark eyes got the door open before he had time. They embraced.

The uniform got on her radio. "Sam one-fourteen to King nine-eleven."

George Dorcus came back at her. "I'm rolling. Go ahead."

She knew he was in his car. "Okay sir, your citizen has just been eyeballed opening the door from the inside, and since I arrived a half hour ago her vehicle has not moved." Just for measure, she scribbled the tag number of the tall man's car.

Dorcus said unhappily, "Okay, Jeannie. You're clear."

His used and abused cop car lurched into traffic as he pulled away from the hospital emergency room ramp where the ambulance had taken Emory Jacobs. Somebody somewhere in the chaos had recognized their famous patient and called the news media, so now there were TV station vans squirreling around, sliding up the ramp and parking and pissing off the hospital security guards.

Dorcus wanted the coldest beer he could find in the darkest shabby beer joint he knew. Whether Emory lived or died that night, Dorcus knew what he had to tell Rachel the next day, and he knew she wasn't going to like it, was going to throw one of her explosive shit fits and get all in his face. But somebody had to say it. She was starting to look like a lunatic or something. There was talk.

He was going to give her tonight to be in there with Emory. Tomorrow, hell or high water, he was going to level with her. Judging by the black clouds writhing among the streaks of lightning, it was going to be hell *and* high water.

He pressed on the car's brake at a traffic light and his shoes squished swimming pool water. He wasn't all the way dry. He didn't care.

=49=

The morning tricked everyone and came up to be a strikingly beautiful clear day. Out the windows of Emory's drab hospital room, Rachel thought of so many of these kind of days, the perfect kind when the world is an oasis. It was on these days that she drove the cart and Emory played the course—he never used a cart unless she went along. She would sit and read a book and hear the swack and then the sound of wings as the golf ball sailed. She would look up at him shielding his eyes, stop action, his lean frame locked in concentration. And her heart would flutter with love.

She turned to him. He was watching her. She said, "What?"

He said, "I feel like a fool. Get me out of here. Did you send all those flower arrangements to the children's hospital? Look at this breakfast tray. Are those scrambled eggs?"

She soothed him. "Honey, you had a close call. They just wanted to watch you overnight. You were face down in a swimming pool, and you scared the shit out of us all."

He waved a big hand at her. "I was pretending to be dead so that whoever shot at me might not shoot again. This coffee is disgusting."

"There was blood in the water, honey."

He pushed the tray away testily, opened his newspaper. "I clipped my chin diving into the pool to get out of the goddamned way. I told you that in the ambulance."

A battleship of a nurse came in, fiddled with him, checked his blood pressure, then asked for his autograph. While he signed graciously she said, "I have to give you one more pill, Mr. Jacobs. Man, my husband is going to die when I bring this autograph to him. Here. Swallow this."

Emory grimaced. "I don't need a pain pill."

If her name wasn't Flo, it should have been. She barked, "You can't get well while you're hurting. There's a bunch of stitches in your chin. You start moving and pumping blood, they're going to hurt like the dickens."

He sighed, greatly agitated, then swallowed. The nurse bustled out.

Rachel got right into the bed and curled herself up into his steady warmth. "There are reporters everywhere. All your sponsors have called. Nike. Pepsi. Geritol." She smiled.

He folded himself around her. "Very funny. I love you, Rachel." He was growing dim from the pain medication.

She touched him, a finger along his tanned arms, her palm against his warm chest, lips on his cheeks and in his hair. She felt a little saucy; her smile was a little too sinister.

"Emory," she whispered, "will you marry me?"

He tried, but was too groggy to look at her when he said in a low breath, "Sure, sweetheart, anything you want."

Nurse Battleship charged in with some papers. "Sign these and he can go right after lunch. Unless you want to be swamped by sports guys, we better take you out the back."

Rachel hugged Emory sweetly in her arms and told the nurse, "Whatever you gave him, give me a shit wad of it to take home, would you?"

=50=

The newsroom crackled with the eclectic bustle of laughter, a police scanner's chatter and the droning of people in cubicles speaking into telephones while typing. Daniel punched the "Send" button on his lengthy news story, which moved it electronically to the computer screen of one of dozens of copy editors across the room.

He sighed with satisfaction and stretched back in his chair, making a big show of moaning and groaning.

The flirty reporter beside him glanced from her screen. "That sounded orgiastic."

"No such word, Goldstein. The word is orgasmic. You must've gone to journalism school up north."

"Hey, chill, Nystrom. I once saw in a story of yours where you used the word 'snuck.'"

"Never. I always say 'sneaked.' And I always say 'dragged,' never 'drug.' You actually read our paper?"

"I'm the one, Nystrom. You're outa here?"

Daniel eased into his corduroy sport coat. "Taking my kid to a three o'clock movie and then to eat. Then I go to the gym and pump flesh." He smiled at his own private joke. He would be pumping flesh, all right, Kelly's delicious warm skin.

The girl reporter raised an eyebrow at him. "But you just sent your story to the desk. What happens if they send it back or have questions or changes? You vain son of a bitch." She started to laugh pitifully. "You know they won't send it back, don't you? Goddamn. How does it feel to be you?"

"Today," Daniel said as he stepped past her, "it feels great. Now don't you tell them I snuck out of here."

She called over the din of noise. "I'll tell them I drug you back here, Danny, but you were rushing to get to a story about a man who hung himself."

"Hanged!" Daniel yelled as he disappeared toward the elevator. "A man who was hung hanged himself today! One is a long penis, the other is a short jump!"

He could hear her laughter fading. The others on the crowded elevator looked strangely at him as the doors opened on his last sentence. Daniel crowded in sheepishly.

=51=

The fancy Italian restaurant was deserted at 5:00 P.M.; all the linen cloths and pristine place settings were poised for the dinner crowd, but it was empty this early. Daniel and Pete ordered spaghetti and meatballs and iced tea.

Pete was yakking while banging the silverware together annoyingly. "My best part of the movie was when that hairy thing—"

"Bigfoot."

"Yeah, Bigfoot, when he got the radio on his head outside Goofy's car and was dancing. That was real funny. Is Bigfoot real, Dad?"

"Some say. Quit banging the silverware. Some people claim to have seen this creature that lives in the mountains. But he's harmless. Pete. Don't kick under the table. That's me you're kicking."

"I wouldn't want to see him. Bigfeet. Would you, Dad?"

"I'd hide behind you, Pete. You're the one who's had all the karate."

"Oh, sure. But I don't got a belt. Tony Barrow has a yellow belt but Mom says when I'm bigger I can get one. Dad, when we caught those fish last week and cut their heads and skin off, did it hurt them?"

"It was last summer, honey, and no, I don't think fish have the part of a brain that feels pain. They don't think or anything. They just do things by instinct."

He was stirring his water and slopping it onto the linen cloth. "So. What's a in . . . stint or whatever."

Daniel grinned. "It means you do something because it's natural and you don't have to be told. Like you definitely don't have the instinct to put away the stuff in your laundry basket into your drawers."

"So. I'm just a kid, Dad. No! Don't cut my spaghetti! I hate it when Mom does that! I'm big enough to eat it longways. Don't, Dad."

"I thought you were just a kid!"

"Yeah, 'cept I can eat spaghetti longways."

Pete said without prompting as they chewed, "Mom got pretty today. We went to this hair shop and they had all these fake heads with hair on them that you take off, they even had green hair, and Mom got one."

"A green one?"

Pete giggled. His chin and cheeks were speckled with red sauce. "No, Dad. She got a white one like her old hair was. Then Kelly and I got grocery stuff while Mom got some new fingernails. And dad, she better not pick her nose or I think she'll cut off her head with those fingernails!"

More silence after the laughter, and then Pete said in his way, the five-year-old way so economic of words. "Dad, how did you turn out to be so bad?"

Daniel's throat clogged. "Pete." He frowned profusely, and Pete could only blink absently. "Who told you I'm bad? Did Grandma Hale say that? Did Mommy's mommy say that in front of you?"

"I don't know."

"Mommy doesn't tell you that, does she?" Daniel's head panged with a sharp pain of anger. "Is that what you hear while I'm working all day?"

"Well, no. Sometimes. I guess she does. Can I have ice cream? Mommy said that pretty soon she'll be well and she'll be my best friend again, like before. We can go to the museum and the skating rink and she can read to me like before. She said after she's well you won't have to bother with me so much."

Daniel contained his voice but his hands trembled. "You are not a bother to me, Pete. I love you."

The boy said weakly, ashamed. "I know. Could I go to the

exercise place with you tonight? There's kids down in that big playroom. They have Nintendo. But we can't tell Mom because she says that the kids who go to day care are common and will give me colds and teach me bad stuff because they have Mommies with jobs."

Daniel sighed heartily. "No, Petey, not tonight, you can't go. But I'll get you home early enough so you can play with Will next door for a while. I'll tell Mommy to let you."

"She'll yell at you. You'll be in trouble again."

There is a love triangle here, Daniel admitted in his simmering thoughts. There is me, my wife and then there is the woman I love. There is Kelly. Someone, he muttered as Pete flushed in the bathroom and Daniel doused water from the sink onto his own tired face, someone has to go.

And there is my son, he considered as he drove home through heavy traffic and whipping spring wind that brought blue darkness with it, my son. Pete chattered more, but Daniel was following his own privately racing thoughts.

She hasn't loved me in years. She stopped being my lover because she commanded it, with no thought to my feelings or our commitment. Then she got sick and being sick made her meaner, not more appreciative of my caring. I am in love with someone else who is also in love with me, but to please everyone around me, especially the wife who tortures me with her dependence and her anger, I am not allowed to have the happiness I want.

His breathing was dangerously rapid. He was speeding as he drove. Pete had fallen asleep. Daniel spoke aloud.

"It's over, Julie. I've had enough. This pressure cooker triangle of hateful marriage to you and sex with Kelly, it won't work. Someone has to go."

Pete awoke as the garage door lumbered shut. He was droopy eyed and whined, yawning, "You said I can go to Will's. He got a new turtle. You said I could go."

He walked the boy to the house next door, feigning chit chat as they all handled the box turtle and agreed that Pete would call home in an hour.

Then Daniel marched across the wet lawn, went inside his house and slammed the door so the windows rattled.

=52=

She was dressed in clothes, not a rumpled bathrobe. And she did indeed, as Pete warned, have on a blond wig that resembled her long, straight hair. She was sitting, gingerly frosting a cake and humming, and when she smiled up at him like a porcelain angel, Daniel sat slowly.

She said softly, "Hi." The frosting was pink and so were her cheeks for the first time in two months, albeit dusted on with a cosmetic brush. She was as thin as a concentration camp survivor; the long-sleeved flowered dress did not hide the gauntness. "How was the movie?"

Angel again. Daniel hung his head in despair. "Fine. You're feeling okay today?"

"Yes." Her waif eyes sparkled at him. "Danny, I talked with Reverend Rose today. He says we can come before the congregation, tell our troubles and ask for special prayer."

He replied listlessly, "You're not serious. I thought you were the queen of privacy."

She touched him. He felt repulsed. "Danny, the congregation can heal us. They're not strangers or outsiders. The church people are like . . . our conscience. You've seen how it's done. We go before them, talk it all out and they forgive us."

He looked up at her. He simply didn't care about the tragic pain etched in her pretty face.

She told him quietly, "If you love me you'll do this for me."

He couldn't speak. He hated her, how she used him and

chastised him. What he hated most was how he had stood by so long and let her prove over and again how stupid he could be. Now she was stroking him, seducing him with her power as the wife. Their family. He couldn't stand her touch and pulled his hand away. He felt crazy, like he couldn't decide whether to laugh in hysteria or shriek in rage.

"Julie," he said, trying to maintain his composure, "you expect me to sit in a church full of holy rolling, narrow minded cretins and let my own son watch me appeal to these . . . gossipy assholes . . . for forgiveness? So they can sit over supper and discuss our sins because it takes the heat off their own sins? Reverend Rose uses the choir like a harem, Julie. When does he ask for my forgiveness in front of a crowd?"

"How dare you," she spewed. "You're so depraved."

"No, what's depraved is to ask me to sit in public with you and blubber my guts out while you blubber your guts out and then a . . . cult of brainwashers goes home and uses my humiliation to jazz up their boring stupid little lives." He stood. He felt the heat on his face. "You go up there and tell those people one damned thing about me, Julie Ann, I'll get a lawyer and sue the whole godless lot of you for defamation of character. You got that?"

"Danny," she leaned into his ashen face. She touched his hair. His skin prickled from revulsion. "He told me to make love to you tonight."

"What?" He screeched it.

"Reverend Rose said that I must take part of the blame for the decline of our marriage. He told me to publicly admit, especially to you, that I have not been the wife I should be, so if you have drawn away from me—"

He laughed. It had a shrill madness in it. "Oh, so you're the martyr; you're the good person. You take the blame and all the hillbillies praise God that they have reached you, and then I'm the asshole bad guy because I won't come and atone to them. I can handle this, Julie! I am a man!"

"Make love to me."

He yelled, "Why? Because you fucking say so?"

She reeled backward. He jammed the knife into the center of the cake, furious, finished.

"Why, Julie, why are you giving me sex this time? Because you feel guilty about how much the wig cost? Fuck it. I don't care. You can have all my money! Or do you want to have sex because you need me to run some cake to your church group or because you want me to fix a cabinet door for you or hammer a nail somewhere or fold the laundry again. What is it? After the sex tonight, Julie, what demeaning fucking thing do I have to do to thank you for it? HUH? Or maybe you just pity me finally for all those years of begging. But one thing's for goddamned sure. You don't want sex because you love me, because if you love me you wouldn't tell my own precious little son that I turned out to be BAD!"

She grabbed hold of him. "I did not tell him any such thing! Danny, stop! You're so upset! Here. Hold me. I'm sorry, Danny. Don't go. Please don't go."

She was sobbing again. Always fucking sobbing. He cringed as she pressed herself against him.

"It's not you, Julie." He backed away. Her face was horrified. "It's not you."

She came toward him. "Yes, it is. I've been unkind. Please forgive me." She screamed when he took up his keys. "No. No! Don't go! I'll kill myself if you go out tonight!"

"I've heard that shit for years, Julie. You won't do it. You wouldn't miss out on the next twenty years of watching me snivel at your feet. What a yuk I am. I'm a great reporter, do you know that? I've got awards, big damned awards. And I'm a great father. Did you also know that? And for ten years I've been a great husband, but do you know why? I've been a great husband just to shut you up."

She fell to her knees sobbing. "Daniel. I have cancer."

He was panting. It felt like internal bleeding. He did not go to her.

"Give me a few hours alone. I'll be back. Just. . . ."

There were no more words. He shut the door and left her

there in a pile of hysteria. As he backed away he could see her at the front door, waving wildly for him to return. The wind blew the dress against her body and he could see she was nothing underneath but a frame of human-shaped wire.

Down the street he pulled over, opened his car door and vomited.

=53=

Lester Graff's cloudy, oily eyes followed Kelly. They were the only body parts that still functioned, and even at best he could see only a narrow tunnel through them.

His legs were gone long ago from the diabetes. His hands were atrophied from crippling arthritis. His heart was a sticky gob of blocked arteries and dead tissue from past heart attacks. Three strokes had muddled his brain so he could no longer speak. He could only moan like a distant foghorn and smack his toothless lips in pain.

But he knew that the milkmaid was his nurse. Sometimes after she left he could breathe better for awhile when each inhale didn't feel like he was sucking in splinters of glass. She did all her usual stuff with the thermometers and the pressure cuff, drawing blood samples and listening to his chest. She gave him a shot, a good one, that made him woozy and took him in his mind to a place where he was still a mule of a young stud working on the railroad. He liked the hallucinations and most of the time hardly felt the finger size tubing go past his gag reflex. The sound of the mucus being torn from his lungs even sounded like the grating of the big iron wheels where he stood all those years, switching different trains to different tracks.

The merciful milkmaid said, "Your fever's down, but your blood sugar is bad. It has to be today, Mr. Graff. You're out of time, which means I'm out of time."

He didn't get it. It sounded to him like talk through cotton in his ears. But he reached for her hand, the white pudding she often set into his tree bark palm, and he squeezed.

Rachel got to the restaurant and thought immediately of the Mafia. Red and white tablecloths on wooden tables, a gargantuan Italian kid behind the bar, Lurch with black hair and tee shirt sleeves rolled up. He swabbed. Dorcus was sweating even though the doors were propped open and a refreshing breeze ran through the whole place. His one strand of hair that ran sideways across his head was askew.

She sat. He poured red wine into her glass from a big carafe on the table and lit a cigarette.

He said to Lurch, "Hey, Tony, this is her. You can bring the stuff now." To Rachel, "We're having fettucine."

"You don't look so good, Georgie. Did you call me here to tell me bad news about your health?"

"No, I called you here because the waiters have guns, so if you start shooting at me I have back up." He grinned. His fat cheeks wadded into fleshy pads. "I saw Emory's press conference on CNN when y'all was leaving the hospital. He looks pretty okay."

She sipped the wine. It was the good stuff, Chianti. She hadn't known that Dorcus knew wine came in bottles. At his house he poured directly from the box. "His hands and arms are insured for two million each." She laughed. "Isn't that amazing? Say, did you check all that stuff I asked you to?"

He pulled at the hair sticking out from his ear. "Yeah. That's what we got to cut up together here. You want the official line or the unofficial sticky stuff first?"

Lurch set down salads, stood like Mama Leone until Rachel tasted and then nodded at him. "Official."

"It was a .44 from about fifty feet away, the distance from the pool security fence to where Emory was sitting. Somebody tried to Dirty Harry him and missed. Wasn't even close. We got the shell from the wall of the cabana."

Lurch put on Italian ballads. Rachel and Dorcus lovers? Could Lurch really think that? She said as she chewed, "Anybody see anything?"

"Private security force saw a blond on a bicycle, wearing a backpack, a half hour before on Em's street. Said she had a ponytail, ball cap and sunglasses. Showed him Kelly's photo, he couldn't be sure. You ain't going to eat your anchovies?" He picked at them, said sullenly, "I asked if this blond had big tits and great legs. He said yeah, but they all do in that neighborhood. They have the same plastic surgeon." He chuckled wryly and shoved in more food.

"The phone call?"

"Pay phone. Public library branch about a mile away. In the women's john. Nobody saw no gorgeous blond toting a .44 go in or out."

"But we know it was her." Luciano Pavarotti belted "La Donne e Mobile." Lurch tossed pizza dough like a native. Rachel added, "We do know that, Georgie."

Dorcus went pasty and sweaty again, slugged deep into his wine glass and poured more. He ate like a prison inmate, scooping food and leaning on his elbows. He said, "Well, that brings us to the unofficial stuff." His droopy eyes sagged at her. "I'll give it to you the way you like it, straight, no ass kissing. Collazo, you're getting all nutso over this nurse. Like obsessed or something. Everything that happens you're starting to imagine it's her. People are starting to say you're," dread clouded him, "like jealous of her or something. Now, there it is. You got to lay off her. Not because I say, but because it's getting around that you're goofy about it, making shit up on her, like trying to put those suicides on her. Here. Here's the fettucine. Say you like it or Tony will strangle you with a thin wire."

Lester Graff didn't even gag. Kelly smiled. I'm that good, she said to herself. The tubing came out coated with atrocious amounts of slime from his lungs. With protective gloves she ran her finger the length of the line and squeezed the pneumonia bacteria into a sterile lab dish. He began to rasp, needing his injection badly. She waited. To nobody anywhere she said, listening to Lester labor for each breath, gurgling painfully, "Poor Lester. Don't fight the respiratory failure. It's inevitable. Go on now. You deserve some peace." She looked at her watch. In five minutes she would call an ambulance. It would be too late.

Rachel actually laughed, but a thin membrane of uneasiness made her angry. "Jealous? That's ridiculous. That's Tillery's horse shit theory?"

With cream sauce on his chin, Dorcus said seriously, "After somebody thought Emory was shot, while he was playing possum in the pool, somebody went inside and took two of his trophies. Reckon a blond on a bike could do that? Reckon a serial killer would suddenly become a burglar?"

"She put them in her backpack. To make it look like burglary. Jesus, Georgie, she's smart! She's after me."

He gloated. "Why, Collazo?"

"Because I know about Iverson, Esterhaus and both of the Merriams. Because she's scared of me." She looked up at him, drew him into her face. "You don't believe me?"

Over the rim of his wine glass he looked like Mr. Potato Head wearing the sad plastic eyes. "It looks, Collazo, like you're out of control on this deal. Are you?"

Kelly dialed. She stuffed the tubing hastily back down Lester's limp throat, certain that he was dead. What kind of fool would order an autopsy on an old man so eaten alive with rampant diseases? Nobody. Nobody would know that she oversedated him and caused his rickety heart to stop and his brittle lungs to fill with fluid. Nobody would care. She was doing her best to intubate and he simply had failure of all of his organs. There. She reached and closed his eyes.

Rachel walked. Fast. To nowhere. Through the historic West End of Dallas with its cluster of restaurants and nightclubs and babbling, bobbling tourists. She almost jerked her car door off, then drove like a maniac to the one place she knew she could find reason in all of this lunacy.

The paramedics waited while Kelly called Wahlstein. Wahlstein said logically, "Well," he said, a dull voice because he had been taken away from a Sunday afternoon cocktail party on his patio, "just, uh, have them bring the death certificate around tomorrow. You sign as the attendant. List the cause of death as heart failure."

"Do we need an autopsy?"

Maybe he smiled dryly. "No, no. It's obvious. He was multisymptomatic. There's nothing more to do."

She drove, feeling open and ecstatic. The pneumonia bacteria glowed at her from the lab dish in her purse, glowed like it was blushing and laughing with fiendish delight.

=54=

On the patio you couldn't hear the yelling from inside so much, Pete thought to himself. Besides, Kelly was there with him, letting him sit on her lap while he put nighttime sounds into his tape recorder. So far they had three sounds, the wind, crickets and, neatest of all, bugs frying in the bug zapper hanging from the tree.

She knew other cool sounds Pete would never have thought of himself, without her. She said to tape record the leaves blowing. The neighbor's dog barked once, and they got that sound. A car door slammed next door. The wind chimes barely tinkled, but he got it on tape.

When the yelling got the loudest through the patio doors, Kelly felt to Pete like she had taken a deep breath and not let it out.

He said to her flatly, "Don't be scared. They do it all the time and nobody ever wins."

"I have to do the chemo soon, Petey." She sounded like his preschool teacher did the time she said that the principal was going to spend the day watching in their room. "Pretty soon I'll have to interrupt them."

They sat a while longer. He could hear that Dad wanted to go to opening night of a baseball game and take Pete because at the newspaper they got free tickets, and Mom was screaming that it was Sunday and Dad couldn't go because he had to take Pete to church. So that was the subject, except that it got lost like a crayon, so his Mom and Dad picked up other colors and started drawing with them—meaning that they were yelling about other stuff and the lost crayon, the baseball game, was too far under the bed to go and get it. Now they were screaming about how Dad never came straight home from work anymore and that Dad had a right to go to the gym for an hour after working all day if he wanted to if it relaxed him.

Then Mom called Dad a name—one of those names Pete knew not to say unless he wanted to sit in his room for like four days or something—and Dad said he was tired of being treated like Mom's pet dog. And then it went on from there.

Pete asked, "How can I get the sounds of the dark time?"

And Kelly said, running her nice fingers through his hair so it felt like warm water, "Here's the sound of nighttime, Petey," and she sang him a lullaby about buying him a mockingbird. He got it all on tape and hoped the yelling that came through the opened window wasn't on the tape, too.

When Uncle Mitch came through the garage toward them, he looked like someone had just bumped his car with theirs, sort of scared and confused. He sat by them.

"I drove up and heard the screaming from the driveway. What's going on?"

Pete said pleasantly, "No baseball game. Mom said. Dad has to take me to church. So you have to go by yourself or take Kelly."

Kelly hugged Pete. Uncle Mitch didn't smile. The screaming sounded like a movie that Pete wouldn't normally be allowed to watch.

Finally the doors banged open and Dad stomped over and said, "I'll go get you a Happy Meal first, Pete, then I'll come get you for church later. Mitch, you can go on to the game."

His dad's words were like rust, like it was wearing out. He stopped once at the step and turned to look back. And Pete followed the line to Kelly's face. Everybody's eyebrows were crinkled and wrinkled, but nobody said anything.

Julie wanted no company while the chemo flowed.

"I'll be right out here when you're finished, Julie, if you need anything."

She said, severely brittle and enraged, "I need my husband to understand that he is going to live as a Christian lives. Period. That's it. God will punish him. I'll pray for that punishment every day."

"Yes, Mrs. Nystrom. Try to relax. When you're finished I'll give you something so you can sleep."

The patio was sinking in purple shadows and breezes that felt oddly tropical. Pete plunked comfortably onto the kitchen tile floor where he could hear Kelly's and his mom's voices. A man called to Kelly loudly from the garage. Pete didn't bother to check if it was his dad or his uncle Mitch, you couldn't tell without looking because they sounded just alike.

Kelly came, looked scared, like Pete felt when he walked in and saw the dentist's chair. She said, "Pete, go in your room for a minute, honey," and Pete scrambled. Halfway he remembered that he'd forgotten his tape recorder, but he'd get in trouble—yelled at—if he went back to get it.

The recorder spun silently, inches from the open garage door where Kelly stepped into the shadows and the urgent whispers.

She: "Oh my god, you're so pale. Are you ill? What is it? You're trembling. Here, sit on this step. Calm down."

He said, "It can't go on. Nobody should live this way. Nobody should be put through this by another human being."

She said, "You're the only one who can change it. It's your family."

He said, "Please. Help us figure out a way. Please. What's it doing to Pete? Oh god, Kelly, help somehow. You say that you love me. So talk to me."

She said, "All right, darling, don't be so upset. You're hyperventilating." Carefully now, so she had a way out if he freaked. "I can do something. It's quick, but it's not painless. My god, you're having a cold sweat. Stop, you'll go into shock. Come here. There now. Calm down."

He was perspiring and shivering.

She said, "Do you know what I'm talking about, darling?"

Her face, so beautiful, was all he had ever wanted. The joy of cupping her breasts in his hands while sliding inside the wetness. The way she sat there like a Madonna while the screaming went on around her. Her protective shielding of Pete. She could stop the madness that was destroying the family.

He, dry as a desert riverbed, said, "Yes. Oh Jesus, I want there to be another way."

She said, "She's getting well. It can go on for years."

He said, "No!"

She, a ravishing vampire, said, "All right, all right. Tomorrow. It will be over by Friday. Kiss me. Yes. More."

He asked, "What if they catch you?"

She replied, "Even if they catch us, they can't prove it. I know what to do. I know exactly what to do. . . ."

He said, "Can I see you in the morning? Can I have your luscious, gorgeous body and do anything I want with it?"

"Yes." The word from her, the magic of eroticism, the core of his manhood. "If you don't contact me before tomorrow afternoon, Julie will die in just a few days."

He skipped a long beat, then said tiredly, "She's dying anyway. Isn't she?"

The lie. "Yes, that's it, darling, it's like we're killing a corpse. Nothing more."

Pete's toy tape recorder spun quietly, a noose tightening, taking in every word they had spoken. When Pete looked for it later, he would find it where he left it.

In his room, into the jumbled and cluttered toy box he would drop it, with all the others, inside his special, secret cigar box, knowing that on the tape were all the sounds of the nighttime. Sometime soon, he thought, he would have to play the night sounds for his grandmother. He was not aware of the voices on the tape, or the danger and the horror.

=55=

The stained glass windows that rose to the sky throughout the huge cathedral made a vivid web across the parishioners. Rainbows of colors arced softly over the long, shiny pews.

Rachel sat alone. After the spectacularly showy high Mass she had not filed out solemnly with the others. She stayed and kneeled for a while, a tiny speck among all the looming porcelain saints overhead with their benevolent faces.

A priest flowed down the center aisle toward her, his lily-white hands tangling in his robes. Hiking boots beneath. She grinned. He sat beside her and kissed her cheek softly.

He said, "Hey, little sister, you all right? Beautiful day for an afternoon walk, get some wine." He glinted mischief. "Or we could play cards in the rectory."

She smirked. "I was twenty-five years old before I figured out y'all had those things marked at home. You and Rusty and Jake owe me at least a half million in my allowance I lost to you. Hey, Patrick, thanks for going by the hospital and seeing Emory. He appreciated it."

"Of course I went. He gives us whopping big checks."

She smiled. "Pat, you're a nut." It was their mother's amorous, girly glint and panged at his heart.

He asked her easily, "What's up?"

"Aw, man, I'm all messed up."

Wisely, he said, "The nurse you told us about at the last family dinner. You had another swing and a miss with her, right?"

235

She made an expression of disgust. "Pat, it's really, really piss—" She glanced at Mary, worldly and stoic, suspended over their heads. "It's really making me mad."

"Remember what Emory always told me on the golf course, Rae. The madder you get the worse you play."

She sighed heavily, bunched her fists in the air. "I cannot catch her. Now it's getting around that I'm flipping out about it, getting delusional because I'm—" she winced in exasperation, "—jealous of how good-looking she is."

Dejected, with a poofy bottom lip that made him recall her warmly as a feisty little girl, she added, "Yes sir, that's what I'd like to be, a wanton, sleazy, psychotic hussy who kills married men and their wives."

He waved a fair hand. "Never mind all that. What comes out of people's mouths is oftentimes common vile. All that counts is what's in your heart, Rae. If you believe she's guilty, then trust yourself. Focus on that. Don't consider for a moment the ramblings of the human tongue. It's no more than smelly hot air we have to walk through sometimes."

She pouted. "I can't go back for another affidavit to search or arrest her. There's no new information for the judge. All I can do is wait for her to do it again, and that scares the sh . . . crap out of me, Patrick. I walk around naked in the dark at night dreading the thought that she will kill again, and I can't do anything about it."

"There must be something," he said thoughtfully. "Bring her in for questioning. Trip her up. You're the master."

She felt a surge of frustration. "Well, that's kinda why I'm here. I'm having her hauled in after midnight tomorrow. Just me and her for a talk. I was hoping that while you're clicking your beads tonight, you'd ask God to make her screw up and spill her guts before she hurts anybody else."

He laughed deeply. "All right, Rae. Anything for you," and he pulled her next to him, kept his arm behind her shoulders and patted her gently.

He said, "Remember the time you knocked me unconscious?"

She smiled wearily. "You had it coming. I thought I had killed you, but no such luck."

"You tried for years to really deck me. But I was much bigger than you. When you finally socked me cold, what was it, what was different about that day?"

She put her head on his shoulder. "I'd had a lifetime of crap from all of you, but especially you, I guess because we're so close in age. Remember when you hid my bicycle in that moving van down the street and it went off to Pittsburgh before you admitted it? My whole life was like that, wondering what nasty little trick you guys would pull on me next. So one day I got enough, and down you went like a clay pigeon. You deserved it."

The organ music was lulling and soothing like Patrick's voice. "Yeah, Rae, but what did I do that day?"

She cringed. "You peed in your water gun and ran through the house chasing me, squirting me with it. It was the absolute last straw."

"Did you hate me that day?" he asked complacently.

"No." She met his pastoral eyes. "I hated being pissed on."

"Rae, stop hating the nurse. You'll think more clearly if you're not clouded by your personal emotions. And stop letting her piss on you. Incidentally, I shot you with my pee because you deserved it."

She balked. His face was bright and innocent. He said defensively, "Surely you remember what you did. Denise Jenkins? The love of my life?"

Rachel rolled forward laughing. "Oh, yeah. She came for dinner. Your first crush, as I recall. Me and Rusty and Paul thought it'd be real funny what we did." Her laughter echoed through the colorful web of stained glass sun streams.

Patrick shoved her lightly, bathing in their laughter. He said, "You thought it would be funny if Denise went into the bathroom and found you dangling and drooling from a fake noose around the shower curtain rod? You and our brothers thought it was amusing when she ran screaming, terrified, from our house? No wonder I'm celibate."

The organ boomed. Their giggles made the sacred music sound like a carnival calliope.

=56=

Julie hobbled, one scraggly white arm clawing the wall. More than anything, more than ever, she wanted her dignity back. It had come to that as she stopped in the hallway toward the breakfast room and leaned for a few breaths of strength.

She didn't look at herself anymore when she passed mirrors. The bald monster in the mirror with the sword points for cheekbones and black craters beneath sunken eyes who looked back at her was too awful to behold and contemplate. She could see each tiny bone protruding along the lines of her feet and hands, some refugee victim too far gone for relief supplies. Her skin was like white ashes. Her bones were stiff so she scooted when she walked, bent over and decrepit. The first weeks of chemo had not taken such a toll, but now she looked and felt poisoned. She leaned on the wall, put a hand to the barren skin flap that had been her breast, and she wept.

Pete found her, came to her in the slanting evening light that crossed paths between windows, held out his small hand. "Come on, Mama, I'll help you to the table."

It was a cherub's puffy grasp he had, warm and steady as they went, the tiny boy patiently abiding the tiny steps his suffering mother had to take as they walked slowly. The house was a cluttered wreck. Daniel had stopped tidying things like he once did, and Julie was allowed no visitors during the chemo to prevent infection. At the table she pushed away an encrusted plate of yesterday's waffles to look forlornly at the gruesomely yellow eggs Daniel had scrambled for her. He read a newspaper. Pete ate eggs and licked at a chocolate milk mustache dutifully.

She tried. "Hi, Daniel. You're home from work early."

He glanced, unfriendly. "Pete has soccer. Eat something."

Pete chirped, "Maybe I could feed you like you used to feed me."

His sweetness panged in Julie's concave chest. "No, Petey, that's okay. It's chilly, Daniel. Pete should wear his sweater."

A grumble. "Get your sweater, Pete. We have to leave."

Pete scampered, skipping. Julie lifted baleful, listless eyes to her handsome husband. "It's not the sort of thing you can hate someone for, Danny. It isn't fair."

As usual of late, he rolled his eyes. "Sorry, Jules, I don't understand your code. Break it down for me into words that make sense."

"You shouldn't hate me because I have cancer. It's not my fault."

He was oddly, hatefully cool. "Don't be silly. I take you to every doctor's appointment. I take care of our son. I give you your medicines. I am your husband. I meet all the obligations that implies. What more would you like, since no matter what I've ever done you always wanted more."

Her bottom lip quivered. She felt a seismic rush of sorrow flood her body. "Maybe you could just hold me."

He stood. She sensed a threat. "My goodness, Julie Ann, you must be delirious with fever. For years when I tried to hold you, you balked and resisted. You told me that desire was demonic wantonness. Why would you want to be touched by someone who repulses you so?"

"I hurt all over, Danny, all the time. I'm sick."

Hatred streamed from him. "You're in remission. Wahlstein said so last week. He said your chances are very good."

Her sob came as a gasp. The eggs smelled putrid. "I want to be me again. I want to be pretty and smell good, to play in the park with our son, to shop and cook and go to church choir. I want to be whole again." Her soft, sad gaze met his stony glare. "I want you to hold me again. And I want you to forgive me."

He reached gently. He could manage only a hand on her shoulder, the slumped, brittle shoulder of a withered great-grandmother. She put the sheath of her bony hand on top of his.

"Eat, Julie. Please." An anchor. The food. He could care for her like he cared for the cat or a homeless bum on the street. "You need some nourishment."

She put her cheek on his hand and felt him jolt into stiffness. "Danny. My Danny. I remember it all. Our wedding night, I came out of the bathroom all dressed like a saloon girl in that lingerie and there you were in some silly pair of giant red lace panties for me, trying to be funny. When I got pregnant you twirled me in your arms and lifted me over your head for joy. In the delivery room I looked down at my feet and you were there in a catcher's mask, clowning for me, smiling. When my father died you stood there at that funeral with your warm hand on my back the whole time, every minute, and I could feel those constant little love pats from you, just tapping me, just saying I'm here. Daniel. My Danny. Much misunderstood by me, but always the same guy, always my rock."

She kissed his hand with pitifully dry, cracked lips. He squeezed her shoulder gently. Then he bent to her, and the sight of his face so close made her smile through the fatigue and the agony and the terrible fear.

"Julie, I thought you didn't—"

She pressed a finger to his lips. "Shhh. I thought I didn't either. Even when I thought I did love you, I imagined that you didn't deserve it." She touched his cheek, kissed it. "But I do, Daniel. I do love you. Dying has taught me so much about life."

"You're not dying. You're going to be okay."

"Please, Danny, say that we are going to be okay. Say that we aren't dying, either. Carry me to bed, would you? Some days . . . these days . . . it seems so far to walk alone."

He did. And he lay beside her and told her funny stories, and Pete knew he was late for soccer but he didn't care. He sat quietly, proudly on his choo-choo train bed listening to his mother's long lost musical little laughs and his dad's rumbly voice. It was like just before he went to preschool, when he was big enough to go number two in the potty but number one still tricked him sometimes, whatever age that was. It was like when they used to leave his bedroom door open at night, and their door, too, and he remembered. His dad's voice would rub low and his mom's voice would tickle high, and hearing them back then was as good as feeling them. Like now.

He put on his sweater. He had some stars that his mom had helped him cut out of paper the day before and cover in glue and then sprinkle with glitter. He was going to give them to his teacher. Special stars.

He was turning them over and over in his hands, trying to figure out what made glitter shiny—was it a trick or did it come off the glitter vines that way?—when he thought that hearing the night sounds might be nice along with his mom's and dad's pleasant voices. He took the recorder and the tape from his toy box. It was the red tape with his name written big on it in tall black letters his mom had made for him the way moms do, straight and neat. He plugged it into the tape recorder, flopped his nubby finger on the button that made the tape whistle forward really fast. It made a sound like his dad's teapot when it steamed hard.

He stopped the button, but the tape was still on Reverend Rose talking from church back when, sometime, the night he had the booger sticking out of his nose like a marble. He pressed again. The teapot squealed again. This time when Pete stopped he heard the windchimes. He leaned in close, watching the tape spin, and thought of a merry-go-round. The dog barked on the tape, and Pete giggled.

Danny came into Pete's room. The tape spun. Pete had the volume all the way up because then it was like the big burly dog was right under his bedspread, so Daniel had to talk loudly.

"Pete, let's roll! I've got your water bottle!"

"Dad, wait! Next is the toilet flushing and then the dishwasher. It's way cool!"

"Later. You're goalie tonight!" His dad came, punched off the tape player. "Play it for me when we get home."

"It's night sounds, Dad. Night stuff that I bet you never even hear when you're doing regular stuff." He dropped the tape player, tape inside it, back into his secret cigar box and slid it under his choo-choo train bed where he was sure no one would mess with it.

=57=

The muddled sunset was lonely, but Julie needed it on her skin like a salve. She sat on the patio alone, watching clouds begin to scar the blue bowl of sky. She sipped water from a fancy stem wine glass and wondered why she had never learned to enjoy wine like people did.

They had told her when she was young, they had shouted from the pulpit that wine was a sin. They had told her that sex was a sin and dancing was a sin and sleeping late on Sundays was a sin. So she married a galumph of a boy who liked—no, loved—to do all those things. "I guess," she thought to herself, "I showed them."

She thought of Chaz, so fierce and brown and beguiling. He had given her an orgasm the way he might have opened up his rough hand and shown her a beautiful jewel. He had found a spot in the middle of her and danced himself against it, gently at first, and then unrelenting when he heard her puppy moans. Without warning her soul had expanded and exploded. They had told her that infidelity was a sin, that even in a loveless decrepit marriage, the honor of a woman was in the suffering. Never in the self-satisfaction. "I guess," she thought, "I showed them."

The tree tops hula danced over the fence line. Her garden was dead, last year's kaleidoscope of blooms now merely mangled sticks.

She saw Kelly then, standing at the gate, black medical bag in her hand. Something went through Julie, a hollow, fleeting shiver as if she had heard a groan behind her in a graveyard and turned. There was Kelly. Gliding toward her. So breathtakingly lovely, she was. And Julie knew where Daniel should and would go when his bickering cold wife ascended. It came over her like a favorite blanket. Daniel should and would go to Kelly.

She put out an arm as weak as a loose rope. "Kelly," she said, "hi. Talk to me a minute before we do the checkup."

Kelly sat. If her body was a Vegas stripper's, her face was still a nun's. "Okay, Julie."

"I haven't told you, Kelly, how much I appreciate you. You take away the pain. You take away the cancer. Whether I live through this nightmare or not, I think of you as my friend."

And with that, Kelly explained that on this evening she would need Julie to breathe deeply on an inhalant Kelly had brought with her. It was a preventive treatment for the asthma, Kelly pronounced like a loving professor.

"But Kelly, my asthma hasn't acted up in years."

The clear wind banged like sacrificial drums. "Well, Julie, we certainly don't want it to complicate things now, this close to the end of your treatment. It's a little uncomfortable so I'll need to sedate you a bit. I promise you, you won't feel a thing."

Inside, on her bed, the inhalant tasted like mint and made her lungs tingle. The shot Kelly gave her first made Julie feel the way he did. Lovely. Free. Secretive. Juicy. The shot made her feel the way Detective Diablo had, and that is what she dreamed of as she slipped away under Kelly's care.

The pneumonia germs scattered into her bronchial system like wrathful, deadly assassins sent to burn and destroy every living healthy cell.

Julie slept. Kelly smoked a black cigarette on the patio and began to contemplate. "Now," the breezes muffled her words, "carefully, we kill Pete. Then Daniel and I must bring life back into this poor, dead garden. What a neglected pity."

=58=

Before Rachel saw Chaz standing in front of her desk, she heard the urgency in his footsteps. When she looked up, she saw that the Bronze Joy Boy was pale and miserable.

"Collazo, I have really bad news."

She studied him, set her pen down slowly. The sun was gone for the day, and her office felt like a capsule of cruel white light and lonely silence.

Chaz said stiffly, "On my own sometimes, when I catch up with her at the nursing service office, I've been following Kelly. Randomly." He trembled and finally sat down. "Two mornings this week she went to Danny Nystrom's house."

Rachel lost a breath. "She's Mrs. Nystrom's nurse? Danny's wife is having home chemo?"

He answered in a desolate monotone. "When I got her current patient roster, my source inside wouldn't give me the names of Kelly's patients, only the diagnoses. Then when I found the pseudomonas pneumonia among them, my source did give me Graff's name so we could talk to him. But I never got the other names. I never knew one of them was Julie Nystrom."

She lay her head in her hands. "Is that the worst of it?"

"No," he said sharply. "From horrible it goes to disastrous. Two nights this week I sat for a while outside her place. Both nights Nystrom showed up. I don't think she's his new handball buddy. They stay in, lights off. He's fucking her."

Rachel started miserably, "Oh, my god—" But Chaz cut her off.

"The night Emory was sniped, Collazo, we sent Jeannie Renaldo to Kelly's, remember, to see if she was home, and you remember Renaldo radioed that Kelly's car was there, and a tall blond man showed up. I talked to Renaldo today. She told me the tall man and Kelly made a big sloppy kiss at the door before he went in. She wrote his car tag number, Rachel. I checked it."

Her palms were sweating. "Nystrom."

Chaz put his elbows onto her desk and jammed his face into hers. "Yeah, Nystrom. Mitchell Nystrom. Danny's brother."

Rachel laughed. It just came out, an uncontrollable giggle at how squirrelly and bad things could really get in her world. Chaz snapped backward and frowned at her.

"You think it's funny? She's fucking them both. She's Julie's chemo nurse. And she's a killer."

Rachel walked to the window. The sky was the same damp gray as the street, an infinity of barren degradation. She said, "We're still on. Dorcus is bringing her in at 2 A.M."

"I don't know why you don't want us in the room with you."

She poured coffee, contemplated the barren infinity another moment and said sedately, "We don't do that Hollywood shit around here, Diablo. No good cop bad cop nonsense. Some teams do that, but not me. I don't sit people under blaring lights and humiliate or pistol whip them. It isn't my style."

"She doesn't have to come. You have no warrant. And she can ask for an attorney."

The coffee tasted like lukewarm cough syrup. Rachel said, "She'll come. She's been very careful, and she knows that, and she knows if I could've caught her I would have already. And if she asks for an attorney I'll comply. Until she does ask, however, six lawyers can stand out there and scream to be let in, and it won't do them a bit of good. She's got to ask. She won't ask. She wants to mind fuck me all by herself."

Instinctively Chaz whispered, "I've got to warn Nystrom."

Rachel twisted toward him, a look of amusement. "Wait a minute. You're the rules-and-regulation kid. Telling Danny anything about Kelly is a violation, a defamation of her character. I thought you never violated the rules, what with your dreams of being—" she mocked him, "—with the Bureau and all."

He was not amused. "I don't give a shit about Danny Nystrom or the rules or the Bureau right now. I give a shit about Julie Ann Nystrom."

Rachel pondered him. "You know Danny thinks he's in love with Kelly. If you tip him, will he tell her?"

"No. He's a natural born investigative reporter. He won't believe me, but he'll do his own checking on her. He's like us, he's got sources on the up-and-up. Plus some sources on the down-and-out. He'll handle it."

Rachel felt eerie, weak, terrifically concerned. She said, "I've got everything I need on this girl except . . . Jesus, except probable cause."

Then Chaz did chuckle grimly. "Don't mention that to her."

Her confidence surged. Rachel knew that she knew this gory business of interrogation, the nuances of a murderer's behavior, the psychology of seducing them into her confidence. She asked Chaz, "What do you hear about me?"

He was droopy eyed, fatigued. "I hear that even if you are a girl, you're the toughest son of a bitch in the game. I hear that in the interrogation room you're friendly and polite and that you convince killers you're their priest and their mother. Then they confess, they realize it was all a bullshit act and they hate your fucking guts."

She smiled a wicked-witch smile and told him, "My Emory shot a sixty-three today at the seniors' pro-am in Augusta. That's a birdie on every other hole, Diablo."

"I know. I heard the uniforms talking. They say it isn't even human, what your boyfriend did today on the golf course. And what the hell does that have to do with anything, Collazo? Shouldn't you be getting psyched up for McLaughlin instead of pining for Emory's putter?"

She said, "Boy, you got no finesse. I'm sitting here thinking that when Emory wins at what he does, the greatest part is that he has just beaten his own personal best. He has no teammates to rely on, no whining, unruly opponents. It's just him out there, and all he's got to do is be better this time than he was last time. You see?"

"He has opponents."

"Naw. Golfers don't play against each other. They play against the golf course. I'm not playing against Kelly McLaughlin when she comes in here tonight. I'm playing against that big entity known as the criminal mindset. I have to go slow. I have to measure responses. She's not a person when she's in here. She's a profile of savvy insanity. It isn't about winning. It's about me using everything I know to do the best I can."

He plunked down the newspaper he took from his satchel, pointed at the front page. "This front-page picture should be of you, not me. You missed a chance for great publicity."

She eyed him kindly. "Yeah. I saw the cameras and I ducked out. I figured you could lead the motherfucker into the jail by yourself, Lone Ranger."

"But Collazo, I didn't catch him by myself. You did the hard part. Your strategy caught him."

The copyrighted story had Daniel Nystrom's byline in bold above it. From the videotape she had doggedly managed to find, the FBI had identified Lisa Canton's kidnapper and murderer. He had been brought to jail that morning in a haze of news fury known before only to Lee Harvey Oswald. Rachel had given Daniel the exclusive details as promised.

She looked down at the huge picture of Chaz Diablo yanking the arm of a scruffy handcuffed child killer.

She said, "You look good, Diablo. The Bureau loves that stone-faced hero shit."

His vanity had slipped some. She reached to sweep back her pretty hair, and he caught her hand in his.

"Rachel, make them frisk Kelly. You're going to be alone with her. Please."

From another woman, someone not so beautiful, someone not smiling at him like any second she was going to wink, it would have sounded repulsive and crass. But from Rachel it was reliable infamy when she jerked away her hand and said, "Fuck frisking her. This no-good cunt takes a run at me, I'll knock her frilly ass into next week. Now scram. I'm due at the gym, time for Cujo to beat my butt to a pulp again."

=59=

Suddenly the atmosphere began to tick. It was as if Kelly put reason and righteousness in a box, lighted the fuse and mailed it to Rachel. The moments led to detonation. Death would soon reign.

Chaz walked purposefully in the blustery evening, unaware of the downtowners shuffling past on their way to cocktails or suburban cottages. He ducked into the newspaper's outer foyer, spoke crisply to the fat, bald security guard, then dialed the phone. Daniel Nystrom answered on the first ring.

He appeared moments later when the elevator doors opened. He was sunny until he saw Chaz's cheerless face. They walked a crowded concrete path, angling around the block together grimly, through anonymous skyscrapers. The sun was setting, bathing everything in pale yellow and light purple.

"The nurse you're fucking, Nystrom. Watch out for her."

Daniel's long stride slowed. He frowned into the space beneath Chaz's gimmee cap from Saint Edwards University. "What?" was all he managed.

"I can't say anymore. She'll sue if we're wrong. But we're not wrong. Watch her. Get her away from your wife and your son. Stop fucking her."

Chaz's eyes were black, shiny pellets. The wind blew Daniel's hair boyishly but his face showed an angry man. "The goddamned police are following me? I'll get a lawyer—"

Chaz poked him hard in the tie. "Nobody's following you. Nobody cares about you. You're a big boy. But your family needs protection. Ditch the nurse. It will be the first honorable thing you've ever done for your family."

Daniel fumed. "Hey, fuck you, Chaz—"

Chaz pushed him. Daniel slammed backward into the brick wall of the alley. Chaz growled, "You've got two heads, you bastard. It's time to think with the one that understands how slowly and meticulously covert investigations have to go. I'm warning you." Daniel stepped forward. Chaz shoved again, harder, and left his fist balled into Daniel's chest. "I'm warning you, Danny. For Julie Ann's sake. The nurse hurts her and I'll shoot you point blank the first time you look my way."

Daniel laughed rudely. "Jesus, Chaz, what is all this cloak-and-dagger bullshit? You got something on Kelly, then arrest her. Otherwise this is pure police harassment."

"When you're in her house next time, look for anything related to the names Ray Esterhaus and Jeff Iverson. You'll see the pattern for yourself. Married men. And now dead men."

They separated. Daniel paced, fingers through his hair. Chaz lit a cigar, planted his boots firmly into the damp alley to block Daniel until he was through with him. Under the cap and the halo of smoke, he looked sinister.

Daniel said, "Kelly's profession calls for intense background checks and constant clearances. I know her. She's good to my wife and my little boy. She gets these loving thank-you notes from her patients. She's," he searched the sinking streamers of gold sunset, "she's the best thing that ever happened to me. You wouldn't wait if you had anything." He fell into Chaz's gritty glare then, asking, "What's with this surfeit of emotion toward my wife, anyway, Chaz?"

Chaz thought. The son of a bitch deserved to hear it and be hurt by it. Julie Ann didn't. He said, "She's in danger. My job is to protect people like her."

Daniel started away muttering, "Yeah, I didn't figure even

you would be horny enough to want to fuck that crazy bitch."

"Turn around, Nystrom."

Daniel did, and instantly, more frightened than he'd ever been, he stepped back from the gruesome killer look in Chaz's shadowed eyes.

Chaz approached. He heard Daniel's plaintive swallow, saw the furtive wincing. He said, "You know that with one hit I could kill you."

"And I know you don't. You won't hit people for that reason. Let this be, Chaz. My wife and my mistress are none of your business. We have no more to say to each other, you and me."

Chaz didn't blink, wasn't fazed, spoke coldly. "I know men like you, Nystrom. Vain, petty, sleazy fucks who use their situational ethics to justify the notion that when a man doesn't love a woman anymore, then he has to hate her." He blew a stream of blue cigar smoke insolently. "If I could hit you, I'd break your ribs first, then your cute Nordic nose and some of your bright, white teeth. It would take four seconds."

Daniel straightened himself. "They make jokes about what a whore you are."

"Yeah. I fuck a lot of women. But I don't fuck women around. I don't assume a woman is too stupid to deserve the whole truth. I don't stay someplace just because I'm scared to leave."

Daniel's laugh was open impudence. "I'm finished here, James Bond. You got anything else to say?"

"You're warned, Nystrom. Get the nurse out of your house and out of Julie's life. Now."

He watched Chaz stride away, overcoat flapping, head held high, cigar smoke trailing. To himself Daniel muttered sarcastically, "I guess this means we're not friends anymore. Asshole."

A half hour later he had rationalized it all away. By dark, Kelly was writhing beneath him, crawling under his skin, giving him wave after wave of sexual pleasure so intense that he sometimes lost his breath and all his logic.

In a strobe of harsh, springtime lightning he saw Kelly through the candlelight that glowed from the bedside table. Through a rumble of distant thunder he spoke.

"Julie has a very slight fever. Janet Bachman called me today. I should go so my mother can go home."

She said as saccharine, "Okay, darling." Then she straddled him. In the candlelight he could have evoked her, his dead sex slave, to come back through this seance. But she was real. He reached for her, dropped a strap on the soft pink chemise and became a man starving for the fruit of her moist breasts.

She told him, "I'll check on her tomorrow. If she's worse, even slightly, Wahlstein will put her in the hospital."

He confessed slowly, "I was ready for her to die. I want my work because it's my happiness. I want my son because he's all my dreams. And I want you, because you never say no."

She moved down his belly. He moaned wildly. Kelly tossed her golden hair away from her face and then dipped all of him into her warm, hungry throat.

=60=

A frown flickered across the usually placid face of Daniel's mother. She said to Julie Ann, "That cough doesn't sound good. You should call Dr. Wahlstein."

She stood at Julie's rumpled bed where Pete sat playing absently with his tape recorder. As he pushed the buttons they heard random blips of songs from kids' TV shows, pieces of silly commercials, a lash of Reverend Rose's fervor from the pulpit, even their own voices.

Julie was touching Pete's soft hair, watching him intently, feeling devastated at the thought of dying and leaving him. She said, "No, Elva, it's okay. Kelly comes for a checkup in the morning." She sighed and it sounded ominously like paper being crumpled, then a long, rattling cough seized her.

"You're sweating, Julie."

"Elva, it's okay," she answered tersely. She shivered, felt it shimmy down her spine and out into her bone-thin arms and legs. Her face was splintered in pain. "The right side of my chest hurts."

Daniel's mother felt gnawing alarm. Julie looked horrible, waxen and collapsed, worse than usual, more pale than ever. All day the cough had been dry and hacking and unrelenting, coming in sudden bouts that held Julie for a few moments like a vice.

"You've obviously caught a cold, honey. You probably need to be in a hospital—"

Julie gasped. She had been nicely fingering Pete's clean,

254

narrow bare feet, but at the word she clutched them and felt seized by tears. Her breaths were labored. She cried out, "No! The hospital is at the . . . last." She breathed in but was beginning to feel less and less air with each breath.

Pete said innocently, "Listen, Mom," and pointed at the spinning tape, "it's you telling me Goldilocks." And then they heard the melody of Kelly's voice singing ". . . don't say a word, Mama's gonna buy you a Mockingbird . . ."

Daniel's mother hit the stop button irritably. "Petey, it's almost nine, sweetie. Let me take you to bed."

Julie smothered him in kisses as he was lifted away. He chirped at her, "Here, Mommy, you keep the tape recorder and listen to it. It's got all kinds of neat stuff to make you smile."

She lay alone in pain, vigilantly fighting off the thought that the wheezing and shortness of breath were coming stronger, not easing. She pressed the play button and heard the rest of Kelly's mellifluous song.

". . . and if that cart and bull fall down, you'll still be the sweetest baby in town."

She stopped it, pushed it away, gripped her chest suddenly as a sharp pain clinched her right lung. Holding the bed and then the dresser and finally the wall, she made it to her small bathroom. The coughing spell was horrendous. She pressed a damp towel over her face to cover the terrible sounds, and when she drew the towel away she saw that she was now coughing up a mist of bright red blood.

"Oh my god . . ." she backed away, fell to her knees from weakness and struggled along the floor to the telephone beside her bed. She dialed.

"Kelly, oh my god, Kelly, I'm sick. Please come. I'm so scared. Please come and give me medicine to stop it."

"Have you called Dr. Wahlstein?"

The breaths were like a child rattling a box of tiny rocks. "No . . . I want you. Not the hospital, please, not yet. Please, help me."

She pulled herself back into the bed and waited, coiled in dread under the covers. She was trying to breathe now through a great, heavy cushion of mucus. She coughed again and had to bend forward into the damp towel. Blood.

Kelly drove, feeling an expansive kind of joy. The night air was fresh and ripe with flowery breezes. Quick ripples of lightning winked at her. This was going to be way too easy, she congratulated herself. Of course when she got to Daniel's she would have to call an ambulance, but it would be far too late for anyone or any drug to save Julie. And of course Julie would die the next day in a hospital, so there would be no autopsy.

When Daniel had left her two hours earlier, he said he was going to swim at the gym and then ramble through the grocery store. Kelly slowed her car. Best to let him arrive home first. As she passed under a street lamp it exploded in her path, hit by lightning that came from the sky like God was throwing knives. Kelly looked back at it, the peculiar and violent little shower of effervescent light. She smiled.

When Kelly arrived, black bag in hand and proper panicked urgency in her face, Elva Nystrom all but reached out and threw her into Julie's room. Daniel was crouched beside the bed. Julie was soaked with fever and breathing like a hot little puppy, head back, tongue out grotesquely.

"Call an ambulance," Kelly snapped.

Elva raced to the kitchen phone.

Daniel looked up at Kelly, winsome as a choirboy as she worked around Julie with the equipment.

He asked, "What's happening to her?"

"Stay calm, darling. Let me write these numbers. Hold on."

From behind them in the doorway, Elva Nystrom heard the "darling." She saw her daughter-in-law dying and her son backing away in terror. She put one trembling hand to her mouth and then slowly the other—to keep her vicious thoughts from coming out in words.

Kelly said into the telephone, "Yes, Dr. Wahlstein. Pulse one-oh-six. Temperature one-oh-four. Respiration rate is bad, too, at forty. Blood pressure," she faked a sinking spell in her voice, "eighty over sixty. Yes, I know. She's slipping into shock. The ambulance is here. Okay, sir."

The ambulance roared away. Kelly loaded her black bag silently. Elva Nystrom lived and breathed propriety. Elva Nystrom prided herself on embodying the premise of "live and let live." She watched Kelly and asked simply, "Are you going to the hospital?"

"No, ma'am. The medical staff there will handle it."

"Is she bad off?"

The answer was somber and soft. "The medications are miraculous, Mrs. Nystrom. How is Pete?"

She felt her fists clench, wanted to strike Kelly and scream and then fall down and cry. But ladies don't, and Elva only said dryly, "He's fine. Good-night, Kelly. I need to call Julie Ann's mother. See yourself out. I'm sorry."

=61=

She checked on her grandson sleeping peacefully. She checked in the kitchen to see that there was plenty of cereal and milk and things for school lunch. She checked the liquor cabinet and made herself a vodka on ice before she dialed.

And now, everything done that could be done, she carried her drink and her smoking ashtray to Julie's room and began to make things tidy. With the toy tape recorder in her shaky hand, she played one minute of Pete telling nonsensical jokes. His voice was so precious. Elva labored a smile.

And her smile darkened suddenly. The tape was grainy, but the words were distinct, like the soap opera that played mindlessly on the television when she ironed at home.

Julie and Daniel were screaming at each other. "It's opening night of baseball, damn it! He goes to church every week, there's only one season opener. Let him be a boy, let me be a man and decide for our son!"

"He's going to church! I'm glad my father's not here to see what a heathen you have become—"

"Yeah, your father's glad he's not here too; all the poor man did since he married your mother was follow orders!"

She switched it off. It was too awful. She hit the fast forward button and then play again. For two whole minutes she listened without taking a single breath.

"Do you know what I'm talking about, darling? Yes, oh Jesus, I want there to be another way. She's getting well, it can go on for years. No! All right, all right, tomorrow, it will be over by Friday, kiss me, yes, more. What if they catch you? Even if they catch us, they can't prove it. I know what to do. I know exactly what to do."

She buckled onto the couch weeping, and sat that way for as long as it took for the shock to weigh in. She talked to herself, "Oh, Daniel." Her haunting bubbled to the surface.

"Oh, my poor son. Always such a good boy, such a fine man. Oh how I do love you. My son. In whom I was well pleased." She looked around the gloomy room. "What in the devil's name have you gone and done?" She took the tape, went into the most innocent room she could imagine, Pete's.

She hid the tape under Pete's mattress. In the kitchen she made herself another drink. In the attic she found the big box of Easter things and went through the house, setting each little decoration into its properly cheerful place. She put the tape out of her mind, comfortable with the knowledge that as soon as she had reason to drive by the lake again she would drown the terrible tape forever.

The ambulance wasn't really happening, Daniel said to himself over and over. I'm not here. This isn't real. The siren was a hysterical screaming. The paramedic moved frantically around Julie, barking into a radio and doing what some calm person in the emergency room was confirming that he should do. Daniel felt tight chested and light headed. Julie was tentacled now with wires and lines, and the paramedic said, ". . . going to ventilate. . . ."

She opened her eyes. Daniel bent to her and wiped away the warm tears that had dripped down her temples and dampened the scarf tied around her head.

"They're going to give you something to help you breathe, Julie, some oxygen." He put his hand on her forehead, and a gulping sob came from down inside him where the long-ago loving husband still wanted the girl he had married to raise her head and love him.

She reached. Her hand was a skeletal claw. She whispered to him between rattling short gasps, "We should . . .

have . . . had more fun, Danny . . . life should . . . be more . . . fun. People . . . should love and . . . laugh more. Let Pete . . . be . . . happy always."

She gagged violently as the tube was pressed into her throat and down into her lungs. Daniel turned away. The ambulance swerved madly on the slick streets.

=62=

Dorcus knocked. Rachel lifted herself from the chair and strode with purposeful calm to open the door of the interrogation room. She wore blue jeans, the kind that on her long legs had been known to crack men's contact lenses when she walked. She wore a white button-down shirt with rolled-up sleeves, dark blue leather cowboy boots, her hair pulled back in a plain rubber band. No make-up. She wanted the "we're just here talking on the porch at a family barbecue" look.

And she wanted authority. She put her silver and black badge in view on her belt, right beside the hip holster where her .44 poked out like a rocket launcher. This was the "don't forget who the hell you're lying to" part of the costume.

Dorcus's flabby face broke into a wide grin. "We get there, Good Legs, she's banging Nystrom's brother, comes to the door naked. We give her thirty seconds to get dressed. She don't say a word driving over. You ready?"

"Did she say anything at all?"

"'Please can I put on some clothes?'" And "'Thank-you, yes, I would like a cigarette.'"

Chaz clipped down the hall toward them. His trench coat sparkled from mist rain. His long, Apache hair was braided and damp so it shined navy blue.

"I want to watch through the two-way," he said. "Is she here?"

"Came along like a little sheep," said Dorcus.

"Let's go," Rachel said. "I'm staying in there as long as it takes. Nobody in or out, Georgie, unless I call." Her eyes flashed a daredevil thrill. "Bring me our sheep. I'll give you back a wolf."

Dorcus brought her in. Rachel looked twice as she poured them coffee, catching herself thinking that even at two in the morning Kelly was still what every man wanted when he rolled over in bed with a hard-on.

"Hi. Have a seat there. I'm Detective Collazo." She set down the coffee on the side of the desk where Kelly sat. "Rachel, if you like. You want cream or sugar?"

"No. I want to know why I'm here in the middle of the night. Am I arrested or something?" It played out as guileless, but sophisticated, not naive.

"Is it the middle of the night?" Rachel glanced at her watch. "Well, hell, who knew that? I work such weird damn hours. Oh. That's a two-way mirror there, but nobody's on the other side. We're alone. You and me."

"Detective Collazo, do I need an attorney?" asked Kelly.

"I don't know, Kelly. Do you?" Rachel countered.

She smiled a dim kind of girlish demure. "I guess I watch too many TV cop shows. So why am I here?"

Chaz watched. He smiled. Rachel thickened the Texas accent so she sounded remotely illiterate. She pulled her chair around to Kelly's side of the desk and sat. Chaz muttered, "Nice. No barriers. And Rachel's chair is higher, looking just a little bit down on her. Good plan. Kelly's coiled, arms crossed, legs crossed, hands locked, shut off, nobody gets in or out. Bad body language, Nurse Nasty. You don't look like you want to be very honest. Hmmm."

"Kelly, I'm looking into the death of Ashley Merriam. You were her home chemo nurse."

Chaz from inside the glass: "Ah. An inkling of relaxation, Kelly. Arms unfolded so slightly."

Kelly answered, "Yes. She got pneumonia. It was so tragic. We were very surprised."

"We?"

"Wes and I."

"Uh-oh. We. She was more than the nurse," Chaz observed.

Rachel saw the relaxation. She said, "I was wondering if you were surprised by his suicide. Was there hostility between them? Did they fight when you were around?"

Kelly said placidly, "I got the impression they were very close. You don't think he killed himself?"

"Whoops. She wants to know what you know, slugger."

Slugger nailed it. "Well, in my experience the consistency doesn't vary too often. People hang onto what's important to them. Women rarely shoot themselves in the head because they don't want to mess up their faces. And men, jeez, I can't imagine a man fucking up his own balls like that. You know? Men almost always use a gun or a noose."

"Arms crossed again. You're too close, Rachel. She's checking her watch to avoid you. She changed position in the chair. You're getting warm, Collazo," said Chaz.

Rachel saw it all. Her innards grinned. Kelly allowed, "That would be your expertise, not mine. Why are you asking questions about Ashley's death anyway?"

"Because I know she was murdered." Rachel sat very still and barely swiveled the chair. "I'm absolutely certain of it. And he was murdered, too. I know how. I know when. I even know why." She glared.

"Bingo! She's picking lint from her sweater! Lie alert! You're good, Collazo," said Chaz.

Kelly's mouth felt dry. She said, "So what do you want from me?" She did not whine. It was pragmatic.

Rachel leaned back, sipped, sat a moment. Then she said, "Lots of men who know you end up dead."

Kelly stiffened. Rachel saw fear instead of anger. Then Kelly caught herself and forced the relaxation along with a petulant grin.

"What a stupid thing to say to me."

Rachel, calm and cool, "Stupid, huh? You ought to hear the list of geniuses who helped me put you with all these poor, dead bastards. LifeCodes, the DNA lab. The American Academy of Forensic Sciences, criminalists, toxicologists. The Medical Examiner. Crime scene experts. Fingerprint experts. Chemical analysts. Latent fingerprint analysts. A biophysicist and a little old lady with a Ph.D. in molecular biology who compares hair fragments."

Kelly's belly imploded. Chaz laughed loudly behind the soundproof glass. Her thoughts were racing. It had to be reined in, it had to stop here. The bitch cop was lying. There had been no mistakes. She was careful. It was all lies. They had nothing or they would arrest her.

She said primly, "Anything of mine you found at the Merriam's house was supposed to be there. I worked there, remember? So your experts did all that experting for nothing. Could I have a cigarette?"

It shook in her hand. Rachel noticed as she touched it with a flame. She asked, "Did you give Wesley Merriam a sedative the night his wife died?"

"If I did I would have gotten permission from Dr. Wahlstein and noted it on the chart. I must not have."

"A non-answer. Red flag," said Chaz.

Kelly smoked like Cleopatra, fluidly and with contempt. She said flatly to Rachel, "You can't think I had anything to do with Ashley Merriam's death. I was her nurse. I couldn't have hurt her. I wouldn't have hurt either of them."

Chaz said, "Aw, yeah. The couldn't and wouldn't. So she's a murderer but she doesn't like to lie. She can't bring herself to say that she didn't. Couldn't. Wouldn't. You got it, Collazo."

"I think you did. Otherwise we wouldn't be here, honey."

The moment simmered, poison in a cauldron. If she wanted a lawyer it would be now. Rachel surged.

"Say, Kelly, you hungry? I could get food for us."

She was breathing too fast, had to slow down, stop. Think. "No, thanks. I'm not hungry. Detective Collazo, if you think I killed someone, why don't you arrest me?"

"Oh no. Don't take the bluff, slugger. Raise her one. Stay in the hand."

"You just told me you couldn't and wouldn't do such a thing."

"And I couldn't."

"Okay. Let's talk about Ray Esterhaus. You knew him."

"Yes."

"Where were you on the morning of his suicide?"

Kelly shifted again in the chair, adjusted a ring she wore, passed a hand through her hair. "Probably on my patient rounds. That's what I do all day. I don't remember specifically where I was at that time on that day."

Chaz said, "A gap. Not good, Kelly."

"He gave you a necklace that day." Rachel took the duplicate box from the drawer. "This necklace."

Alarm. Oh shit. Oh damn. She answered in a monotone. "No."

"Yes, Kelly. I have a witness."

"You do not."

Chaz saw the sweat. It gently appeared first as a fine sheen over Kelly's top lip. Dorcus came beside him. Chaz said, "Collazo's all over this bitch, man, and Kelly still thinks that Kelly is in control."

=63=

For three hours Kelly and Rachel went through every angle of Kelly's relationship with Esterhaus. When Rachel asked about benign specifics—where they did it, was he a good doctor, that kind of banality—Kelly was direct. When it came to the day of the suicide and the necklace, Kelly fidgeted, averted and spoke open-endedly.

Chaz and Dorcus pulled up chairs and ate sausage sandwiches and slurped apple juice.

Rachel said, "Now one more time, back to the necklace."

Kelly had washed her face in the bathroom, brushed her hair. She looked less disheveled, but slightly haggard from the cramped position in the chair and the burning tension in her neck and head.

"I told you he didn't give me the necklace."

"I told you, Kelly, that I know he did. He bought it the day before he died. You went there the day he died. He gave you the necklace. You shot him."

She yelled, knees rounded up to her chest, "That's insane! I would not shoot someone!"

"But you were there that day. You had sex with him just before he killed himself. Are you that good of a lay or that bad? Everybody who fucks you decides death would be easier! And with Esterhaus you left a big hunk of physical evidence. It had to come through sex unless out of respect for his marriage vows you were only willing to take off your panties and let him chew them!"

"All right." She said it playfully. "I saw him that morning. He came to my apartment."

"What time?"

"Eight-thirty. After his first procedure."

"He took a phone call to his home from the hospital at that time."

Dorcus said, "There wasn't no phone call."

Chaz replied, "Yeah. Kelly will find that out when it's too late."

Kelly said defiantly, "Then it was earlier or later. But it was my house, not his."

Dorcus said to Chaz, "You going to eat them fries? My money's on the nurse. Only reason she ain't ran out of here yet is because she's enjoying this. Thanks. Give me the rest of your biscuit, too, if you're done with it."

Rachel said, "Okay, okay. Jeffrey Iverson."

Chaz said, "Hoo-hah! Look at her hands gripping that chair cushion!"

Kelly said easily, "Jeff and I were friends."

"Lovers."

"Yes."

Dorcus, chewing crudely, said, "Man, this gal has fucked more boys than the draft."

Rachel took off her glasses and rubbed her eyes a long time. Kelly chain smoked. The sun limped up.

"You know where you were when he killed himself?"

"At home. Asleep."

"Alone? For a change?"

Kelly smirked at her. "Yes."

The city beneath the wires crossing the window was stirring. Early birds were stalking Big Business worms as they skittered toward the skyscrapers. Rachel was tired and hungry. Kelly was irritable and impenetrable. There were no hairs or fibers to connect her to Iverson. Only the photograph. She turned to Kelly.

"Marcus Chang. You gave him the staph bacteria in the cough syrup."

"Prove it."

Chaz sat up. "Uh-oh. The wolf just growled. It's turning."

Rachel: "I can prove that Ashley's pseudomonas pneumonia bacteria came from Lester Graff."

Kelly's locked fingers unlocked. "Then do it."

"You made her breathe those germs. They attacked her lungs like fire ants on soft flesh. You did the chemo on Monday, and told Janet Bachman that Ashley had requested you to do the re-check on Wednesday. On Thursday you made an unscheduled visit and sedated Wes Merriam so he would be too drugged to hear her cries for help in the night." She stepped within striking distance of Kelly. "I know about it all."

A psychopath looked up at Rachel, the eyes of a lunatic.

"Kelly, I know you've been careful. But between Chang, the Merriams, Esterhaus and Iverson, don't you know you've screwed up along the way? I also know that you're a good nurse." Rachel sat beside her. "It's just that these men, these fucking asshole men, they dick us around and then they deserve to be killed. I know that."

Chaz said, "Look. Killer just lowered her hands and uncrossed her feet. She's relaxing."

Dorcus said, "Or maybe she's getting ready to jump on Good Legs." He unsnapped the strap on his gun holster.

"Kelly, I want to kill someone about every fifteen minutes. I get so goddamned angry that they don't appreciate how valuable I am. I know how you felt about these men. They make you love them and then they shit on you."

She went away. Rachel saw a soul exit the eyes so they became hard, blue, empty shells. "I want to go home, Detective Collazo. Can I go home?"

"Iverson wasn't carrying any chloral hydrate in his sample briefcase, Kelly. Wes Merriam couldn't have cut his femoral artery so clean while he was so fucked up on booze and pills. A witness puts you with Esterhaus that morning. Lester Graff's DNA is all over Ashley's—"

She jerked. "It is not. The host's DNA supersedes—"

She stopped. She lit another cigarette, dragged a hand through her hair. "I'm a nurse, Detective. Don't try to bullshit me about medical analysis."

"You should've left a bottle of Seconal at Wes's murder scene." It was a lame try.

"I wasn't at Wes's murder scene."

"How did you know to always wear white cotton? How'd you know the fibers are untraceable?"

She stared at Rachel and imagined pulling a leather belt tightly around her throat and watching her face explode in blood, hearing the gags, feeling the death spasms.

"Kelly, I know these killings are not your fault. And part of me knows that part of you would like to stop." It was as intimate and private as a French kiss. "I can help you." She put her hand delicately on Kelly's knee.

Chaz said, "Nurse Nasty is contemplating. Look at the wonder in her eyes. She's scared."

Dorcus said, "If she don't crack we ain't got shit."

"I know, Kelly, that you want to put it all behind you and not do it anymore and have a regular life with someone you love. Maybe a baby or two. A man who adores and is devoted to you. I can help you."

Chaz: "Yeah. Up onto the lethal injection table." He and Dorcus laughed meanly.

Kelly blew smoke, chewed a nail. Her plaintive eyes went to Rachel, away from Rachel, back and forth. She felt weepy.

"It isn't always murder to kill somebody, Kelly. I can help you explain and prove the difference if you'll just trust me. Right now they're after you. I'm your only friend."

A tear fell. "Ray was a dick. When we traveled I had to fly ahead alone and act like a stranger to him."

Rachel: "What an arrogant prick. How unfair to you."

She sniffled, flicked ashes. "I was in love with Jeffrey. He had this great house and these great kids. His life was so perfect. Sometimes he said he was out of town and stayed over with me, and I'd watch him dress in the morning, and I'd just . . . crave for him to be my husband." More tears. She left them, and they dripped. She left the snot, no self-conscious wiping. Rachel had never seen a person so sad.

"They abandoned you, Kelly. It wasn't fair."

She and Rachel stared at each other, lips so close they could feel each other's exhausted breaths.

"You can't help me."

"Yes, I can. Now and only now. Not later. Later they'll eat you alive, and I won't be there to rescue you."

"I have to go."

She walked out, gorgeous despite the ordeal and as dangerous as ever. Rachel turned to the two-way glass, put her head against it and screamed, "FUCK!"

=64=

The fine gentleman in tasteful plaid slacks, a vibrant red sweater and blindingly white golf shoes swung. High above him went a fluid arc which then smoothly ran along the ground as quickly and gracefully as a natural waterfall.

Rachel applauded. "Liquid gold, that swing of yours, Em. You were born to do it."

She splotched open a beer and swigged, still trying to wash down the sour aftertaste of that morning's foul confrontation with Kelly. Emory was beside her, shading his eyes down the course. She drove the cart.

She chided him. "You're great in bed, too. We've got it down to a skeet shoot, you and me. You yell 'pull' and my pussy explodes for joy." She smiled brightly. "I love you!"

Emory teased her lovingly. "In times of more gentility, sweetheart, you would have been known by the parlour crowds as a ruffian, I believe."

He kissed her hair and swaggered down the course to his ball. Rachel squinted into the cool sunshine. Emory was on one knee, sizing up the slope of the green. She watched and felt all the love under that glorious sun rush through her heart.

Afterward they ordered martinis in the country club grill. She sipped hers complacently while across the room Emory signed autographs for a group of gawking college boys. He listened politely to their accolades. Rachel nibbled on her cold cocktail onion and enjoyed admiring her tall, handsome lover from afar. The martini burned her eyes deliciously, and she said aloud to herself, "Ah. Sometimes life is good."

Emory joined her, apologizing. He dove into his drink. Eight or ten quick times she kissed his nice lips and cooed silliness at him.

She said as usual, "Emory, will you marry me?"

He said, coy and modest, "I should, shouldn't I?"

"Ah. A crack in the veneer. Or maybe it's the liquor."

"Dance with me, Rachel."

"There's no music, baby."

"I'll sing."

"I'll make your bail when they cart you off."

"You must remember this, a kiss is still a kiss, a sigh is just a sigh . . . the fundamental things apply as time goes by. . . ."

He hummed. They swayed so close together she could feel his steady pulse. "Emory, when you played golf that day with Danny Nystrom, did he mention the nurse?"

"No, sweetheart. During golf, men discuss sex. Not love. He is in love with her."

"Hey, Emory, you know what makes a man a great lover in bed?"

"Yes. What he does to her and for her out of bed. Like diamonds and dances and believing in her dreams."

Rachel loved him too much and had too much polish to be the coquette. She asked him, "After your wife died, before I snagged you, you were a real true playboy, weren't you?"

He showed his immense love by making his honesty always so kind. "Before you, Rachel, sex was always easy to come by. But it was never, ever so much fun." He kissed her mouth.

When the flip phone rang on their table she wanted to ignore it, but he danced her toward it. She answered. Chaz was huffing and puffing.

"She's dead, Collazo. Julie Nystrom died this morning in the hospital. Of pneumonia."

"Get the warrant. Charlie will sign now."

"I've got two warrants. I'm busting Danny Nystrom's ass, too, by god. I'm sending uniforms to get Kelly."

"Diablo, we've got her. Calm down."

He was as sharp-edged as a razor. "Goddamn that Nystrom. It's our fault. We should've arrested her."

"We tried. Hey, Diablo, we did our best."

"Goddamn that Danny Nystrom. I hope the fucking she gave him was worth the fucking he's going to get from me."

=65=

The handsome, married lawyer went down on Kelly, sweet as chocolate syrup slides down vanilla ice cream. The cabin in the woods where he had brought her for the afternoon was owned by his prestigious law firm and was totally secluded in woods along the undeveloped lake region.

He flicked his tongue over her milk and honey neck, over her pillows of breasts and nipples, along her creamy slate of flat belly, until he found the deepest spot that made her moan and beg.

She needed it, the release. The morning episode with Rachel Collazo had been a nightmare. She had teetered on insanity. But now in her element of seduction and murder, she was fixated and controlled again. Rachel Collazo was a million miles away and had no physical evidence at all. If she did, Kelly knew she would be in jail, not in bed with her next victim.

Elva Nystrom sat in the morbid silence of Daniel's house, quieting her own crying so she could hear the muffled bleating of Pete from his room as Daniel tried to explain that Mommy was never coming home. She could only hear the cracked and terrified tiny voice imploring. "Why, Daddy?" And then, "She wouldn't leave us . . . can't you go and get her? Can Batman go and get her? No, Daddy, don't say that. . . ." Her heart shattered finally. She hung her head and wept, leaned forward into it and cried out to God.

Daniel touched her shoulder. "You go be with him, Mom. I've got funeral arrangements to make." He looked frightening to her. His eyes were blackened from fatigue, his hair matted, his skin sallow. He seemed thinner, like concentration camp photos, and his voice sounded old. The phone rang and he answered.

"Yes, this is he." A quizzical look. "Why? Who? Well, if Wahlstein says to, but it's so obvious. The autopsy seems unnecessary to me. Can I object to it? It's just a physical massacre—yes, all right." To his mother he said hollowly, "The police have court ordered Wahlstein to release Julie only to the county Medical Examiner's office, not to the funeral home. Jesus."

"What does that mean, Danny?"

He told her squarely, "It means they think she was murdered."

When Kelly sat up on the lawyer's belly, her cheeks were flushed with excitement. "Let's play a game, Artie. You like it rough. You hate that old missionary married safe stuff. Let me tie you to the bed."

He watched her thin, naked body move around him, first the wrists and then his feet tied to the four posts of the bed with neckties from his closet. He was splayed and naked. She titillated him for a long time. Played with him and licked and bit him. When she went to the bathroom and he was alone, he felt more silly than scared.

When she came back, when he saw the scalpel and the dead eyes and heard the lunacy in her voice, he was terrified. He struggled. She stood over him. He thought she was salivating.

"Don't struggle, darling. You won't get free. I was a Girl Scout. I can tie a heck of a knot." She stuffed a wad of white cotton into his mouth and said, "Now if it hurts too much and you suck in air, you be careful not to suck the rag down your throat. We don't want you to suffocate. Yet."

She put on surgical gloves. Artie the lawyer began to whimper like a whipped dog.

* * *

Chaz pushed the front door so hard it drove the door knob through the plaster inside. He knocked Daniel to the floor and was on top of him instantly, cuffing him and grunting.

"Resist arrest, please. Give me half a reason to break your neck in self-defense."

He slung Daniel up, gnarled in his face, "You have the right to remain silent. Anything you say can and will be used against you in a court of law. . . ."

"Chaz, relax man. I know what you think—"

"I'm arresting you for murdering your wife. Because you had the motive, Danny boy, you didn't love her anymore. And the somebody else you do love is a nurse who's done this many times before." Chaz had wild eyes. Daniel felt choked. "By the way, lover stud, she faked it with you all those years. But I talked to her and got her relaxed so she could have a real orgasm. So it wasn't that she didn't like sex; she just didn't like sex with you. You're Mirandized. Walk, you murdering piece of heartless dirt."

"My mother and son are down the hall, Chaz. Don't make this a scene."

Chaz pushed him forward. "You're a criminal now, Nystrom. You don't matter anymore. Shut the fuck up."

She slapped him twice so hard in the face that he saw sparks. He felt the blood her open hand drew as a fingernail cut his cheek. She was gone, over some mental ledge, screaming at him.

"You cheating married men really piss me off, you know that?"

He tried to talk, but the rag was big and stuffed too deeply. She croaked at him, "What? What are you trying to say, darling? You have to go home to your wife now? You have to leave your little poodle mistress all alone because it's Christmas or Halloween or fucking Mother's Day? You have to go home to the REALLY IMPORTANT woman in your life? Is that what you're trying to tell me, darling?"

With all her might she crashed her fist into his nose. He felt the cartilage shatter with the impact of a sledgehammer smashing an orange. He began to choke on the gush of blood in his throat. She had something, a rope or a belt, and was beating his torso violently with it. With each slap his tied arms and legs reflexively jerked to cover himself.

Chaz put Daniel in the cage, the backseat of the police car that had no handles on the doors and a metal screen protecting the front seat. Daniel tried to talk.

"Chaz, you're wrong, I'm going to sue your fucking ass."

"Oh, well, then let me just stop right here and let you out and dust you off and apologize. Most people I arrest never say that. Let me tell you something, old friend, I don't like you anymore. Don't talk to me."

"You fucked my wife? Julie let you have sex with her?"

"Yeah. And afterward she gave me cherry pie and fresh coffee. She was a real lady. Of course she's dead now. Because you thought killing her would be less inconvenient for you than divorcing her."

Daniel shrieked, "That is not true!"

"Never heard that one before either. You talk again, I'll slam on the brakes. You'll hate what hitting that metal screen does to your face. Slices it like Brie cheese."

Kelly was finished. She stepped back, admired her butchery. She stood over him and peered into the sockets where his eyes had been before she gouged them with the scalpel. He was making blubbering sounds.

She cooed at him. "What, darling? You want to talk? I thought you didn't have time to talk. I thought your little wife needed you to hurry home because you had respectable guests coming for dinner and chit chat. Oh. You want to know why I've blinded you and tortured you and given you a sex change operation?" She kissed his cheek. "The wages of sin, I guess. Bye, love. Next time you cheat on your wife, try not to be such a condescending shit. And pick someone sane."

From the trunk of her car she took the gasoline can. She stayed a few moments outside to watch the fire fully engulf, and then she drove away.

=66=

From outside the interrogation room door Rachel and Dorcus could hear the manic screaming. He handed her some coffee.

"Hey, Good Legs, reckon ol' Don Juan is killing him in there?"

"Naw. Nystrom has a lawyer. At least I think it was his lawyer. Kind of looked like a mobile home salesman." She blew into the coffee. Dorcus sat by her on the crummy bench in the hallway.

He said, "Nurse Nasty was not at her domicile when they hit with the warrant. You know, if she gets away, you and me will finally get to be on *America's Most Wanted.*"

"Lord, when they film us I hope I don't have PMS. It really fucks up my hair when I have PMS."

He cut hound dog eyes at her. "Collazo, point out to me some day when you don't have PMS."

"You love me."

"I sure do. Let's get drunk tonight."

Daniel and Chaz's loud yelling scratched through the door. They heard a clamoring heave.

Dorcus said, "There went the table."

Rachel told him, "I guess I better get in there and mop up Nystrom's blood. Oh, man, I wish he hadn't been so horny."

Dorcus chuckled, "Or we could wish his wife had been more horny. Either way."

She went in. Daniel looked like a homeless bum, shirttail out, hair wild, unshaven, glasses cocked wrong. The lawyer, who Rachel was sure had his goofy hair permed, maybe a Mike Brady fan, sniffed like the air went bad.

Rachel pulled a chair next to Daniel. He smelled bad, like old sweat and stale cologne. "Hey, Danny, we can't find your girlfriend. Where is she?"

"I don't know."

"You see this girl every day for months and now suddenly you're clueless as to her whereabouts?"

"Rachel, what is going on here?" He looked caught in the headlights.

"She's a serial killer. She has this regular life like they all do. And by night she's a murdering loon. She's killed six people, including Julie Ann."

He shouted hoarsely, "Then why the fuck didn't you arrest her?"

Rachel signaled, "Diablo, uncuff him. Because we couldn't prove it. Until now. Now the deaths of Ashley Merriam and Julie Ann Nystrom are more than coincidence. Now it's a pattern." She leaned back for space to watch him. "When did Julie first get sick?"

He had spit dried at the corners of his mouth. He rubbed his sore wrists. "She got a dry cough on Thursday morning. Janet Bachman called the doctor. He said the fever was just minimal, but that she should be checked the next day. It was Kelly's day, Friday. Kelly told us that Julie was better—"

Chaz interrupted harshly, "Couldn't you tell she was sicker?"

Daniel's head drooped. "This morning we could. My mom begged Julie to let her call Wahlstein, but Julie refused. She was afraid of the hospital. She called Kelly."

Chaz moaned, "Oh, shit . . . having the wolf guard the hen house."

Rachel said, "Well, maybe all you had to do was sit back and watch. You and Kelly planned giving her the pneumonia bacteria, and all you had to do was make sure nobody got her to the doctor."

He yelled, "Bullshit!" and stood, but Chaz pushed him down again.

"Or maybe," Rachel said coyly, "maybe Kelly told you

how and you gave Julie the bacteria. She died of a hospital pneumonia, Danny, Erin has already ruled on it. Nosocomial pneumonia resulting in septic shock. Exactly like another of Kelly's patients. We've got her, kid, and we've got you, too."

The lawyer yapped, "Don't say another word, Daniel."

Rachel said, "Hey, somebody give Fido a biscuit. He just gave his client some good advice." She stood, towered over Daniel, who was sniveling. "Nystrom, did you kill Julie?"

"No. I did not. I swear to God I didn't kill her."

"Did you love her?" She pressed. If he lied on this then he was lying to her all the way.

"No. I didn't love her. But I did not kill her or help anybody else kill her. She is my son's mother. Jesus."

She said, "Cut him loose. Nystrom, like they say in the movies, stay in town. And if your girlfriend comes to see you, don't bother to call me. Call 911. You're next."

She heard Daniel scowl at Chaz, "You slept with my wife."

Chaz popped off, "You slept with your wife's killer. Now go home to your boy and help put his world back together."

Rachel said outside to Dorcus, "He didn't do it. But I'm not going to be able to convince the grand jury that he wasn't in on it. He'll get indicted, and he'll do time. His life is a bucket of shit. Whether he did it or not, when we find Kelly she's going to say he did. Nystrom is finished."

"You're the detective, Good Legs. You're the brains."

Rachel joked, "Yeah, boy. That's why I get the big bucks."

As they walked Dorcus said, "This Nurse Nasty was so careful for so long. Then she went and did Julie Ann exactly the way she did Ashley Merriam. That sounds kind of dumb, don't it? I mean, you've got her. Circumstantial shit alone will get her forty to do. How'd she get so ignorant all the sudden?"

"Georgie, honey, if murder was easy, we wouldn't need prisons. Nobody would get caught. The truth is, it's damned hard to kill somebody and get away with it. Kelly didn't get ignorant. She got caught."

=67=

As Rachel stood in the fog under a useless rim of light outside the county morgue's night entrance, she was keenly aware of the darkness and of the fact that Kelly was loose out there.

Erin's voice came on the intercom, then the door buzzed and Rachel started down the most treacherous hallway toward the autopsy rooms.

Erin was in full scrub garb from head to toe. Her midriff section was gobbed with human goo. The body on the table was skinned in the middle like a side of beef.

Rachel said, "You rang."

Ellie Mae Clampett came to mind again. Erin said, "Listen, sugar, on the witness stand I can do the math for the jury. Two women being taken care of by the same nurse and dying of the same rare infection is . . . horse shit."

Rachel grinned. "Oh, how you do sling that science jargon."

Erin said, "I called you because I want you to see this nice fellow. He was a lawyer. Now he's a dead lawyer—"

Rachel quipped, "The best kind."

"Anyhow, from his shirt in that bag over there, I got me one long, blond hair, about shoulder length, about like Nurse Nasty's in the photo you showed me. I think Hot Rod Counselor here was a member of her fan club. She's getting more violent. Didn't bother with that hair mousse I found on the others." Over the mask her gaze was solemn. "He was castrated. I looked all over for his balls. Finally found them . . . in his throat.''

"Did she leave anything?''

"I've scraped for vaginal secretions on him, but there's so much blood. I'm doing fibers, hair, the Polilight on his skin. Prints at the scene. Damn thing is, you touch the same surface more than once and all the prints are smeared to hell, no tracing. All the criminals go around wiping up fingerprints when all they have to do is slide their palms over everything and then it's impossible to get the prints. What I care about right now, Rae, is that she's gone over the edge. A rampant, murderous edge. If she can get to you, you'll be next. And then maybe me. Anyone who knows anything about her.''

Rachel hugged herself. "Or maybe Danny Nystrom. He was her latest screw buddy.''

"He's arrested, too, as an accomplice to his wife's death?''

"No. But he will be. There's enough circumstantial on him.'' She whispered as if the dead could hear her. "I know you're licensed to carry. So do it tonight, loaded and cocked, all the way to your car and into your house.''

Over the mask Erin showed a certain dread. "I can put her away for you, Rachel. You did good, seeing the pattern and staying on her.''

Rachel sighed. "She's still out there, rambling around in the fog like the damned wolfman.''

"Let the night guard walk you to your car, Rae.''

Rachel chuckled, "Hell, if Nurse Nasty's body slammed me out there, Jerry would have a heart attack from just seeing her cleavage.''

"I'll watch you out, then.''

The silhouette of Erin's face in the windowpane faded as Rachel locked her car doors and pulled away into the streets rolling with creepy, crawly fog.

=68=

Daniel drained two beer mugs in one swallow each, and then leaned in the darkness over his sink to slap water onto his aching face. Then he leaned farther down into the sink and wept until his gut hurt.

The figure behind him in the dark hallway fell back into the shadows.

He slapped a whole package of ham between two slices of bread, turned on the living room light and hit the machine to play back phone messages. There were soupy condolences from people who mostly never met Julie and some who had met her and probably, he thought, hated her. He ate the sandwich in four bites. He called his mother. She said Pete was fine. She had given him the children's Tylenol as the doctor recommended, and Pete was sleeping okay, crying out some for Mommy, but resting as best he could.

Daniel turned off the light. The secret figure crouched.

He got into the shower and turned on the water as hot as he could stand. She seized the moment, moving through the house to turn on every gas outlet. In each of the two fireplaces, on the kitchen stove top. She opened the oven door and turned on the gas so the fumes would spew freely. Then she left quietly, locking the door behind her, running free and feeling free.

The phone rang as Daniel toweled himself. The house was dark, and in the shadows of moonlight through the sheer curtains he didn't see the back and forth movement of the thing dangling dead at the end of a noose. If he had turned he would have seen the fat striped cat twisting in the cold wind, casting shadows of a gruesome pendulum.

His lawyer said into the phone, "They're moving to arrest you. Probably tomorrow. We'll go, you turn yourself in. That makes you seem more innocent."

"I am innocent."

They talked a few more moments and then hung up. Daniel lay back on his bed, taking deeply troubled breaths and feeling so sleepy that he never noticed the slices of darkness the dead cat made as the noose swung listlessly.

He drifted slowly. Finally he slipped into an oddly heavy slumber that he welcomed with each deep inhale of odorless poison.

=69=

Rachel set her burglar alarm and stood at the window with a glass of wine. The night was peculiarly bereft and quiet. The fog came like a pall. Emory called. He was in Palm Beach doing commentary on national television for a golf tournament. She flinched that she had not heard a word of him that day on the TV. He said that was all right because television golf commentary was only slightly less boring to those not of the ilk than watching water boil. She said, "I love you," and he said, "I worship you," and they hung up.

She was alone. Not scared. It wasn't fear she felt inside like people do when they hear a noise in the dark closet. Instead of fear, Rachel felt the tug of vengeance.

She thought of Julie, trying so hard to live for her son, and of Danny out fucking the nurse, such total disregard for the human condition, such blatant sin. She searched the carpet of fog. She drank wine. And she waited.

Nothing came. No inspiration that she hadn't already thought of and used. No killer Kelly down the chimney. No Nystrom calling her to confess and make a deal for immunity to help them prosecute the nurse for multiple killings and thus make it into capital murder. So Rachel got herself and her wine glass into the shower, too, and let the hot water lavish her.

When the electricity went out and she was dunked suddenly into complete blackness, the burglar alarm went off. It whooped like the horn on a huge steamship, and she stepped from the shower into the ridiculous blaring sound and the choking darkness.

She saw the gun. Kelly said, "Turn it off with the code."

Rachel said, "All right. I have to walk past you to the panel."

"I'll shoot you if you run."

"I know that." She put a hand up. "Just . . . be cool."

At the panel she punched the right numbers. The whooping died. "They're going to call, Kelly, the alarm people. If I don't answer the cops will come."

"So you'll answer. You'll tell them you're fine. And then we'll talk. Light a candle and carry it into the living room. Turn on a light. And pour me some of that wine you have in there."

Rachel knew the drill. She put her hands on her head and walked steady. She asked, "Can I get a robe? It's on the chair in my bedroom."

The remark was icy and lascivious. "I don't know. You look awfully good. Maybe before I kill you I'll force you to let me go down on you for a while."

"Well, if you do, then follow up on the killing part, because I'd die of embarrassment. I like lesbians as my friends, but I'm not one."

She put on a robe, tied it and took a hairbrush from her vanity. She noticed then that her gun was not in its spot.

"That's my gun you have, Kelly?"

"Yes. But I brought a big knife. One to start the fun with, the other to finish. We're going to tie you up."

Rachel turned. She noted crucially that Kelly hadn't cocked the revolver. "No, we're not going to tie me up. Shoot me now. No hours of fun and torture first. Fuck that. Kill me here."

Kelly pointed the gun at Rachel's face. Rachel didn't blink. Kelly said, "Get some of your bras. I'm going to tie your hands and feet."

"No. Shoot me. It'll draw the neighbors and then this will be over. No fun and games first with me."

The gun lowered. Kelly arced an eyebrow and said, "I don't want to fuck you anyway."

"No, I wouldn't think so. I'm not married."

Kelly frowned. "Get the candle and light it. Remember, I've got your gun right by your head."

In the living room the candle glowed singularly between them, making eerie shadows. Kelly sipped wine, watched Rachel menacingly, sometimes with a nasty smile.

The phone rang and Kelly followed her to it. The voice said, "We got an intruder alarm at your residence, Miss Collazo. Is everything all right?"

"Yes, everything's fine."

"Okay, ma'am, I just need your password."

"My password. Triumph." Her password was hole-in-one.

The voice said, after a knowing pause, "All right, then. You do require assistance?"

"Yes. Thank you." She turned to Kelly, the gun extended right at her chest, and said, "You be careful with that gun of mine. It's a revolver. It never jams. Not like an automatic. They'll clog up on you. But not a revolver. Not as many shots, but hell, if you can't get out of someplace with six shots, you're dead anyway. So be careful unless you mean to do it. That sucker will kill me."

Kelly said, dead as the sound that had come from the corpse on Erin's table, "Shut up. Go to the couch and lie face down."

Rachel walked. She knew she was done for if she did lie down. Within the candlelight, when she could reliably see more than six inches, she turned again. Kelly came at her, whipped her in the head with the gun butt once, and Rachel felt the gnash of pain in her temple.

"You were good, Rachel. I almost admitted everything. You made me want to admit everything. Like I could just put my hand in yours and you'd kiss my wounds and it would all go away." She came into Rachel's reach with her ghost-white face. "You think I won't kill you? I killed my own fucking mother. Once you've done that, killing a bunch of fucking lying bastards and their fucking leg chain wives is no trouble at all."

Rachel straightened herself. The go-to girl was on point.

She said, "You know there is just one problem with revolvers."

Kelly blinked, confused.

Rachel said, her right hand twitching at her side, knowing this was it, "Like I said, automatics jam. But revolvers, all you have to do to stop a revolver is this—"

She reached up and as strong as a vice grip clamped her fingers over the cylinder. "Now look, Kelly, I'm holding the cylinder. It hasn't been cocked so it won't fire. Try. See. You pull the trigger. Nothing happens. That's why with a revolver you ought to always keep your distance. But I guess you didn't know that."

Kelly drew back her hand. Rachel smiled big.

"Kelly, Kelly. Never fight like a girl. Never draw back to punch. Man, for a psychopathic killer you sure are a . . . wimp."

With three whips of her free fist, Rachel hit Kelly. Cujo would have been proud. The first slam ripped Kelly's eye, the second crushed her nose. The third powerful jab—and Rachel heard the mighty pop—broke Kelly's pretty jaw.

A uniformed cop was pounding. She opened the door and Dorcus scooted in, weapon drawn Hollywood style. Rachel's hand hurt and she wondered if it was broken. She shook it and blew on it and knew it needed ice badly.

Kelly was unconscious and bloody on the floor, sprawled.

Dorcus said, putting away his gun, "We heard the call over the radio to your residence. I knew it was her. Is she dead?"

"I don't know. But I need a doctor for my hand."

He grinned at her. "Good Legs, you're straight out of the Wild West. Hey, where're you going in your housecoat with wet hair?"

She took up her car keys. "To check on Nystrom. Tell a uniformed unit and Diablo to meet me there."

=70=

Chaz was closer. He got there first and walked the perimeter of the flatly dark house twice, bending past low hedges to look in windows. Nothing. On the front porch, he drew his gun and banged on the front door.

Daniel's car was in the garage. He could see it through the small squares of tinted glass along the top of the door. He felt the metal garage door for heat and listened to see if the engine was still cooling and popping, but the silence was cold. This time he banged on the back patio door, hit the metal part of it with the butt of his pistol and called Daniel's name loudly. Nothing.

In his car he used the radio and got Dorcus in his unit.

"How far out are you?"

On the radio Dorcus sounded like Fred Flintstone. "Ten, maybe twelve, minutes. I wasn't given code." He meant he wasn't speeding or using lights or the siren.

Chaz said somewhat sarcastically, "Sergeant, are we operating here on the presumption that the resident inside is in peril of his life or possibly injured?"

Dorcus, not a man for urbane cop stuff, said slyly, "Yeah, slick, go on in. Hey, you do know how to crack a lock, don't you, without mucking up your manicure?"

Chaz sneered at the radio. "Ten-four on that, sarge. I'm an Apache. We can get in through cracks in the wall even with a hangnail."

He used his pocketknife and stepped inside the narrow marbled foyer, and he instantly knocked over a potted plant on a stand. It startled him so he jumped and pointed his pistol and then felt supremely amateur.

"Danny! Police! It's me, Chaz! Danny! Don't do anything stupid. Come on out."

He knew about Daniel's gun case in the office upstairs. If Nystrom is setting up on me, he reasoned, he'll be up there waiting. The stairs were through the living room.

Chaz scooted along the wall for a few feet, into the wide den. In the ripples of moonlight he studied the deck outside and saw nothing moving except blown tree limbs. He found his way to the kitchen, reached for the light switch, and he was deadly seconds from flicking it. The smell of rotten eggs hit him, a noxious wave that rushed at him when he came through the dining room and slid back the kitchen door. Gas. With a moment of weak fear, he backed away from the light switch and mumbled.

"I am standing inside a ticking bomb." He could hear the stove top gas jets hissing by now and realized the fatal fumes were curling all around him like flames. In unfamiliar darkness he found the stove top knobs and cut off the hissing there, then he turned off gas fumes streaming from the oven.

"Danny!" He stayed against the wall, through the dining room again and into the living room. "This is not the way, pal! Call out to me! We'll talk. Don't go out like this! Oh, shit, the kid. Pete. Oh god. It's down here, his room is down here. Wait. I need light."

Scrambling back to his car he opened living room windows along the way. Gulfs of cool air waved through all at once. In his car he found the flashlight.

Back inside, in the hallway, he found Daniel. He knew when he turned Daniel over that it was worse than bad; he was apple red and had urinated on himself and was barely breathing. Chaz saw Daniel's finger twitch.

"Danny, can you hear me?"

No sound, faint pulse. Chaz left him, running to Pete's room. The bed was neatly made. Okay, he thought, he's in Daniel's room. He went quickly, calling Pete's name frantically, looking under beds and in closets, anywhere a kid might go when he started feeling real sick and couldn't wake up his daddy. Chaz yanked up the bedroom telephone and hit 911.

"Yes, we need an ambulance. Signal 51 attempt by gas fumes. Please alert Sam one-fourteen to have officers turn on NO LIGHTS as they enter the residence, and Collazo," he had to think, "uh, she's William three-twelve in her unit, tell her, too. I'm letting in new air now. Get the main gas flow to this address turned off immediately by the city's switch."

The voice, a salve, "Okay, Officer Diablo, you are on the scene, no lights. Your exact location in the residence for identification? Notifying Lone Star to shut off main flow now, sir."

"The main hallway. It's pitch dark so tell them it's me in the hallway. With a weapon. Plainclothes."

"Will do. Plainclothes officer in the main hallway. With weapon. Ambulance is dispatched sir. Shall I stay on line when you lay down or disconnect, sir? Prior units apprised now."

"I'm clear. I have to see if I can get my friend breathing."

"All right, sir, help is on the way."

Chaz clamored to the hallway. Daniel was not breathing. Chaz kneeled over him.

"Nystrom," he said with cool diffidence, "time for you and me to kiss and make up."

He put his mouth over Daniel's and began to breathe for him. Soon he could hear the ambulance, Rachel calling to him, and he could see the bliss of red and blue lights flowing all around him through the windows.

=71=

One week later, as he stood looking through the bars of his jail infirmary room, birds were singing and Daniel was considering limply just how incongruent that was. A pretty sound dancing through such a dismal place.

His hospital stay had been brief. The first morning that he was considered stable, he was put under arrest in his hospital room and transferred to this secure place. His door did not open outward. He was beginning his first long, lonely night in lockup and had so far only one visitor, his lawyer, who came to bring him candy and a copy of the indictment. There was no telephone or television, no wires or glass. He knew he was under suicide watch because the mirror had the dull, silken look of a two-way.

When the door clicked, he felt a weird kind of thrill, even if it was the execution squad, at least it was a break from the boredom. He saw Rachel's comely face step in, and his stomach wrenched. He turned away, pissed and indignant. She said, "Let's talk."

"They're burying my wife in an hour, and I don't get to go because I'm considered too dangerous to society. What shall we talk about? Are we going to discuss the phenomenon that if one is an infidel then one is also a murderer?"

She dragged up a chair by his empty bed and sat. "This isn't the time for your Ivy League sanctimony against the corrupt elite system. This is the time for you to get down and dirty with me."

He sat on his bed, washed and frail in the brash sunlight.

The bars made the sunbeams ribbed, so his face appeared to have bars across it, too. He said, "I did not help Kelly kill her. Period."

"She says you did. Well, she wrote that you did. She can't talk too good with her jaw wired together in pieces." Rachel grinned insouciantly.

Daniel whined, "Why would she do that? Why would she say that?"

Rachel handed him a stick of gum from her pocket. He took it and chewed mindlessly as she said, "If she's going down—and she is, for a long time—she doesn't want to go alone."

He spat, "Bitch."

"Little late for character assessment, Danny. Best to do that before we slide between the sheets with somebody. Diablo warned you. Why didn't you listen?"

He lay back, arms folded under his head like he could have been on a bale of hay. He had become gaunt. "You want to know why? I've thought of nothing else since Julie died. Why didn't I listen to Chaz and leave Kelly alone?" He glanced at Rachel and let it stay there.

"Sex. Good sex. Constant sex. Easy, nasty, unbridled sex. My wife made it very clear that she was through with me, and Kelly couldn't get enough. Yeah. My kingdom for a piece of ass. I wish I could attach some literary pinnacle to it. But there isn't one. You do brain surgery on nine out of ten men, you'll open up their skulls and find their testicles. Sorry, Collazo. Not a pretty picture."

"So it was Julie's fault?"

With great derision he laughed and said, "My wife wanted me to put a nail in a door frame that had come loose one day. I wouldn't do it. Just to piss her off. Like whatever she wanted was beneath me. That's the kind of shit wives get. We stop putting in little nails, so to get even they stop nailing us. Marital dynamics. No, it was my fault. But I didn't kill her or help Kelly kill her."

Rachel said again for emphasis, "She says you were her accomplice, that she did it because you begged her to."

He went sappy. "I can't believe she would claim that."

Rachel laughed loudly at his intense frown. "Nystrom, let me get this straight. She knows that to be with her you have to lie every day—in every way—to your own family. And every time she looked at your son and ailing wife, she was lying to them, too. You and she are the big spiders in this web of constant, heinous lying. She gases your house to try and kill you. And you're shocked she turns out to be dishonest?"

She slapped her knees like a country girl, saying, "Danny, you laid down with a dog and now you got fleas." She cocked her head at him, studying. "Wasn't there a moment . . . some salient flicker of time . . . when you knew this broad was nutsola? Did you ever wonder why a gorgeous babe like that wanted a married man, instead of a bachelor who could take her home to Mama?"

He turned on his side and said dryly, "Yeah. There was a moment, an epiphany. She offered to kill her cat if I'd stay with her."

Rachel flinched. "Jesus. Kill her own cat to have a man? Do you know, Danny, that a woman who'd do that is just one step from driving the kids into the lake and then watching the car sink while they scream?"

"Oh yeah, you're so intuitive, such a fucking psychoanalyst. My wife fucked Chaz Diablo, my virginal saintly wife who told me sex was a sin, and she lets some slimy cop on top of her like she's a common slut. You want to explain that, since you're so damned erudite and shrewd?"

She smiled coyly. "That's an easy one, Danny boy. It was our idea, the woman's idea, remember, to bite the apple."

"I thought she was a Christian."

"She was a woman, Danny. Not a slut. Not common. Sometimes we women do things to see if you losers have gotten any smarter since the Garden of Eden. The answer is usually no." She stood. "You're not getting bail. They think you'll run. For what it's worth, I don't think you were involved in Julie's murder. I have no idea how I'm going to prove you weren't, but I won't give up. You're welcome for the chewing gum."

He was decrepit. "Where are you going?"

"To your house. To see if I can find anything to help you out of this mess."

=72=

In all his born days, Mitch Nystrom had never seen his mother look like anything but an elegant, tailored lady. And, most bizarre to him, she had never showed up unannounced to his busy office. The secretary buzzed.

"Your mother is here to see you."

"My mother? Well, okay. . . ."

She was facing him in a flash, standing there out of character.

He said, "Danny's in more trouble? What happened now?"

She was always a smiling woman, the smile of a long ago beauty queen who'd kept her poise and her good looks. She was not smiling now. Her face was creased in worry and despair. She clutched her purse to her chest, wouldn't sit.

"It's not Danny," she said like a mummy. "They're moving him to the jail tomorrow so we can see him. Are you going to let them do this? Are you going to let him take the blame?"

Mitch felt a throttle-down in his gut. "I'm paying his lawyer whatever it takes. Mother, they will never convict him of helping that nurse kill Julie Ann. Calm down. Sit down. Let me get you a drink."

He chunked ice into a highball glass, poured and handed it to her when she finally sat, stiff as an upright ironing board. She said, "Mitchell, I love you."

He bit his lip, paused and then said, "I know that. I love you, too."

"But I don't know you." She swigged deeply. "I only know about my sons' lives what you want me to know. That is the privilege of finally becoming an adult. You get to run things your way, to live your own values."

"Mom, you're blathering. Danny will be okay. I've hired the toughest lawyer in the state to defend him. Kelly's not a credible witness against him. You don't understand this stuff, so don't meddle. Don't talk to the press or the cops, because you don't know anything."

It was the evil eye he got, the one he used to get when he giggled in church, the one that promised an ass whipping if he didn't lay off immediately. "Oh, but I do know something, Mitchell Eugene."

He made a steeple of his fingers and leaned back calmly. "I should have a doctor look at you, maybe hospitalize you for emotional trauma. You're making no sense."

He wished for tears from her, some sign that she was cookie-baking Mom inside there, but the steel resolve that hit him took him to his knees.

"You knew about it. You discussed it with her, how Julie needed to die because Danny was so miserable. She told you when she was going to do it, and you sat back and did nothing. I'd call you a son of a bitch, but that would reflect on me." She slammed down the highball glass, jabbed a torch of a finger at him. "And I was a good mother. If you turned out to be a crooked, conniving sex fiend, it was not because of what I taught you, but because you rejected what I taught you."

He found his usual suave self speechless. But he stood. She didn't back away. He felt the world close in, a blow of real terror to his belly. He had to ask. "Mother, if what you're saying is true, how would you know?"

"There's a tape, you ninny. Didn't I tell you that God was always listening to your evil thoughts? Well, he was. And this time he recorded it on your nephew's little toy tape recorder and I found it." She glowed like a meteorite slicing toward him.

"Where is the tape?"

"I'm not turning you in, Mitchell. Yet. I'm going to give

you twenty-four hours to search your own conscience and do that yourself."

He gritted his teeth. "Where is the goddamned tape!"

She threw the drink on him, at his face. He let the ice cubes clank to his desk and the vodka burn his eyes.

She hissed, "Twenty-four hours. And then if you won't do the manly thing, I will. God help you, Mitchell."

=73=

Danny's and Julie's empty house had spooks in it. Rachel could hear and feel them. A thump here. A distant chorus of whispers in there. She had learned to like the spooks that swirled around her head in the homes of murdered people. The spooks were her friends. They led her to secret places.

She stood in Julie's abandoned convalescent room. Nothing had been touched because it had been declared a crime scene, so the medicine bottles and nightgowns and books were all strewn the way Julie had last seen them. There were toys around the room. Grinning dinosaurs. Tiny fierce robotic people in space helmets. Crayons.

The sun was fading, but there was enough light to work even without the electricity. She bent and handled each object, smelled the medicine bottles, capped them. She yanked back the sheets and was hit with an ether smell, the smell of convalescence. She looked under Julie's bed and dragged out a red and blue toy tape recorder with no tape in it.

In the living room shadows she sat on the couch and noticed the silence. All sound was missing with no utilities humming. No refrigerator buzzing dimly. No clocks ticking. It was a palpable silence that she could be aware of, the omission of life's daily appliances.

"Hey, Julie, talk to me. I'm here, baby. Come on."

A crow cawed on the deck, a sound like car gears grinding. She went to the deck and surveyed it. Something was hanging, a limp lump with a definite form, to the side of the patio near the bay doors into Danny's room. She went out and toward it, then felt her feet pick up with dreaded alarm. She finally ran.

"No, no, not Kelly's kitty. Please." She reached it, instinctively reached out, and then panted to herself, "Oh, god. Don't touch, Rachel. Don't touch. You can't save him. He's evidence now. Jesus." She turned from the gory cat and massaged her temples, mumbling. "Come on, Julie, honey. What is it I'm supposed to find here? I'm running out of daylight, baby. Walk with me." She took a step. The wind rattled leaves. The dead cat twirled and twisted. Rachel stared, feeling utterly forlorn.

In all the potted plants on the patio and the deck she stuck her fingers, looking for anything. In Daniel's room she went through every pocket she could find, pants, shirts, coats, sweaters, fished all through his shoes and drawers. She went thorugh his tackle box, past all the lures and hooks. Under his bed.

She stood. Darkness was inching in like quiet waves at her feet. "Yeah." She felt a stir. "Yes, Julie. I feel your cold spot behind me. It's okay. Come closer."

She went through kitchen drawers and cabinets, through a chest of place mats in the dining room. She picked up and put down every item in Pete's room and was walking out when a flowery sigh tickled the stale air around her.

She turned back to the cluttered room. "What? I looked everywhere, except. . . ." She walked to the bed and lifted the mattress. A red cassette tape. She held it and read the label, an adult's handwriting. She felt a quick tear. A mama's loving handwriting. It listed in tidy script, "Mom—Goldilocks, Dad's tool shop, Kelly—mockingbird song, Night sounds." Rachel carried it to Julie's room where she had left the toy tape recorder.

The sun slipped lower while she sat on the floor and listened. The happy sounds made Rachel cry. Kelly's song made her shoulders hunch and shiver. The night sounds made her smile sadly.

And then Danny's voice came with Kelly's harp of a seductive tone. The plot. She heard it all. Rachel sat stone still. The troubled ghost moaned with the wind outside.

She and the ghost heard the click of a door at the same time, followed by nothing, no calling out or footsteps. But somebody was in the house with them. The cold spot around Rachel intensified. She had nowhere to go and no time to go there. As she reached under her arm to free her revolver, he loomed, abominably desperate, in the doorway. Her escape was blocked.

He said, "I'll take that tape." His shotgun was a cannon leveled at her chest.

"And then do what? Shoot a cop?"

He weakened, wiped his mouth, and she saw that his free hand was shaky. "I wanted it . . . for Danny. To set him free. Her abuse was sickening."

Rachel didn't answer. She knew that the one who talked most in an armed standoff would lose. Mitch went on, his voice cracking from dryness.

"She could talk anybody into anything, Detective. She was so beautiful. The sex was so electric and savage. No one could resist. Even when I knew she was insane, finally, when I knew she was so demented with desperation for endless lovers, I couldn't look away from her." He had been crying. Rachel could see it. He was terrified. The shotgun barrel glared at her. It was pumped.

She asked slowly, "So it's you on the tape? Not Danny."

He had an oval of sweat on his shirt at the chest, but he kept the shotgun squarely on her. "We wanted to save him."

Rachel's palms were sweaty. This freak was scaring her. "You love your brother enough to help murder his abusive wife, but you didn't mind screwing the woman of his dreams?"

"Loving your brother, Detective, has nothing to do with getting laid."

"I reckon not," she said easily, "so if you didn't love

Kelly, why is she protecting you and dropping Danny in the grease?"

He fought a vain smile. "I asked her to marry me."

"Your wife didn't mind?"

"It was just a game. To buy time in bed with her. The other men made her feel like a whore, but I told her I would leave my wife as soon as my son finished high school next year. And the dumb bitch. She believed me. It was just a game, an experiment. Nothing more. Nothing meaningful."

She tried to stand. He screamed, "Stay down, goddamn it, or I'll shoot you, I swear to god I'll blow your head off!"

From behind him a deep voice said, "I don't think so."

Mitch reeled with the shotgun. Chaz fired. It spun Mitch sideways. His face fell so near Rachel's lap that she heard his head crack on the hardwood floor. Sideways, his fisheye wobbled in its socket at her. Whatever he was trying to say couldn't get past the blood gushing out of his mouth.

Rachel said, shaky as ever, "Nice shootin'."

Diablo helped her up. "I missed once trying to save my partner, remember? I don't miss the target anymore. What were you looking for? Why did you come here?"

Rachel dusted herself. "A woman called me. Anonymous. She said there was something here, that if she brought it to me or if she didn't, either way she would burn in hell. But if I found it, she said, then it would be God's will."

"What woman?" Chaz asked, smoothing Rachel's hair as she bent futilely to feel for Mitch's pulse.

"Elva Nystrom. Thank goodness for caller I.D., huh?"

He took her hand, pulled her up, took her face in his hands. "Hey, Collazo, you okay?"

"Yeah. Let's get this tape to Tillery. It exonerates Danny. Then we've got to hold a proper funeral for a poor dead kitty. Afterward let's get a beer. You got any money?"

Chaz smiled nicely at her. He said, "Quantico called. I'm going to miss you. You should come, too. The Bureau would like you."

She picked up the phone, said playfully, "Yeah. Until I told some pinhead superior up there that he's a stupid son of a bitch and threatened to choke him if I couldn't do things my own damned way. You know what I mean, baby doll?"

Chaz laughed. Rachel winked at him.

Into the telephone she asked for an ambulance that Mitch Nystrom would never see or hear.

=74=

Doak got into Rachel's face like a panting cactus. "You do it today like I showed you, you get ranked. Don't fuck it up. You got no headgear, so watch for her to swing high more times today. You stick with going for the torso. You got me?"

Rachel was jittery. "Yeah. You got the white towel?"

He rolled his bloodshot eyes. "Put your mouthpiece in. And remember, the crowd incites Cujo. We got three, two-minute rounds. It's the main event, kid. But you're out there alone." He popped her aside her head. "You ain't a girl anymore. You're a fighter. Cold as ice. Mean as hell."

They were all there, the rabble rousers, to watch her. Never before had she come into the gym's old arena to lights and music and applause, so it all threw her, and she wanted her mama real bad. Cujo, the living punching machine, was in her corner getting a massage and chewing what Rachel was sure was human flesh. Since they sparred last. Cujo had lost a front tooth and gotten shaved into her buzz haircut, "I hate you."

Ding. Rachel pattered into the middle of the ring. Cujo lumbered, shoulders like anvils. The Vaseline on her face showed no sweat; Rachel's Vaseline was melting under it. Cujo came in first, a lethal swipe that connected to Rachel's belly. She wanted the luxury to double over in pain, but she knew Cujo would bend down and take a bite of her if she did.

So Rachel ran. She turned and ran to the ropes like a

bunny rabbit. Cujo had a what-the-hell look, then gnawed on the mouthpiece and started for her. Rachel ran again, shamelessly, to the other side of the ring.

Doak yelled something so profane that Patrick Collazo crossed himself. Emory covered his eyes. Chaz winced, it didn't look good out there, what with his partner skittering all over the ring to avoid being hit. Her friend Narda threw popcorn, Melvin screamed, and Pauline asked someone next to her, "Is she supposed to run away?" Dorcus answered, "No, but it might be the best plan at this point." Mark Tillery shouted, "Kill her!" but his allegiance was very suspect, maybe he was urging Cujo. Mrs. Pickett pulled her sweater tighter at the neck and covered her eyes.

A half-dozen uniformed police officers tried to start the wave, but Cujo's side of the bleachers mooned them.

The chase went on long enough, Cujo coming in and Rachel darting away, so that Cujo went palms up to the referee. He came to Rachel.

"You're running from her, Collazo."

"You expect me to stand still and let her hit me?"

He put his hand up and then dropped it. "Now fight."

Okay, okay, Rachel loosened her shoulders. Her silks were white and Cujo's black, so that meant she should be the good guy, the one in white, so okay. She moved toward Cujo and got hit so hard and fast in the face that her dancing feet hardly felt the mat. She pushed herself up, covered her face with the gloves and moved in. Cujo knocked her backward, into the bench where Doak stood.

He growled, "Don't look down at the blood."

Rachel said, "Right over there. You can hand me my gun."

"Hit her. She's dumb and slow."

"Somebody should tell her that."

By chance, Rachel connected a damaging blow to Cujo's right eye. Half of the misfit crowd booed, Rachel's half whistled and whooped. Cujo clamored up onto her immense haunches and looked none too pleased. Cujo's eye was bleeding badly just as the bell rang.

Doak toweled her, rubbed her, gave her water to spit that

came out bloody. "She won't see from that eye in about five minutes. Listen, you've got reach. Swing from outside more."

"Okay, and then I'm switching to aerobics."

Cujo came in bent over. Rachel aimed for the taped eyebrow and got it with a sickening splat. A fireball came from the direction of Cujo's left and creamed Rachel's right side. It felt like shit, and she cried out, but didn't go down.

Once at her granddaddy's farm, Rachel had walked off far down the pasture to sit under a tree and read. She looked up as the sun began to set and saw standing four feet from her a badass bull with six feet of horns and snot drooling. He stamped one foot at her, and she knew if she ran he'd catch her and kill her. Cujo had that look now. Kind of carnivorous. Rachel's lip was busted. Cujo's eye was swollen shut. They were injured and gooey with sweat. The round ended that way.

Doak said, "You're losing on points. I need something out of the hat. I need her on her ass. It's more tiring to swing and miss than to wait and get a hit. Step in more now. She's tired and half blind. Your feet are off. You don't got your feet down each time you swing. Don't swing when you're up on the dance. Go. Keep down and lash out."

Cujo's cyclops watched Rachel twit around lightly on her feet. She had learned how long Rachel's arms were, even if they didn't match her force. From nowhere Cujo came in pummeling. Rachel felt her kidneys burn from the blows, then her shoulder and the left side of her face. She went to her knees no matter how she yearned and prayed to keep standing. It hurt, everywhere, all at once, and Cujo didn't stop.

It was over that quickly. The invincible reigned. Cujo took the match. Rachel staggered to the locker room. Cujo jumped and hooted and stood supreme in the spotlight.

=75=

Emory found his beautiful girl in a bloody, sweaty heap. Her silks were massacred. She was wiping her face, a piece of clear tape on the tip of her lip.

She said, "I lost."

He set down his light overcoat and sat by her. "No, sweetheart, you showed up, you suited up and you went the distance."

"Emory, I choked. I ran from her."

"Wisely so. Here, give me that towel." He tended her, pushed away her sweaty ringlets of hair. "You were fabulous out there."

"So, marry me."

"Whenever you say, Rachel."

She shrugged girlishly. "Sure. What else could you say to a woman still wearing one boxing glove?"

He started to untie the glove, said to her, "I would like to point something out to you."

"Okay. Point with a hundred-dollar bill and I won't bullshit you."

"The last three times you have asked me to marry you, I have said yes. And you," he wiggled his hand like a fish, "you have veered away from my answer."

She pulled a bright purple Texas Christian University sweatshirt over her bloodied silk boxing tee, and she said flatly, "Oh."

He stared, so she resumed it. "Well, I thought, you know, after twenty years it would make you feel more . . . loved by me. Isn't it time for one of us to ask, Emory? Isn't it proper that by now I should want to marry you?"

He was as handsome as a man could be, and she reached out to touch his face. He asked, "Would it make you feel more worthy, being my wife?"

She didn't mean to sound shy, but she did. "No. I just want you to know that I love you enough to marry you if it's time, if it's proof of something. Asking you seemed kind of—"

"Rachel, look at you, all beaten up and bloody and nurturing me!" He tilted back, laughing kindly. "What a heart you have! What a level head! Sweetheart, you have nothing to prove to me."

She flinched when he put medicine on her cut, and she said, "I just didn't want to end up like those nuns at my high school. Bad shoes. Intolerant. And having one of those funny moustaches. Getting married seemed like insurance against losing the feel for intimacy."

"No, no. That's from not making love, from not being committed to love someone always, no matter what. The moustaches aren't caused from staying single. Now, ask me again."

"Emory, will you marry me?"

"Any time."

She bumped him playfully, and she admitted, "Yikes. Sounds like it's time to quit asking." She put her forehead to his and said sweetly, "Don't you kind of like it the way we've got it, Em? I mean, isn't it okay?"

His eyes sparkled at her. He said, "I do. And you, Rachel, do you like it the way it is?"

She kissed his lips and said proudly, "I do. Like for twenty years we've been having a good time sitting on the front porch together, in the breeze, sipping cider and holding hands. And marriage, well, it'd be sort of like having to get up and go in the stuffy old house, wouldn't it?"

He laughed loudly, and he put her cape around her, the one Dorcus had given her that said in brazen letters across the back, "The Go-to Girl." They strolled, and when she had to limp from the aches and fatigue Emory held on to her tightly.

She said, "I should shower first."

Emory gloated, "Heavens no. All your buddies and Doak will want you at the pub just like this. It's very earthy and very you. Clobbered. Beaten up. But never broken down."

Daniel was just outside the door when they stepped into the alley. Emory gestured that he would wait ahead.

Daniel said softly, "I didn't come inside. How'd you do?"

She shrugged. "There's always next time, so they say. How's Pete?"

He looked away, into his pain. "He wants to stay at my mom's house for a while. I said he can. He's kind of mad at me."

"Why exactly?"

The good and wise Daniel came into focus, and Rachel knew he and Pete would be all right. Daniel answered, "Because he has to blame somebody for his mother's death. But the counselor said it's okay, that Pete knows it's safe to be mad at me above anyone else because he can count on my love. I'm going to give him a little time, and then I'm going to take him fishing." His smile was dreary but a real effort.

Rachel asked, "You want a beer with us all at the pub?"

He said dimly, "You think that's a good idea?"

She tried to grin but the lip cut twinged badly. She said, "Danny, you've got to live in this town. Mend whatever fences you can. Apologize only once, and mean it, and then get over it. Folks who don't like us, well, to hell with them, I say. Some of them will call you names." She limped a step forward. He took her arm to help. "But Danny, remember, just because somebody says something about you, that doesn't mean it's true. Screw 'em."

"I expected you to cuss me out, Collazo, ream me for being so selfish and blind. In all the years, I've never seen you cut anybody any slack. Are you mellowing?"

She considered his nice face and then used her hack saw logic on him. "Eat shit, Nystrom. Take the invite to the pub or not, I don't care. But I won't stand around here and baby-sit your ignorant wounded pride while there's a cold Guiness out there with my name on it." She cringed. "Ouch. Damn. I hurt."

He shoved his hands into his jeans pockets and said, "I wouldn't know what to say to Chaz. He screwed my wife. Shot my brother dead."

She winced painfully as they walked. "Yeah. Your sorry brother had a pumped shotgun leveled on me. And if we're nut cutting here, let's admit that your wife wanted to be screwed. In the world of religious chumps like you and your brother, what's a little fucking between friends, anyhow?"

He pouted. "So I say what to Chaz? Ho-hum, think nothing of it?"

She hobbled. "Say that you're buying. Jesus, Nystrom. Stop whining. Isn't it your whining that started all this?"

Finally he saw her, the cuts and swollen cheek, the blood soaking through into her TCU sweatshirt and the places where he knew bruises and bumps and cuts would swell tomorrow. He said, "Thanks, Rachel, for believing me."

She said flatly, "You're welcome."

He said, "I've got my car. You and Emory want a ride to the pub?"

"We like to walk. You can snuggle closer that way."

"You get him to marry you yet?"

She grinned, cocky and cute at him. And she said, "I ran a bluff. He called it. Life is just so damned interesting."

Daniel passed Emory, and they nodded to each other. Rachel hobbled more, and Emory asked, "You're up to the walk?"

"Sure. It only hurts when I don't laugh."

They linked arms, the leggy, pretty brunette and the distinguished, silver-haired golf legend. Down the road, as her cape flowed and her boxing hightops sagged and the words "The Go-to Girl" flapped in the gusts of a spring dusk, Emory took her arm and raised it high.

"The winner!" he sang out. "And still champion!"